Evolving Elizah: Aeturnum

Book 2

C.J. Hall

ISBN: 978-1-7350537-3-8

DEDICATION

For the friends I met in Presidio, Texas—

You lift me higher than I ever imagined. I hope you enjoy the book. I'll bring some copies, and a Topo Chico, to the Lizard Lounge. For anyone else who might want to join us… Follow the Rio Grande to the other side of nowhere. Be careful you don't miss it. There's not much there, only everything that matters.

PROLOGUE

Now she is alone—She Who Needs No Name. Her aloneness stretches out almost longer than she can remember. It fills her mind, encroaching upon everything else she knows about herself.

Unencumbered by a dense physical body, she is a pure energy cluster, meant to ascend by elevating her vibration through knowledge and experience. She wasn't born or hatched but simply created from the great black womb of nothing from which all of creation emerges. She has no parents, other than the great creatrix, but others have come before her—those with experience to teach and mentor her. She can still remember others of her kind, although the memories now only come with effort.

She thinks back to the moments before her great aloneness. She was with the others, preparing for an ascension—a new level of growing and becoming. She had quieted her thoughts. She had listened to her teacher as she created a sacred space to receive her lesson. She had opened herself up, waiting for the flood of brilliance that accompanied her prior ascensions—joy, perhaps, or maybe just expanded being. She waited, but it didn't come. Instead, something strange happened.

She became distracted, by a dense creature she'd never seen before. She had a fleeting sense that it was alive, surprised that any spark of life could survive in such a dense little body. A fraction of a moment later, she was washed in a strange energy, and then she was alone.

She must have failed the test. Her teacher must have found her unworthy of ascension, or perhaps unready. But isn't unready the same as unworthy? As she ponders this strange and lonely place, she thinks it is.

She might think this place dark, if she knew was darkness was. But she creates her own light. Besides, she has no physical eyes to discern dark from light. She sees with her awareness, and she can push her awareness out well beyond the confines of the space that embraces her.

Maybe I didn't fail the test, she thinks. *Maybe this is the test.* She likes this explanation, although it seems implausible. None of her prior ascensions involved tests like this. Perhaps this is the first.

She needs information, so she starts with what she has— her awareness. She pushes it out beyond the matter immediately around her, dense matter from which she knows planets are made. She is in a planet—a planet she can sense teeming with a nearly overwhelming variety of strange, dense life. The life seems to sense her as well, and it shrinks back from her energy—painfully so. She remembers her teacher telling her that denser, simpler life can be overwhelmed by her higher vibration—even damaged. She pulls her awareness back, considering what to do.

I can't give up, she decides, knowing that persistence is key to passing any test. She tries again, concentrating very hard to spin a thread of awareness so fine it almost isn't there at all. She waits until she can sense the life around her, barely able to detect the vibration this time because it's so low. *Are they afraid?* she wonders. She doesn't have any direct experience with creatures dense and low enough to know fear, but her teacher has talked about such things. She waits, proud of her own patience. The life around her begins to normalize again. As the collective vibration rises, she can perceive it a bit more clearly.

Hello, she whispers, waiting for a reply. None comes, but she feels the energy around her dip and knows they perceive her. She lowers her own vibration, trying to meet them where they are. But she's young and inexperienced. She can only lower it so far, and she's not sure it's far enough.

She listens intently. Slowly, she begins to perceive whispers—whispers of many voices. *Did you hear that?* they ask. *What was that? Something is different. What is different?*

She withdraws her thread of awareness to process the situation. What will she do now? The beings seem harmless, but their vibration is so low. She has been well admonished by her teacher that working with low beings is dangerous until a certain level of ascendance is reached. She's not even close to that level. Are these beings dangerous to her?

She doesn't know.

So she gathers her energy back toward her core, pulling it into a tight ball that soothes her. She feels the sand and the stone and the molten rock around her. It hums a melody of sound as it changes with light, heat, and movement. The sand transforms to molten rock, which cools to stone. The stone pushes its way up and out, only to be worn down to sand again. It has a rhythm she can immediately sense, even though the cycles never take the same amount of energy. Or time. *They would think of it as time,* she realizes. She must be in linear time.

The gravity of being within time excites and scares her. She's heard that time can feel oppressive, even though it means nothing to her given her state of ascension. It will mean something now, though, as along as she is in it. How will she use her time? She ponders this for a moment, or perhaps a millennia—she doesn't yet know how to gauge it.

I'm not alone, she reminds herself, even though she feels so very alone. Surely her teacher is watching, from somewhere just beyond her awareness. Surely help will come if she needs it, although she doesn't want to need it. *I've only been in this place for a moment,* she reminds herself, even though it feels like forever. It hasn't really been forever, has it?

Her thoughts turn back to the frail, dense creatures around her. She must be here to learn something about them, or perhaps about herself. She is far more ascended than they are, and she knows her higher vibration could destroy them. If she harms them, she might fail the test, so she needs to be careful.

I will experience linear time, she decides, *and learn something about these lowly creatures.* Regardless of what the lesson is, this is what she will do, and having the sense of direction reassures her. Some lessons seem difficult or outright impossible, but they aren't. All of her lessons are meant to be passed.

She returns her focus to her awareness. She needs to spin fine threads of it, finer than she's ever spun before. And she needs to practice lowering her vibration, lower than she can ever remember being. Then she will push her awareness out again, to touch the beings she can sense on the edge of this ball of matter in which she landed. She will do this to pass her test, and then she will return to the others of her kind.

CHAPTER 1

OPENING PERFORMANCE

***

OCTOBER 22, 2059—WEDNESDAY

Ruth feels the age of her weary body as she sits by the light of the crackling campfire. She has lived an eventful eighty-two years, but—as it must—her life is winding down. That's okay with her. She knows that in the grand scheme of things, she's nothing more than a small cog in the vast machine of existence. Nothing she has or hasn't done will change the fate of humanity. But despite knowing this, she still feels the weight of the world on her shoulders. Even here, in this beautiful garden and surrounded by the people most precious to her, she feels completely alone.

The children prepared a play, which they are performing at tonight's story time. They call it *Liz Saves Us at the Depot*. The title lacks flair, but Ruth is proud they want to preserve the story of what happened that fateful day. It's important to Ruth that they remember. She hopes they understand that Liz saved more than their lives. She saved the things that make life worth living—hope, a sense of possibility, faith that good will prevail, and the belief that the human heart is more powerful than hardship or bullets or even fear.

Or, maybe it's all a dream. Maybe Ruth will wake to find herself still in the cave that sustained them for nineteen years before they fled to the depot. Maybe she will rise from her meager bed and steel herself once more, determined to do whatever she can to keep her people alive for one more day.

Ruth closes her eyes. If this is a dream, she wants to remember it clearly. The wooden bench presses against her legs, a sturdy promise that she will not fall down. A hidden brook provides a backdrop of sound to the children's voices, burbling assurance that all is well. As she breathes in deeply, a panoply of smell floods her senses.

She loves the intricately woven perfume of roses, wisteria, and jasmine that overlays the clean smell of pine trees. But the strongest scent, and the one she wants to remember most clearly, is lilac. It's her favorite flower, and that's why she chose this particular seat around the campfire tonight, next to the bush with the glorious blooms. Ruth surrenders her attention to its perfumed embrace. It's spicy but delicate, exotic but familiar, a series of contradictions braided impossibly together like dark and light, death and life.

The garden is a microcosm of paradise—heaven on earth. Except, they aren't on Earth. They are on Level 20 of the Green Grow 3, billions of miles from Earth and catapulting into deep space in what strikes Ruth as a bizarre strategy to get home. Instead of heading back toward Earth, they are moving faster and farther away, toward a turnaround point called Omega. It makes no sense to her that they have to go so far just to turn around, but she knows that people smarter than herself devised this plan. This is what they are doing, she's come to accept, and they have to speed up to make it work. They have to speed up a lot.

Two weeks ago, Captain Harris announced they would accelerate gradually, to give everyone time to adjust. It didn't sound terrible to Ruth. Couldn't she endure anything for a few days? She no longer knows. After three days of "gradual" accelerating, they reached 1.5G. Ruth feels like she gained half her body weight—it's challenging, although not impossible, to function. That part gets easier as time goes on, but then the captain added bursts that are nearly unbearable.

Captain Harris calls them controlled accelerations—4G for ten minutes every morning and evening—and they render everyone useless. All anyone can do is lie in bed and try not to pass out. Each time he tells them to prepare, Ruth hopes it's the last. It's miserable, and she doesn't want to think about it right now. She wants to enjoy the garden and the play, so she opens her eyes and watches the scene unfold before her.

A soft voice asks, "Don't you have room in your heart for one little baby?" Something deep inside Ruth withers as she remembers posing that question to Liz at the depot. She and her people were standing outside the fence, a New Generation raiding party bearing down on them fast. Liz seemed only marginally human then, dressed in a flight suit with tinted goggles and a breathing mask. Ruth had begged the nameless, faceless person to take at least one of the children to safety, if not all of them. She didn't know how to persuade her. That was why she asked the question—*don't you have room in your heart …*

Ruth refuses to talk about that conversation. In fact, she refuses to recount the day at all, although the children plead with her terribly at story time. It hurts too much to think about, and she doesn't need to tell them, anyway. They were there—they all witnessed everything that transpired.

Zachary, in particular, heard the entire exchange with Liz, and he apparently can recall every word. Ruth remembers how tightly he clutched her dress, how she pushed him through the gate roughly when he didn't want to leave. How desperately she wanted him to survive, knowing he might be the only living legacy of the group. He's playing himself tonight, clutching Gabriella's dress just like he clutched hers that day. His small face is fuller than it was then, although Dr. Harris says that he may never grow very tall. It's enough for Ruth that he's still alive.

The children seem to think she favors Zachary, which is why they sent him to ask her about the play. They wanted her to play herself, at least the first time they performed. But Ruth refused. Gabriella agreed to take her place instead, and she's doing a fine job. The young woman doesn't seem as broken as she used to be, and she even let Ellis hold Luke while she performed. It's the first time she's trusted anyone with the baby since he was born.

Ruth doesn't love Zachary any more or less than the other children. It just so happened that Ellis drew his name when they chose which child to save. She didn't want to choose—she loved them all so much. Ellis said he would carry the burden of choosing. But his words didn't make it any less heavy as he wrote down all of their names and drew one out of a bowl.

Zachary didn't know that his ticket to salvation was bought with betrayal. Jackson gave them a head start when they fled the cave, agreeing not to loose his raiding party on them for another day if Ruth would smuggle the memory stick onboard the Green Grow 3. Ruth cried as she sewed a small pocket in the seam of Zachary's frayed shirt, a hiding place for the stick.

Did she think this was a good deal? Of course not. She couldn't even be certain he would keep his word, but she had to take whatever chance Jackson offered, for the sake of her people—for the sake of the children. It was the only chance they had. Her people were starving, weak, diminished. Sure, they would fight if they had to, down to the last man and woman, down to the last breath, but it would be a losing battle. They couldn't fight off a whole raiding party.

The first time she saw a New Generation raiding party was back in Oxford. She hadn't yet drawn any conclusions about the New Generation, although she'd heard plenty. She wasn't sure what to think, at least until the raiding party came through town.

They only passed through that time, riding motorcycles that roared in a silent world. Their faces were smeared in black and red paint, their leather clothes tattered and adorned with scraps of metal and bone. They carried machetes and spiked clubs, spears and guns. Her heart raced when one of the motorcycles began to slow, approaching two young girls who immediately clutched each other, trying to shrink back into the doorway of an abandoned drug store. The man on the bike, if he was still human enough to be considered a man, cast a jeering smile at the girls, and Ruth could see yellow teeth filed into points.

But before he could stop, a voice snarled from the front, "Another time! Get moving."

Ruth can still remember the face of the man who barked the words, blackened with paint and scarred. The beads in his long, matted hair had an uncanny resemblance to human teeth.

The raiding party did far worse when they returned days later. Ruth tries not to think about her old neighbor, Steve, but the memories refuse to be contained.

She looked out her kitchen window when she heard the rumble of the motorcycles. Steve's electric car flew into his driveway, wheels screeching as he screamed at his sister, Nora, to get her children into the house. But it was too late. The motorcycles were upon them, enclosing them in a roaring circle of exhaust.

Ruth can still hear them chanting, fresh in her ears as if it's happening anew. She smells the exhaust, mixed with the scent of grease, blood, and unwashed human bodies. She feels her back pressed against the kitchen wall as she shrinks into a corner, peeking out through a gap in the lace curtains that cover the open window. She can see the beastly woman who licked Nora's blood off the blade of her knife after she stabbed her twice and-pushed her to the ground. The smell of lighter fluid filled the air, and time stood still as understanding hit her like a sledgehammer. Then the match dropped, a single spark of flame that transformed Steve into a screaming, thrashing heap of pain and suffering.

The New Generation seemed barely human that day, and their humanity disappeared altogether over the years that followed. They only grew stronger as her own people grew weaker, and when Jackson offered her the memory stick that day in the cave, Ruth knew she needed to take it. What remained of her people stood no chance against a raiding party, but maybe she could save a few of them. Jackson would have to spare at least one, someone to carry it to the space farm. That was why she and Ellis drew the name, why they chose Zachary.

Ruth had to turn away when the children used a similar method to decide who would play Liz's role in the opening performance. They all put their names in a bowl and asked Ruth to choose one. But she never wants to choose a name out of a bowl again, not for anything. Luckily, Ruben was there with her, and she asked him to draw a name instead. He made a show of choosing, making them all laugh, and Ruth was especially grateful for his easy way with the children, even though he still doesn't speak.

Sophia won the part. She was a thoughtful girl, who took the responsibility of playing Liz's role very seriously. Of course, it was only for the opening performance. All of the children want to play Liz's part, and they'll take turns—boys and girls alike. And why shouldn't they?

The children idolize Liz, and that's just fine. Liz was the heroine they needed that day at the depot, descending from the sky like a goddess of justice—fierce, strong, and fearless. She flawlessly chose to save them all, literally opening the gate to their salvation and ushering them inside. Ruth had been certain that most of them would die that day. They would have, if Liz hadn't stepped outside the gate, risking her own life to unleash a righteous fury on the New Generation. Redemption sounded like gunfire, each bullet declaring to Ruth anew, *You are worthy.*

Now, she glances over at Liz. The woman's impassive face is softer by the light of the fire. She hasn't been the same since Albert Wyndham died two months ago. Ruth doesn't know what they meant to each other, but Liz must have meant something to Albert—he killed himself just a few yards away from her, leaving her tied to a tree. And if Albert didn't mean anything to Liz before, he surely must now. It's hard to know, and Ruth doesn't pry.

She turns her attention back to the play. Sophia is leading the newly saved group into the depot, telling them that they must come back with her to the Green Grow 3. And just as Ruth did, Gabriella says, "We'll go. All fifty-two of us."

It sounds so simple, so good and honest. But the children only know what Ruth said in that moment, not what she was thinking. Ruth was thinking about the memory stick pressed in the bloody arch of her blistered foot, hidden in what remained of her sock. She'd ripped it out of Zachary's shirt as soon as they were all inside, frantic to relieve the child of his treacherous burden. Ruth was thinking that as much as she despised Jackson Goeff, the chain of events he set in motion saved her people, and that was enough for her. She kept her end of the bargain and smuggled the stick aboard.

But that was only the beginning, wasn't it? Why did she keep helping him?

Ruth could argue that she never meant to betray Liz. She could cling to the confusion she felt at Liz's hatred toward the New Generation, the organization led by her own brother. She could point to the question that penetrated her mind like an arrow when she realized who Liz was—*Did she bring us onboard because she knew we had the memory stick?* Ruth could not conceive of the notion that anyone would save them simply for the asking. Nor could she imagine that Liz truly didn't know her brother Jackson was the regional captain of the very organization she claimed to despise.

All Ruth knew when she arrived on the Green Grow 3 was that she owed a debt of gratitude she could never repay, not to the Green Grow Corporation or to the New Generation, but to Liz Goeff. But by the time she came to understand the depth of Liz's convictions, Ruth had already betrayed her. She had already delivered the memory stick, which she later learned contained the specifications for the strange tablets Jackson used to communicate in real time and command mutiny.

Ellis tells her that she's too hard on herself, that she couldn't have known what would happen. But that's no excuse. Ruth knows that this is how evil takes hold—a few innocuous acts followed by a series of benign orders, all mindlessly completed. She is responsible. She is the one who carried the memory stick onboard and instructed Will to sneak out of the quarantine and deliver it to the kitchen. The one who agreed to do the things Jackson subsequently asked her to—everything except kill Captain Harris. That, she refused, but the other things he wanted seemed so inconsequential, a small price to pay to maintain a relationship with a man who might one day be in a position to yet again decide her people's fate. Jackson is formidable, possibly even undefeatable, and he clearly has his sights set on overtaking the Green Grow 3.

Part of Ruth wants to tell Liz the truth, to tell her everything and let the chips fall where they may. But what would happen then? Would Liz despise the Fifty-Two like she despises her brother, or would Ruth bear the burden of her hatred alone? And what would Captain Harris do? He seems fair-minded, but that may not bode well for her. He executed the other traitors. Why would he treat Ruth differently? And what would happen to the people she ordered to complete the tasks Jackson set before them? What would happen to the children? Haven't they already lost enough?

No, Ruth cannot tell Liz the truth, even though she knows it makes her a coward. Bearing the consequences of her actions is too frightening, even though she knows she deserves whatever happens. But it's what it might mean for those she loves that scares her the most. Besides, there's a chance that Jackson is finished with her. He hasn't been in touch in weeks—maybe his negotiations with the council have overtaken his need for spies. Hopefully that's it, but she can't shake the feeling that his silence should terrify her more than it comforts her.

Men like Jackson don't go quietly into the night, but if Ruth can spare Liz the pain of knowing she's been betrayed, she will. If she can spare her people the trauma of being blamed for her own treachery, she will. She thinks about the children, how deeply they respect and adore Liz. They wrote the play to honor her, and it's a beautiful, heartfelt production. Ruth has no right to desecrate their work, or their devotion, by telling Liz the horrible truth. The truth would change everything, and Ruth doesn't want things to change—not that way.

She closes her eyes again, feeling the warmth of the campfire on her face, breathing in the smell of the lilacs. Has she made the right decision? It doesn't matter. Right or wrong, her decision is made.

CHAPTER 2

CLAM CHOWDER

***

OCTOBER 23, 2059—THURSDAY

Liz perches as high as she can in the branches of a pine tree on Level 13—the same level where Albert Wyndham tried to exact revenge upon her for his brother's death. It's so early that it's still late, the trees lit with the silvery simulation of night that won't turn to day for another two hours.

An hour ago she was in Seth's bed, knowing that she needed to get up even though she didn't want to. Liz wanted to marinate in the warmth of his large hand covering the small of her back, the hand that pulls her close to him and away from everything bad. She wanted to yield to his arms around her, the arms that hold her tightly as he whispers in a sleepy, early-morning voice, "Don't go yet." She wanted to bask in the look he gives her when his eyes blink open, that adoring gaze that she's come to love. It's fresh and new, as if he's seeing her for the first time. She feels beautiful when he looks at her like that, like she hasn't been diminished by the sum of her actions, torn ragged by the demons of her past.

She'd rather be there, but she's here, perched in the tree, because she wants to know what Jackson is hiding. Her brother seems so earnest in the negotiation calls, comparing notes with Claire about breakthrough medical treatments and puzzling through yield problems with his hydroponic farm. His childlike curiosity is practically endearing, and in those moments, even the scar that frames his face seems less severe, pitiful almost, like he's just a child who suffered a tragic accident.

It would be easy to hold on to that side of Jackson, to choose to believe him when he tells her that his only motivation is to improve life on Earth. But there's another side to him that Liz cannot deny, a dark, angry side that appears whenever Seth becomes involved in the discussion. Jackson's face grows cold and hard, his demeanor menacing, fearsome. He becomes the man Liz remembers from the mutiny he staged, and she can't help but remember the people who died on both sides when he ordered his spies to rise against Seth. Jackson still has spies on the Green Grow 3, Liz knows it, and he still communicates with them regularly. It's a constant reminder that she cannot trust his intentions. She needs to find out what he's hiding.

And so, she's here, hiding in a tree.

The branch seems eager to move beneath her weight, so she remains perfectly still as she turns her attention to the burly chef known as Chub. He's standing beneath her perch, oblivious to her presence. Liz knows his given name is Ronald Baker, although no one calls him that. She knows because she's pored over his personnel records, trying to understand how he might be connected to her brother.

She met Chub the day she arrived on the Green Grow 3, a frightened girl who had lied her way onboard the ship.

She needed to fit in quickly and inconspicuously, and she was trying to gain her bearings without attracting attention to herself.

Seth hadn't yet finished fabricating her employee records, but he'd managed to assign her a job in the orchard and quarters. That was where she first met Willow Brown, one of her roommates. It was late, well past dinner, but somehow the beautiful, dark-skinned woman sensed that Liz was hungry. She pulled her out of their room and toward the cafeteria, assuring her that there was still food to be had. Liz followed two steps behind Willow, afraid of being turned away or, worse yet, caught.

"Hi Chub," Willow said, walking into the cafeteria as she did every room—just like she owned it. Liz froze, heart jumping to her throat. Did Willow just call this man chubby? But the man turned to face them, a broad smile spreading across his ruddy cheeks in response to Willow's own radiant grin. Liz could see that he wasn't fat, although his barrel chest and stout build might mislead the untrained eye. He looked old, but Liz didn't know if it was years or weariness that had worn on him.

"This is Liz," Willow continued. "It's her first day on the ship. She just got here a few hours ago, so I'm showing her around." Liz felt scrutinized as Chub turned his gaze toward her, but his smile only widened.

"Welcome aboard, Liz," he said heartily. "You're in good hands. Are you working in the orchard with Willow?"

"Yes, sir," Liz replied quickly—perhaps a little too quickly. Chub laughed, and Liz flinched.

"You definitely are new here if you're calling me 'sir.' People call me Chub."

"Chub?" Liz asked, trying out the word but not liking how it felt on her tongue. She wanted to be casual, like Willow, so she laughed. "It sounds like there's a story there."

Chub blinked, and Liz instantly wondered if she'd made a mistake by asking. But then he smiled again, and his eyes seemed to sparkle.

"I had two brothers. Twins. They were quite a bit older than me, and they weren't keen on my tagging along everywhere. At least, not until they realized that the girls thought I was cute, which meant my brothers could start up a conversation with anyone they wanted. So they started taking me everywhere, telling each other to 'get the chub' before they went to town."

Liz didn't know what to make of this, and evidently the frozen expression on her face gave her away. Chub only laughed again.

"A chub is a bait fish. They're too small to eat, and besides, they taste terrible. Mostly, they're a nuisance. Fishermen used to catch them and use them as bait to get the fish they really wanted."

Liz managed a smile as the explanation came together in her mind. She was so nervous she wanted to go back to her room and vomit, but Willow spoke before she could turn away.

"I didn't know you had brothers, Chub!"

"You never asked," he retorted playfully. "Besides, they're gone. But the name stuck." He said it casually, like it didn't hurt him. Maybe it didn't—Liz couldn't tell. Clearly, she had a lot to learn about the people on the ship.

Now, in the darkness, Liz finds it ironic that nothing has changed. She still has a lot to learn about the people on the ship—those who are left, anyway. She shifts slightly in the tree, moving only enough to relieve the hint of numbness she can sense in her right leg. Can't afford for anything to go numb in case she needs to move quickly.

Chub starts pacing back and forth just a few feet directly beneath her. She can smell his acrid sweat, the smell of anxiety. He's so close that even in the dim light, Liz is sure he'd see her if he looked up. But she knows she's safe—he won't.

This is why trees are the best place to hide. Liz learned on the surface that people rarely look up. She'd spent many a night perched high in dead pine trees, hiding as she tracked New Generation raiding parties to find her brother. She followed them closely, sometimes so closely that she knew they could sense her. She'd watch them from above, especially when they camped at night, so close that she could see their skin prickle. Sometimes they would even look for her—every way but up.

Now, she watches Chub's head shift from side to side, his barrel chest wrenching every few seconds to look over his shoulder. Liz is certain he feels something amiss. Even the most oblivious people perceive danger, although she wouldn't call Chub oblivious—just unaware of her presence. In fact, Chub was actually quite discreet. Liz wouldn't have suspected him at all, except for the clue Albert gave her before he died. *They have code words,* he'd told her. *Words that are completely out of context, like "hashbrown casserole" when there is none in the cafeteria.*

Liz's first lead was Mathilda Greenberg, Jackson's spy on the council. Mathilda was completely infatuated with her brother, and she wouldn't go long without contacting him, even after she was discovered. But the woman was smart enough to know she needed to be careful—all of her communication was being monitored, so she asked Chub to contact Jackson on her behalf.

Liz watched from a distance, hidden behind stacks of trays, as Mathilda approached him in the cafeteria. "I'd really love some clam chowder," she said nonchalantly. But there were no clams on the ship, and chowder had never been on the menu. When Chub told her that he'd see what he could do, Liz started following him instead, and that led to a series of new discoveries.

He must be waiting for someone, she thinks now, as he continues to pace. This is exciting—she's never seen him meet anyone. He's hidden some of Jackson's tablets on several occasions, though, and retrieved them as well, depositing them in a different place each time, generally just outside the range of video surveillance. The spies are careful, waiting for hours or even days before collecting the devices—too long for Liz to monitor, although she did see one of Charlie's dock mechanics collect a tablet once. She tried to follow him but didn't learn anything useful.

A rustling comes from the trees. A shadowy figure emerges, but Liz can't see who it is.

"I thought you weren't coming!" Chub whispers.

"I can't get it." It's a man's voice.

"You need to figure it out," says Chub. "I've been asked for it, and I mean to provide."

"Then find another way. I don't have access to the medical unit, and I'm not going to risk blowing all our covers—especially mine." He sounds vaguely familiar, but Liz has heard so many different voices, it could be anyone.

"Wasn't this the whole point of getting you assigned to the maintenance staff?"

"No, I don't believe it was. I got assigned to maintenance to access parts stores and to plant bugs. And to manage the video feeds while the rest of his lackeys run around the ship, manufacturing parts for his mystery machine." Liz's heart falls. There have been six new assignments to maintenance, all of them members of the Fifty-Two.

"But I gave you a cover story." Chub sounds desperate.

"Dr. Harris maintains very strict access to her lab. The story won't pass muster, and I'm not keen to catch a bullet in the head like Willow, or that guy Zag. Besides, didn't you say he's negotiating with the council? If Dr. Harris already gave him the specs for the bone mender, why wouldn't she be willing to give him information about her DNA repository? I hear it's mostly farm animals and birds, anyway."

"You've heard what's in it, but you can't get me a simple list?"

"No, and I'm done discussing it. Stop asking. You're putting us all at risk."

"We're already at risk," Chub mutters. "I don't like it any more than you do. We're in too deep, and we can't change that. We have to see it through—prove our worth. If we can't be valuable, we'll be disposable."

"Find another way! We're done here. I set the loop to thirty minutes, so we need to get out of here now before the video starts up again."

This seems to instill urgency into Chub, who hesitates only a moment before pushing through the trees, grumbling under his breath.

Liz waits until they're both gone before she jumps down from her perch. She's hesitant to follow them, even though that's the only way to know for sure who Chub met. A beam of bright light silhouettes the two figures as they open the door to the stairwell. They step through, and the door closes, returning her to darkness. Now it's too late.

Maybe she doesn't really want to know who Chub met. An image of Ruth flashes in her mind. The woman's tan face is varnished with wrinkles, her eyes the color of pine bark, with an edge of bluish haze. Liz can see the campfire they sit around each night, glowing light flickering across Ruth's face as she talks about the way things used to be. Liz's dreams for the future are built upon those stories, upon the wonder and hope she sees in the children's eyes as they sit captivated.

She thinks about the play the children wrote in her honor, how everyone wants to play her role. Their adoration redeems her humanity, transforms the blind rage she felt toward the New Generation that day into something heroic, something useful. It's unbearable, knowing that one or more of the Fifty-Two has fallen from grace, that they are helping the very people who were so eager to slaughter them outside the Denver depot.

Does Ruth know her group has been compromised? Of course, she must. Nothing happens in the Fifty-Two without Ruth's knowledge. Liz doesn't want to think about what this means, but she can't ignore her perennial questions. How did fifty-two people survive in a cave for nineteen years without getting caught? What did Ruth do to keep them alive? What did she compromise?

Liz breathes in the smell of darkness, deciding what to do next. *This was a waste of time*, she thinks, realizing that she's learned all she can from tailing Chub. She needs a different way of getting information. Turning deeper into the trees, away from the stairs and the main lift, she heads toward the utility lift, which is outside the range of the cameras. She'll take it to Level 7 and exit from the orchard. No one will know she was here, especially the Fifty-Two.

Her pace slows as she hears the lapping of water—the reservoir. This is close to the spot where Albert died. He brought her here to kill her, but he wasn't a killer. In the end, the only life he could bear to take in his suffering was his own.

Liz only has to close her eyes to remember how it went down. Will the pain of that memory ever go away? Does she even want it to? Albert's death made her realize that her priorities were all wrong. She'd been so busy hating her enemies, she forgot that she needed to love her friends. It was a hard lesson with a steep cost. Doesn't she owe it to Albert to remember?

Some memories have no right to be forgotten, and this pain has no right to be healed. Liz sits on the ground, leaning against the rough bark of a large pine tree. It presses into her back, scraping against the scar that remembers how she fought to get free of the ropes. Albert's grief-stricken face flashes through her mind, how he fell upon her knife just beyond her reach. She can hear her shoulder popping as she tried to free herself to help him. The smell of his blood, the taste of her own bitter words when she did the only thing she could to comfort him—she sang him a lullaby. She remembers until she cannot bear the remembering, and then she reminds herself that the past is gone. Only the present remains, and the possibility of the future.

She's got to flip him. Chub will be in the kitchen, preparing to open for breakfast. Now is the time to get what she needs, while he's still flustered and scared.

***

Liz stands in the kitchen, waiting for Chub to notice her. He freezes when he sees her, a large sheet of uncooked biscuits in his hands. His face flushes red, and Liz is sure his first instinct is to yell at her to get out. Crew members aren't allowed here, unless they have a work assignment. But the words seem to catch in his throat, and he swallows hard as his eyes take her in. He shifts his weight from foot to foot.

"I want to talk to you about clam chowder," Liz says, eyes locked on his. He momentarily freezes, eyes popping open before he quickly blinks them back under control.

"We don't have any clams," Chub says gruffly. "I keep asking the genetics lab about it, and they keep referring me to Harry Goodworth, telling me they can only breed clams after he makes a saltwater habitat for them, but I know there is such a thing as freshwater clams." His mouth clamps closed. Liz thinks he may have bitten his tongue by the way his eyes are watering.

"We can either talk about this here," she says evenly, "or we can talk somewhere more privately—the brig, perhaps. But I know you have information, and I intend to get it from you right now." The blood drains from his face, a stark contrast to the red flush from seconds ago.

"Let's go to the dining room," he says, wiping his hands on a towel before tucking it into his long white apron.

When they get there, he takes a seat at a table. "What do you want to know?" He presses his lips together as if he's trying to guard his expression, but his eyes betray his fear and doubt.

"I want to know everything."

"To what end? What do you intend to do with the information I give you?" Chub's voice is dripping with fear, but he seems determined to resist. Liz studies him as he waits for an answer that she has no intention of providing.

"I won't be the reason someone else takes a bullet to the head," he says doggedly. "If you expect me to betray someone else to save myself, forget about it. I'll take the blame."

"This isn't about blame, Chub," Liz says calmly, speaking to him as she would to a wounded, cornered animal.

"Oh? Then what is it about?"

"It's about survival—ours."

Chub asks again, this time with less panic in his voice, "What do you want to know?"

"Are you sure you want to talk about this here?" Liz asks, noticing a handful of other people at nearby tables.

"It's as good a place as any." His voice is gruff now. "I don't want to be seen going off with you."

"Why is that?"

"I just don't."

"Are you afraid it might be the last time anyone sees you?"

"Would it be?" His eyes are uncertain.

"I guess that's up to you," Liz replies softly.

"Was it up to Albert Wyndham, too?" he asks. A bead of perspiration forms on his lip.

"Yes, it was," Liz says tersely. She doesn't want to think about Albert right now.

"If you say so," Chub mutters. His eyes drop to the tabletop before him.

"You don't have a credential. Why not?"

Chub shrugs. "I don't need one. I haven't been to the surface in years."

"So how did you get hooked up with the New Generation?"

Chub meets her eyes again, calmer than before.

"Willow Brown recruited me, after Captain MacAbee disappeared." A mist gathers in his eyes as Liz waits for him to continue. "She was so convinced that she knew the truth, wasn't she? She was the most fearless person I've ever known." His voice turns wistful, and Liz remembers Willow's way of owning every room she entered, with grace and confidence. She wanted so desperately to be like that woman when she first came to the ship. Could Willow have convinced Liz to turn—even if it meant spying? Liz likes to think she wouldn't have betrayed Green Grow, not after everything Seth did to help her, but Willow was persuasive—and genuine. Who knows what she might have done?

"Why you?" she asks, and Chub blinks away a tear.

"I don't think there was any reason in particular. She tried to recruit everyone she thought would listen. But once I was in, Jackson seemed to think I was especially valuable—at least that's what he led me to believe. Because of my position in the kitchen, you see. I could pass messages to anyone—everyone has a reason to come to the cafeteria."

"Is that what you did? Pass messages?"

Chub's eyes grow narrow.

"How much do you already know?" he asks.

"Why does it matter if you answer my questions honestly?" Liz counters. Chub stiffens, but then sighs a wave of resignation.

"After Willow recruited me, she gave me a radio transmitter—a real small one. People would pass me information, and then I would use the radio transmitter to send it to Jackson, tapping it out in Morse code."

"That must have taken a lot of time."

"It did, but the messages were simpler then—usually updates on new recruits or information about what was happening on the growing levels. He never asked for anything that seemed all that sensitive. Then I guess the stakes got higher, when he learned we were building a propulsion drive."

"Did you tell him?" Liz asks.

"I suppose I could have. There were a few specification reports that took a long time to transmit. They might have been from engineering, but it's more likely that someone else told him."

"Like who?" Liz asks.

"I don't know," Chub says gruffly, his face constricting. "Willow had ways to communicate with him, and I'm sure there were others, high in the chain of command. There must have been someone, because I didn't pass any messages to Zag Bryant—the guy Captain Harris executed for transmitting specs to the New Generation."

"I know who he is," Liz says evenly.

"You mean who he *was*," Chub corrects, meeting her eyes with a defiant stare, back straight even though his bottom lip trembles.

"But now you have a tablet," Liz says, refusing to acknowledge his correction.

"Yes, I manage a tablet," he replies. "Jackson tells me who to deliver it to and when to retrieve it."

"When did you start doing that?"

"About two months ago." His voice quivers, as if he's afraid Liz won't understand his implication.

Or maybe he's afraid I do understand. He could have phrased his response another way, but his point is clear. She brought the Fifty-Two here two months ago. Albert's words ring in her ears—*You brought some of these people on board.*

"So what does Jackson want you to do now?" she asks.

"If he wants anything, it's not from me," Chub says gruffly.

"He's had nothing to say to you since he failed to overthrow Captain Harris?" She looks at him sternly, leaning toward him in a way that makes him shrink back.

"Oh, he had plenty to say in the beginning. Not to me directly, but I picked up things as I passed the tablet around. He wanted something built—some kind of a machine. Lots of instructions about manufacturing parts. No one knew what it was for, though."

"Did we build it?" she asks.

"If there were instructions about when or how to put the thing together, they didn't come through me. Just a flurry of messages—mostly files he transmitted on the tablet. Then Jackson went dark. I haven't heard from him in weeks. The parts he wanted are piled in the airlock on Level 37. You can see them for yourself if you want."

His voice is calm enough, although his eyes plead for mercy, begging her to believe him. Liz takes a deep breath and moves to rise from the table. Chub lurches forward, clutching her arm.

"Don't you want to know why I did it?" he asks. She stares at him. Part of her wants to break the hand he used to grab her, but she has too many memories of this man to truly want to hurt him. She retakes her seat.

"Does it matter why?" This seems to unbalance the chef. His brow starts sweating, and he slumps back into his chair.

"I suppose not," he mumbles.

"Tell me anyway. Why did you do it?"

"To survive, Liz," he says emphatically. Is this meant to sway her? If so, it doesn't. "Look, no one knew what to think when Captain MacAbee didn't come back. Captain Harris didn't tell us anything. We didn't know what to believe. It seemed like just a matter of time before the New Generation came to take over the ship, and none of us wanted to be on the losing side."

Liz feels no sympathy for the floundering man, although it's true that Seth had little presence among the crew until recently. Maybe if he knew how to do that—how to be the leader they needed—none of this would be happening now.

He left a gap Jackson was more than happy to fill, although Liz knows that Seth can't be blamed. The ship had already been infiltrated under Captain MacAbee's leadership. Besides, Liz meant what she told Chub—blame is a luxury they cannot afford. Blame will get them killed.

"And are you still on the losing side?" she asks.

"I'm pretty sure I've already lost," he says, crumpling forward on his elbows as if the strength that held him upright has broken. "What's going to happen to me now?" His words strike deep at Liz's core, fanning a smoldering flame of anger. He's not the first person to ask her this question, as if she is the decider of fates, knower of the future.

The anger leaks into her voice.

"You're going to go back to the kitchen and go about your business. Keep this conversation between us, and I want to know about any future communications between you and the New Generation." Liz pauses for a moment, commanding his full attention. "All of our lives depend on this, Chub. You can't trust the New Generation—none of us can."

"But Jackson is your brother," he ventures.

"Then you should take my word for it, shouldn't you?" she says stiffly, rising from her chair.

"Liz?" The man's eyes brim with tears. "Did Captain Harris really have to kill Willow?"

Liz remembers the woman pleading to the crew, screaming before Seth shot her.

"Didn't he, though?" Turning, she walks away without looking back.

CHAPTER 3

THURSDAY'S COUNCIL MEETING

***

Liz studies the familiar faces seated around the table in the captain's conference room for the daily council meeting. They need to work together to get back to Earth in one piece, but the dynamics are more dysfunctional than ever. The meetings are necessary but barely tolerable. Is this why Jackson so often seems to work alone?

Her brother has no patience for dissent, and thus no patience for the council. He clearly believes that he alone can solve the problem of getting the Green Grow 3 back to Earth, and Liz is afraid he might be right. The council could certainly find a way home, if they'd only work together. But they never do. They continue to argue, regardless of the circumstances or urgency involved, especially where Jackson is concerned.

Claire and Mathilda support everything Jackson wants them to do, while Harry and Jarrod protest. They don't seem to understand the importance of solidarity, which is dumbfounding given how little they know about what Jackson intends. They see only what he chooses to show them, and there's no way it's the complete picture.

Jackson claims he wants to improve life on the surface, to lead the New Generation to a brighter future, but it seems like what he really wants is power. Restarting and controlling the food supply from the Green Grow 3 would give him leverage over the other New Generation factions he's told Liz about. It would give him power over everyone who would come to depend on the food. What would he do with that power, and who else does he want to control?

Does Jackson really mean to improve life on the surface, or would everyone still live in fear? He presents himself as an educated, thoughtful leader on the video calls, an agent of change who's redirecting the errant ways of the New Generation. But this is misleading at best, and disingenuous. His raiding parties still take what they want. They pillage and destroy anything in their way. They still think of women as property, using them for entertainment and diversion, buying them for the price of a motorcycle and confining them to breeding centers for procreation. They still look and act and think like savages, and despite how Jackson presents himself on the calls, Liz knows he must be well-versed in savagery to maintain his position. She isn't convinced that Jackson has the ability to change the core values of the New Generation, an organization that dominates its members with shows of force. He doesn't even seem to want to try.

What does Jackson intend to do with the crew of the Green Grow 3 when they return to Earth? The council worries about this, but not nearly enough. It's as if they believe by the time they get back to Earth, Jackson will have forgotten that they were once enemies. This couldn't be further from the truth, Liz suspects.

She believes Jackson when he says no one will harm her, but his promise of safety doesn't seem to apply to anyone else. Will Seth survive the New Generation? Jackson ordered his spies to kill him during the mutiny, and the fact that they failed seems to make him despise Seth even more. Will the Fifty-Two survive the New Generation? It certainly didn't look that way when Liz saved them at the depot. She's not even sure that Jackson's supporters will fare well—Claire, Mathilda, the spies in the crew. The New Generation subjugates or kills those it conquers. It's that simple. Yet, the council continues to believe they have the luxury of bickering instead of working together.

Jackson may appear to be civil, but his pleasantries seem like a thin veneer, one that is already wearing through. He still refers to the meetings with Liz and Seth as negotiation calls, but there's increasingly little negotiating. Jackson sets clear expectations and gives them instructions, instructions that Claire and Mathilda call advice and Jarrod and Harry call orders.

More often than not, they do what Jackson wants. They have to if they want the formula he promised, to generate thruster fuel. The council claims they can't figure it out themselves, although Liz isn't sure they've tried hard enough. Instead, they try to meet Jackson's demands, but he's not satisfied with the progress they are making. In fact, it seems that nothing is capable of satisfying him. Over the last two months, he's increased his demands far beyond the sharing of medical technology and bioengineering knowledge that originally seemed enough. Now he's trying to run their operations.

"And what exactly are we going to do with the crops when they are ready to harvest?" Harry demands, incensed that Jackson has given them very specific instructions to restart growing on all the abandoned levels. "The rice he wants will take three months to grow, and we need another month to clear and prep the levels. That's four months, but it's going to be years before we get back to Earth's orbit. Why would we want to use our resources managing new crops? We need our people focused on maintaining the ship, especially given the strain of the controlled accelerations. What good will any of this do if we don't make it back to feed anyone?"

Harry looks expectantly at Seth, who appears deep in thought. When he doesn't respond, Harry continues.

"Seth, you know there's no way we'll be back to Earth in six months. And now he wants us to breed all the livestock, too? I don't understand how any of this is a good idea. How are we supposed to manage this along with the controlled acceleration?"

"Yes, the livestock could be a problem," Seth says, his brow furrowed, eyes drilling holes into his tablet. It's only been a few hours since Liz left him asleep and content in his bed, but he already looks tired. The corner of his eye begins to twitch, and she knows that something is on his mind—something more than the accelerations and the calls with Jackson and the bickering of the council. "Claire, is the additional livestock feasible? I expect the lab to turn its full attention to the thruster fuel as soon as we get the formula."

"We can manage," Claire says, and Liz isn't surprised by this answer given what she's seen on the calls with Jackson. Claire falls prey to his charisma time and time again. It feeds her ego and sustains her delusion that she has some measure of influence over him. "Once fertilized, the embryos will require some monitoring, but it's not a heavy demand. We have limited gestation ability in the lab, but we can implant the embryos into our existing stock with a few hormone treatments. It can be done."

"But should it be done?" Harry demands.

"Why not?" Claire asks, a familiar curtness in her voice. "The ship has a much greater capacity than we are using right now. What's the point in leaving it dormant, even if we don't get back to Earth right away? Jackson told us to be ready to distribute food in six months. I'm certain he has a plan to distribute it, and we should be ready. Isn't this what we've all wanted? To get back to the business of feeding the earth? We need to push ourselves here."

"We need to be careful of Jackson Goeff!" Harry cries. "We don't know what his intentions are for this ship, or what his intentions are for us when we get back. Why are we relinquishing control of our operations to him now?"

"We're not relinquishing control," Claire replies. "We're working together. We're building peace!"

"Do you really believe that?" Jarrod asks, breaking the rhythm of the argument between Claire and Harry. "I'm with Harry on this one. Jackson has given us explicit orders regarding nearly every aspect of operations on this ship—the course he plotted, the velocity he's demanding, when and how to engage the propulsion drive. Meanwhile, he dangles the promise of thruster fuel before us but has yet to deliver. Is that your standard of a partnership?"

Claire studies Jarrod's face, her chocolate-brown eyes bright and alert.

"We need to reach terms," she says firmly, "and we need to make sure they are good terms, or we will all be doomed when we get home. Besides, what's our alternative? I don't need to tell you that this ship wasn't built for deep space travel. We have to go home, so there's no point in trying to hide from Jackson or lie to him. He still has good sources of information on this ship, and there's no point denying that we've been infiltrated."

"So it's basically reaching terms by surrender, is it?" Harry demands.

"No," Claire replies, "but perhaps that's how you choose to see it."

"How I choose to see it? It looks plain enough to me—no choosing involved. You're the one suggesting we choose to overlook the obvious. And what will be the cost of that choice, Claire? How much will it cost your son, in particular? Or do you also choose to believe that Jackson has somehow grown fond of Seth over the last two months?"

"Enough," Seth interjects firmly. "Nothing has changed. We'll continue to work toward his demands until we get the full specifications for the thruster fuel. Perhaps then we can reassess. Harry, use whatever resources you have available to prep Levels 14 and 15 for rice production. Send me a timeline and growth projections by the end of today for all of the crops Jackson has requested. Claire, I want a detailed plan on ramping up livestock numbers, including timelines and competing priorities. Don't sugarcoat it. Jarrod, what's the status of the new thrusters?"

"I'm working out some issues with my team, but we're on schedule."

"Mathilda, are we still on course?" Seth asks. The plain woman with the liquid brown eyes and heavily rimmed glasses clears her throat.

"Yes, we're still on course. The scanners Jarrod built have not detected any substantial impediments, and the Hubble data Jackson sent us indicates this sector should be clear of any major debris."

"What's our current timeframe to the turnaround point?" Seth asks.

"Factoring in our continued acceleration, we should arrive in eleven years. I don't know what Jackson intends us to do in six months, but we won't be anywhere near Earth."

"The man is insane," Jarrod blurts out, his face turning purple. Liz is becoming accustomed to his emotional utterances, although it still surprises her sometimes just how strongly he hates—or perhaps fears—her brother. She doesn't doubt that Jarrod's emotions are on point, but it seems to debilitate him, paralyzing his mind instead of sharpening it. "And we're insane if we do what he tells us. I'm not surprised that he expects obedience without question, but I am surprised that we continue to comply. We are literally flying blind through space faster than any human has ever gone, to appease a man who hasn't been honest with us! We're counting on the formula he promised for thruster fuel, but then he tells we have to build completely different thrusters before he'll give us the formula. And the design is so simple and obvious, I could have come up with it myself. Why didn't he give us the formula when he sent the sent the specifications for the new thrusters? How do we know he'll give us the formula at all, and what if it doesn't work? He's a fraud, and we cannot trust him."

"And yet," Mathilda says dryly, "despite the simplicity of the solution, it didn't occur to you, did it? Obvious or not, he gave us a solution we didn't consider. What did you expect? A magical recipe to make argon gas out of compost? We can't produce appropriate fuel for the existing thrusters, but we can build the new ones and generate a nearly endless supply of fuel. I'm sure he'll deliver the formula, and I'm sure it will work. Perhaps if you had spent your time working on the shield we discussed instead of tinkering with your homemade scanners that we don't need, we'd all be feeling better about this. Interstellar dust is a far more pressing issue at these velocities."

Jarrod inhales deeply and sits back in his chair, fingers raking through his hair.

Seth glances down at his tablet. "Are we ready for the morning acceleration?"

"Yes," Jarrod confirms, "repair teams are ready."

"Harry, any concerns?"

"We'll be ready," Harry replies. "We're confining the livestock as we speak."

"Claire?" Seth asks, looking at his mother.

"We've had a few visits—headaches, earaches, vertigo, those kinds of things. I think we're still within our tolerances, though. We could push a little harder if you wanted to."

"Really, Claire?" Harry demands, his face flushing. "Push a little harder for how long? This has been a roller coaster ride from hell. I'm not sure how you think anyone can or should be pushed harder."

"Liz," Seth interjects, speaking calmly as if there's no argument building around him, "when is our next meeting with Jackson?"

"He said we'd talk tomorrow," she replies.

"Good." He stands to conclude the meeting. "You have your assignments. I want the usual reports after the acceleration. Jarrod, I'll meet you on the bridge and make the announcement as usual. Everyone is dismissed."

Liz remains seated as the council files out, studying Seth, who makes no move to rise from his chair. He seems preoccupied. What's on his mind? If they were cocooned within the seclusion of his quarters, she'd cradle him close to her, stroking his hair and whispering the question into his ear. *What's wrong?* Behind closed doors, they are lovers—two halves of the same heart. But outside the walls of their refuge, he is the captain of the Green Grow 3, and she is simply an advisor, as well as the sister of his enemy. The weight of the world rests upon his shoulders, the fate of everyone onboard the ship. Out here, she can't hold him in her arms. She can't ask him what's wrong, but she can give him something useful—information.

"I have an update," she says. Seth's tired eyes dart right, then left, then right again. He rises from his chair, motioning for her to follow him to the bridge, the only place he's confident Jackson can't bug. It's the only location he's comfortable speaking openly about her investigation.

"Jackson must realize we can't get back to Earth in six months," Seth says in a low, serious voice as they exit the room. "He must know that it's impossible for this ship to even approach the speed of light, much less surpass it. He must know this—he's too smart to be that dumb. What do you think he's planning?"

"I don't know," Liz responds honestly. "Maybe he has a solution we don't know about. Or maybe we're making the wrong assumptions. He never actually said we'd be back to Earth in six months. He only said we should be ready for regular food distributions."

"True," Seth says thoughtfully, "but what's relevant about that distinction? What are we missing?"

"I don't know," Liz says again. "But if we can manage it and still ensure the safety of the ship, maybe we should get the crops underway. What would it hurt?"

Seth nods, brow furrowed as if he is deep in thought. "I'll make a decision after I get Harry's reports."

The door to the bridge hisses closed behind them. Seth sits in the large captain's chair, activating a control panel and pressing a sequence of buttons that scan for any unauthorized transmissions or electrical impulses in the bridge. The scan comes back clear, and he activates another command that starts a low-grade static noise, further encumbering any potential attempt to intercept what they're saying.

"Okay," he says, facing Liz squarely. "Tell me what you found."

CHAPTER 4

DARK SIDE
OF THE MOON

***

Seth sits strapped in the captain's chair on the bridge, surrounded by the rest of the council. He requires them to be here for every controlled acceleration, despite their objections. Actually, his mother is the only one who voices concerns, but she's been clear that she finds it tedious and disruptive to report to the bridge twice a day. Nonetheless, each acceleration is momentous and must be done carefully. Seth cannot allow it to become routine.

"Approval code confirmed," he says, activating the propulsion drive.

"Propulsion drive engaged," Jarrod confirms, just before a mechanical voice counts them down.

The ship accelerates, and the ten-minute countdown begins. Seth closes his eyes as the world blurs around him, the pressure in his head increasing. His body grows heavier and heavier as they reach 4G, and he focuses on the air going in and out of his lungs. *I choose to stay still,* he tells himself. He has no choice, but something about the affirmation keeps him from panicking. The next ten minutes will be miserable, but Seth can use the time to think. He's incapable of doing much else, plastered in his seat by a rate of acceleration the human body was not built to endure.

Turbulent thoughts batter his skull as he considers everything Liz told him. How could she have learned so much but so very little at the same time?

He cannot reconcile Chub's betrayal with everything he thought he knew about the man. Chub has been a fixture on the ship since Seth was a kid. In fact, Seth can't remember a single day that he hasn't seen the man onboard. Why would someone who spent no time on the surface involve himself with the New Generation? Why would he use his position in the kitchen to undermine their safety?

He asked Liz those very questions, and she recounted Chub's explanation of being recruited by Willow Brown, as well as his alleged fear after Captain MacAbee failed to return. It sounded like a bunch of lies and excuses, and it was no justification for compromising the ship's security. *Hasn't he heard of self-fulfilling prophesies?* How could anyone be afraid of the New Generation overtaking the ship, while simultaneously helping bring it about?

We've lived together here for years. Why did I not see his fear and weakness? But Seth knows why—he didn't used to think about people in those terms. It's only now, since dealing with Jackson, that he thinks of people as strong or weak. But doesn't he need to see them that way? That's how Jackson sees them, and Seth needs to see the world as his enemy sees it. Jackson is strategic and opportunistic, a formidable opponent in a game Seth never asked to play.

Does he really think it's all a game? The thought hits Seth hard, ringing true as he considers his enemy's

Machiavellian ways. How could so many lives be reduced to a mere game? It's unsettling, but even worse is that Seth knows he's unprepared. If his only way out of this is to match Jackson's intellect and strategic prowess, he will lose—not just his command, but his life as well. He's known since the broadcast inciting the crew to revolt that Jackson wants him dead. But knowing how deeply the crew has been infiltrated makes Seth feel vulnerable in a way he hasn't before.

And what about the machine on Level 37? There wasn't time to see it in person before the acceleration, but the pieces sat in plain sight on the airlock's video feed. He and Liz saw it together, on the bridge's large panoramic screen—stacks of panels, cartons of bolts, boxes of circuit boards, and a few oddly shaped pieces that Seth couldn't identify offhand. What is it meant to do? Is it a new weapon, or another communication device? Are all the parts even there, or is it only partially complete? Is it anything at all, or just a diversion intended to send him on a fool's errand? Anything is possible.

His thoughts shift to Liz's Fifty-Two. They are the only new assignments to the maintenance staff. Undoubtedly, they've been compromised, although Seth can't make sense of that, either. He's convinced they brought the specifications onboard for Jackson's tablets, the ones he uses to communicate in real time over impossible distances. But then, when Jackson hacked the broadcasting system, they fought by Liz's side, subduing his force with great skill and no hesitation. Now it seems they are helping him again. Why? And how will Liz respond when she can no longer deny that the people she saved, the people she's come to love dearly, are working for her brother?

Seth's head begins to throb painfully, forcing all of his thoughts and questions to the background. He looks at the countdown clock on the large screen, squinting his eyes to make sense of the blurry numbers. The controlled acceleration is almost done, and he's grateful despite needing much more time to think. He waits for the pressure on his body to ease, to feel relief from the heaviness that makes it hard to breathe and impossible to move.

How much longer can he bear this? How much longer can the crew? The moment Seth is certain they can produce thruster fuel, he'll put a stop to this nonsense. There is no way they're traveling eleven years to a faraway planet to turn around. It's a ridiculous plan—even Jackson must know how absurd it is.

The only sensible option is to slow down. Enough that they can turn around earlier. But they need thruster fuel to do that. If they could engineer the fuel themselves, they would already be slowing, despite Jackson's threats and intimidation. But the council claims they can't do it, and Jackson finds reason after reason to delay giving them his formula. He's stalling, but why?

What does he really want, and why does he insist they head toward this planet, Omega? There must be something out here that he can't get on Earth. Seth can't imagine what, but he's starting to get the idea that Jackson isn't the only one who wants something only the Green Grow 3 can provide. He thinks about the strange message he received when they began accelerating—a message he's shared with no one—and he realizes he can't ignore it any longer.

The control system's mechanical voice confirms that the acceleration has reached 1.5G. Seth takes in a deep breath, just because he can, and tells himself that the world around him is normalizing.

"Jarrod, commence the post-acceleration system scans," he says, repeating the same protocol they follow every time they accelerate.

"System scans commenced," Jarrod confirms, and then they all wait. Seth can see his mother out of the corner of his eye. Her eyes are still closed, and it's just as well. He doesn't want her to look back at him, only to study the woman who gave him life, the woman who is teaching him just how hurtful a mother's abandonment can be. *Don't wallow,* he tells himself, letting his mind drift to the future.

He dreams of a place he and Liz can be together, a place where they can be who they are instead of who the world has made them. Somewhere no one knows he grew up on the Green Grow 3, or that he served as its captain. Where no one knows the name Jackson Goeff, or that Liz ever even had a brother.

Seth doesn't bother dreaming of a quiet, simple life with Liz. No, she's too expansive for that—too fearless and adventurous. Liz can't help but change the world—she's certainly changed Seth's. He only wants to be with her when she does it, loving and protecting her. He will be hers, and hers alone, and her love will sustain him in return. The thought of it makes him smile. He won't have six hundred crew members relying on him, questioning him, betraying him—certainly not trying to kill him.

"We've lost gravity on Levels 13 and 16," Jarrod reports.

"Great," Harry interjects. "Why can't we lose gravity on abandoned levels?"

"Isn't Level 13 abandoned?" Claire asks, sounding groggy.

"Technically, yes," Harry replies, "but we're using the reservoir to grow bacteria. There will be globules of water floating around, and it'll take days or weeks for it to drain properly back into the reservoir."

"Jarrod, deploy repair teams. Level 16 is the first priority," Seth commands, not interested in bickering or thinking about Level 13. He knows well enough what's there—the place where Albert Wyndham died, where he found Liz tied to a tree, babbling incoherently with a dislocated shoulder. He'll never forget the sound of lapping water, or her whimpering cries and unintelligible words as he carried her to the medical unit.

"We also have one water processing station malfunctioning. It's one of the backups, not a primary system."

"Acknowledged," Seth says. "Is it the same one that shorted out two days ago?"

"No, Captain," Jarrod confirms. "That repair appears to be holding. A maintenance team has been deployed." The bridge goes silent as the remainder of the tests run, until Jarrod speaks again. "The rest is clear."

Seth unlatches his seat restraints and stands, feeling battered and sore.

"Sounds like we got off easy this time," he says as everyone else prepares to leave. "Jarrod, can I have a word?"

"Is it about the new thrusters, Captain?" Jarrod already has too many things to do, but Seth isn't sure anyone else can help him, not anyone remotely trustworthy, anyway.

"No," Seth says, quickly scanning the bridge to make sure everyone else is gone and the door is sealed. "I have some questions about a message I received. I haven't spoken to anyone else about this, and it needs to stay between us for now."

Jarrod looks curious, but he says nothing as Seth pulls the message up on the panoramic screen before them. His eyes quickly scan the words before freezing, wide as saucers.

"Is this for real, Captain?" Jarrod asks, still glued to the screen.

"That's what I need to know." Seth glances at the words he's read so many times he knows them by heart.

> *TO: SETH HARRIS, ACTING CAPTAIN OF THE GREEN GROW 3*
> *FROM: GREEN GROW EXECUTIVE BOARD*
> *WHAT IS THE STATUS OF YOUR SYSTEMS? PLEASE CONFIRM YOUR LOCATION.*

"I've been getting them for days—ever since we started accelerating," Seth says. "It's the same message, coming to my ship-to-ship communication box on some kind of transmission loop."

"It's a ship-to-ship communication?" Jarrod asks, standing motionless.

"Yes." Seth is certain that he knows what the man is thinking. "If it's real, it means the executive board is alive and well—on the Green Grow 2."

"Just like Jackson told us," Jarrod whispers.

"Can you tell where it originated?"

"Yes." He moves toward Seth's chair. "May I?"

Seth stands and motions for him to sit down. Jarrod's fingers fly over the keyboard, his eyes filled with furious intensity. Strings of characters fill the screen. His gaze freezes, and his mouth falls open.

"Every ship-to-ship message has an encoded time and location stamp," he says, his voice barely more than a whisper. "And look—it's right there. The message came from the Green Grow 2." Jarrod's eyes fly up to meet Seth's. "Captain, if the executive board is on the Green Grow 2, why didn't they communicate sooner? Why didn't they help us, and where is the ship?" Before Seth can respond, the man's fingers once more fly furiously over the keyboard, scrolling down through the lines of code. He copies a series of numbers and opens a new application, pasting them in an empty box. "We can find out where they are," he mumbles, seeming oblivious to Seth's presence as he waits for results. With a gasp, he looks up once more, his eyes wide but this time with rage.

"They're right there!" Jarrod proclaims. "Captain, they're right there! Why didn't we pick them up on our scanners?"

"Where?" Seth asks.

"Earth's orbit." He types more codes to pull up a star map, then zooms in on a location. "Wait. No. No!"

"What, Jarrod?" Seth asks, eyes flitting between the man's angry face and the nonsense on the screen in front of him.

"Captain, they're hiding behind the moon. Look, they're right there!" He jumps up from the captain's chair, running to the large screen and pointing at a series of numbers. Seth isn't sure what the numbers mean, but he gets the point. Jackson was right. The executive board fled the peace summit and left the Green Grow 3 cut off and vulnerable, floating in Earth's orbit like bait.

Moving back to his chair, Seth sits down heavily, confounded.

"Could Jackson hack the system?" he asks.

"It's unlikely." Jarrod's brow furrows. "Although I can't say it's impossible. I'm not sure why he would do it."

"Who knows?" Seth asks. "A distraction? A trick? Maybe he thinks I'll respond. Maybe he just wants to annoy me."

Jarrod nods, lips pursed. "If the message is transmitted on a loop, I may be able to track the signal back and confirm the source. Let me see what I can find. And there are some other tests I should run as well. Did you respond, sir?"

"No." Seth shakes his head. "And I don't intend to until I know more."

CHAPTER 5

WORLDS
WITHIN WORLDS

***

Once again, she is alone—She Who Needs No Name. All her energy is gathered around her in a tight, comforting ball as she dims her awareness into the humming churn of the planet. Its cycle of construction and destruction brings her comfort still, although not as much as it used to.

She could go anywhere and do anything, but why? Going to a different place here in linear time won't solve her problem. It won't help her pass this test, if indeed it is a test. She is beginning to wonder, although part of her deep down already knows—it's not a test. It's a mistake. Something unexpected happened to her, and she doesn't yet know how to make it right.

She can hear the lives of the small, dense creatures on the surface much more clearly than ever before. She's gained much skill at lowering her vibration. In fact, she can lower it so much that her own energy starts to feel very dense, and it becomes harder to remember who she really is. But, it's the only way to sense the creatures around her, at least for now.

Her presence in this time and place seems to have affected the creatures, or some of them anyway. Their vibration has risen, not a tremendous amount but enough to inspire a curiosity in them, a desire to learn more from her and raise their vibration higher.

She felt strangely good when she first realized this, which then made her sad because it made her think about home, where she was fully herself before arriving here. Thinking of coming here makes her angry—a new emotion she's discovered when her vibration dips too low. Anger courses over her in waves, and all she can do is pull herself into a tight ball, withdrawing from the creatures and retracting her awareness so far within that all she can sense is the cyclical reformation of the rock around her, from solid to liquid to solid again.

She finds it increasingly difficult to raise her vibration when she's angry, and each time she wonders if the brief respite from her loneliness offered by the creatures is worth the way it makes her feel. She wonders if she should keep to herself and wait, but wait for what? No one is coming to save her.

She has only the creatures now, and they seem to wait for her when she withdraws. She noticed how a few of them took up permanent residence on the part of the surface closest to her, and they now seem to listen for her whispers all the time. No matter how angry she gets, the feeling eventually passes, and she emerges once more, possibly due to boredom or—if she's optimistic—hope. And she begins her own cycle again, whispering to the creatures, teaching them things that seem to fill all the space of their narrow minds.

The small, dense beings possess a vast ignorance that

confounds her. The simplest things mystify them, but she can sense they want to learn so desperately. She knows that the capacity to learn is a trait the creatures share with her, although it may be the only thing they have in common. All beings grow through learning, no matter how primitive or low. The creatures frustrate her, but she reminds herself that they deserve the same patience she required as a student, the patience she will undoubtedly continue to require once she gets back to her teacher—if she gets back.

"It's true," she tells them again, feeling the threads of her mind grow tighter with the strain of being patient. "All life is connected."

"How can it be?" a perplexed mind whispers back. "The others here are different, weak. Aren't they meant to die so we can eat them?"

"Broaden your perspective," she commands. "You are weaker than I. Does this mean I should extinguish your life, and consume your energy for myself?"

She senses a combination of emotions surge through the group—fear, but also insight. This pleases her, although she's not sure which is more pleasing: to be feared or to be illuminating.

"Please don't," they cry. "We are worthy!"

"You find yourselves worthy, even though you are so weak and pitiful compared to me? Then what of the other creatures—are they still unworthy?"

"But what will we eat? How will we survive?" She senses their fear growing. Perhaps she shouldn't find this amusing, but she does. Is she wrong to feel this way? Her teacher would likely rebuke her for being amused by someone else's fear, and this makes her angry—perhaps at herself, perhaps at her teacher. How can her teacher judge her feelings, especially after abandoning her in her time of greatest need? She reminds herself that her teacher has judged nothing. She is projecting her own thoughts onto another and has no right to be angry. This does not stop the seed of anger from budding.

She snaps at the creatures. "Did I suggest you stop nourishing your own bodies?"

"We cannot eat them if they are, indeed, our brothers." The whisper comes with conviction. If she were calm, she might be proud of this insight. But she's angry, and she doesn't care what the creatures consume. They are all insignificant, and she has no opinion on the rightness or wrongness of what they do. There are many reasons for life, and perhaps a short, simple life that culminates in a sacrifice to feed another is a legitimate experience—it's only the body that dies, after all.

She can sense their anticipation as they wait for a reply, and this annoys her. She chooses to reply, as she often does, by telling them that there are many ways to solve problems. A harshness carries in her voice that she doesn't intend, but she's too preoccupied with her own thoughts to care. If there are many ways to solve problems, why can't she solve her own problem? Why can't she go home?

She is ready to withdraw again, to pull her energy into a tight ball below the surface of the planet, and then she senses it—a surge of disconcertingly familiar energy, the same energy that washed over her before her great aloneness. Her awareness reels as she sends threads of it in every direction to pinpoint the source. The energy disappears almost as quickly as it came, but not before she hones in on its origin. Something very interesting remains where the energy originated, a world within a world filled with strange creatures she's never encountered before.

She's tempted for just a moment to turn back to the

steady rhythm of the planet, but she cannot ignore the magnitude of what just happened. A spark of curiosity grows inside her, a spark that reminds her who she really is. She sweeps aside her lethargy and spins a thread of awareness, casting it far into space to explore this tiny vessel that contains worlds within worlds.

CHAPTER 6

WELCOME ABOARD

***

OCTOBER 24, 2059—FRIDAY

Liz steels herself for another hour of bickering as she sits in the captain's conference room. Seth convenes the meeting, and Harry immediately begins to detail his concerns, yet again, about Jackson's request to cultivate the unused levels. Then Liz's ears register a clicking noise that shouldn't be there, and her eyes jump to the conference room door. The handle is moving, but no one else should be coming. All of the council members are here.

Seth also seems to have heard it. He jumps up from his chair, raising his pistol and squaring it as a man walks casually into the room, followed by a woman who looks around curiously from behind his torso.

"Jackson Goeff!" Seth barks as the rest of the council falls into a stunned silence. Time slows to a crawl as Liz's eyes grow wide as saucers. She finds herself standing as well, not to intervene but because her body needs to move, to prove to itself that she's not dreaming. *How is he here?* she wonders. Nothing her brother does should surprise her, but it does.

"Indeed," Jackson replies. Liz recognizes his voice from the video calls, but now she also hears how deeply it resonates through the air, taking up all the space in the room—surprising her again. Her heart skips a beat as she takes him in. He's tall—almost as tall as Seth.

"What are your intentions?" Seth growls, finger still on the trigger. Liz studies her brother, who scans the room casually. There's something like arrogance in the way he stands, straight and proud like he's never known any other way. Has he ever? She digs back into her memories, trying to rewind as fast and far as she can, but her mind gets stuck on that last day—that day he made her the only promise he never kept, the promise to come back. Jackson was fourteen, and Liz was eight. He stood tall and proud that day too, appraising her solemnly and instructing her to take care of their mother.

"I'm here to continue our negotiations, of course!" Jackson raises both hands in the air. "I am unarmed." Liz breathes in the strange scent of him, a fresh and clean smell that permeates the air. It takes her a moment to recognize it —ozone.

"Who else is with you?" Seth demands, pistol still aimed at Jackson, who glances at it dismissively before matching the captain's intense gaze. Liz takes in his clothing, disconcerted by its strange familiarity. He wears an open leather jacket over a shirt cut from crudely woven cloth. The shirt is surprisingly neat and well-fitted, with well-placed buttons to keep the collar comfortably closed. His long, fitted pants appear to be soft, dark leather, elaborately stitched at the seams. He's cleaner and better tailored than the New Generation raiding parties, but Liz knows his clothes are cut from the same cloth.

"It's only the two of us. I will be happy to make introductions," he says icily, "as soon as you holster that pistol. I won't have anyone hurt." Liz's gaze rests on an elaborate chest plate that hangs from his neck, intricately constructed from polished metal beads, strips of leather, and what appear to be bluish-green stones. It must signify his rank in the New Generation. It marks him as her enemy.

A sarcastic scoff escapes Seth's throat, but he says nothing. Liz glances at him, and he returns it with a cocked eyebrow, pursed lips, and a nearly imperceptible nod. *Play it cool*, Liz's signals with her eyes, and Seth seems to agree. What else can they do? He lowers the pistol to his side, finger no longer on the trigger, but doesn't holster it.

"Is this how you treat your guests?" Jackson demands, still fixed on Seth. Liz thought from the video calls that his hair was short, cropped close to his head, but now she sees she was mistaken. It's long and darker than hers, less like sunshine and more like damp desert sand, shiny and straight and loosely tied back at the nape of his neck.

"Guests are not allowed in this room, only council members," Seth growls in reply.

A wide smile dawns on Jackson's face. "Wonderful!" he booms. "I shall join the council!" He turns his attention to Liz, his eyes a paradox of sparkles and ash.

"Lizzie," he says softly, as if they are the only two people in the room. He takes a step toward her, extending two large, rough hands that are studded with silver rings. He is more alive than she ever thought possible—her greatest hope and disappointment, her protector and betrayer, her enemy, her brother.

Without her permission, her feet close the gap between them. She feels herself fold delicately into his embrace, inhaling the scent of his leather jacket and memories of Earth. Her mind and spirit want to push him away, to bury her knife in his chest, but her heart merely wants to crumble as she exhales a breath she's been holding for a very long time.

"I can't believe you're here, brother," she whispers, taking in his eyes, framed by the severe, ropy scar that covers one side of his face. He has the same serious look she remembers so freshly now from when they were young and still innocent.

"We have a lot of catching up to do," he says, breathing in her hair.

Liz pulls away tentatively, turning her attention to the woman who stands patiently behind Jackson, although she exudes a confidence that suggests she is no one's subordinate. Liz instantly thinks of Willow Brown, who walked into every room like she owned it. The woman looks small next to Jackson, barely reaching his chin, but her delicate frame stands tenacious and unapologetic, crowned with long, unruly curls. They fall free, wild, unbroken and uncontained. Her hair is such a deep brown that Liz might think it black if it weren't for the reddish glow toward the ends, and her skin is the gold of dark honey. Her heart-shaped face is beautiful, with high symmetrical cheekbones and a small chin. She studies Liz with large brown eyes, dark pools of mystery that seem intensely unafraid. Her fitted leather leggings rest atop chunky combat-style boots, all topped by a loose tunic. Her long leather jacket is the color of buckskin.

"Lizzie, meet my wife, Shelby," Jackson says.

Wife? Liz thinks. *Why didn't he ever mention being married? And why did he bring her here to the Green Grow 3?*

Liz can hear a whisper of a gasp from the place Mathilda sits, the sound of heartbreak.

Shelby offers a small smile, revealing a perfect dimple on each cheek. "I've heard so much about you," she says, her voice smooth and silky, infused with a lilt from a place Liz is sure she's never been.

"Welcome aboard," Liz offers, unsure what to say. She turns back to Jackson, questions flooding her mind.

"How did you get here?" she asks, not unkindly, as she takes a step back and sits at the table, beckoning the others to follow. Jackson sits across from her, and Shelby remains standing.

"I devised a way to move instantaneously across broad stretches of space, by folding the space-time continuum." He says it casually, as if it's no big deal. Liz looks to Seth, seeking a cue about whether to continue. One eyebrow lifts, and his eyes shift, perceptible only to her, telling her to continue before he turns his attention to his tablet.

"I see," she says. "Is this how you intend to return the ship to Earth?"

"No," Jackson says, chuckling. "The process is complicated, and I don't know how to move something as large as this ship. Not yet, anyway. Besides, the Green Grow 3 already has a way home."

"So why are you here now?" Liz asks, perplexion transparent in her voice.

"You need to speed up to get to Omega on time, and I'm beginning to doubt your council's ability to follow my directions."

"And then what?" Seth asks, eyes cold as steel.

"And then I have affairs to tend on Earth, where I intend to return," Jackson replies stiffly.

"What else do you intend?"

"What do you mean?"

"Surely you didn't come all this way to tell us yet again that we are going too slow," Seth presses, unyielding.

"No, I didn't," Jackson says plainly. "There are other matters to discuss. Matters of food distribution, for instance."

"We can't do that over video chat? You went to such great lengths to smuggle this advanced communication technology onto the ship, to interact in real time. Shouldn't we use it?" Seth's voice is sarcastic.

"No." Jackson sounds impatient.

"And what are your expectations while you are here, Jackson? Surely you don't expect free range of the ship."

Jackson lets out a bitter laugh. "I already know what I need to know about the ship. I expect to be treated courteously and to be included in the council meetings. Beyond that, if you wish to try to keep my presence a secret—if you wish to lie to the crew yet again about what is going on beneath their very noses—then I am content to remain on Level 1, as long as all of our needs are met. And what of you, my love?" He turns his head to look at Shelby. "Do you have expectations while we are here?"

"I have nothing to add," she says in her strange tone.

"Jarrod," Seth says, sounding composed, although Liz is sure he's anything but, "prepare Level 1 quarters for our guests with appropriate security. Harry, make sure they have food and everything they need in their quarters. Claire, brief them on the procedures for the 4G acceleration. We're continuing as planned. Everyone, we will conclude for now. Liz, please stay."

"Indeed," Jackson says, looking amused. "I'm sure you have many matters to tend at the moment." He stands and turns to face his bewildered sister again. "Lizzie, I do hope you'll stop by so we can catch up. It's been a long time, and there is much to discuss. I've missed you terribly."

Liz doesn't know what to say, how to feel, or what she wants to do. She casts him a tight smile, then turns her attention to Seth, who rises from his chair and ushers everyone out of the captain's conference room. Ellis is already waiting outside, having responded to a message Seth sent him to come immediately.

"Lock them down tight," Seth whispers to Ellis. "If they so much as look at you funny, I want to know, and if they try to leave their quarters, shoot them." He walks stiffly toward the bridge, and Liz knows he expects her to follow.

***

"Holy bearcats, Z!" Seth cries out as the bridge doors close behind them. "Did that seriously just happen?" His hands fly to his hair, pulling at the dark strands while he paces in front of the panoramic window that stares into the endless depths of space.

With wild eyes, he sits heavily into the captain's chair, pulling up security cameras on the window in front of them. "Let's see how much of his story we can corroborate."

Time seems to flow backward as they rewind the camera footage, tracing Jackson's arrival back to its origin. They start with the moment he arrived at the conference room door, straightening himself before entering, then scroll back through the corridor and the lift, where he placed a card over the digital access panel to gain entrance to Level 1, all the way back down to Level 37, the last level on the ship—the one housing all the parts to his mystery machine. They track him farther back, to the airlock where his large machine appears first intact, dismantling as they continue to watch the footage in reverse. When the machine reverts to the stack of parts familiar to Seth, they track Jackson back out of the airlock, back to the woods from which he emerged. They watch him until he disappears from the frame, to wherever he originated on the level.

"The hull was not breached," Seth observes, "but he's clearly coming from the trees. Whatever vessel he used to arrive here must have arrived directly on the level." He types more codes into his access panel and the view switches, moving quickly in real time as Seth deploys a drone camera on the level. He tracks back the direction Jackson traveled, and it only takes a few minutes before a large, opaque, egg-shaped capsule comes into view.

"What the fresh hell?" Liz asks breathlessly.

"I don't know, Z," Seth replies. "It's your brother we're talking about—it could be anything. We don't have time to sort it out now."

"So he arrived in that capsule, with the woman?"

"It seems that way. Then he assembled his machine before hopping right onto a lift and riding it all the way up to Level 1. There don't appear to be any other New Generation with him, so that part of the story must be true."

"But how do we know his army won't appear at any time?" Liz asks, eyes narrowed.

"We don't." Seth's voice is flat.

"We can't hide their presence," Liz says bluntly. "There's no way to keep it a secret."

"Agreed. I'll make an announcement to the crew today." A steely determination shines in his eyes. "Look," he continues, "I need to talk to Jarrod about bridge security. Find Mathilda, and see what she knows about Jackson's arrival."

Liz nods, turning to leave, but Seth catches her arm, pulling her back into him. His arms wrap tightly around her, and she can feel his heart racing in his chest. His lips press hard against hers before he buries his face in her hair.

"I love you so much," he whispers into it, squeezing her for another moment before letting her go. Liz knows he's afraid as he tells her to be careful, but she feels no fear. She walks off the bridge overwhelmed by a numbness that makes her wonder if she's really in a dream.

***

Time is of the essence, but Seth doesn't know what he should be doing at the moment. Jarrod is validating security protocols for the life support systems, navigation, and propulsion drive. Liz is talking to Mathilda, and his mother is preparing Jackson and the woman for the controlled acceleration. Ellis is standing guard outside Jackson's newly appointed quarters, and the crew is preparing for the controlled acceleration.

That's what everyone else is doing. What should I be doing? Seth wonders, his eyes still glued to the panoramic screen where the video of Jackson emerging from the trees on Level 37 plays on a continuous loop. Seth cannot afford to sit here and let himself be overwhelmed, but his mind is still reeling from the man's unexpected arrival, and from Liz's seemingly warm welcome.

How do I think she should have responded? he wonders, reminding himself that she looked just as shocked and surprised as he felt the moment her brother walked through the door. She's clearly been confused and conflicted about Jackson ever since he hacked the ship's broadcast system and Liz discovered he was still alive. *No,* he thinks, realizing he cannot read anything into her words, *Liz didn't know he was coming.*

But did his mother know? Seth wants to brush the thought aside, but he can't dismiss his doubts about her. She's taken Jackson's side too many times over the last two months for Seth to be confident about her loyalty. Could she have betrayed him?

Seth stops the video loop, rising from the captain's chair. Part of him wants to sit back down, to look at the live feeds in case more New Generation appear. But Charlie is doing that in the security office, freaked out like the rest of them that Jackson incomprehensibly materialized on Level 37. When Seth pointed him to the video and directed him to monitor the live feeds, Charlie asked if he should mobilize all the security forces. But Seth told him to hold off. "He's here alone," he said, "with a woman, and I don't want to create unnecessary panic."

But maybe they should all be panicking right now.

You are the captain of this ship, Seth reminds himself. *Stop hiding like a coward, and go see what you can learn.* He leans over the console to make a call, refusing to sit back in the chair in case he can't bring himself to rise again.

"Charlie, I'm going to Level 37 to investigate the arrival point."

Charlie hesitates, sounding unsure when he speaks. "Do you want backup, Captain?"

"No, there's no time. Keep your eye on the monitors as long as you can, and then prepare for the controlled acceleration."

"We're still doing a controlled acceleration this morning?" Charlie sounds disoriented and confused.

"Yes, we're proceeding as planned."

"Roger that. I have a cot in the security office, and I'll be here for the acceleration. I'll monitor your progress on the video feeds and send officers if anything unexpected happens."

"Thanks, Charlie."

Seth ends the call and leaves the bridge, drawing his pistol as he steps onto the lift and rides down to the bottom of the ship. He presses himself against the wall as the doors open, waiting a moment before quickly peeking out to make sure the level is clear. A strong smell of ozone fills his nostrils. He walks into the trees, holding his pistol ready as he makes his way to the place where Jackson arrived.

Every hair on Seth's body stands on end as the capsule comes into view. The drone footage didn't prepare him to see it in person, and his heart races as he approaches it cautiously, moving from tree to tree in case he needs cover. But the vessel seems barely large enough to accommodate Jackson and the woman, too small for a third person to be hiding inside.

It sits slightly lopsided, oblong like an egg, with a square opening on one side where Jackson must have emerged. Seth holsters his pistol and moves closer to inspect the smooth and seamless surface. There's no metal or framing to provide structure, just the deep emerald-green material that looks to Seth like a hardened, plant-based composite.

He moves closer to inspect the opening, peeking inside to find a hatch, carefully placed against the inside wall. It's the same size and shape as the opening, with no apparent hinge or handle; it has to be secured from the inside, using some other method. Otherwise, the vessel is empty, containing no controls, seats, lights, or any kind of electronics.

The capsule must act as a barrier, but Seth can't tell whether it's supposed to keep something in, or keep something out. He taps the green surface, wondering how he can chip a piece off. The green material seems to be a consistent thickness, approximately two inches.

Jackson's motives may be beyond his understanding, but Seth knows enough chemistry and biology to figure out how this capsule was made, if he can get a sample. But when he decided to come down here, he wasn't thinking clearly enough to bring a knife or any other tools. *I'll have to get a collection kit from Mom's lab,* he thinks, his stomach instantly constricting into a ball of anger. *She's probably thrilled he's here. Now she can ingratiate herself with him in person.*

It takes only a few minutes to get the collection kit, and only a minute more to scrape off a sample from the opening in the capsule. Seth returns to the lab. He needs to hurry. Everyone is preparing for the controlled acceleration, securing themselves in their quarters, and he needs to be back on the bridge in ten minutes.

After preparing a slide, he studies the sample through the microscope. Just as he thought, it's a biological substance, mostly algae with shreds of other plant material, pressed together with some kind of a binding agent. He studies the algae more closely. The cells are alive, or some of them anyway. Jackson must have created this capsule right before he came, with living algae.

Seth looks at the sample again, increasing and then decreasing the magnification. There must be something more he can learn. He needs to get back to the bridge, but he still has a few minutes. Then he sees it. The sample is degrading. Zooming in on a cluster of dead algae cells, Seth can see that the binding agent is breaking down. He can't be sure about the timeline, but it looks like a matter of days before Jackson's capsule disintegrates.

***

Liz's heart pounds with urgency as she turns toward Mathilda's quarters. She needs the woman to be there, because she's not in her office. In truth, Liz is thankful Mathilda's office is empty. She can't bear the thought of squeezing herself between the ever-present mountains of paper to attempt a meaningful conversation. But the conversation needs to happen now, and Liz needs to find her.

It's doubtful that Mathilda had anything to do with Jackson's arrival, but she needs to be sure. Besides, Mathilda seems to have history with Jackson, and she may have insight into his intentions. But will she be forthcoming about what she knows? Liz is pretty sure there are things she's been holding back even after she was discovered spying. Mathilda has been protecting Jackson—or at least that's what it seems like. What will she do now that she's met Jackson's beautiful, exotic, graceful, mysterious wife?

Liz knocks on Mathilda's door and waits. The door remains closed, but she can hear someone shuffling behind the door. She knocks again and waits. Nothing.

"Mathilda," she says quietly through the door, "it's Liz. Let me in. I'd like to talk."

Silence, and then more shuffling.

"I'm as surprised as you, Mathilda," Liz says. "I'm just as confused, and I'm not going away until you talk to me. I need to know you're okay."

She waits as the shuffling gets closer to the door, and finally it opens.

"I am not okay," Mathilda says, her thick-rimmed glasses absent. She quickly turns and shuffles back into her darkened quarters. Liz follows her tentatively. She's never been here before, and she is surprised at how sparse the space is compared to her paper-packed office—a small dining table with one chair, and one armchair in the living area with an end table and a lamp. Otherwise, it appears empty.

Mathilda flops into the chair, seeming to forget for a moment that Liz is there. She takes a new tissue from a box sitting on the end table, blotting her eyes before miraculously producing her glasses from the darkness and placing them back on her face.

"If you'd like to sit down, you'll have to bring the dining chair over," Mathilda says, voice shaking as she gives a small wave of her hand. Liz's eyes adjust to the dark, and she can see the woman's expression, mouth twisted and eyes swollen. "I know, there's not much in here," she says with a bitter laugh. "I don't spend much time here—mostly just to sleep—and strange as it may seem, too much stuff stresses me out."

Liz doesn't bother with a chair. She sits on the floor at Mathilda's feet, taking a moment to adjust the pistol and knife strapped to her belt. This seems to surprise Mathilda, as Liz leans up next to her legs, eyes focused on the floor. They sit in silence for a moment. Liz isn't sure what to say, and she's surprised to find the darkness and Mathilda's presence soothing. Her own thoughts are still in turmoil—expressing them to someone else feels impossible.

Mathilda seems to gather herself first, blowing her nose vigorously and shamelessly into a tissue. "Did you know he was married?"

"No," Liz replies. "Did you know he was coming here?"

"No," Mathilda says, in a voice too pained to be lying. Liz lets a silence stretch between them until the woman speaks again. "How could he bring her here?"

"I don't even know who she is, much less why she's here," Liz replies, then pauses. "I can't pretend to understand his thinking."

"He didn't give you any indication he was coming?" Mathilda asks.

"No," Liz says, still processing her own confusion. "He said several times there were things best discussed in person, but I assumed that would be years from now—back on Earth. I certainly didn't expect him to show up here. I mean, is it really possible to bend the space-time continuum and instantly travel billions of miles? Who could possibly do that?"

"Apparently, your brother," Mathilda says, a hint of humor infusing into her voice before she chokes back a sob, removing her glasses once more and placing them on the table beside her. Liz waits as she cries. Maybe the tears will wash away the delusions Mathilda has about her brother. She reaches out to touch the woman's leg, hoping to provide some measure of comfort but unsure how.

Mathilda dabs her swollen eyes again.

"He didn't acknowledge me in the conference room!" she says. "I might have thought he was protecting me, but we all know I was helping him. He didn't even look my way, or say my name."

"When did he stop communicating with you?" Liz asks. Mathilda's legs shift slightly against her body.

"I guess it started after I built the first tablet, the one I slipped into your laundry. As soon as he started chatting with you, it became harder to get ahold of him. I built a second tablet, the one he wanted me to give to … Well, I passed it along to someone he designated."

"Chub," Liz whispers. "I know."

Mathilda's body grows tense beside her.

"How do you know?"

"I made it a point to know."

The woman sighs. "Yes, I gave it to Chub to manage. I kept waiting for him to deliver it to me, or for any other sign that Jackson wanted to talk to me, but it never came. I thought it must be a mistake. I managed to configure one of my computers to communicate with him, but he never answered my calls. I was sure he'd left me a clue or message somewhere, so I dove into the data sets he sent—the star charts—looking for hidden messages. But there was nothing for me."

Mathilda starts to choke back another sob but seems to rethink it, and instead lets it flow, taking another tissue from the box. Liz turns to face her, sitting up on her feet as she places both hands on Mathilda's knees and seeks her eyes.

"He used me!" she cries, wadding the tissue angrily and throwing it into the darkness. It lands on her own lap, too light to travel any distance, and this seems to make her even angrier. She bats it onto the floor.

"Don't you think he uses everyone?" Liz asks softly, watching the emotions play on Mathilda's face in the dim light. "Why would he come here like this, Mathilda? What do you think he wants?"

"Well, he certainly didn't come here for me!" she grumbles, but the anger doesn't seem intended for Liz. "Maybe he came for you, to rebuild your family!"

"But why now? Why this way?"

"I don't know," Mathilda says weakly. "Why does he do anything? There could be a hundred reasons, or no reasons at all. Maybe he wanted to see the ship in person. Maybe there's information he wants. Maybe this is a test run for a bigger arrival, or maybe he just wanted prove he could do it. Or, maybe he simply wanted to take his *wife* on a nice vacation."

Liz tries to suppress a laugh but fails. Mathilda pulls away, as if offended.

"For someone concerned about his motives, you seemed awfully happy to see him walk in, Liz. You even welcomed them aboard!"

"I don't know how to feel about him being here, but I know he's dangerous. I also know you're hurt, but you have to set that aside. It's time we both see him clearly. He's not the man you thought he was."

"Then who is he?" Mathilda asks.

"I don't know. I'd like him to be the boy I knew as my brother, but I'm sure he's not that person either. My brother wouldn't have abandoned me the way he did."

"He sure threw me away, didn't he?" Mathilda chokes back another sob. "Discarded me like trash."

"I have not discarded you," Liz says urgently, rising from the floor, "and neither has Seth. Help us find out why he's here. I'll see you on the bridge."

She turns to go without another word, leaving Mathilda alone with the weight of her grief.

CHAPTER 7

ELECTRICAL SURGES

***

The mechanical voice counts down, and Seth waits for his vision to blur and his breath to grow labored as the ship accelerates to 4G. Since Jackson arrived, not even an hour ago, Seth has been moving, doing, and directing. But now he's still, whether he wants to be or not, with only his thoughts and the fear that's been stabbing him like a knife since he laid eyes on the man. It feels like everything in his world has been yanked out of his control.

Seth feels vulnerable strapped in the captain's chair on the bridge. Is the ship safe during the acceleration? Could more New Generation arrive, like Jackson did? That seems unlikely. Even if they did arrive, they would be subject to the same G force as everyone else. And if they weren't lying down, as everyone is required to, blood would pool in their feet and they would pass out, maybe even die. But isn't Jackson a master of the unlikely, and even the impossible?

Stop it, he thinks, feeling panic rise in his constricted throat. He can't let his fear consume him. No one else is coming. Not now, anyway. And Jackson is under guard, secure in his quarters, although Seth has no illusions of truly containing a man who literally appeared out of nowhere from billions of miles away.

Why did he come, and for what purpose? Sure, there's what Jackson said in the conference room, but Seth believes none of it. Did he really fold the space-time continuum? It's hypothetically possible, but nothing like that technology exists, not yet. Then again, how else could he have gotten here?

There's no way that green capsule could be a spacefaring vessel. There's nothing in it, and Seth can't think of any scenario where it could accelerate enough to catch up to them and then slow down quickly enough to intercept the ship. It would have to approach the speed of light to get here that quickly, and that feels even less likely than folding the space-time continuum. Besides, Seth would have seen the video footage if they'd entered through the airlock. His head begins to hurt as his mind spins, searching fruitlessly for other possibilities.

This isn't productive, he thinks, knowing that until he has better information, all he can do is accept Jackson's explanation. The man has a history of using unlikely technology—the credential with the blue light, and the modified tablets that communicate in real time across vast distances. Seth feels the panic rising in his throat again. *I don't stand a chance against someone like Jackson.*

He has to stop himself again. So what if Jackson is brilliant? So what if he's mastered the impossible? *You're not trying to outsmart him. You're only trying to survive, and give the crew a chance to survive.* There must be something working in Seth's favor. Jackson cannot have all the advantages. Seth thinks back to when they orbited Earth. The man didn't expect them to build the propulsion drive, and Seth is certain he didn't know they were doing it until it was almost finished. Then he thinks about Jackson's broadcast, inciting mutiny. He didn't expect to fail, but he did. Even the negotiation calls aren't going as Jackson intended.

I can be unpredictable, Seth realizes. Perhaps that's his advantage. He needs to keep being unpredictable, long enough to devise a plan to escape when they get back to Earth.

The decomposing capsule returns to his mind again. If Jackson needs it to return to Earth, he can't stay more than a few days. But does he still need the capsule? Maybe that's why he assembled his machine. Or maybe he plans to create a new one while he's here. Another possibility occurs to Seth, making it even harder to breathe—maybe Jackson doesn't plan to leave at all.

Seth thinks back to the negotiation calls, combing through his memories for some shred of insight into the man's intentions. He thinks about the information they've shared, the demands Jackson's made. He smiles when he thinks about Liz standing up to her brother, screaming at Jackson that as long as they have possession of the ship, he doesn't have the upper hand.

Liz. Seth's smile fades. Jackson appealed to her directly when he hacked the broadcast system, and he insisted she be present in all negotiations. Seth knows that the man has been using the calls to work on her, to reestablish their connection. Didn't he tell her there were things they needed to discuss face-to-face?

Is he here because of Liz?

She looked confused when Jackson walked into the conference room, but part of her must want to reconcile with her brother. Will his arrival change Liz's feelings? Will she lose sight of how he abandoned her? Will she forgive the harm he's caused to so many?

No, Liz won't be deceived by this. She's too strong to be swayed.

But didn't she see what she wanted to see in the Fifty-Two? Something about the group triggered her on the surface, making her want to protect them even though it was completely irrational. And Liz still refuses to see the old woman clearly. Who's to say she'll be rational about her brother, now that he's here?

It's not the same, Seth thinks firmly. Liz saved the Fifty-Two without hesitation, but when her brother hacked the ship's broadcast system, her first instinct was to kill every one of his supporters, call him a liar, and fight her way to Seth's side. And even though Jackson despises him, Liz has chosen Seth again and again, supporting and helping him in every way. Just as he helped her by smuggling her onto the ship that first day at the depot.

Not even Jackson can break their bond. The thought comforts him, but only for a moment. As far as Seth is concerned, Liz is the best thing that's ever happened to him. She's his home, where he belongs. He thinks she needs him as much as he needs her, but does she? And is it enough? Hopefully. But when has hope ever made a difference in his life? Her words from the conference room ring in his ears. *I can't believe you're here, brother.*

Seth wonders what Liz is thinking, strapped into her own seat on the bridge with her eyes closed. If only he could pull her close to him, not just to protect her but also to claim his place in her life—by her side. He can't, though. Liz makes her own choices. She's chosen Seth in the past, and the only way they can be together is if she keeps choosing him.

He needs it more than anything else.

"Deceleration to 1.5G complete." The automated voice shakes Seth from his thoughts.

"Jarrod, commence the post-acceleration system scans," Seth says, working the straps that secure him to his chair. He looks over at Liz, who's unbuckling her own straps.

"System scans commenced," Jarrod confirms. "Captain, we've got electrical surges on Levels 4, 5, 6, and 17."

Odd. That hasn't happened before.

"Captain, the surges appear to be moving into our primary systems."

"Shut down the servers," Seth commands.

"I'm shutting down and rebooting systems now, but I'm not sure where this electricity is coming from. It appears to be from some external source, and not our own drives. I've cut all power to these levels, but the current is still flowing."

"How much current? Is it enough to damage our systems?"

"I'm checking. I—wait. It's gone. The energy is gone. Our servers are rebooting. Running diagnostics now. We have damage, Captain. We've lost lights on Levels 5 and 17, but the gravity seems to still be intact. I'm deploying repair teams. Our primary servers appear to be undamaged, but I'm getting strange readings on our backup servers. I'm deploying a repair team to the server room. I assume this is our top priority?"

"Is Jackson Goeff still secure?" Seth asks, feeling a ball of anxiety in his stomach.

"Jackson, sir?" Jarrod looks confused but then seems to regain his focus at Seth's stern look. An image fills the large screen on the bridge—a hallway camera. Ellis is stationed in the hallway. He appears to be rising from a cot.

"I installed surveillance in his room, Captain," Jarrod says. "Pulling up those cameras now." The screen fills with static snow. "The cameras must have been disabled during the acceleration." An edge of panic creeps into his voice.

"Or Jackson disabled them," Seth grumbles. Then he remembers that Ellis is carrying a radio. "Ellis," he continues, feeling the aftereffect of the acceleration as he raises his arm to activate his wristband communicator, "confirm that Jackson Goeff is still secure in his quarters."

"The entrance to his quarters remained secure for the entire acceleration, Captain."

"Thank you," Seth replies. "I need visual confirmation that he's still in there."

Jarrod switches the camera feed back to the hallway, and Seth watches the large screen as Ellis briefly knocks and then uses a keycard to open the door. He steps inside and disappears from the screen for a few moments before reappearing again, closing the door behind him. Seth watches him activate the radio again, and his voice lags only a moment behind.

"Jackson and the woman are both inside," Ellis confirms. "They appear disoriented, but they are present. They're sitting on the bed."

"Thank you. Check in with me at the end of your shift."

"Yes, Captain." The screen before them goes dark again.

"Maybe the surges were a fluke," Jarrod offers.

"Perhaps," Seth says, although he doesn't believe it at all. The timing is too uncanny. "The servers take priority."

"Will do, Captain," Jarrod says.

"I should see to Jackson and Shelby," Claire says, sounding weary as she unbuckles herself from her chair.

"They cannot leave quarters without my approval," Seth barks.

"And what if they need to go to the medical unit?" she

snaps, her weariness transformed to the dogged anger that seems to surface any time they talk about Jackson.

"Then notify me, and they can go," Seth responds through gritted teeth. "Jackson Goeff does not have free reign of this ship—nor does his companion."

"Fine." Seth watches her stalk off, feeling the connection between them die just a bit more, as she goes to check on the man who wants him dead.

"I'll go with her," Liz says. "Maybe I can find out why Jackson is really here." Seth smiles at her, trying not to look like he wants to cry, before turning his attention back to Jarrod.

I'm not sure which is falling apart faster. Me or the ship.

CHAPTER 8

HALF A SANDWICH

***

Liz sits on a couch in Jackson's quarters, watching Claire worry over the two new arrivals. She's already called the medical unit twice, having long compression socks delivered as well as an EKG machine to make sure their hearts are beating correctly under the strain of the acceleration.

What happens if they aren't beating correctly? Liz idly wonders. Would life be easier somehow if Jackson's heart stopped beating altogether? What if Seth had shot him when he walked into the conference room? *Is that what I think he should have done?* A year ago, it's probably what she would have done herself. But not Seth. He's better than that.

The weight of the lives she's taken presses down on her. It's easy for her to kill people, and much harder to actually work through the problems she may have with them.

"The socks will help with your circulation," Claire explains to Shelby, who eyes the long tubes of fabric suspiciously. "It probably seems fine now, especially compared to the 4G acceleration you just experienced, but 1.5G can still have an adverse effect on your body, especially your circulation. It's like instantly gaining half your body weight and trying to function normally. If your feet or ankles swell, or if you feel lightheaded, please come see me. Or at a minimum, lie down and elevate your feet."

"I see," Shelby says. "I suppose the body adjusts to this over time, does it not?"

"To a degree," Claire says cautiously, "but it doesn't happen quickly. Some of the crew is still adjusting to the 1.5G, and the 4G accelerations are hard on everyone. Even now." Claire glances over at Liz nervously. What does the woman not want to say in front of her?

Jackson folds the long socks Claire gives him and places them on the bed next to him. He looks at Liz and smiles. "Do you wear these?" he asks, playfully motioning to the socks.

"Yes," Liz says, pulling up one leg of her pants to reveal the compression socks underneath. "I didn't think it would be a big deal at first, so I didn't, but they help quite a bit. Mobility is more important than my pride."

Her brother nods vigorously. "Smart, Lizzie. Very smart." Liz wonders if he will wear his, but he seems to have forgotten all about them, discarded on the bed.

"Thank you, Dr. Harris," Shelby says. "If there's nothing else, I think I'll go put these on now." She rises with great effort and takes labored steps to the bathroom.

"There's a bathtub in there," Claire calls out to her. "You might also find that soaking in the tub brings some relief."

"Thank you for this, Claire. Rest assured that I will take good care of Shelby." Jackson looks at her expectantly, waiting for her to get the cue that it's time for her to leave. It takes Claire longer than it should, which makes Liz think of Mathilda. Jackson was able to build her expectations so easily.

"If you need me, don't hesitate to call," Claire says forcefully, giving Liz another cautious glance. "You are restricted to these quarters, but I will come if you need me. And I can get you into the medical unit for any treatment you need."

She's trying so hard to please him. Claire seems just as enamored with Jackson as Mathilda is, albeit in a different way. She's too eager to put him in charge, too eager to dismiss her son's own strength and resolve, as well as his role in leading the ship back to Earth.

Claire prepares to leave, holding the briefcase-sized EKG with both hands. Liz catches a glimpse of Ellis guarding the door as Claire opens it. Hopefully he'll be diligent about keeping Jackson in his quarters—Liz can't think of anyone better. The door closes behind Claire, and for the first time since Liz was a little girl, she is alone with her brother.

She realizes she's nervous, unsure what to say, sitting on the couch and clasping her hands in her lap as if preparing herself to be reprimanded for some wrong she didn't commit. *Ridiculous,* she tells herself, trying to push all of her boiling emotions aside so she can learn something useful. Jackson never liked to see her look weak. He was always telling her not to cry, to be strong. She needs to be strong now as well.

"Why didn't you tell me you were coming?" she asks. "Seth might have very well shot you when you walked into the conference room unannounced."

"I did tell you we would speak today," he says patiently, making her feel like a child again. "And why would Seth shoot me? Aren't we negotiating peacefully? Isn't that what we're doing?"

"I assumed we'd be talking over video chat."

Jackson smiles and waves a finger at her. "Never assume,

Lizzie. That's where most of our misunderstanding lies—in our assumptions." Liz feels a rush of annoyance. Her brother seems adept at allowing people to read into his words and intentions. She vows she will not make the mistake again.

"I heard what you said in the conference room, but why did you come?"

"Do I need a reason to visit you after all these years? There are things we need to discuss in person."

"Yes, you do need a reason, and speak plainly, so I don't make any mistaken assumptions. I wouldn't want to come to the wrong conclusion about why you're here." Her voice is harsh.

Jackson looks startled but then smiles.

"I hope to gain many things by coming here, but please don't minimize my desire to see you face-to-face. I know you're hurt, and I can't make it better if I'm billions of miles away, talking to you over video chat."

Liz feels a vein of emotion pulse deep in her heart. She tightens her jaw, determined to keep it from bubbling up.

"Why else did you come, and what did you assemble in the airlock on Level 37?"

"You see?" he asks softly. "This is what I'm talking about. Whenever I try to talk to you about us, you shut down."

Liz feels her fists clench, her mouth tighten.

"Do you expect me to believe that you set out to fold the space-time continuum solely for the purpose of forcing me into conversations I don't want to have?" she demands. "Bushwa! I don't buy it."

Jackson sighs, shaking his head dismissively. "You under-estimate your importance to me, but as I already told you, I hope to gain many things by coming here. As for the machine

I assembled in the airlock, I call it my transporter. I came to assemble it properly, something I cannot trust anyone else to do. And I must personally oversee its use."

"What does it do?" Liz asks.

"It creates wormholes between two designated points in space. I used a similar machine on Earth to transport Shelby and myself here, and it's how I anticipate starting emergency food shipments to Earth."

"That's why you want us to ramp up production?" Liz is incredulous. "Why didn't you tell us, Jackson?"

"I owe the council no explanations!" He closes his eyes and breathes deeply. "Lizzie, the situation at home is dire. We can't afford to wait for the Green Grow 3 to return to orbit to start distributing food. Even small shipments can make a real difference, and I don't have time to argue with the council about it. I chose to solve the problem, instead of creating more delays by trying to school them on technology well beyond their understanding. We have no time to waste if we are to have any hope of rebuilding civilization."

"How do you know it's safe?" Liz asks, eyes narrowed.

"If I thought it unsafe, would I use it to transport myself here? I've taken as many precautions as I can. We have to restart to the food supply."

"I don't disagree," Liz concedes. "But do you understand that by coming here—by simply appearing out of thin air with no explanation and no warning—you've created an entirely new threat to the security of this ship? We'll have to be on constant guard, wondering who else might show up, and when. Who else has this technology?"

Jackson reaches out, taking Liz's hands in his own.

"You are safe, Lizzie. I, alone, developed this technology. No one else has it, and no one else will. We will only use the transporter to ship food. I intend to honor the negotiations with the council, frustrating though they may be. If I intended otherwise, you'd already be overrun. The fact that Shelby and I arrived alone and unarmed should speak clearly enough about my intentions."

Liz studies him, doubtful.

"But trust goes both ways," he continues, "and I find myself questioning the council's intentions."

"Their intentions?" Liz grows angry. "The council isn't spying on you. Nor did the council stage an invasion of your home and attempt to annihilate you."

Jackson nods. "True. The council has done nothing, while those of us on Earth continue to wither away. Given the sluggish response to nearly every request I make, I wonder if that's exactly what the council intends—nothing."

Liz feels her mouth fall open, but she cannot deny the validity of his concern.

"It's not always easy to convey the challenges we face over video chat," she concedes. "The controlled accelerations are particularly demanding. Perhaps this will be easier to understand now that you're here."

"Yes." Jackson nods solemnly. "I'd like to see the problems firsthand."

"I'll arrange a tour for tomorrow," Liz says.

"I'd like that."

"I'm sure Seth can make the time to join us."

Jackson's face falls, but he says nothing. Liz hears the door to the bathroom click open, and Shelby emerges.

"How do the socks feel?" Jackson asks.

"I'll grow accustomed to them, I'm sure," the woman says. "I'm glad to have them."

"Would you like fresh clothes?" Liz asks. "I could have

some things delivered from the laundry." Shelby looks repulsed, but she contains her expression quickly.

"Thank you, Lizzie," Jackson says quickly, "but we will be fine in our clothes. They are quite fresh from all the ozone generated by our arrival." Liz nods, wondering if Shelby is as disgusted by the idea of Green Grow as Liz is by the New Generation.

"Jackson, why didn't you tell me you were married?" Liz asks.

"It's a personal matter," he says, "not something I'd want to discuss over video call. You should understand this, Lizzie. You still haven't officially told me of your involvement with Seth Harris, so who's the one keeping secrets now?"

Shame washes over her, like she's a young girl being scolded—followed by anger. What does she have to be ashamed of? Liz doesn't talk about her relationship with Seth to anyone. It's their business, although she's certain everyone around them has drawn conclusions about their involvement.

"How long have you been married?" Liz asks.

Shelby smiles and answers before Jackson can. "Our souls are bound for eternity. I knew the moment I met your brother that I have always loved him and always will." He smiles at her affectionately.

Does either of them know how to answer a question directly?

"Shelby and I found each other three years ago," Jackson says softly.

"Do you have any children?" Liz asks, curious as to how much he hasn't told her.

"Not yet," Jackson says, "but perhaps they will come, if we are meant to have them." Shelby smiles at him as they share a glance, one that makes Liz feel like she's intruding on a private moment. She's flooded with embarrassment, then anger—she's done nothing wrong. The whipsaw of emotion makes her panic. *I need to get out of here.*

"I'll have sandwiches delivered for lunch," Liz says, rising to leave.

"We still have food from this morning," Shelby assures her, motioning to the remains of a tray of fruit, cheese, bread, and cured meat.

"It will keep, my love," Jackson says, smiling broadly at Liz. "Will you join us for lunch, Lizzie? Stay and let's catch up."

Liz wants to say no, to run out of the room and away from her brother. But she doesn't. *It's a chance to gather information,* she thinks as she forces a smile and utters a choppy, "Okay." She steels herself for more conversation as she retakes her seat.

***

"There's so much food here," Shelby says, sounding dismayed at the plate Ellis places before her. It contains a chicken salad sandwich, French fries, and a cookie.

"If you can't eat it all, we'll save it for later," Jackson says, quietly.

"In the cafeteria, the food is served buffet style, so you can take as little or much as you need," Liz says, a familiar wash of shame making her feel the need to explain that food is not wasted on the Green Grow 3. But this only seems to upset Shelby more.

"People here can take whatever they want?" she asks, incredulous.

"Hoarding is not allowed," Liz says, not sure if this will make the situation better or worse. "Nor is it necessary. We take what we need, and that's all."

Jackson pats Shelby's hand, as if sending her a signal to relax.

"Enjoy your sandwich, my love," he says. "Things will be this way for everyone before you know it. Here, let me help you." He takes a knife from his plate and carefully cuts Shelby's sandwich in half. Liz watches, washed in memories of Jackson portioning out the meager food they once had. Her eyes fill with tears, and she wipes them away, hoping he won't notice.

"What is it, Lizzie?" Jackson sounds concerned.

"Nothing," she says quietly, wiping her nose with her napkin. Both of them look at her curiously. "Jackson used to do that when we were kids," she says to Shelby. "He cut everything in half, giving me as much as he had, even though he was bigger."

"Of course I did!" he exclaims as he turns his attention to his own food. "You're my little sister, and I wanted to take care of you." This makes Liz want to cry again, and she fights to hold back the tears.

"Your brother is as generous now as he was then," Shelby says, looking at Jackson with sparkling eyes.

Has Liz been too hard on him? She calms herself enough to eat her sandwich, noticing how her brother seems to savor every bite. He looks so lean, and she's sure he's too thin under his jacket. They're both thin—probably they rarely have enough to eat. Enough to survive, maybe, but not enough to be healthy.

"Tell me something else from your childhood," Shelby says, smiling at Liz between bites. "Jackson says so very little about his early years."

Liz considers for a minute, then speaks. "He was always very serious." She smiles as she calls his young, somber face to mind. "And he liked to teach me things."

"Oh?"

"Yes, he taught me how to swing, and how to read. Mom tried teaching me, but she never made it as interesting as Jackson did."

"I did say I could teach you faster," Jackson recalled.

"Yes, and it was true!" Liz laughs, thinking back to their small farmhouse. She felt safe there with Jackson, oblivious to just how bad the world around her really was. Is it possible to feel that safe again?

"I'm a man of my word, Lizzie. I always have been." Liz's smile falters, as she remembers how much she trusted him, how she was so certain he would come back because he said it was so. But he didn't, not even when she needed him the most. She turns her attention back to Shelby.

"When he was eleven, he built a wooden cart with two bicycle tires for us to take to the depot. We'd each grab a handle and push it along behind our mother, while Jackson told me about all the things on the shelves."

"That sounds very efficient," Shelby says, turning her attention to him. "It doesn't sound like you've changed all that much from when you were a child, my love." She caresses Jackson's hair and he returns her smile.

"No, I haven't," he says, "other than growing more handsome."

They all laugh. For a fraction of a second, Liz feels better than before, and then she's ashamed of herself for falling prey to the moment.

CHAPTER 9

EVENING ACCELERATION

***

When the tones sound, indicating that a ship broadcast is forthcoming, Ruth is walking down the corridor to her quarters. Other people pass her, seemingly eager to get their destinations, but Ruth feels no rush. Eighty-two years of living entitle her to walk as slowly as she wants. Another day is almost done—meals eaten, work completed, story time finished. The only thing left to do is survive the evening acceleration.

Ruth despises the accelerations, although she tries to be positive. She's not a complainer, and she needs to set an example for her people. None of them complain about it, not even the children, even though she knows it's unpleasant for everyone. She tells herself it's merely a time to rest, although it's not the least bit rejuvenating.

When she hears the tones, Ruth wonders if the broadcast is related to the acceleration—special instructions, perhaps, or maybe one of Captain Harris's pep talks, the ones he gives to try and make them all feel better about what they're doing. The talks don't make Ruth feel better about anything, but she likes that he tries. Captain Harris is doing his best, and he's a promising leader, albeit a young man with a lot to learn.

It must be a pep talk—they haven't received one a couple of days. Nonetheless, she's edgy, her mind a cacophony of paranoid whispers that the broadcast could be something else. Perhaps Jackson is trying to overtake the ship again. Perhaps the small tasks Ruth completed to help him will make the difference between success and failure. What will become of her if he succeeds?

Despite the assurances Jackson is so quick to give her, Ruth knows she would fare poorly in his regime. And the rest of the crew would fare poorly as well, something they must sense just as certainly as she does. Does Jackson still have enough supporters to try another coup? She knows how beguiling the man can be, how he enamors people who so quickly become oblivious to the other, darker side of his nature.

Given the terrible things she's seen the New Generation do, Ruth should be immune to Jackson's charm, but she's not. When he showed up in her cave, claiming to be alone, part of her wanted to believe he had their best interest at heart—in spite of everything she'd seen and lived. Part of her wanted to believe that he was offering to save them. It must be the part of her that wants to believe there are simple answers to complex problems, that goodness always triumphs over evil. The voice of her naivety, which only speaks when she closes her eyes and covers her ears to everything happening around her.

What will her bargain with him cost her? What will it cost

her people? The truth has a way of revealing itself, and Ruth knows it's likely just a matter of time before her treachery is discovered. Thoughts of how and when it might happen torment her waking and sleeping moments. Will Liz confront her? Will she be executed by Captain Harris, like the other two people he shot? Will the children be disappointed by what she's done?

She, alone, brought the memory stick on board, but that was only the beginning of her betrayal. Perhaps things would be different if she had refused Jackson when he contacted her via the strange tablet. Perhaps if she hadn't blindly manufactured the machine parts he wanted, she'd be less culpable. Perhaps if she'd refused to give him the information he wanted, innocuous as it seemed, she'd have a more defensible case. But she did help him, and she will accept full responsibility.

Ruth tells herself it was to protect her people—four of them are still on the surface, and Jackson made it clear that their well-being depended on her cooperation. She tells herself that it's not a matter of choosing sides between Green Grow and the New Generation, that humanity can only have one side to survive. But she knows those thoughts to be lies—excuses.

Helping Jackson was really just the path of least resistance. It allowed her to keep her options open, trying to forge many welcoming paths for her people—even though she knows that the only reason her people even have a path is because Liz forged it for them. Liz is a force of nature, but couldn't the tables turn at any time? Couldn't they? Ruth chastises herself again, knowing that turning tables are the product of many hands, that despite the magnanimous way that Jackson presents himself, he is not all-knowing, all-seeing, or all-capable. If the tables turn in his favor, Ruth's own hands have helped it come about.

It disgusts her, the things she's done to gain Jackson's favor. She should spurn him at every turn, but that's the response of an idealist, not a survivor. Ellis tells her she's too hard on herself, but she doesn't think she is. She no longer wants to wrap herself in the comfort of her own lies.

Ruth redirects her attention to the video monitor as Captain Harris's face fills the screen. He looks somber, which worries her given the urgent call she knows Ellis received to report immediately to the captain's conference room for a security matter. Ruth hasn't heard from him since, and he didn't come back to his quarters to endure the morning acceleration.

"Good evening," the captain starts, his face serious but otherwise unreadable. "I have important news to share with you tonight, but first I want to reiterate my thanks and appreciation for everyone's patience and support with the controlled accelerations. I know it's not easy, but these accelerations are an important step to getting us back to Earth.

"As you know, we are in ongoing negotiations with the New Generation, working toward a peace that will not only ensure our safety but also allow us to resume full production of food that we can distribute to the surface. And now, thanks to a miracle of new technology, we are able to continue those peace talks in person. That's right—Jackson Goeff arrived in person on the Green Grow 3 earlier today, with a small contingency, to hash out details of how we can help the people of Earth now and when we return to orbit."

Ruth feels her stomach drop to the floor. She leans heavily on the wall, focusing on the captain's voice through the ringing in her ears. Jackson is supposed to be on Earth. How is he here?

"As part of this planning, I will be touring the ship with Jackson tomorrow, so please do not be alarmed if you see us. This is merely another step—albeit an important step—in the negotiations that I, your captain, am leading with the New Generation. While the New Generation contingent is here, our operations will continue as normal, including the controlled accelerations.

"Thank you for your cooperation, and I will continue to keep you apprised of important developments. Please prepare for tonight's acceleration, which will happen as scheduled. Thank you, and goodnight."

Ruth finds herself unable to move, unable to tear her eyes from the blank monitor, unable to close her mouth. Jackson Goeff is here. How? And where is Ellis? Has he been detained? Is he taking the blame for her decisions? Is it time to pay the price for what she's done?

Then a new question enters her mind, one that makes her want to vomit. What kind of machine did she help Jackson build? Was it a transportation device? Did she help bring him here? The world spins as her heart pounds. Part of her wishes it would stop beating altogether, although she knows she doesn't deserve such mercy.

Ruth cannot continue to delude herself about who Jackson is or what helping him might mean. She must set aside her excuses. She must stop believing her own lies. But is it too late? Has she already doomed not just herself but her people, too? And where is Ellis? She can't lose him. A wave of panic washes over her, catapulting her body into motion. She runs faster than she thought her eighty-two-year-old legs could carry her, down the hallway to a phone, where she calls the security office. Charlie's voice answers.

"Charlie!" Ruth is breathless. "Where's Ellis? What's

happened to him? I just saw the news that Jackson arrived here." She feels hot tears running down her cheeks.

"Ellis is fine, Ruth." His voice is calming.

"How do you know?" she demands. "He's been gone all day. Jackson Goeff is here, Charlie! He's here! How do I know Ellis is fine?"

"I know Jackson is here." His words are slow and soft. "I know you're worried—we all are. I don't even know how he got here. But don't worry about Ellis. He's taking the first shift guarding Jackson and his contingency."

"His contingency?" Ruth is frantic. "How many of them are there? What do they intend?"

"I don't know," Charlie says, "but you need to calm yourself. I probably shouldn't be telling you any of this, but I know how upsetting all this is. I'm sure your people are especially upset given well … your history. Best I can tell, there's only two of them. Jackson and a woman. Captain Harris asked Ellis to stand guard outside their quarters."

"Where are they being held?" she demands. "The brig?"

"They're on Level 1. Look, I can't tell you anymore. I'm on my way to relieve Ellis now. He's the most qualified security officer I know. I'm not surprised the captain summoned him."

Ruth stands in the hallway, holding the phone to her ear even after Charlie disconnects the call. She needs to clear her head, because her problems have just escalated to a new level. She will have to be patient and wait for Ellis. Surely, he will have news—he must. All she can do now is endure the acceleration.

***

"Did Charlie take over?" Seth asks Ellis.

"He did, but I'd like to add a second person."

Seth studies the older man, considering what to say. "Did he try to get out?"

"Not exactly. He asked to go to the medical unit, to meet with Dr. Harris. I explained I would need your permission for that, and he told me not to bother. Said he'd do it another time."

"Did anyone try to get in?"

"Ms. Greenberg asked to speak to him."

"Mathilda," Seth whispers. He shouldn't be surprised, and it's not surprise that he feels. Disappointment, perhaps, although he tries to dismiss it.

"She was rather insistent, but I told her I'd need your permission."

Seth stands, turning his back to Ellis, thinking. He fills the silence with a question.

"How did you fare during the morning acceleration?"

"Dr. Harris had a cot delivered. She insisted I lie down on it, but I could still see the door to Jackson's quarters. I think it's a viable solution, especially since he's pretty unlikely to try and escape during the accelerations." Seth can't help but smile. Hearing Ellis tell him they were sitting on their bed disoriented is the most uplifting news he'd heard all day. He shouldn't wish ill on the woman—she's probably just another pawn like everyone else. But he's glad Jackson is suffering. The man has certainly made Seth's life difficult for the last several months. He pushes the thought aside, hiding his emotions again.

"I want them guarded at all hours," he says. "Who do we have?"

"I'm not sure the security staff is trained up enough yet for someone like this," Ellis begins. Seth turns to face him, curious about what he means. "Captain, he's New

Generation. The same face that incited rebellion on the ship two months ago. And somehow, he manages to simply appear today. Add that to the reputation he already has, and it's intimidating, sir."

"Who do you suggest?" Seth asks.

Ellis doesn't falter. "I suggest pairing a member of the security team with a member of the Fifty-Two. I can ask Ruben to come up and stand guard with Charlie."

"Ruben …" Seth considers this. "He's the one that doesn't speak?"

"Yes, sir, but he's capable and trustworthy."

Seth turns away, hands clasped behind his back. Trustworthy? No one is trustworthy. He's certain some of the Fifty-Two helped manufacture the parts for Jackson's machine. So did the rest of the crew. He can't choose on the basis of trust, or no one will guard Jackson. He has to choose a capable team, and hope they understand the stakes.

He turns to face Ellis again, his face calm and his eyes steady.

"I don't know what Jackson's intentions are—not for me or the council or the ship. I don't know what he intends for the crew, including the rest of Liz's Fifty-Two. I have no doubt that others on the ship—them included—have more experience with Jackson than I do. I have no doubt he's made threats and promises and everything in between to get people to cooperate with him."

He pauses, studying Ellis's face. Some emotion is playing below the surface, but he doesn't know Ellis well enough to discern what it means. Seth looks away before he continues talking.

"Jackson is here now. His machine is assembled and fully in his control, although I have no idea what it's meant to do. He has extensive information about the ship and the people on it. None of us should assume we know his intentions. None of us should assume we carry his favor. He cares for no one but himself."

Seth pauses, but Ellis only continues to listen, standing at attention.

"Did you know he abandoned his sister and mother?" Seth asks, meeting Ellis's gaze and waiting for a response.

"I don't know the details, Captain, but I've heard the high points of the story."

"She was only eight years old when he left," Seth says, thinking of Liz's face. "He left her in charge of their mother so he could join the New Generation, and he never came back. He never tried to make contact with her, not until the day he incited the mutiny. Do you think she would have survived if she were anyone else?"

"No, Captain," Ellis says, still standing at attention. "It seems highly unlikely—not on her own like she was."

"As a child, I spent very little time on the surface," Seth continues, pacing a circuit back and forth while Ellis remains standing in the same position, wearing a neutral expression. "I've had no interactions with the New Generation prior to Jackson Goeff. But that doesn't mean I don't understand the stakes others have faced. It doesn't mean I can't see the appeal of his vision, even though I suspect it's mostly lies. Do you know why I executed Willow Brown and Zag Bryant?"

Seth stops and turns to face Ellis, waiting for him to respond.

"They were spies, Captain."

"Yes, they were. But I didn't execute them because they pledged loyalty to Jackson Goeff or took his credential. I executed them for decisions they made in real time that put all of us at risk. Zag was transmitting specifications for the anti-matter propulsion drive, and Willow used her credential during the insurrection, screaming at her compatriots to kill me and take command of the ship. I didn't execute them for decisions they made in the past. None of us can do anything about the past. None of us can do anything about Jackson's machine or his arrival, or whatever he intends to do. All we can control is what we do now, and that's how we must be held accountable."

He can see that Ellis's expression has changed, but he still doesn't know what it means. Just what he hopes it means—what he needs it to.

"I didn't ask for this job, you know," Seth continues, and Ellis looks surprised at this comment. "The prior captain—Captain MacAbee—went to a peace summit with the New Generation and never returned. Until recently, I thought the New Generation killed him and the rest of the executive board. I couldn't see any other possibilities. But now I see that I may have even been wrong about that. Ellis, all we have left is each other. To others, we are nothing but cannon fodder, collateral damage in a game we never asked to play. If we can't stick together, we'll be torn apart."

"I understand, sir," Ellis says emphatically. Seth can see an intensity in the man's eyes that he likes, but is it enough?

"Do you? I need to be sure. Jackson Goeff cannot continue to operate in the shadows, nor can he be allowed to undermine my command. All of our lives depend on it. I'm afraid even Liz's life depends on it." Seth pauses to let this sink in. "He abandoned her before, left her to die. What's to say he won't do it again, after she's served his purpose? We can't let that happen, Ellis. Not to her."

"No, sir," Ellis says, and now he's shaking his head

emphatically. Seth doesn't know if the Fifty-Two feel any loyalty to him. He's not sure they can solve his problems even if they do. But he knows how they feel about Liz. Everyone knows how she and the old woman love each other. If nothing else, Seth needs to know they will take care of her.

"Thank you for everything you've done to help me since you've been here. Thank you for fighting next to Liz during the rebellion, and for watching over Jackson today. If you say that Ruben is the right person to pair with Charlie, call him. And if Jackson attempts to contact anyone or do anything covertly—or if he uses this woman Shelby to do it on his behalf—I need to know about it immediately. All of our lives depend on it."

"Yes, sir," Ellis says, his expression steeled. "I'll pick up the watch in the morning."

"Very good. I'll see you then. And please extend my regards to Ruth as well."

The two men study each other for a moment, but Seth believes there's a mutual understanding. He watches Ellis leave his office, back straight and feet sure. The Fifty-Two are a formidable asset, but they're a resource Seth has shared with Jackson Goeff until now. If he can change that, he might just have a chance.

***

Ellis lies next to Ruth on a bed he's pushed next to hers so he can hold her hand and they can talk. Ruth is grateful he's here, grateful for the time together, grateful for his touch. It's not easy to form words, even though she knows what she'd like to say. It's not easy to do anything while accelerating at 4G except wonder when it will be over, but they have no more time to waste. Ruth needs to know what Ellis knows, and they need to decide what to do.

"I don't get the sense that he knows details, but he knows." Ellis's voice is hushed and strained.

"What's going to happen to us, Ellis? How much does he know?" Ruth feels her heart racing.

"It doesn't matter," he says. "All that matters is what we choose to do now. The captain made that clear. He said the past doesn't matter—not anymore."

"Do you think he really means that?"

"I think he does. He's a smart man. I think he knows that's the only way forward."

"So he trusts us?"

"No, but how could we expect him to?"

"What are we going to do? Jackson is insane, and we've been helping him. Why did we help him?"

"Stop it, Ruth. What's done is done." She doesn't respond, and they marinate under the weight of the acceleration and their silence. Then Ellis says, "Mathilda Greenberg tried to convince me to let her into Jackson's quarters."

"Mathilda Greenberg? The chief astronomer?" Ruth thinks about this carefully. "Maybe she can help us."

"Help us do what?"

"Help us find out what Jackson is up to. We have to do something to redeem ourselves, Ellis."

He doesn't respond right away, but she can feel the warmth of his hand on hers.

"I need to give the captain my full time and attention. But perhaps you can find out something from Mathilda."

Ruth remains silent, her mind already whirring with possibilities for how she might connect with the woman.

"Ruth?"

"Yes?"

"You're only human, you know."

Ruth grunts in acknowledgement, not interested in making any more excuses for herself. She can see now that Captain Harris may have compassion for them, or at least a use. That may be enough to save them—for now.

She thinks about Liz and can't help but wonder what the girl is thinking and feeling right now. Is she happy to see her brother? Ruth's mind flashes back to the day at the depot, the words Liz spoke as she picked off the raiding party, fearless and unforgiving. *Not today, you disgusting filth.* She thinks of the way Liz fell to her knees when Jackson hacked the ship's broadcast system and she saw his face on the screen. She rose, despite her devastation, and made her hatred of the New Generation known. No, this can't be a joyful reunion for Liz. Ruth feels her heart breaking yet again, for how much she loves the young woman, for how much betrayal Liz has endured, and especially for how Ruth knows she's added to that burden. Liz is one of the fiercest people Ruth has ever known, but her heart is pure. It doesn't deserve to be broken, but when Liz finds out what Ruth has done, it will surely shatter.

CHAPTER 10

MUTINY AND THEFT

***

Seth lies stretched on his back in his quarters, one arm propped under his head, the other wrapped loosely around Liz. His fingers absently trace her scar, the wide bumpy one just under the ridge of her left shoulder blade. It's where the pine tree scraped her flesh nearly to the bone as she tried to free herself from the rope Albert Wyndham used to tie her to the tree. She has many scars on her body, but this one is the freshest, the one Seth most wishes he could heal. He should have prevented this scar, but he wasn't there when she needed him. He failed Liz just as surely as Jackson abandoned her.

Seth looks at his pistol, loaded and within easy reach on his night table. He shouldn't be concerned about Jackson barging into his quarters, but he is. Jackson used to be a far-away, hypothetical problem, but now he's a clear and present danger. So close, in fact, that his smell still saturates Seth's nostrils—leather and ozone.

He thinks Liz might have dozed off, but he doesn't know for sure. Her body is soft and relaxed, molding against his own. He'll let her rest, although he'd like to talk to her about the messages from the Green Grow executive board.

He received a second one today, moments after Jackson strolled into his conference room. The board is demanding that Seth return the ship to orbit and report for a hearing. Apparently, he's facing charges of mutiny and theft. Mutiny? Theft? Seth isn't sure whether he wants to laugh or scream. The charges are ridiculous and insulting.

He thinks about the last time he saw Captain MacAbee, on the dock before he piloted a shuttle full of food and supplies to the Detroit peace summit alone. "I'll be back in a day or two," he told Seth. "Just keep your head down and basic operations running, my boy." Seth had been so sure the captain would return, so quick to believe that something catastrophic must have happened when he didn't. He never imagined that Captain MacAbee would abandon them, that the executive board would flee to save themselves, cutting off all contact with the Green Grow 3.

Seth remembers how helpless he felt as the days passed, waiting for the captain to return, waiting for someone to tell them what to do. Surely a new leader would come—someone qualified, someone with a plan, someone Seth was not. But no one did, and now the executive board wants the ship back, with no explanation of where they've been or why they went silent.

Is it coincidence that the message hit his inbox moments after Jackson arrived? Or is the propulsion drive the common thread? Jackson attacked them in orbit to stop them from using the drive, and now that they are using it regularly, the executive board appears out of nowhere. The timing is uncanny.

Seth wonders again if it was a mistake to build the propulsion drive. Maybe Jackson would have approached them more peaceably if he wasn't scrambling to keep the ship from leaving orbit. Would the executive board have reached out at all? It's impossible to untangle the gordian knot of events that led to the present situation.

Perhaps all that matters is that, in the end, Seth got what he wanted from the propulsion drive—a measure of safety, and leverage to negotiate with the New Generation. The drive put them in a position of some power, instead of waiting to be overrun. But was it worth the cost? Eighty-two people died quelling the mutiny Jackson orchestrated, and those weren't the only lives lost. Seth thinks about Willow Brown and Zag Bryant, condemned and executed by his own hand. He thinks about Sam Wyndham and Ellen Ryan, who died on the mission to retrieve antimatter from the surface. So many lives were lost, and those who remained were lucky to have survived the G force when the ship was flung out of orbit.

Was it worth it? *Not yet, but if I can get the ship back to Earth and negotiate peace with Jackson, maybe it will be.* It's a tall order, and whether Seth can do it remains to be seen. He shifts his fingers on Liz's skin to a smooth, un-scarred place between her shoulder blades. She sighs deeply, throwing one leg over his. He'd like to tell her about the mes-sages, but what can she do about them? For that matter, what can he? For now, he intends to do nothing, and Jarrod agrees that this is the best course of action. He said there were things he needed to look into, and Seth didn't have the energy to press him about what. Surely he will find out soon enough.

CHAPTER 11

TURQUOISE
AND HUMMINGBIRDS

***

OCTOBER 25, 2059—SATURDAY

Liz opens her eyes to greet the morning alone in Seth's bed. She buries her face in his pillow, breathing in the smell of him, unsure whether she wants to jump out of bed and face the day or hide under the covers until she dies.

She chooses to lie still, eyes fixed on the void of space in front of her. She tries to assimilate her brother's arrival, to integrate his presence with everything else she knows to be true about her world. He's really here, just a few doors down the hallway. They are no longer separated by time and space, but she doesn't know if this is good or bad. The highs and lows she felt yesterday have led her to no conclusions.

Warring emotions rage. She's glad Jackson is here, but she wishes he never came. She loves him, but she hates him. She's curious but terrified. She's glad he's alive, but she wants to kill him. Yesterday, the shock of his arrival left Liz numb, but this morning she realizes she's furious at him for taking away the time she thought she had to work through her feelings.

She thought she would have years of video chats to engage with him on her terms from a distance. She thought he understood that she wasn't ready to talk about his leaving, the way he abandoned her and what happened after he left all those years ago. She was pleased when he stopped pressuring her in the video chats to speak to him alone, to talk about the past. It seemed like a good sign when he told her that some things would be better discussed in person.

She didn't expect him to do something crazy, like fold the space-time continuum and simply appear in the captain's conference room as casually as if he'd always been right down the hall. But that was what he did, and now he's here. Her forbearance has expired, the deferral come due. She realizes she only deluded herself. Once again, Jackson didn't exactly lie to her, only allow her to read in to his words. What other lies has he allowed her to believe?

Get up, Liz tells herself. *You have to face him.* The stakes are too high to hide in bed like a child, not just for her but for everyone on the ship. She may be the only one who can find out why he came. She may be the only one who can protect the crew, and she wants to protect them, even the ones who spied for Jackson—especially them, in fact. She has to try to protect them, because even though she's not ready to face it, she knows the Fifty-Two are part of that group— the betrayers. Strangely enough, she still wants to save them, even though the thought of Ruth lying to her cuts her soul to the quick.

Jackson claims he came to improve their relations, and Liz knows she needs to try. She has to set aside everything she thought she knew, especially about the New Generation. It's the only way she can build a relationship with Jackson, but she fears the forgetting will be too hard—not for her mind but for her body. When she thinks about the New Generation, her adrenaline surges, and her heart races. Her hands crave the comfort of her knife handle or a pistol grip. Her first instinct is to destroy, to crush her enemy. Then, she remembers that enemy is her brother, and she instantly wants to vomit as her child-heart screams in agony at the ferocity of her hatred.

Until Jackson walked in yesterday, Liz didn't know that heart still existed—the one that remembers squealing in glee as he pushed her on the swing under that old cottonwood tree, the one that remembers the wonder and pride she felt as he taught her how to sound out words by the light of a dying candle. Her child-heart wants to beg him to forgive her for letting their mother die. It wants to believe everything he tells her, to once again become the family they used to be.

That heart cannot accept that he betrayed her. It doesn't believe that he didn't try to find her, even while she sacrificed so much to look for him. No, that pain lives in a different heart—a woman's heart, scarred and shaped by privation and hardship. One that has no delusions about what Jackson has done, to her and others.

She dresses quickly, brushing her hair and leaving it loose, falling in soft waves around her shoulders. She tries to steel herself as she stands at the threshold of the door and the threshold of the day, the first day of the rest of her life. Will her brother know that she didn't sleep in her own bed last night? Why does it matter? It shouldn't, but nonetheless, she cannot dismiss the thought.

She summons composure, walking with purpose to meet Jackson and Shelby for breakfast. They will go to the cafeteria since Seth decided they can move around the ship, with the condition that either Seth or Liz accompany them, as well as the security detail.

Liz's child-heart whispers that she should be happy—this is a victorious day. She's safe with Jackson, they are together, and neither of them will be hungry. It might be a dream come true, except her woman-heart knows that such dreams often turn into nightmares. Liz finds it ironic that she isn't the least bit hungry. Isn't all of this ultimately about food? But in this moment, food couldn't seem less relevant.

She turns a corner and sees that they are already waiting in the hallway. Just like yesterday, her brother stands straight and tall, like he knows no other way. His eyes are narrowed, scanning his surroundings purposefully, almost robotically. But why? Is he looking for her? Is he taking in his surroundings? There's not much to see, just the plush carpet beneath their feet and the richly stained wood-panel walls, lined with doors to other quarters.

Liz sees Ellis standing guard along the wall a few feet down from Jackson's door. His eyes are fixed on Jackson and Shelby, but he doesn't seem nervous or anxious. Does Ellis know that the Fifty-Two have been compromised? How could he not know? How could Ruth not?

If Ruth knows, Ellis knows, Liz tells herself, although it still makes little sense. Liz and Ellis risked their lives for each other—Liz at the depot and Ellis in the orchard. She'll never forget his words after Jackson hacked the broadcast and tried to overtake the ship. *If you don't hide, we don't hide.* Surely that means something, because if risking one's life for another has no meaning, then how can anything be meaningful?

She looks away from Ellis, back at her brother. He's wearing the same clothes as yesterday, the leather pants and jacket over a crudely woven shirt. Liz can see the chest plate, woven metal and stone. It gleams of death to her world-weary eyes, although part of her is intrigued by its beauty. Shelby wears the same outfit as well, the flowing tunic and buckskin jacket only slightly softer and less fearsome than Jackson's clothes.

Liz watches Shelby's lips move, her dark eyes focused on Jackson. Her words are too quiet to hear, but Liz can see that her brother always hears Shelby's words, no matter how quiet. He's giving Shelby his full attention, his chin tilted down and posture relaxed.

He respects her. Liz is stunned by this simple realization, because it contradicts everything she's come to believe about women in the New Generation. She's seen firsthand how they are treated in the raiding parties, like inhuman playthings. She's heard of the place women go to have babies, where they are warehoused like sentient bundles of flesh with no right to be free. She thinks of Gabriella, sold like a slave for the price of a motorcycle. But now, standing before her, she sees something different, something irreconcilable. She can see that this woman has power.

As if Shelby can sense her thoughts, her dark eyes settle on Liz, rich pools of mystery. Her mouth turns slightly up, a hint of a smile that whispers, *Yes, I have power.* Jackson notices the change in Shelby's gaze and turns to greet Liz.

"Good morning!" he says excitedly. Despite herself, Liz hopes his wide smile is genuine.

"Good morning," she says in reply. "Shall we go?" They walk in silence to the lift, Liz lost for words as Ellis trails two steps behind. She presses the button for Level 4, but the lift stops on Level 3. The doors open to reveal six crew members chatting amongst themselves. The conversation stops abruptly as, one by one, they realize who stands before them. Almost in unison, their eyes dart to Jackson, then to Liz, then back to Jackson.

"There's room if you care to join us!" Jackson says in a loud, jovial voice.

"No!" one of them answers quickly before quickly training his eyes on his feet.

"I think I forgot something in my quarters …" a woman standing in the front mumbles before quickly turning away.

"We'll catch the next one," another person utters, his eyes also finding the ground. Liz gets the feeling that none of these people want Jackson to see their face. Why? Are they simply scared of him, or are they afraid he'll recognize them?

"Strange people," Shelby lilts as the doors close, and Jackson grunts in acknowledgment, his hand finding its way to the small of her back. The doors open again moments later, and they all exit onto Level 4.

***

If Shelby or Jackson have a reaction to the cafeteria, they don't reveal it to Liz. She watches them take in the scene, but it's a mechanical assessment, seeking out the logistics of everything before them. Liz hands each of them a tray, then takes one for herself.

"There are baked and prepackaged goods over there"—she motions to racks and refrigerated cases along one wall—"and the rest is buffet style."

She does her best to look casual, willing her feelings of guilt to disappear. She's been through this breakfast buffet so many times, and she has nothing to regret—she's wasted no food. At no point has she taken more than she needed. But as her brother stands beside her, on the edge of her peripheral vision, she knows his body is gaunt under his strange clothes. His searching blue eyes are judging everything he sees before them. Liz has had free access to everything she needed while he struggled to survive on the surface.

How do you know that? Liz asks herself. She knows nothing about Jackson's life on the surface. Maybe he does have everything he feels he needs. Maybe she shouldn't assume he suffers. Besides, didn't he choose his own path? She turns her attention to Shelby, who seems to be appraising her options carefully. Liz watches her delicate hand hesitate before she wraps her fingers around an apple. She adds it to her plate, which contains two pieces of toast and a slice of ham. Her easy grace reminds Liz of Willow Brown, although Willow always seemed so confident about what she wanted. Willow's hand would not have hesitated.

"Coffee?" Liz asks, trying to loosen her smile and relax her shoulders. Jackson's eyes jump to hers, and he smiles broadly.

"What a treat that would be! Shelby, love, have you ever had coffee?"

"I'm sure I haven't," she replies. Liz leads them to the coffee station.

"Let me make one for you," he offers Shelby, and she nods her agreement. Liz watches his hand hesitate as well, just like his wife's, as he drops two spoonfuls of sugar into her cup. It's like he's relishing the very existence of the substance he is giving her to consume. He carefully pours a drizzle of cream into the cup to finish it, and Liz isn't sure whether she's glad to share this with him and Shelby or whether she's ashamed it exists at all.

Liz chooses a table for them, and the surrounding tables

are quickly vacated as startled crew members seem to lose their appetites. Jackson and Shelby look unconcerned as they sit. Shelby raises the coffee to her lips, sniffing it first and then taking a tentative sip. A quizzical look flashes across her dark eyes before she takes a more substantial drink.

"It's wonderful," she says, "but why grow coffee instead of something that can feed more people?" Liz assumes the question is directed at her, but she sees that Shelby has fixed her gaze on Jackson.

"Indeed," he says gravely, "a fine question." He places a bite of scrambled eggs into his mouth, chewing it carefully before he responds. "Green Grow didn't intend these ships to feed the masses. All you have to do is look at the original specifications to know that they were intended to serve exclusive populations—gourmet items like tropical fruit and exotic spices. Isn't that so, Lizzie?"

Liz looks at him, unsure what to say. It's true that there are many exotic things growing on the Green Grow 3. Different choices could have been made to feed more people.

Jackson continues, "Even the vast DNA repository on the ship was intended to provide exclusive items to exclusive people. Does that surprise you? Did you know?"

"Very little surprises me anymore," Liz says.

"That's how they got the Green Grow 1 operating so fast," he continues. "They were already building it, not to save the world or feed North America but as a novelty for people who could pay the price of space-grown food, or to visit the ship." Jackson looks at her expectantly, but what can she say? Liz doesn't know why Green Grow decided to build the ships, only that they did. Does it matter what they were intended to do? Isn't it more important to focus on what they can do now?

"It could change," she replies. "We can grow whatever is needed. It's only a matter of seeing it done."

"Yes," Jackson says. "That's why we're here." Liz detects a familiar enthusiasm in his voice. It's the same voice that praised her when she was little, when she tied her shoe correctly or read aloud. It's the same voice that taught her so many things, like how to filter ash out of her water and where to hide if strangers appeared. Maybe there is something left of the brother she knew, but what? They aren't those children anymore.

Jackson turns his attention back to his food. Liz watches him put another bite in his mouth, closing his eyes as if he's savoring it. A vision of Ruth flashes in Liz's mind, how she savored the bread the first night in quarantine, and the image sends a shard of pain through her heart.

"What's it like on the surface?" Liz asks, hearing the words come out before she's given her mouth permission to speak. "Would you have breakfast this morning if you weren't here on the ship?"

Jackson and Shelby both freeze, looking at her with surprise. Even Ellis seems to be looking at her as he stands nearby, as if he's curious about the answer. Jackson studies her for a long while before responding.

"I could say it's been harder to make do since the depots closed," he begins, "but it would be more accurate to say that it's been a different set of challenges. We've had to adapt, and it's been harder for some to adjust than others. But the future is looking brighter. We still can't grow food on the surface, but the underground hydroponic farms are doing well, especially since I've been working with Claire. I recently expanded the operation to a series of large underground caverns, and I'm optimistic about what that will yield."

He considers her for another moment before he says with resolve, "We are surviving, and if you were with me on the surface today instead of me being here with you, we would have food to eat. We wouldn't have as many options as you have here, and we would be served a rationed portion. We get two meals a day instead of three, but it's enough for now. It's better than it used to be, and six months from now, it'll be even better—by leaps and bounds."

"And the raiding parties?" Liz asks. "Are they learning how to work on these hydroponic farms?"

"I'd be lying if I said we didn't still need scavengers and scouts and soldiers," he replies. "But, I am redirecting what you call the 'raiding parties' to the extent possible. Some of the crews assimilate better than others."

"Assimilate?" Liz asks, feeling a spark of incredulity. "What does that mean, Jackson? Does it mean you're having a hard time making farmers out of butchers and thugs?" Jackson's mouth opens and then closes again.

Shelby interjects, her eyes filled with a sharpness that permeates her soft, lilting voice. "That's a fascinating question coming from you, isn't it? How many lives have you taken, Lizzie? Have you not relished the blood you have shed with the knife your brother gave you? And yet, you also worked in the orchard. Apparently, butchery and farming are not mutually exclusive."

Liz's eyes narrow as she meets Shelby's gaze. She detects an undercurrent of animosity, and something about Shelby's words irritates Liz, although she cannot deny the truth of what she implies. Does she despise Green Grow as much as Liz has come to detest the New Generation?

"I'm sure we've all done things we find necessary, if distasteful," Jackson interjects. *Distasteful?* Anger flares in her chest. "We are far from utopia," he continues, "but we are making progress. Don't forget, Lizzie, we still face threats on many fronts. Canadians subsisting in conditions more dire than our own are trying to force their way south, and disputes sometimes arise between factions of the New Generation. We don't yet have the luxury of laying down arms, but perhaps one day we can."

Liz studies the food that remains on her plate, taking the last few bites in silence. Is she the hypocrite Shelby accused her of being? She dismisses the thought, knowing that she can't afford to second guess herself now. Nor can she afford to spend her time with Jackson quibbling about his ideals, not when his reason for coming is still unclear to her.

***

Liz watches Jackson stack his and Shelby's plates neatly on his tray.

"What shall we do after breakfast?" he asks.

"I think you should spend some time with your sister," Shelby says quickly, rising from the table. "I'd like to go back to our room and refresh myself before the council meeting."

Jackson stands quickly, his hand instinctively finding the center of her back. "Are you unwell, my dear?"

"No, love," she says. "I'm just tired. It's been a long few days. Spend the time with Lizzie."

"Ellis can see you back to your room," Liz says, nodding her head in response to Ellis's inquisitive look. "We still have an hour before the council meeting. I have a place I'd like to show you."

She watches Jackson as he watches Shelby walk away. His knitted eyebrows fold into a deep crease above his nose, as if he's trying to compress all the problems of the universe into his mind at the same time. Maybe he is. Has he always been this serious? Liz doesn't remember. Then his face softens, and he smiles—not the broad, toothy grin he often gives, but something more genuine, softer. A smile that makes her want to like him.

What might have been a crowd waiting for the lift immediately dissipates as Jackson and Liz come near. The doors open and three people scurry off, wide eyes glued to the floor moments after they register the sight of the siblings. Liz hears Jackson chuckle as he follows her onto the lift, astutely watching her press the button for Level 20.

"You find it humorous that they're afraid of you?" she asks, looking at him curiously.

"Perhaps," he says.

"Why?"

"Wouldn't you find it humorous if you were visiting me and my crew scattered before you in fear?"

Liz considers this and decides to answer honestly. "Probably. But would they do that? Scatter in fear before me?"

"Like cockroaches," he says. This makes her laugh, a moment of levity that passes as she considers everything that she wants to ask him. There's just so much she wants to know. Why did he come? Why does he have to be her enemy? Why did he abandon her all those years ago? Didn't he know how desperately she needed him? When did he become a monster?

As the lift doors open onto the paradise of Level 20, Liz steps out for the first time with her brother by her side. The profundity makes her bones quiver, her stomach tremble, as she wonders how long he will be at her side and where they might go together. The lift doors close behind them, leaving only the song of birds and the sound of running water. Jackson stops, blinking quickly to compose himself. Liz wonders what he's feeling, but she doesn't ask. She sees his chest expand and hears him breathe in deeply. Does he smell the lilacs? Or perhaps the wisteria? Both are in bloom.

"What is this level for?" he asks, his eyes resting on a bed of tulips lining one side of the gravel walkway.

"It's a place for the crew to gather."

"It's quite lush," he says, eyes scanning left and then right. "Isn't this where the rice should be growing?" This is a small stab to Liz's heart. She was hoping he'd like the place.

"No, the rice will go on Levels 14 and 15," she says. "All we currently grow on this level are memories and dreams." They continue walking the winding path, the metal tube of the lift disappearing behind them, severing their connection to any tangible cue that they are on a space ship.

Liz tries to decide what to ask first. How he acquired the technology to get here? Whether he intends to overrun the ship with troops? If he really means to go back to Earth? But her mind sticks on a different question—*why did he abandon me?* She stops on a wooden footbridge that spans the burbling brook, gazing into a series of waterfalls that flow over large rocks. *When did he turn into a monster?*

"Would you really blow all this up?" Jackson asks, his voice sounding distant and choked. Startled, Liz turns to face him, but he's staring into the falling water. "That's what you said when we first spoke, that you'd rather blow the ship yourself than witness the carnage you knew would follow if I found a way on board. I'm here now. Are you going to blow us up?" Liz feels a knot in her stomach, remembering the exchange. She can't decide if it's anxiety or anger as she studies him.

"Speak plainly about your intentions," she says, "and

let's not find out."

"You always were headstrong," he says, one eyebrow cocked. "But I'm glad. I have no doubt it's kept you alive."

Didn't he know how much I needed him? How could he not know?

Liz opens her mouth to ask him again why he's here, but different words tumble out. "Did you know that the last time I went to the surface I brought back fifty-two survivors?"

"I'm aware."

"They have a nightly storytelling tradition, and I've found it quite enjoyable. We made a space on this level to continue the tradition—it's farther down the path."

"I see," he says, as they cross to the other side of the bridge, continuing under a series of wisteria-laden arbors. "Is that a hydrangea?" Jackson sounds breathless as he fixes his gaze on the huge violet and pink flowers. He quickens his pace. "Where did all of these plants come from?"

"Some of them came from Claire's lab," Liz explains, "but many of them were planted here by the crew. You were right—the whole level used to grow rice. It was the first level Captain MacAbee closed and had planted with trees. That was when the strange plants started showing up. Best I can tell, crew members preserved them from surface trips. I'm sure some of them were dormant for years—waiting for a place to live where they could grow and thrive."

Liz continues on the path. Jackson lingers a moment longer at the hydrangea and then catches up to her in a few long strides. They walk past banks of bright yellow and or-ange lilies, finally stopping at a rose bush just before a thicket of trees. Liz steps forward to gently take a large bloom be-tween her fingers. She lowers her head to meet the velvety petals, brilliant pink near the center and yellow on the edges.

"It's just like Mom's," Jackson whispers hoarsely.

"Wouldn't she love this place?"

"I don't want to talk about her," he says. Liz hears a hint of vulnerability under his commanding veneer. *There's my brother.* She wants to ask what happened to him, how he became a captain in the New Generation, what happened to his face. But those aren't the words that come out when she speaks.

"I couldn't save her," she says.

"What do you mean?" His eyes narrow, becoming sharp and hard.

"I couldn't save our mother, Jackson." Liz meets his critical eyes squarely.

"You weren't supposed to save her. You were a child."

"I told you I would take care of her, and I didn't." Liz feels her child-heart beating and breaking inside her, washed in confusion and the shame of letting her older brother down.

"She was the parent, Lizzie! She was supposed to take care of you."

Liz's confusion ignites into anger, burning away the chaff of her dead innocence. "Then why did you tell me to take care of her until you got back?" she demands. "Why did you make me think it was my responsibility?"

Jackson doesn't answer right away. Did he find her question unworthy?

"I wanted you to have a sense of purpose," he finally says. "I was a kid, too, and I didn't know how pitiful she was. She wasn't strong enough."

"Pitiful?" Liz's voice crescendos, commanding his full attention. "What was she supposed to do? There was no food. No one else to help. Her only option was to take a picker job at Green Grow and leave me alone on the surface for weeks at a time. She refused to leave me alone, and it cost her her life."

"No." He turns to face her, reaching out as if he might place his hands on her shoulders. But then he pulls them back, letting them fall to his sides. "There is always another choice."

"Bushwa!" Liz's hands ball into fists. "What other choice?"

"Lizzie, don't be coarse. Such language does not suit you."

"Coarse?" Anger surges through her veins. "Fresh hell, Jackson! I'll tell you what's coarse. Watching our mother starve is coarse. Wondering and waiting and watching every day for my brother to come back is coarse—knowing that he would because he said so! Why didn't you come back? Why didn't you find me?"

She cannot stay the well of tears spilling over her cheeks, tears that burn with guilt and sorrow—heavy drops laden with all her unanswered questions. Jackson steps forward and wraps his arms around her, and before her mind can object, her body folds into his embrace, the strange chest plate cool against her cheek and his clothes a mix of earthy dust and ozone.

"Lizzie, I cannot justify my actions. I should have come back sooner. I was a stupid, idealistic kid, and I thought our mother would take care of you. I was wrong."

"She was so thin, Jackson. We ran out of food, and she wanted me to go to the depot alone. She knew I wouldn't do it. I wanted to carry her. I told her I'd pull her in our cart. She knew I wouldn't leave without her, and so she cut her wrists. I was right there, watching the life flow right out of her. It happened so fast. I froze. All I did was sit there and watch."

"I am so very sorry," he murmurs into her hair. "If I could go back and do it differently, I would. But I can't. All

I can do is be here now."

"I tried, but I didn't know what to do. I tried to take care of her, but I failed. I should have done more. I could have done something."

"Don't cry," he says sternly, backing away slightly to take her by the shoulders and seek her eyes with his. "You didn't fail—if you don't know that, you should. You're a grown woman now. Stop seeing it through a little girl's eyes, and you'll see that it wasn't your fault. Would you expect a child to save you, Lizzie? Would you expect a child to solve your problems?"

Of course not, she thinks, too bewildered to say anything aloud. She feels a wash of shame again, this time for her self-pity. Jackson is right, or is he only trying to absolve himself?

She blinks away her tears, just like she used to do when they were little, those countless times when he told her to stop crying. She doesn't want to feel this way anymore. She doesn't want to talk about their mom, so she wipes her face with the sleeve of her tunic and commands her mind to clear. She takes a deep breath and changes the subject.

"Why can't you go back and do it differently?" she asks him. "You seem to be able to do anything you set your mind to. Why can't you just go back in time and do it differently?" This seems to surprise him.

"Well, yes," he says. "I technically probably could find a way back, now that I know how to fold the space-time continuum. But time travel poses a unique set of challenges. You see, with every decision we make, we create parallel realities, and ..." He stops to study her, looking confused as she smiles at him. "Was that not a serious question?"

There's my brother, she thinks. *He's still in there.*

"No, Jackson, it was not a serious question, although it might be a fair question. Some of your technology is mind-boggling, to say the least."

One corner of his mouth turns up. "I can see how it might seem that way."

"Did you invent the credential, too?"

"The chip that creates the blue light?" he asks. "Not really, no. I came across the specs when I hacked the Antarctica files."

"Antarctica files?"

"Yes, I've been collecting information for some time, important information we need to protect and rebuild our country. When I first accessed the old Pentagon servers, I came across a series of encoded files transmitted from secret bases in Antarctica. It appears our government used the bases to study extraterrestrial life and technology."

"Seriously? You got the chip from an alien?"

"I don't think so. Well, maybe. I don't know. It was just there, in the files. Maybe it has extraterrestrial origins, or maybe it's something our government developed."

"Why, so they could prove their membership in some kind of elite galactic club?" Liz is surprised to find herself joking with him. At least, she thinks she's kidding.

"Perhaps," he says, studying her face with a measure of amusement. "I don't know. I modified the chip to project the New Generation credential. The original technology appeared to be intended to store maps. And admittedly, it is nice to hold the world in your hands." He presses a spot on the top of his wrist with one finger, then opens his hand to reveal a blue globe of light. "I installed a version on myself similar to the original one I found, and the storage capacity is tremendous."

He does indeed appear to be holding Earth in one hand, using his free hand to manipulate the image, zooming in across the Pacific Ocean, through the rugged topography of the Rocky Mountains, and then stopping and zooming in further at the base of the mountains. "Look, that's where our old home was." Lizzy can see the creek marked on the map, and the old road that ran in front of their house. "I have star charts stored on here, too."

Liz gazes at the glowing map a moment longer, and then a wave of anger washes over her—anger at herself for getting off track. How can she be sure of his intentions? His story seems so simple, so innocent, but she looked for him so hard. She posted inquiries on the same billboards he used to recruit the crew—her coworkers who spied on them, deceived them, tried to overtake the ship and kill her and Seth. She reminds herself that technically they didn't try to kill her, and then she chastises herself for splitting such a meaningless hair. This isn't the information she needs, but will he tell her what his true agenda is if she asks him? Can she believe anything he says?

"How did you rise so high in the New Generation?" she asks instead. "And how did you get that scar on your face?"

He studies her for a moment. "I can answer both questions with the same story," he says. "I had to fight for my command, and that's how I got the scar. But perhaps we should wait until we have more time. I'm sure we need to head back soon, and I have something I'd like to give you before we go."

"Let's keep going," Liz says, motioning toward the stand of trees. "We're almost there." Jackson nods, and they continue on as he reaches into his leather jacket. Liz hears him inhale deeply.

"I'd forgotten what the pine trees smell like," he says. "Do you even remember them from Earth, when they were alive?"

"No," Liz says. "I remember the dead ones, though. I used to hide in them, when I tried to find you."

"You tried to find me?" Jackson seems surprised.

"Oh yes," Liz says, feeling that familiar wave of hurt and anger pulsing through her breastbone. "I searched for years, but perhaps we should save that for another time as well." They continue to walk, until Jackson stops suddenly. Liz can see a small flutter of wings, pausing in the air before them and then flying off.

"Is that a hummingbird?" Jackson asks, tracking the flitting creature with his eyes.

"Yes, I believe it was. They are great pollinators, and they live all over the ship. We tried to contain them at first, but it was impossible to keep them out of the ventilation shafts. So, they go where they want to go."

"I don't think I've ever seen a real one before," he says as they enter the clearing that Liz knows so well. She sits on one of the wooden benches.

"This is where the Fifty-Two have story time," she says.

"The Fifty-Two?" Jacksons asks, as he produces a small parcel, wrapped in a soft cloth and tied with a piece of twine.

"Yes, the people I brought back. The crew calls them Liz's Fifty-Two."

Jackson smiles and hands her the parcel.

"I am sorry I missed yet another birthday," he says, as some unknown feeling stabs Liz's heart. She turned twenty-five a few short weeks ago, an event that she recognized but did not celebrate. She takes the gift tentatively. The only other person who gave her a gift was Seth, but this seems different somehow. Liz unwraps it carefully, holding her breath without realizing it. The fabric yields a shiny silver chain with a large, bluish-green pendant at the end, similar to the stone in Jackson's breast plate.

"It's turquoise," he says. "People used to believe that turquoise would protect you, not just in battle but from all sorts of danger, so I thought you should have some. I found this piece in the desert and had it polished and set for you." *Will it protect me from you?* Liz wonders, feeling guilty the moment the thought enters her mind. But what does she have to feel guilty about?

"It's lovely," she says, running her fingers over the richly colored stone. "It doesn't have any superchips or tracking devices implanted in it, does it?" She's only half joking.

"Of course not," Jackson says. "I have far more advanced ways of knowing where you are." As if the question is written on her face, he laughs. "No, it's just a rock and some metal, crafted into something I hope you find beautiful. But I don't intend to lose sight of you again. Can I help you put it on?"

Liz lifts her hair while he clasps the chain around her neck. The large stone falls just below her collarbone, resting solidly on her chest. She likes the way it feels, like it somehow soothes the burns and scars on her heart.

"Thank you, Jackson," she says, rising from the bench. "Let's head back."

Jackson stands next to her, his eyes sweeping the trees and the lilac bush and the wisteria that frames the path back to the lift.

"You created a beautiful garden here, Lizzie," he says. "Is this what you imagine, when you dream of the future?"

"The future?" Liz asks, surprised by the question.

"Yes," Jackson says as an amused smile plays across his

face. "We must have a clear vision for the future. Otherwise, what is it all for? You and I don't fight for the world of today. We fight for the world of tomorrow. We suffer and bleed and sacrifice for the world of tomorrow. What do you want that world to be?"

Liz appraises him skeptically. She's not sure how to answer his question, nor whether she wants to. Jackson laughs, as if he knows what she's thinking.

"Don't be afraid to dream, Lizzie," he says. "Don't be afraid to share your dreams with me. I will only ever try to help you achieve them."

Liz's eyes drift to the lilac bush, to the place where Ruth likes to sit.

"I want the world to be more like it used to be," she says, "before the quakes." It sounds ridiculous to her, even as she says it. It sounds naïve and overly simplistic. She waits for Jackson to laugh, but he only nods, thoughtfully and earnestly.

"What do you remember about the world before?" he asks, clasping his hands behind his back as he tilts his head down to look at her with unblinking eyes.

"Not much," she admits quietly, "but I listen to the stories the Fifty-Two tell each night, about the world before. They tell them so everyone can remember."

"I see. Then tell me about the world they remember."

"People lived together in communities," she begins. "They helped each other. There were schools for the children, where they learned and played and made friends. There were sports and parties and movies and concerts. Music and art, books and newspapers. People took vacations to faraway places—islands and beaches. They weren't afraid to go. They weren't afraid to fly or sail or drive in cars. There were many places to go, many things to see and do. They were safe, and they were fed."

"Yes," Jackson murmurs, "they were happy, weren't they?"

"Maybe not all the time," Liz says, "but at least they had a chance of happiness—a real chance. What chance did we have?"

"None," he replies softly, still looking at her attentively. "Do you want to hear about the world I dream about?"

Liz nods, remembering how she felt as a child when Jackson would ask her if she wanted him to read a story before she went to sleep.

"I dream of a world where families can stay together, in a home of their choosing. A world with enough food and medicine. Clean water and electricity. I dream of backyard barbecues, camping trips to the lake. Disputes are settled peacefully, because no one has to go without the things they need. People sleep soundly at night because they are safe, their bellies full."

Jackson pauses. "Don't you see, Lizzie?" His voice is urgent, but tender. "We dream of the same world. I know sometimes it feels impossible, but it's not. We can build the world of our dreams. The path is laid before us. All we have to do is follow it."

Liz feels her eyelids flutter. Her gaze drops to the pine needles beneath her feet.

"You make it sound so simple," she says.

"I'm not saying it's simple," he replies. "I'm saying we could do it—you and me. We could change everything. We could build the world of our dreams. But we have to do it together. You and me, Lizzie."

What is he asking me to do? Liz wonders as she returns her gaze to her brother, searching his eyes. She doesn't know what to say, and so she turns and begins to walk, back through the garden and onto the lift. Jackson seems content to leave her to her thoughts, walking casually beside her and easily matching her stride.

"Thank you for the time you spent with me this morning," he says as the lift doors close in front of them. Liz presses the button for Level 1, swiping her key card when prompted. She only smiles in return, feeling a strange new connection to her brother. Maybe they really do dream of the same world. Is it really that simple? And what if it is? Could they really build it together?

CHAPTER 12

COUNCIL MEETING

***

Seth convenes the daily council meeting, annoyed that Jackson chose to sit in the seat Liz usually occupies. *I guess he has to sit somewhere.* Or does he? Why can't he evaporate into nothing and cease to exist altogether? Then he wouldn't need a place to sit. The upside is that when Liz saw her usual seat occupied, she chose to sit next to Seth instead of moving farther down the table and bookending the interlopers. Seth didn't realize how much he needed her affirmation until she sat by his side and he felt a wave of relief wash over him.

Now he fortifies himself with the energy she radiates, memories of her warm skin pulsing through his mind. He steels his face and sits straight and tall, which is easier to do since he wore his formal uniform today. It's confining and unyielding, and he can't seem to forget that the last time he wore it, he executed two people in front of the crew. But the uniform reminds him of who he needs to be every moment that Jackson is here—the captain of the Green Grow 3.

"I see we are all here," Jackson says the moment everyone is seated. "My time is valuable, so let me get straight to the point. You, Seth Harris, claim to be the leader of this ship, but you lead no one. You claim to care about the people on Earth—the ones you so carelessly abandoned—but your actions are the true measure of your regard for their fragile lives.

"I, alone, am moving heaven and earth to sustain those struggling to survive back on the surface, without the bountiful resources of the Green Grow 3, which you withhold. I, alone, have undertaken the responsibility of solving all the problems you created when you abandoned Earth. Yet, you resist me at every turn, and your example is infecting the crew with lethargy.

"Literally, all I've asked you to do is follow a few simple instructions to get home, but you fail to cooperate at every turn. Are you truly this incompetent, or are you simply oblivious to needs of the people whose survival depends upon your return?"

Jackson pauses to take a breath, although Seth is sure his rant is far from over. *This has gone on long enough,* he thinks, making sure that his voice fills the room as he begins to speak.

"Perhaps when you see how the ship is faring with the controlled accelerations, you'll better understand why we can't accelerate any faster or more frequently than we're doing. Is there something we can discuss constructively, Jackson, or should we proceed directly to the tour?"

Seth refuses to break eye contact with him, even as the room is draped in silence. The man is clearly accustomed to staring people down. Jackson is testing him, and he doesn't intend to fail. The silence stretches on as they stare at each other, unflinching. The room is so still that Seth can hear his mother breathing to his left and Harry shifting in his chair past Liz on his right. Mathilda picks up a pen to doodle on the paper in front of her, and Jackson breaks the stare, startled by her movement.

"I'd like to discuss food distribution," Jackson says.

"What do you propose?" Seth asks. "I'm sure you wouldn't bring it up if you didn't have something in mind."

Jackson casts a scornful glance his way. "Your response to my requests to seed new crops has been lackadaisical at best. Need I remind you that people are starving? Your responsibility for their suffering grows each day."

"I see no value in growing food that cannot be distributed," Seth replies. "But, since you have mysteriously, and perhaps even miraculously, appeared on my ship, I now see that you may have the means to distribute food before we actually return to Earth. Is that accurate?" Seth sees something like mirth in Jackson's eyes, and he reminds himself that he cannot afford to get angry. It's what the man wants, and Seth cannot concede.

"I see you are finally comprehending the situation at hand," Jackson replies. "I do have a way to transport the food, but I must oversee it personally. The goods must be packaged with precise specifications, and I will not turn my technology over to you." Seth detects disgust in Jackson's voice, but it only makes him want to laugh.

"Frankly, Jackson," he says, "I don't want your technology. It strikes me as dangerous, and not something to be used casually, if at all. I cannot imagine that even you fully understand the ramifications of what you are doing. But I am not here to school you in your own arrogance. I am here to manage this ship and its resources, and this ship is meant to feed the people on Earth. I'd like the details of your proposal, but I have no problem transporting whatever you can accommodate."

Seth sees a fleeting whisper of surprise on Jackson's face. "Indeed," he says quickly, tapping his fingertips together, "I assembled my transporter on Level 37 shortly after I arrived here. Rest assured, it contains layers of security to ensure I am the only person who can use it, but I am sure you will want to see it at the end of our tour."

I can't wait, Seth thinks wryly, shifting his attention away. "Harry," he says, "I want to know, based on our current stores, how much food we can spare."

"I'll send you a report immediately," Harry says.

"And what else?" Seth asks. "Medicine? Lumber? Paper? Cloth?"

Jackson smiles, his eyes betraying a hint of uncertainty that Seth relishes. He's sure Jackson didn't expect him to be so cooperative, and Seth is pleased to catch him unprepared. *Be unpredictable,* he reminds himself.

"The goods must be coated in a protective biofilm," Jackson says. "Dr. Harris should determine how much she can produce, and then I'll have a better sense."

"Of course, Jackson." Claire nods vigorously. "I'm certain we can find a way to produce whatever you need." He acknowledges her with a nod, reaching into a pocket of his leather jacket. He produces a neatly folded piece of paper, his eyes never leaving Seth's as he extends it for Claire to take.

"Here is the formula," he says. She takes it gingerly, as if he's handed her something sacred, and scrutinizes the neatly printed characters.

Seth can't stand the way she defers to Jackson.

"And the formula for the thruster fuel?" he demands, channeling his fury into words. "Are you going to give us that today, too, or is there some new delay you care to explain?"

"I need explain nothing." Jackson leans back in his chair, one corner of his mouth raised in the hint of a smile. "Build the thrusters. Once I'm certain you've built them correctly, I'll give you the formula. In the meantime, focus on the protective biofilm."

Seth glances over at Liz, considering what to say. Then something catches his eye. She's wearing a necklace with a large blue stone. It looks like turquoise— it must have been a gift from Jackson. He feels sick and angry, partly because it's so beautiful. He could never give Liz something like that, although maybe if he'd thought of it, he could have asked his mom to manufacture some kind of a stone. But the fact that Liz accepted it from her brother, and is wearing it right now, makes him wonder whether their relationship is shifting beneath his very feet. What happened between Liz and Jackson this morning? He tries to brush the thought out of his mind, turning his attention back to his mother, who has been looking at the formula Jackson gave her.

"I'll get right on this," Claire says, looking up to meet Seth's gaze. "Are we done here?"

She sounds so eager to please this man, so anxious to do whatever he asks. Meanwhile, the way she's looking at Seth reminds him of when he was a child, when she thought he was being a nuisance, asking too many questions or interrupting her work. He can't stand it now.

Jackson is turning everyone against him, taking everyone away. He wants to rage at him, to fly across the table and pummel him, fists cracking bone. He wants to make him pay for every sleepless night, every anxious moment Seth has suffered since Captain MacAbee left.

"You can get on it after the controlled acceleration," he says tersely, rising from his chair and turning on his heel. "We're done here." He doesn't wait for anyone else to leave the room. He doesn't look at Liz or her necklace, or his mother or anyone else on the council. Instead, he walks straight to the bridge, where he sits heavily in his chair, closing his eyes until it's time to start the acceleration.

I choose to be still. I choose to be still. I choose to be still. He repeats the mantra over and over, riding out the ten minutes and trying to reset his mind, although he doesn't know how. He knows this much—he hates the bursts, but not as much as he dreads the time he will have to spend with Jackson after, giving him a tour of the ship.

When the controlled acceleration is over, Seth doesn't get up right away. Everyone else leaves the bridge, except for Liz, who stands before him, looking at him curiously.

"Are you jake?" she asks.

"Right as rain," he says, managing a smile as he winks at her. His eyes settle on her necklace. "Pretty stone. Is it turquoise?"

"Yes," she says, her fingers moving up to touch the pendant. "Jackson gave it to me this morning. It seems to be seventeen years' worth of birthday presents. I need to see if Jarrod can scan it for bugs or chips or anything else that might be hiding inside."

Seth finds her skepticism comforting. "I suppose we should get this over with," he says, moving to rise from his chair.

"Are you sure?" Liz asks. "Maybe a tour is a bad idea." He looks at her delicate, furrowed brow, her inquisitive eyes. He pulls her close to him, wishing he could hold her for eternity. But he can't, so he just gently kisses her forehead as she squeezes his hands.

"It's a good idea, Z. I just have a lot on my mind. I'd like to talk to you about it, but for right now, let's get through the tour." He starts to move toward the doors, but she grasps his arm, pulling him back to her.

"Jackson can wait," she says. "Isn't Ellis with him?"

"Charlie and Ruben are on," Seth says, "but let's talk later. All I can think about right now are the names and faces I spent half the night studying. I wanted to know the names of everyone working today. Plus, I went over all the inventory and maintenance reports."

Liz's brow furrows again, and she bites her lip. "You'll do great, Seth. No one knows this ship like you."

Seth suppresses a bitter snort. *Is that why I spent most of night studying, like a child preparing for a test I'm afraid I'll fail?* No, it wasn't his ego that drove him to spend hours poring over reports and archived files, fortifying his knowledge of the current and past operations on the ship. He did it because something occurred to him lying in bed, on the cusp of sleep that never came as he cradled Liz in his arms.

Seth used to believe that any attempt to kill him would come in the form of a physical attack. But if Jackson can transport matter at his will by folding the space-time continuum, his options for killing Seth are nearly endless. Although he doesn't yet understand the intricacies of how it works, Jackson could literally make him disappear at any point. *All he needs is my precise location to open a wormhole that could transport me anywhere.*

The idea that he has so little control over his own life, and his own death for that matter, terrifies Seth. But he cannot give Jackson the satisfaction of knowing that he's afraid. Seth hates the idea of playing Jackson's game—he hates the idea that his very life has been reduced to a game. But he must play, at least for now. He must make Jackson believe he is indispensable—for long enough to develop an escape plan.

CHAPTER 13

ON TOUR

***

"You have already seen portions of Level 1," Seth begins, walking with Liz by his side and gesturing for Jackson and Shelby to follow. "In addition to the quarters and the conference room, the level also contains escape pods, offices, and the bridge."

Charlie and Ruben remain posted outside Jackson's door, although Seth knows the guard will change before they get back. Charlie looks happy to see Jackson and Shelby go. Ruben, on the other hand, has the same fearless confidence as Ellis, meeting Jackson's eyes without hesitation. *What is it with that group of people?* Seth wonders, flummoxed.

When they reach the bridge, Jackson looks predictably disappointed that the heavy doors are closed. Seth has no intention of opening them. He's sure the man would love to sit in his chair, to see how the controls work or plant some kind of listening device to help him hack the propulsion drive and navigation system. Those are among the few remaining mysteries Jackson hasn't solved, and they will remain mysteries as long as Seth can keep them that way. He motions them on, and they continue walking.

"And this must be where you shot Willow and Zag," Jackson says, his voice cutting through the air like a sonic blast as they pass through the open area where Seth holds the all-hands meetings. Seth takes a few more steps, pressing the button for the lift before responding.

"Yes," he replies, meeting Jackson's eyes steadily. "This is where the spies were tried, convicted of mutiny, and executed." He turns to step onto the lift before Jackson can respond.

"Level 2 contains more escape pods," Seth continues, "as well as quarters that were intended for officers and supervisors. It's currently abandoned, since we have no need of such space."

"You don't offer the space to the crew?" Shelby asks in her lilting voice that Seth is sure has softened the heart of many men. It doesn't soften his, though. Her innocence is an illusion, a façade that makes him suspicious.

"No," he replies. "I don't want them preoccupied with competing for space."

"In the New Generation, competition is a core value," Shelby says.

"I'm sure it is." Seth glances at her but quickly looks away, unsettled by how much she reminds him of Willow Brown. He can see Willow clearly, screaming before him as she raised her hands to shield her face. He doesn't regret executing her—not exactly. It haunts him, but it was necessary.

The corridors on Level 3 are deserted, a sure sign that the crew is hiding. Seth describes the layout of the quarters and the common bathrooms.

"This is also where the laundry is," he says, motioning to the double doors that lead to the space where the crew drop off and pick up bags of laundry. Seth opens the doors to find two wide eyes, a man he recognizes as one of Jarrod's mechanics. The man slings a bag over his shoulder and quickly ducks his head, taking two steps back and attempting to melt into a corner. Shelby appraises him curiously as she wafts by in her graceful gait, looking out of place in her New Generation clothes.

Seth focuses on a middle-aged woman whose eyes grow wider with every step he takes toward the counter. He makes a point to stand straight as he greets her.

"Good morning, Clarissa." He smiles broadly. "How are you today?"

The woman jumps when he says her name, her eyes roving wildly across the group. Finally she seems to remember that Seth has asked her a question, and clears her throat to respond.

"Good morning, Captain," she says quickly. "I am fine—just preparing for a busy day." Seth nods and turns to face the group.

"Clarissa is starting a two-week rotation in the laundry. Then she will move to the kitchen."

They return to the desolate corridor, moving down to Level 4, where Seth is certain that hunger will prove stronger than the crew's fear of Jackson. The cafeteria is busy, but the crew give them a wide berth, ducking their heads as if they are afraid of being seen.

Seth is surprised to see Chub, standing in the doorway to the kitchen, refusing to look away. His eyes are wide and bloodshot, and he appears terrified. Seth knows he has reason to be afraid of Jackson, that the man could call him out by name and reveal his betrayal. Seth feels no sympathy for the man's predicament, nor does he feel animosity. He feels nothing beyond a glimmer of admiration for Chub's refusal to hide despite his terror. Seth acknowledges him with a curt nod, giving him permission to recede before Jackson sees him. The cook blinks quickly, nodding in return, before taking refuge in the privacy of the kitchen.

Seth leads them through the fitness center and recreation area, empty except for a maintenance crew accessing a broken water pipe through a panel in the wall. Seth greets the three men, watching them jump as he calls them all by name.

"This happened during the morning acceleration?" Jackson asks.

"Yes," Seth replies. "Pipes broke on three levels, and an air handler shorted out. The damage will be repaired before the evening acceleration, but more damage is inevitable. We've expanded the maintenance teams, but it's a challenge to stay on top of the ongoing repairs."

Jackson says nothing, appearing to be in deep thought.

"Thank you, gentlemen," Seth says to the three men anxiously jostling from foot to foot in front of him. "Please return to work, and we'll be on our way." They seem happy to do so, and Seth finally leads the group to the place that he's least excited about going—the medical unit.

***

"This is remarkable," Shelby gasps, eyes glued to the petri dish the lab tech placed under the microscope for her to see. "Is that really a baby goat?"

"It will be," the lab tech says with a smile. "We'll be implanting a batch of embryos like this one into the nannies on Level 16, and five months later we'll have a slew of babies."

"Is it really that simple?" Shelby asks.

"Well," the tech replies, "there are several steps in the process, including hormone treatments for the nannies. It takes a little time, but for the most part, it really is."

Seth knows what they're doing is anything but simple, and he's not enthusiastic about it. Over the last two days, the genetics lab has been working nonstop to expand the number of livestock, not just goats but also pigs, cows, sheep, and chickens. Claire is ramping up faster than Seth thought possible.

Too much is happening too fast, and his mother is entirely too excited about it. He glances over at her, talking in hushed whispers to Jackson as they both lean over a lab table. Liz stands behind them, engrossed in whatever they are saying. He trusts her to monitor what they're doing. Of course, Seth is the one with the background in biology and chemistry, and he's the one who would understand the details of their discussion. But right now, the details don't matter to him. Getting through this tour is the only thing that matters, and his wits are already thin. He can't bear to watch his own mother chat amicably with Jackson, as if he didn't try to slaughter them just two months ago.

He turns his attention back to Shelby and the lab tech, forcing himself to smile. "There's still much to see," he says. "Let's move on." He ushers her toward Jackson and Liz, looking away when the disappointment and annoyance washes over his mother's face.

"Thank you, Claire," Jackson says in a tone Seth finds glib and disingenuous, but just as he imagines she will, his mother smiles warmly and promises to update him on her progress at the council meeting. *How can she be so blinded by his charm?* Seth doesn't find Jackson charming at all, but his mother seems to be allured by every insincere compliment, every fake smile. The captain knows she's just one of many who have fallen prey to Jackson's charisma, but he feels a pang of anguish nonetheless at how quick she is to minimize the man's hatred of him.

She seems to truly believe she can read Jackson's intentions, that she can influence him in ways Seth doubts are possible. She's so quick to dismiss the brutality of the organization Jackson leads, rushing to his defense when the council questions his motives. The way she accepts what he chooses to show her with so much conviction seems like arrogance to Seth, and it doesn't just hurt him—it astounds him.

Seth steels his face and squares his shoulders, determined to set aside the pain of his mother's dismissive condescension. He refuses to behave like the spoiled child Jackson accuses him of being.

***

When the doors open to Level 5, Seth sees the cart he requested parked a few feet away. With a wave of his hand, he ushers everyone inside.

"Now that we are out of the residential area of the ship, a cart will be more efficient," he says, looking forward to the cushioned driver's seat. He watches as Jackson offers a hand to Shelby, helping her into the back seat before he climbs into the cart next to her.

When they are all in, Seth presses the accelerator, motioning to the server room as they drive by. He's glad Jackson can't touch anything, as his mind flashes back to the day the propulsion drive engaged. He remembers the first woman he shot, the one with the blue credential of light beaming out of her palm. He hates Jackson for that, for creating the situation that forced him to take a life—several lives, in fact. Seth remembers running at full speed down the row of servers, launching himself like a rocket at a man who was frantically typing on a tablet connected to the server. Clearly, he was trying to disable the ship's systems, leaving them floating in space with limited life expectancies. Wasn't that what Jackson told the traitors to do when he hacked the broadcast?

Seth finds it hard to hold back his anger, harder than it's ever been. He's tired from too little sleep. His uniform is stifling and hot, and his face hurts from forcing too many smiles. His back aches from standing rigidly straight, reminding Jackson at every turn that he's not the biggest man in the room. Seth is tired of worrying about what he will do next, this man who is his enemy. He wants to end this tour, to go somewhere that Jackson Goeff is not, but where would that be? The man has eyes and ears everywhere—human or electronic.

"We call the first six levels the Survival Saucer," Seth says, trying not to grit his teeth. "Those levels can eject completely from the growing levels and function independently in an emergency."

He hears Shelby's lilting voice from the back, and he forces himself to cock his head, as if interested in what she wants to know. He's not.

"Jackson tells me that you lived here as a child," she says. "Is that true?"

"Yes," he replies, forcing yet another a smile. "I moved here with my parents while the growing levels were still being built. They were part of the first group of scientists to live here, setting up protocols on the ship, testing the systems, and establishing the DNA repository that seeded all of the plants and animals we have onboard today."

"Were there other children?" she asks, and against his will, Seth finds himself intrigued by the question.

"No," he says, keeping his eyes fixed on the path ahead.

"That sounds lonely." Seth isn't sure how to respond. Was it lonely? It must have been, but no more than the underground bunker where he lived before the Survival Saucer. He doesn't remember having anywhere to play, or anyone to play with—ever. But what difference does it make now?

"It wasn't without challenges, but a different set than those faced by people on the surface."

"Indeed," Jackson responds, and Seth knows what he's getting at. The jab might have bothered him two months ago, but now it seems like a minor thing.

***

The trees on Level 7 radiate a peacefulness Seth hopes he can absorb. Light glows above them, and he breathes in the familiar smell that always reminds him of kissing Liz. She tells Jackson and Shelby about the growing cycles and the logistics of maintaining the trees, and Seth lets himself focus on the melody of her voice. It's a nice harmony with the birds singing around them.

"If you try to swat it, it may sting you," he hears Liz say. Shelby squeals in the back.

"It's okay, love," he hears Jackson tell her. "It's a bee."

"I've never seen such a thing!" she cries.

"I know," he says, soothing her as she buries her head in his chest, "but they make a delicious treat called honey."

"And they pollinate the trees and plants all over the ship," Liz adds.

They drive on through the tropical orchard on Level 8, where Shelby spots a hummingbird that makes her giggle. They drive through the field crops on Levels 9, 10, 11, and

12, where Jackson plies him with questions about how decisions are made about what to grow.

When Seth drives off the utility lift onto Level 13, he seriously considers turning right around and going straight down to Level 37 to see Jackson's machine. But the idea of it feels like capitulation, and hasn't Seth failed enough as it is? He can't stand the thought of living up to the opinion he's sure Jackson holds of him—that he is weak and incapable of leading the ship.

Instead, he talks about planting the abandoned levels with trees, and how they use the trees for paper products, building, and soil enrichment. He talks about oxygen management, about the biosphere of the ship, about how even abandoned levels are still important to the ecosystem. He drives them through the trees toward the reservoir, stopping when the soil becomes too soft and muddy for the cart. When the level lost gravity just a couple days ago, water globules floated into the air and then rained down everywhere when it was restored. Most of the water has drained back to where it belongs, but the soil needs more time to dry out.

Jackson wants to see the reservoir, so they get out and walk closer to the shore. Seth wants to scream, "This is where you sister almost died! This is where she watched yet another person end his own life in a moment of despair! This is the path you created for her when you left her alone all those years ago." But he can't bring himself to speak those words, because he was the one who failed Liz that day.

The tour goes on and on. Seth drives through Levels 14 and 15, explaining how they will be prepared to grow the rice Jackson asked for, and how the work competes with the need for ongoing repairs caused by the controlled accelerations. He shows them the livestock on Levels 16 and 17, describing the cascading demands created by Jackson's request to breed them all—increased pasture space, more people to tend them, more buildings to contain them.

Levels 18 and 19 are currently abandoned, but Seth drives through them anyway, describing their size and potential. He remembers when all of the levels were bustling, the ship's crew more than three times the size it is now. Now most of it sits unused. *What a waste,* he thinks, realizing that just as Liz blamed the New Generation for so many things, he too wants someone to blame for the wasted potential on this ship. But who is to blame? Jackson? The Green Grow executive board? Himself?

When he drives off the utility lift onto Level 20, he skirts around the edge of the garden so that Shelby can see it as it was intended to be seen. Driving the cart onto the gravel pathway leading away from the passenger lift, he hears her gasp.

"We created the garden to support the crew's new tradition of recounting stories about Earth each night," he says somewhat dismissively. "It's important to them, or at least some of them, but we can reconfigure the area if we need to. Level 20 is the largest level, and the garden takes up little of the space."

"Indeed," Jackson remarks smartly, "I've heard of Ruth's story time."

Seth doesn't know if Jackson intends to rattle him by invoking the old woman's name, but either way it doesn't work. His nerves are already shot, and there's nothing left to rattle.

"Story time?" Shelby asks. "May we attend?"

"Of course!" Jackson says, without bothering to confirm this with Liz or Seth. Seth looks over at Liz, who meets his gaze. She will have to handle this.

"Let's get out for a few minutes," Shelby says enthusiastically. "Can we?"

"I don't see why not," Seth says loudly before Jackson can say anything. He stops the cart, and everyone climbs out. In truth, Seth is also glad for the break. He watches Jackson and Shelby walk to the wooden bridge that crosses the stream. She stops in the middle, pointing to the waterfall and saying something to Jackson that Seth can't hear.

Seth tries to see it through fresh eyes, remembering how enchanted he was the first time he walked off the lift onto the garden path with Liz. *It's an extraordinary place,* he thinks, and this makes him feel more optimistic. Together, he and the council and the crew made something beautiful, something better than he ever would have imagined.

Moments later, they're all back in the cart again, moving down the ship level by level. Seth feels calmer now, surprised at his own knowledge as he details the history of what used to grow on each level. They continue down until finally the reach the bottom, down to the airlock where Jackson's machine awaits.

CHAPTER 14

MATHILDA'S LUNCH

****

Mathilda is the chief astronomer, and she sits on the council, but the only reason Ruth knows what she looks like is because she saw her up on the dais that night that Captain Harris executed the two crew members. Now, Ruth sees her in the cafeteria sometimes, sitting alone and looking unabashedly forlorn. Such a solitary life must be lonely, but Mathilda doesn't give any indication of wanting to connect with others. People who report to her say that she's aloof and distant, and Ruth has never seen her at story time, although it's possible by the flickering light of the campfire that someone could get lost in the crowd. Ruth has known introverted people, but Mathilda seems to be more than introverted, perhaps even reclusive.

Nonetheless, she's determined to talk to Mathilda today. She got to the cafeteria as soon as it opened, sitting at a table where she could see everyone coming through. But Mathilda didn't come for the breakfast service. Ruth waited until the last possible minute to go back to her quarters for the morning acceleration, and returned as fast as her old body would allow when it was over to wait for the woman to come for lunch.

She's still waiting.

Ruth is supposed to be working on a growing level, but she told Harry that her arthritis was flaring and that she needed to rest this morning. He told her not to worry about it, to go to the medical unit if she needed to. She can't imagine that she's missed. Harry assigned her to a team that rotates between levels as needed, and they always make sure she has something to do, although she doubts any of it is useful. But she doesn't complain.

Most of the time, she drives a tractor. She transports produce, which is loaded and unloaded by others, or sometimes pulls an attachment to plow or cut or fertilize fields. It's an easy job, because all she has to do is drive. Clearly, she's been given this job because of her age, and she appreciates the consideration, although it bothers her to be pitied. Today, however, she will take the pity if it helps her connect with Mathilda. She will sit here all day if she has to.

Eventually, Ruth sees the diminutive woman, carrying a sparsely filled lunch tray as she walks with hunched shoulders. She waits and watches as Mathilda sits at a nearby table, settling heavily in the chair as if she's suffered the worst kind of defeat. The woman appraises her salad, pushing pieces around her plate with a fork before resting her chin on one palm, as if her head is too heavy to hold itself up. She stabs a piece of lettuce, taking a bite that she chews for much too long.

"Ms. Greenberg?" Ruth asks softly, approaching her table. Mathilda's jaw stops working and her eyes jump up, liquid and damp through the lenses of her glasses. Ruth sees no life in those eyes, only a vacant numbness, surrounded by dark circles and puffy lids. "May I speak with you?" she continues, sitting tentatively across the table. "I'm Ruth, one of the people Liz saved at the depot."

"I know who you are," Mathilda replies in a flat tone, placing her fork next to her plate and folding her hands in her lap.

"And I believe I know who you are, too," Ruth says, keeping her gaze even. "I believe that we've both been helping someone who has no interest in helping us, and I'd like to change that. Would you?"

Something sparks in the woman's eyes, something that Ruth chooses to interpret as curiosity.

"It was you," Mathilda whispers. "I knew it had to be you—the timing was undeniable. I got the specifications to build the laptop antennae right after you came …" Her voice trails off as her eyes shift away from Ruth and toward some thought she does not share. Ruth waits for Mathilda to say something else, but the woman only picks up her fork and starts to push her food around again.

"It was me," Ruth says quietly, "and I believe it was you, as well. You had access to information he wanted, like what Captain Harris was planning and when he intended to depart."

Mathilda looks up at her but says nothing.

"Why did Jackson come here?" Ruth asks. The woman studies her, suspiciously, before shrugging and returning to her food.

"I wanted to blow you up, you know," Mathilda says quietly, eyes fixed on her plate.

"Excuse me?" Ruth asks, unsure how to respond.

"When Liz brought you back on the shuttle," she explains. "It seemed like such a bad idea to bring refugees on board. We thought you must be working for the New Generation, and clearly you were. Claire suggested blowing the shuttle, and I agreed. But of course, Seth wouldn't allow it, not with Liz on board."

Ruth studies Mathilda's dispassionate face. *Why is she telling me this?*

"Perhaps it would have been easier if you had," Ruth replies, "but you didn't. And I'm not sure why you, personally, would have been threatened by any relationship we might have had with the New Generation."

Mathilda looks up with angry eyes.

"I was a fool," she chokes.

"As was I," Ruth whispers, leaning in closer, "but I want to change that now."

"Why?" Mathilda seems less angry than curious.

"I'm tired of being afraid. I'm tired of living in the shadows, of undermining Liz and Captain Harris."

"She doesn't know, does she?" Mathilda asks, eyes widening. Ruth wonders if this conversation is a mistake.

"I don't think so," she replies.

The woman nods, retreating into her own thoughts for a moment. "Did you help him build the machine?"

Ruth nods solemnly, feeling sick to her stomach. "What does it do?"

"Apparently, it folds the space-time continuum," Mathilda replies. "Jackson says he built it to transport food back to Earth." Ruth looks at her, confused.

"Is that how he arrived here? With the machine?"

"No, he didn't need the machine to arrive. He assembled it after he got here."

Ruth isn't sure whether this makes her feel better or worse, but she knows it doesn't absolve her.

"Why did you help him?" Mathilda asks, and Ruth is filled with unease. Why did she help him? She's asked herself countless times but has no good answer.

"I suppose I thought I had my reasons," she says. "To protect people who stayed on the surface. Fear. Ignorance. To be honest, I don't know. I see now that my reasons are really only excuses."

Mathilda nods.

"You worked against him before we left, though, when he tried to take command," she says. "What changed?"

"Nothing changed." Ruth shrugs. "We weren't going to let Liz fight alone, not after she saved us. I would never abandon her like that." She hears the contradiction in her own words, but it's the truth as she knows it.

"No one ever does," Mathilda says with resentment. Ruth reminds herself that she wants information from this woman, although it's looking unlikely that they can work together.

"But why did Jackson come alone?" she asks.

"Oh," Mathilda says, voice still bitter, "he is definitely not alone. He brought his beautiful wife, Shelby." Ruth can see that Jackson has hurt Mathilda deeply. She wonders if he knows, and then she wonders if he cares. Ruth is almost ready to call it a bust and end the conversation when Mathilda speaks again.

"Look, Jackson took some big risks in coming here. He must have his reasons, but I don't know what they are—what they *really* are, I mean. My dealings with him seem to have concluded, so I'm afraid you'll be disappointed if you think I can help you get answers."

"Perhaps there's a way we can find out," Ruth suggests.

"We've tried bugging his quarters," Mathilda explains, "but he disables every device."

Ruth nods. "That's good to know."

"What will you do?" Mathilda asks, looking curious again.

"I'll find a way," Ruth says vaguely, "and I'll report anything I learn to Captain Harris." Mathilda looks away, her attention returning to her food. Ruth rises to leave, but turns back once more.

"You are always welcome at story time, dear," she says. "Join us any time." Mathilda looks up but says nothing, and Ruth takes her leave, mind spinning. She has an idea about how to eavesdrop on Jackson's conversations. The thought of it makes her sick, but if she can make it work, perhaps she can provide something valuable to Captain Harris.

She decides to go back to work, heading directly to Harry's office to tell him that she's feeling better and doesn't want him to be shorthanded. He studies her for a moment but doesn't protest, telling her that her team is working in the vineyard on Level 7. "The vines are getting too full to withstand the 4G accelerations," he says, "so we need to harvest what we can before it's ruined."

Ruth likes the vineyard, even though she can't seem to forget the rustling of the large grape leaves and Liz telling them to hide as Jackson's face filled the broadcast screen near the tool shed. So much has changed since that day. As she climbs onto a tractor and starts it up, she reminds herself how fortunate she is, that she is safe and fed and healthy, even if her head is still spinning from Jackson's arrival. She's built a life on this ship, a life worth living.

It feels good to be doing something useful, to be among the greenery and the people. Ruth drives the tractor toward the melodic chatter of happy voices, knowing that this is where she will find her team. They're all tired from the controlled accelerations, but no one complains. They laugh and banter while they work, grasping moments of happiness and normalcy even among the chaos.

Ruth realizes how much she needs this, how quickly she's grown accustomed to the fullness of life on the Green Grow 3. Each day that she lives in this microcosm of paradise, the fear that used to saturate her heart diminishes a little more—fear of hunger and sickness, fear of watching the people she loves suffer. But now she remembers the fear again. It is raw and all-consuming, and she wonders if she can find the strength to co-exist with it like she used to. Perhaps the comfort she's found on the Green Grow 3 has dissolved more than her fear. Perhaps it's dissolved her strength as well.

But does she need to be afraid? Why is that her only choice? Maybe she's overreacting. Maybe she doesn't need to spy on Jackson. Maybe he's done with her, too, and she can simply put the past in the past and forget that she ever helped him. If he arrived without using the machine she helped him build, then she can't be held responsible for him coming.

Ruth is driving the tractor, pulling a trailer loaded with baskets of grapes to the utility lift, and just starting to convince herself that everything will be okay, when the world around her goes silent and she sees them. The laughter and chattering conversation stop so suddenly that first Ruth thinks she's gone deaf, but she can still hear the hum of the tractor. She looks around and sees the faces of her team, silently staring open-mouthed at the cart Captain Harris is driving toward them. Liz sits next to him, and Jackson and the woman are in the back seat.

Liz's voice carries. She's telling Jackson about the irrigation system in the orchard. Then the woman in the back squeals. Jackson murmurs something to her about bees and honey.

Mathilda called her Shelby, Ruth remembers.

She slows her tractor, considering what to do. Her team members are fading into the vines like wraiths. She could hide as well. No one would question her leaving the tractor here for a few minutes. No one would even know—everyone else is hiding too.

You would know, she reminds herself, thinking of the children. How can she ask them to be strong, to set aside their fears and do what needs to be done, while she herself runs like a coward? *Face him,* she commands herself. *Be brave.*

Tendrils of fear grip her fiercely, but it's anger that pushes her forward as she drives the tractor on. Anger at her own weakness. Anger at what she now knows the children must do. Mostly, it's anger toward Jackson for ruining the peace she found in this place.

She keeps her chin high and her eyes forward, refusing to look away from the man's face. She sees his cold blue eyes, the ropy scar that proves he's not invulnerable. He sees her too, and he gives her one of his charming smiles, the kind that doesn't match his eyes. He gave her that same smile the morning he showed up in her cave. She remembers it clearly. It was that beautiful time of morning, when rays of sun beamed down divinely through a collapse in the ceiling, when she still felt strong enough to face whatever challenges the day would bring.

"Good morning, Ruth," he said, approaching her from behind as she was taking inventory of their meager supplies. She whirled to face him, wishing she could scream but abandoned by her voice as she took in his leather clothes and the chest plate made of stone and metal. She knew it marked him as a leader, but she didn't know if that made him more or less dangerous.

He raised his hands, trying to appear harmless. "I'm only here to talk," he told her. *This time,* she understood, even though he didn't say those words. "Your scouts are on their way back, and if you sit with me to speak, I can be gone before they return." Ruth fell to the ground then, collapsing in a heap on her knees as he leaned against a large rock that had fallen from the ceiling of the cave.

He gave her that same disingenuous smile then, the one he's giving her now. She tells herself he's only a man, that she cannot concede by looking away. But it's not a man's face she sees—it's every bad thing that's ever happened to her and her people, every bad thing that could happen in the future. Ruth isn't staring at the face of a man—she's staring at the face of evil and everything it's done to her.

Jackson looks away, turning his attention back to the woman, and Ruth notices the captain looking at her curiously.

"Captain Harris," she says as she drives by him toward the utility lift.

"Ruth." He tips his chin slightly in acknowledgement.

She's almost past the cart when Liz catches her eye, giving her a warm smile. Liz, who she has betrayed. Liz, who has saved Ruth and her people twice from the New Generation—first at the depot and then again when Jackson tried to overtake the ship. Will Liz save them again now that Jackson is here?

Please, Ruth begs with her eyes. *Save us. Save me. I don't deserve it, but save me anyway.* In a moment, Liz is gone. Ruth can hear her telling Jackson about the vineyards, why they're harvesting the grapes and how they will stack them in small crates to keep them from being crushed during the controlled acceleration. She sounds perfectly at ease explaining all of this to Jackson, and for a reason she can't articulate, Ruth finds this frightening.

CHAPTER 15

JACKSON'S MACHINE

***

Jackson's machine is bigger than Liz imagined from the security footage. It consists of a platform about ten feet square, which sits on a solid base about two feet off the ground. Each corner contains a thick metal pole that nearly reaches the ceiling of the large airlock. Liz tilts her head to gaze at the rounded ends of the poles, thinking they must be at least ten feet tall. Everything is made of metal, neither shiny nor dull, and Liz can't help but wonder why a machine capable of such great things doesn't look more remarkable.

"This is your transporter?" she asks.

"Indeed." He looks at the machine dispassionately, which is worrying. He has probably seen it, or one like it, countless times, but she doesn't think that the novelty should ever fade when folding the space-time continuum. No one should ever grow accustomed to altering the very fabric of the universe.

"It looks so simple," Liz says. "Is it finished?"

"Yes, Lizzie," Jackson replies. "Great things need not be complicated."

"Are there no tubes or wires?" she asks. "No control panels or sensors?"

Jackson smiles at her. "The required components are inside the platform, and within the poles. It's all there."

"Do we need additional security around this?" Seth asks, gaze fixed on the machine. His face is devoid of emotion, hands clasped behind his back as he stands tall.

"It's secure," Jackson replies, with a thread of pride, or perhaps indignance, in his voice.

"How do we know?" Liz asks. "We need to be certain that no unauthorized person can attempt to activate this machine."

"Well, Lizzie," he says, sounding again like the big brother she remembers from when they were kids, "there are two layers of protection. The first and most important is that the machine requires special fuel." He reaches inside his leather jacket and produces a small case from an interior pocket. He carefully opens it to reveal a series of glass tubes, each filled with what appears to be liquid metal.

"What is it?" Liz asks, feeling her eyes narrow.

"It's a formula known only to me," he says with a wink, closing the case and returning it to his jacket with a flourish, as if he's making it magically disappear.

"And the second layer?" she asks.

"The machine can only be operated using a special program I designed, a program that is only available on my personal laptop, which is fully encrypted. Without the special fuel and without my program to activate the machine, it's basically just an assortment of metal plates, nuts, and bolts."

Liz looks over at Seth, who gives her a nearly imperceptible nod. He seems satisfied with Jackson's answer. Despite her annoyance at her brother's tone, she knows the machine is well beyond her understanding. *It's well beyond nearly everyone's,* she thinks, remembering Chub's statement that no one understood what it was meant to do. Liz suspects if they did know, they'd be just as uneasy as her.

"Why did you build it in the airlock?" she asks. "Does it require containment?"

"No," Jackson says. "I can relocate it, to a location better suited to staging the goods to be sent."

"So why did you build it here?" she asks again.

"I needed to be sure all the parts were manufactured properly," he replies. *No,* Liz thinks, *you made a mistake.* She reminds herself that despite his seemingly magical technology, and despite his air of superiority, he is just as human as anyone. His clothes are only leather and fabric, his chest plate only metal and stone. He is flesh and bone, like the rest of them, albeit with a mind more curious and sharper than most.

"What purpose does the biofilm serve?" Seth asks, his eyes slightly squinted as if he's lost in thought.

"There appear to be strange phenomena inside the wormhole," Jackson replies. "The conditions will require additional study, but traveling through the wormhole appears to subject matter to harmful radiation. Living creatures die, and electronic sensors and devices short. The biofilm absorbs or deflects the radiation."

"Fascinating," Seth whispers, not looking at him. "Do you know if there are long-term effects on matter that travels through the wormhole?"

"Like I said," Jackson says, a sharp edge in his voice, "the conditions will require additional study."

"I see," Seth says, turning and smiling wryly. "When we relocate the machine, would you like the crew to assist, or do you plan to do it yourself again?"

Jackson's face flashes with anger, or perhaps embarrassment. "Help would be fine."

He's only human, Liz reminds herself, determined not to forget that again.

CHAPTER 16

STORY TIME

****

Ruth waits by the fire for those who wish to gather for story time. She holds a large book in her lap, titled *The Complete Works of Edgar Allen Poe*. It's not her favorite. She finds the stories morbid and bizarre, but it's one of the few books that survived the trials and tribulations of life in the cave, and for some reason, the children love it. She's grateful that it's large and filled with many stories her people enjoy, if for no other reason than that those are the stories they know.

She feels disembodied, her thoughts floating outside the reach of her emotions. She knows she should feel disgusted for considering how to best post the children in the air vents connected to Jackson's room, but she considers it anyway. She sees no other way to eavesdrop on his conversations, and after seeing him in the vineyard, she cannot rest until she finds out what he intends to do.

The children are the only ones small enough to fit in the vents for any length of time, the only ones who can move quickly and quietly in the small space. Ruth knows they are disciplined and capable of hiding for a few hours to listen to anything Jackson is saying. Even the younger children are capable of reporting back what they've heard accurately, although she won't ask them to do it. There are others who can do the job, like Bobby and Brad, the orphaned brothers who are eleven and thirteen. Brad hasn't grown much in the last few years, so he can probably still fit in the vents. Both boys are especially fond of Ruben, and Ruth can make sure that Ruben is posted nearby, farther back in the ventilation system where the air shafts combine into larger tubes. As monstrous as she feels, Ruth is not monstrous enough to send the children completely alone to spy on Jackson Goeff.

She thinks of Axle, who is ten, and Zoe, who is twelve. She thinks of Kelly, a boy of thirteen who is still small, and Courtney, twelve, who has grown in the last month but can probably still fit in the vents. At sixteen, Megan is too big to fit in the smaller vents, but she's close with several of the children and mature enough to be stationed back, to pull them out if it becomes too dangerous and encourage them if they get scared.

Too dangerous. Ruth scoffs to herself. Is this any more dangerous than their lives on the surface? These same children were trained how and where to hide from the New Generation, and they were included in scouting parties as well. Childish ignorance of danger was not a luxury they ever knew, so what's different now? *Don't you dare try to minimize what you're doing,* she scolds herself, knowing that she deserves every moment of sickness and every ounce of guilt she will feel when she tells the others what they need to do.

Ruth can see clearly in her mind how it will all play out. In the morning, before breakfast, she will gather them together, the six children as well as the adults who will be stationed behind them. She will ask Ruben, at least when he isn't guarding Jackson, and Megan. She will ask Noah and Emily, a brother and sister who are twenty-five and twenty-two, as well their cousin Olivia, who is twenty-one and mother to Sophia. After a moment of doubt, she decides that she will also ask Shawn. He's only fourteen, and too big to fit in the vents close to Jackson's room, but he's levelheaded and calm, and Ruth knows the children will feel safe with him.

She will explain what they need to do and how it will help Liz. She will tell them to be strong, and be very clear that they are only to get close enough to hear what Jackson is saying. His voice is loud, and it resonates, which means they can stay far enough back that they won't be seen through the vent cover.

She'll remind them that Jackson is a large man, that he's not capable of moving quickly through the small vents, not like the children who can scuttle out quickly if they need to. He isn't used to the increased gravity, so even if he does chase them, he will move slowly. Ruth will assure them that he won't chase them, because they will be so quiet that he won't even suspect they are there. She'll tell them how they are strong and brave—they've been taught how to hide and how to fight, and that they will not be alone. She'll assure them that they can be as brave as Liz was the day she saved them at the depot, that this is their chance to help Liz by reporting back everything Jackson says.

No one will question her, or disagree. The children will look at her bravely, even though she knows they will be afraid. They will push aside their fear and do what needs to be done. Her people are strong, and Ruth is so very proud of who they are and who she knows the children will become.

Looking past the fire, Ruth's eyes fall on the gravel path

that stretches through the trees. Groups of crew members are starting to arrive. Her own people are coming in groups, too, just as they discussed when they decided to proceed with the event, after Ellis sent her a message through the security office warning her that Jackson might show up at story time. Liz warned him when she and Captain Harris returned Jackson and the woman to their quarters, and she told Ellis everyone would understand if they wanted to cancel.

When Ruth received the message, her first thought was to pinch herself, that perhaps this was nothing more than a ludicrous dream from which she could wake. Was she really being asked if she wanted to cancel story time because it would likely be crashed by the New Generation? She knew her people would respect any decision she made on the matter, but she's weary from the burden of leadership. No mind can contain the answer to every problem, not even hers. She's ready to share the load, for others to guide and lead the group, and so she decided not to make the decision alone.

She gathered those she could find in their quarters to discuss what they should do—Ruben, Melissa and Will, and Nora. Ruben was the first to express his opinion, fiercely writing a note that said, *We didn't come this far to hide, and we didn't hide when he tried to overtake the ship. Haven't we lost enough? Why let him take this away from us?*

"But why subject ourselves to it?" Nora countered. "Why subject the children? It's better to cancel than to let him ruin it." Melissa then asked if Ruth knew for certain he'd be attending. She didn't, nor did she know how long he'd be on the ship, only that he'd been given permission to leave his quarters as long as he was accompanied by Captain Harris or Liz and a security detail.

At that point, Zachary butted into the conversation

from the doorway of the room he shared with his parents. He had obeyed the letter of his mother's instruction to stay in their room but not the intent as he poked his head through the open door, listening to every word of the exchange. "We aren't having story time anymore?" he wailed. "But what about the play? I get to play Liz the next time we perform!" He began to cry, and Melissa scooped him up, trying to calm him as she explained that it wouldn't be forever.

"We continue," Will said with resolve, face stern as he looked at his crying child. "We'll sit close together in case anything happens."

"Fine," Ruth agreed. "Spread the word."

She wonders now if it was a mistake, if the indignance she feels toward Jackson for everything he's already taken from them clouded her judgement. Another group of her people are coming in, the largest intact family in the Fifty-Two—Noah and Ava, their parents Justin and Emily, and Olivia and Sophia. They're pressed tightly together, and it reminds Ruth of that day at the depot, everyone pressed against the fence, clinging to the only certainty they had—each other.

Will and Melissa follow close behind, each of them holding one of Zachary's hands. She sees the glee on his face as they swing him high into the air, his sadness left behind the moment they decided to proceed as usual with story time. She envies his oblivion, and it reminds her to appreciate the beauty of this place, this garden that she's come to love even more than she loved Earth. Ruth cannot allow her fear to tarnish this pristine place, where her beloved lilacs live, and the wisteria and roses that bring her so much joy.

Nora trails the group, arm wrapped around Gabriella's shoulders as she clutches baby Luke close to her chest. Ruth is surprised that Gabriella came, although perhaps the fragile woman found the prospect of being alone in her quarters even more fearful than encountering Jackson Goeff. Nora ushers her to the center of the group, where the children are sitting, surrounded by the adults who form an outer ring of protection like a herd of elephants. Perhaps she will feel more secure there, although Ruth isn't certain that Gabriella feels secure anywhere.

She waits as more people come, trying to dismiss her fear. The wooden benches around the fire begin to fill. Maybe Jackson won't show up after all. Perhaps all of her consternation was for naught. It's almost time to start, and she feels relief begin to creep around the edges of her worry, like the first drops of a summer rain that promise to drench a forest fire. But then she sees him, emerging from the darkness like a demon coming to feast on her terror. Now that he's standing, Ruth remembers how tall Jackson is. She sees how slight the woman is next to him, although her wild hair and leather clothes remind Ruth that the woman's size means nothing. She sees Captain Harris flanking the couple on one side, Liz on the other, and Ruth's mind glitches for a moment as she tries to reconcile what she sees.

Liz, who is good, and Jackson, who is evil, look more alike than Ruth realized. They share a strong family resemblance, similar coloring and features. They move the same way, stealthily as cats, and they have the same lean, athletic build. *They differ in the ways that matter,* Ruth tells herself, but do they? She summons her memories of Liz's sweet face, awkwardly introducing herself that first night in the medical unit, sitting across from her at story time, walking with her down the garden path the first time, asking about the children when she came out of her coma in the medical unit.

Yes. They do.

She sees Ellis trail behind the group, eyes roving across the crowd as he walks next to another security officer whose name Ruth can't remember. The young man looks scared and unsure, reminding Ruth that it's time to don her own brave face, to put away her fear and doubt. Isn't this why they have story time, after all? To provide stability and routine? To ground themselves in their humanity, even if just for a few moments each day?

Ruth manages a smile as she stands, leaving the book on the bench beside her. She raises both hands in the air, the cue that everyone understands to mean that they will begin— everyone except Jackson.

"This will be fun!" she hears him say, and she's almost swept away by anger. Does he think she's here to entertain him, like a court jester? Does he find himself worthy of being here, among her people who are still loving and generous and kind, despite all they've suffered? Does he think himself better than Ruth? *Of course he does, but he can only desecrate story time if you let him.*

"Thank you for coming," Ruth begins, projecting her voice from deep in her belly. "I'm so glad you're all here. Tonight, I will read you a story—a favorite among our children, 'Descent into the Maelstrom' by Edgar Allen Poe."

She focuses her gaze on her people, on the children sitting closely together as the adults shield them from anything Jackson might do. Ruth doesn't know why they like this story so much, only that they do. So she chose it bring them comfort tonight, to bring relief from the burden of fear and uncertainty of Jackson's arrival. She's read the story so many times that her worn book opens right up to the page where it starts. Her eyes focus on the words, although she knows nearly every one by heart.

Her fear and the story and the flames of the fire make her think of the cave, when she and the others from Oxford first took refuge there, thinking it would only be for a short time. Ruth thought it cold then, nearly unbearable at night, but they only made small fires. They still had much to learn about living in the cave—how to survive in reasonable comfort without being spotted by New Generation patrols. It wasn't a body of knowledge Ruth ever intended to acquire, but she did.

Why was she so dogged then? Why did she fight so hard for all their lives? Did she think life would improve? Did she think it would get easier? Did she not see that the situation was as hopeless as the fisherman's plight in the story, as he clings to a floating casket in the maelstrom even though all signs point to his demise? *But the fisherman survives,* she reminds herself, *and so did we.*

Ruth knows why she clung so desperately to life then. The same reason she clung so hard to the impossible chance of life standing outside the depot fence—the children. Back then, it was Melissa and Noah and Emily. Olivia was just a baby, although now she has a child of her own. Ruth remembers how they would cry in fright in the darkness of the cave, after the fire went out and before the sun would shine through the collapsed ceiling. They had to learn to be silent. They had to learn to find comfort in themselves and each other. And so, Ruth would tell them stories.

They learned how to survive in the cave, and then Jackson took it away from them. Ruth tells herself it was a blessing in disguise. Life in the cave was only getter harder, leaner, and bleaker. Life on the Green Grow 3 is vibrant, full, and promising. She thought they'd survived the maelstrom, come out on the other side of the storm. But have they? Or is Jackson here now to rain down fear and privation? Maybe the abundance before her is really just a dream of a dream, here for an instant and gone the next.

Ruth hopes the children enjoy the story, because tomorrow they have work to do. She does the best reading she can, watching their eyes widen in anticipation even though they know how it ends. There are no surprises, but they allow themselves to be surprised nonetheless. *Is that what hope is?* Ruth wonders, knowing that whatever hope may be, she has none of it at the moment.

When she finishes the reading, her people begin to applaud. For a moment, she allows herself to forget that Jackson is here as she smiles and nods in appreciation. At least, she forgets until he stands up, crying out "Bravo!" in a booming voice that shreds the air like a bomb, striding toward her with outstretched arms as if he's going to crush her in a hug, a wide, disingenuous grin plastered on his face.

Before she comprehends what's happening, all hell breaks loose. Gabriella pops up from the center of the group, looking at Jackson and shrieking like a banshee. Ruth sees several hands reach out for her, but she breaks free of the group, running in an awkward gait into the woods, clutching baby Luke so tightly that Ruth worries she will smother him.

Zachary begins to scream, "Hide! Hide!" Ruth sees the children dive under the benches as the adults stand up, facing outward in a closed circle, ready to give their very lives if needed to protect the children. Ellis, who was sitting behind Jackson, jumps up and runs to try to intercept him. Ruth can see his hand on his pistol, and fear washes over her, wondering what will happen to Ellis if he shoots Jackson. But before he can reach the man, Seth flies in front of him, standing tall and bellowing, "Jackson, stop!" Ruth can see his pistol on his belt, but he hasn't drawn it. Instead, he stands with his fists clenched, legs braced. A moment later, Liz is by his side, placing her body between Seth and Jackson.

"Jackson," she cries, "these people are terrified! Stop, please!"

Jackson stops, looking at his sister quizzically as if she's the only one who has said anything worth hearing.

"I only meant to congratulate her on such a fine reading," he says, and Ruth briefly wonders if his confusion is as fake as his smile.

"Please," Liz implores him. "You don't know what these people have endured!"

Oh, my dear, Ruth thinks, *he knows exactly what we've endured.*

Jackson drops his hands to his side, looking around the campfire.

"Apologies," he says, smiling again. "I didn't intend to startle anyone."

Ruth looks back to the bench where he was sitting, where Shelby remains, watching everything transpire. She bears the hint of a smile, a sardonic, hateful expression that makes Ruth wonder, if only for a moment, whether Jackson is the one they should fear after all.

CHAPTER 17

EVENING ACCELERATION

***

Jackson has many trains of thought, all running at the same time. It's both a blessing and a curse to have the capacity for so many ideas, but he doesn't concern himself with it being good or bad. It only is.

His mind is a useful tool, a powerful one that enables him to meet his goals. At the moment, it's also his only companion. He is quite literally stuck on his bed, confined to quarters with Shelby for the duration of the ten-minute 4G acceleration, and she is not capable of talking to him at the moment.

If Jackson were the kind of man to lose control of himself, he would be infuriated. He has too many things to do to lie here for ten minutes, incapacitated. But the brat has banned him from the bridge, which is where he should be with the rest of the council, and he learned the hard way during his first acceleration that the G force is too strong for him to move around or even sit up for any length of time.

When it became clear that he was expected to remain in

his quarters like the rest of the crew, Claire urgently advised him and Shelby to lie flat on the bed for the duration, but Jackson had no intention of doing so. He thought he could use the time to manage his affairs on Earth, and so he tried to sit in a chair with his laptop. But within a matter of seconds, he was dizzy and lightheaded, and all he could do was crawl onto the floor and lie flat for the remainder of the time. Each minute was its own eternity, lying there like a hapless fool while the universe mocked him. It forced him to admit that all he can do during the 4G accelerations is lie with Shelby on the bed and wait.

Jackson now sees why the brat refuses to accelerate faster—or for longer than ten minutes. It seemed reasonable enough when Jackson did the calculations on Earth, especially since Claire assured him it could be done. But now, lying flat on his back for yet another span of eternity, he can see how quickly 4G wears on a person. Claire assures him they could go faster and longer, but at this point, it only makes him question the soundness of her advice.

There is also the matter of the continuous 1.5G acceleration. When he was on Earth, Jackson thought this was too slow, especially since Claire maintained they could safely accelerate at a continuous 2G. He thought Harris's refusal was a power play, that he was merely proving a point that he was still in control of the ship. But now Jackson sees how the increased gravity makes him fight for each step, each movement, and he's starting to wonder if it wasn't a power play after all.

Of course, Jackson would never admit this to anyone, and he thinks he's hiding his own discomfort well enough—but Shelby is suffering terribly. She doesn't complain, but she does admit that the heaviness she feels and lethargy is nearly unbearable. Jackson has noticed that even sleeping requires tremendous effort from her, as he rests beside her and listens to her labored breathing.

He knows that if they stay long enough, they will acclimate to 1.5G, but he didn't plan to stay that long. Now, he doesn't know what he will do. At least if he were on the bridge, he could look around, but the so-called captain stood firm that Jackson was not allowed there—ever. Harris doesn't want him to know how any of it works, and he begrudgingly admits to himself—and only himself—that this is probably a smart move.

Jackson needs some idea of how the propulsion drive operating system works, as well as physical access to its servers to hack it. He thinks those particular servers are housed on the bridge, but he can't be sure without at least a cursory inspection. Plus, he needs some idea of what security measures the brat installed. If he's banned from the bridge, hacking the drive will be more challenging—if he still wants to, that is.

He intended to override Harris's commands and speed the ship up himself. They need to be moving farther and faster to get where Jackson wants to be, which is as close as possible to the Walkabout 2. He knows he's pushing the limits of the Green Grow 3, but he must be the first person to see the probe's data stream—before it reaches Earth. The closer he is to the probe, the more time he'll have to analyze the data. He doesn't know if anyone on Earth is waiting for it, but he has a growing suspicion that someone is.

Shelby says he's paranoid. She rightly points to a lack of evidence that anyone else is vying for the data. But he has a feeling that he's learned not to ignore—the kind that raises the hair on the back of his neck and makes his stomach churn. And when Shelby tries to reassure him, it only makes him feel worse. It's like she's trying too hard to convince him everything is fine, although she must be concerned about his well-being. He can't blame her for thinking he's overreacting—she doesn't understand what's at stake here. How can she?

If Omega is habitable, Jackson has earned the right to be the first human to explore the planet. And he has a tremendous advantage: his transporter. Once he's confident about the conditions on the planet, he can transport a team directly to the surface. Then it won't matter if someone else is waiting for the data. They'll see it eventually, in any case. But he needs to see it first—to be certain no one has tampered with it.

Interfering with the stream would be no small feat, but someone could try to shield or deflect it. Or, they could alter the data and rebroadcast it, just to confuse matters—that's what he would do. Maybe it's unlikely, but he can't take the chance, not with something this momentous.

But neither can he afford to break the Green Grow 3, and he can see now that even the current acceleration is stressing the infrastructure and core systems. Frankly, he's not sure that he should change the acceleration at all, so why bother hacking the system? He'll simply have to keep scanning for the data and hope for the best.

Once he gets the Walkabout 2 feed, he can break the news to the council that they need to stop and turn around. Using Omega to turn around is a ridiculous ruse—the planet is light-years away—but the council seems to believe it. Harris, on the other hand, can be sly and unpredictable. That's why Jackson is holding on to the thruster fuel formula a while longer, until he's sure he has the data.

In the meantime, he'll stay busy organizing the food shipments. Perhaps even earn a smidge of forgiveness from his sister, although thanks to Harris, the situation with Lizzie hasn't worked out like he planned. She feels so strongly about the man, refusing to look past her feelings, not even to make amends with her own brother. The worst part is, Jackson can see what she likes about him. He doesn't want to admit it, and so he won't admit it outright, but he may have underestimated Seth Harris. He may, in fact, be dealing with a wild card.

Jackson has defeated more than a handful of adversaries. But none of them has surprised him as much as Harris. He still can't believe the brat thwarted his attempt to overtake the ship, and the antimatter drive was a complete surprise too. Thankfully, that worked out alright—without the drive he wouldn't be able to intercept the Walkabout 2 data this close to the source. But what else does Harris have up his sleeve? Jackson is intrigued by the man's ability to do bold and unpredictable things despite his own inadequacies, to camouflage his strength with weakness.

As soon as Jackson laid eyes on him in the conference room, his customary disgust was injected with a dose of uneasy surprise. For one thing, Harris is bigger than Jackson imagined. Jackson is a tall man on Earth, a perfect six feet if he stands rigidly straight. He's used to being the tallest man in the room, imposing and fearsome. His height is an advantage, helping him command attention and radiate power. He was shocked to see that Harris is at least as tall as he is, and probably a bit taller.

Of course, height alone doesn't win a conflict, but it's not just the man's height that confounds him. He has a strong, unyielding appearance that Jackson never detected on the video calls. His chest is broad, his body strapped with muscle. His movements are smooth and quick, like a viper ready to strike. Jackson can tell that he's been trained in some form of hand-to-hand combat, even though he's probably never seen a true fight.

The fact that the brat sees the value in fighting skills is noteworthy, to say the least. On the surface, fighting is a way of life. People who lack strength or combat skills are killed or subjugated. But here, within the safety of the Green Grow 3, only a highly disciplined person would acquire these skills, someone who recognizes the inherent value of strength and agility.

And his eyes—there's a look in them, a fearless invitation for Jackson to step over some invisible line, to trip a wire that will start a fray Harris would happily leap into. How can this be? This man who has cowered behind his council—including his own mother—for the last two years ... *Did I underestimate him?* Jackson wonders, although he dismisses the question as soon as he asks it. Jackson Goeff does not underestimate anyone.

But as he lies motionless and uncomfortably heavy on his bed, he realizes that he may need to reassess Seth Harris. It doesn't mean he was wrong about the pesky brat—it can't. If he's wrong about him, he could be wrong about a lot of things. That simply cannot happen. Everything that matters depends on him being right.

Jackson can feel the pressure on his chest start to ease. The 4G acceleration is over—until the next one, anyway. He sets aside his thoughts of Harris and turns to see how Shelby is faring, gently caressing her face until her eyes flutter open.

***

Seth sits strapped in the captain's chair on the bridge. He can feel the pressure start to ease on his body, and he's almost sad that the acceleration is coming to an end. He reminds himself that all things come to an end, or do they? This torturous day with Jackson seems unending, as does the list of Seth's responsibilities.

As usual, it was a hellacious ten minutes, but after the tour with Jackson, and the free-for-all at story time, he realizes that the notion of hell is relative. At least during the acceleration, he didn't have to talk to anyone, or even look at anyone. He didn't have to force any smiles or guard his expression. He didn't have to stand straight or tall. All he had to do was breathe and wait. And for at least a little while, he didn't have to deal with Jackson Goeff.

He thinks back to Jackson's machine, to the biofilm he's using to protect matter from radiation in the wormhole. Is the biofilm the reason Jackson hasn't transported the Green Grow 3 back to Earth's orbit? Admittedly, transporting the entire ship seems impractical, but Seth can't imagine that practicality factors into Jackson's thinking.

What if they coated the entire ship with his goo? Could they pass through the wormhole safely? No, the biological matter would freeze in space and die. But what if they injected it between the inner and outer hull? Wouldn't the outer hull protect them like a Faraday cage when they passed through? Could they produce enough to protect them? Why not? Seth's mind whirs with possibility. Does he want to pursue these possibilities? Seth isn't sure he wants to arrive back to Earth's orbit quickly. He needs more time to figure out what he's going to do when they get back. He needs an escape plan.

Despite the glib half-truths and insinuated promises Jackson gives Liz during the video calls, Seth knows that the New Generation is an organization of savages. They wouldn't wear bone-and-metal body armor and rain down fury on innocent people if they weren't. Savages require spoils, and they conquer without mercy. Jackson will conquer the Green Grow 3, and then he will use whatever leverage he has to save Liz, which means he must make an example of Seth to prove to his followers that he isn't weak.

But, if there is a way to transport the ship back to Earth's orbit, Seth might be able to create a window of confusion that he could use to his advantage. He and Liz could take a shuttle and make their way to China or India. They could offer the shuttle in exchange for refuge, and Seth could return to his work in biology and chemistry. He's certain he could make himself valuable. But Jackson claims the Green Grow executive board is already negotiating with them, and Seth can't take the risk of being turned over to the board. They believe he's a criminal, and Seth has no intention of returning for any hearing.

What options are left? And will Liz go with him? Seth can't rule out the possibility that she will think him cowardly for leaving, and if she makes amends with Jackson, she may want to join him instead. The thought makes him nauseous, but after seeing them together today, Seth cannot deny that the siblings are a lot alike.

He's known since Jackson's face appeared on the ship's broadcast that they shared a physical resemblance, but their similarities run much deeper than high cheekbones and blue eyes. They are both intelligent, ferocious, and single-minded. Neither seems willing to back down from a fight. They even stand the same way, shuffling in unison from foot to foot when they're ready to start moving again, fidgeting their long, slender fingers in the same manner. When questioned, their eyebrows move in the same indignant expression. They can both be proud and forceful, or quiet and subtle. In fact, the siblings seem so much alike that Seth isn't sure how Liz can love him and Jackson hate him, although he's heard that the line between love and hate is thin and often smudged.

When Jackson arrived, Seth was sure the man had no power to break the bond between him and Liz, but now he can't help but wonder. Jackson is her brother, her family. They are connected by blood and history that Seth can't pretend to understand. Nor can he predict what Liz will do, not with Jackson working so hard to wear away her anger. She welcomed him aboard, and she accepted his turquoise necklace. Maybe their reconciliation is only a matter of time, too.

The mechanical voice of the control system confirms that their acceleration has been reduced back to 1.5G. Seth takes a deep breath, trying to center himself in the expansive feeling his chest always gets after the 4G acceleration ends. It's the closest thing to freedom he knows at the moment.

"Jarrod, commence the post-acceleration system scans," he says, repeating the same protocol they follow every time they accelerate.

"System scans commenced," Jarrod confirms. Seth is certain he will report more electrical surges, which have been happening at all hours since Jackson arrived. Jarrod still can't pinpoint the source of the energy, although now that Seth has seen Jackson's machine, he doubts the transporter is causing the surges. Jackson must be affecting the ship some other way, although Seth doesn't have a clue how.

"All systems are clear," Jarrod says, much to his surprise.

"Really?" Seth asks, as he unbuckles himself from the seat.

"Yes, Captain."

"That's the best news I've heard all day," he grumbles, feeling an ache deep in his bones as he stands. His head hurts again, like it does after every acceleration.

But as he turns to leave the bridge, he sees that his mother has lingered behind. He doesn't want to talk to her, but neither does he have the energy to refuse her. Liz looks at him questioningly, her eyebrows raised in the same expression Seth now knows Jackson dons on the rare occasions that he's surprised. He nods for her to go on, a signal that he'll catch up with her momentarily.

"You look tired, Mom," he says a moment later. "Maybe Dr. Singh should check you out. You take care of everyone else—someone should take care of you."

"The accelerations are wearing on everyone," she replies, "but I'm sure I'm fine."

"And yet, you want us to accelerate faster, and for longer?" Seth asks.

"All I'm saying is that it's possible. At least it would shorten the duration of this trip." A hand instinctively goes to her neck, rubbing the knotted muscle where she usually holds tension. "How did the tour go?" she asks.

Seth considers her, unsure what to say. He's in no mood for banter or games.

"What is it you want to know, Mom?"

She eyes him wearily.

"I want to know if you've come to terms with Jackson," she says. "We don't know how long he'll be here, and this is your chance to prove you're not his enemy."

"Aren't I, though?" he asks, feeling the familiar stab of irritation at his mother's apparent infatuation with Jackson. "The man tried to kill me and overtake the ship. I'm sure he still intends to kill me. What part of that do you not understand?"

"There is a way through this," she says through gritted teeth, "but you need to stop challenging him."

Seth's eyebrows rise. "Do I?"

"Yes," she says. "You need to help him see that you were thrust into this position and you are only trying to do your job. You need to convince him that you have no intention of retaining control of this ship when we get back to Earth."

"Oh? And what am I going to do when we get back to Earth?"

"You're going to be a biochemist," she says fiercely, "and you'll work with me in my lab. It's the only way I can protect you. Don't you see? It's why I'm trying to make myself valuable to Jackson."

Seth is too tired to be anything but honest. He sighs. "You really don't know who you're dealing with." Anger rises in her face, and he finds it strange that it doesn't bother him. For most of his life, he would have hated to make his mom angry, but things are different now. He's different.

"I'm sure Liz can help as well," Claire says. "Jackson will listen to her. She can help protect you."

Now it's Seth's turn to get angry. He doesn't want to, but it happens anyway. Does his mom really believe that his fate is to be protected by two women, skulking behind their skirts?

"Mom, I do not believe anyone can manage Jackson Goeff's ambitions. Not you. Not Liz. Not anyone, except possibly this woman Shelby, and she has no reason to help me. I certainly cannot change Jackson's plans for me, and frankly, I'm not sure I want to try."

"You're talking nonsense," she spits in reply. "Get over yourself, and see the situation for what it is. Play the cards you've been dealt."

Seth considers the many things he could say to her. He could tell her she's delusional. He could tell her she's wrong. He could tell her that he's a man and doesn't need her intervention anymore, and that even if she intervenes it won't change anything anyway. But he doesn't waste his breath. There's no point using what's left of his energy that way. Instead, he only shakes his head and ushers her off the bridge. Surprisingly, she goes, despite her angry expression, and Seth realizes that she's probably as exhausted as he is.

CHAPTER 18

VEILED BEINGS

***

She Who Needs No Name reflects on everything she's learned about the tiny vessel she discovered. At first, she thought the vessel itself was alive, sentient and intentional. She was excited about this, hopeful that she may have found a kindred being. She has desperately longed for someone to converse with, someone besides the dense, ignorant beings on the planet she's come to consider her own.

The vessel was open and inviting, transparent and accessible to her. She found it easy and natural to allow tendrils of her awareness to flicker along its branches and veins of energy. As she explored further, however, she was disappointed to conclude that the vessel itself was not alive. Amicable and intelligent as it seemed, it couldn't interact with her spontaneously and showed no signs of volition. But it contained information, a wealth of information about the creatures on board.

At first, she found the data overwhelming, but once she understood the structure and rhythm of the information, it was easy enough to interpret. Paired with her own direct observations, the information has helped her learn a great deal about the vessel's inhabitants, but there is much more to learn. She studies the information until her awareness is full and then retreats to the space within her planet to process what she's gathered.

In many ways, the life within the vessel is similar to the life on her planet. It contains hierarchies within hierarchies, existence nested within existence. She can discern the same cycles of creation, growth, reproduction, and destruction. She can sense the same interconnectedness between the various life forms, the way they sustain each other through giving and receiving. They are independent and dependent at the same time—interdependent, perhaps.

None of this is new to her, not anymore. But the enigmatic masters of this vessel are more complex and paradoxical than any other being she has encountered. Based upon the information they store in the vessel, she believes they are capable of vast and profound insight. Yet they have not achieved it, not consistently anyway.

Their curiosity for learning rivals her own, yet they often ignore what they've learned. They create and they destroy, but not in an intentional way. They are erratic and fearful, while also brilliant and endearing. They seem to understand the interconnectedness of life, and yet they veil themselves, dimming their connection as if they cannot tolerate the life around them.

She tried to touch several of the creatures with threads of her awareness, to no avail. She couldn't connect in even the most basic of ways, much less communicate with any of them. She can only conclude that it's impossible to reach them, that their tightly swathed veils of ignorance are impenetrable. But she must find a way. She does not know how they pulled her out away from her home and into linear time, but she needs them to reverse what they've done. They must send her home. They seem unaware of what they've done, so she must find a way to tell them.

She studies them, more intensely than she's ever studied before. She studies them in groups, and she studies them alone. She observes their patterns and notices their deviations, pores over the information stored in their vessel, and her labor is fruitful.

There is something different about one of the beings. The thickness of its veil seems to fluctuate, and when it thins, the being's energy is stronger and its vibration higher. If she can calibrate her own energy properly when the being's veil is thin, perhaps she can connect. And if she can connect, she can communicate.

She studies this being intently, looking for patterns in the fluctuations. She looks for relationships between action and the frequency of vibration. She develops and refines hypotheses, and she calibrates her own energy again and again, trying to connect. Each time, she fails, but she refuses to give up hope. When frustration and anger overwhelm her, she retreats back to her planet, drawing her energy in a tight ball until she can raise her vibration and try again. Again and again, she whispers *hello* and waits to be heard.

CHAPTER 19

GOING HOME

***

OCTOBER 26, 2059—SUNDAY

Liz sits with Jackson in the cafeteria, watching him sip coffee as she wonders whether Shelby's absence makes her feel more or less uncomfortable. She claimed she had plenty to eat in their room, leftovers from a dinner she didn't finish the night before, but Liz suspects there is more to her absence than meets the eye. It makes her edgy, wondering why Jackson wants to spend time alone with her.

She cannot read his expressions, and this unsettles her. This is her brother, whom she was so close with as a child that she thought they might actually be two halves of the same person. But after all this time, she doesn't recognize the man in front of her—not even after the series of video calls they've had over the last two months. All she can know with any certainty is that something is on his mind, because he's been quiet for the duration of the meal.

She wonders if she should say something, if for no other reason than to break the silence, but what would she say? She is lost for words.

Finally, Jackson takes his last bite of food, sets his fork next to his plate, and looks at her appraisingly. She sees doubt in his face, a question that she suspects he is about to articulate.

"Lizzie," he says, hands folded in his lap, "would you consider coming back to Earth with me?" This isn't what she expected, but his face seems earnest and vulnerable. It seems like a genuine question, and so she considers what to say.

Just a few days ago, it would have been impossible. But it seems that nothing is impossible now, even though his words feel surreal swirling in her mind. She thinks back to that last day at the Denver depot, when she found the Fifty-Two. She remembers taking off in the shuttle and uttering her last wish for those who remained below. *Burn in hell.* Her life is here now, on the Green Grow 3. She can't imagine leaving, but neither is she ready to tell Jackson no.

"What would I do on Earth?" she asks.

"You would help me," he says, looking hopeful that she didn't refuse him outright. "Now that we have a way to transport food to the surface, we need to set up distribution channels. And you have practical experience that will be invaluable in the hydroponic farms. My people have much to learn about growing and harvesting food."

"Your people ..." she whispers, thinking back to the depot, back to the raiding party rushing the fence with their homemade weapons, faces filled with evil glee in anticipation of killing. Were they his people, too? A question forms in her mind, and she gives him a curious look. "You mentioned expanding into a new series of caves recently," she begins. She sees a door close in his eyes, as if he knows what she will ask. "The fifty-two people I saved lived in a cave—a big cave with a growing room painted in mirrors. Is that where you expanded your operation?"

"Yes," he says quietly, looking down at his plate. "The people you brought back from the depot chose to leave. They could have stayed. I gave them the option."

"And the raiding party I encountered?" she asks. "Were they your people?" Another door closes in his eyes.

"The one you nearly decimated?" he asks, as if to imply that she is no better than him.

"Yes, that one." *He has no right to judge me.*

"Yes, they were one of my crews."

"What would have happened had I not intervened?" she asks, her heart growing cold. He looks at her for what seems like a long while.

"I cannot say precisely," he begins, and his vague answer ignites anger in her, anger that Jackson seems to sense as he continues. "My crews have standing orders to bring any survivors they encounter back to camp."

"And if they don't want to go?"

"Lizzie, everyone must work together if humanity is to survive. We cannot rebuild a society scattered in groups of twos or threes."

Or groups of fifty-two. "And if they refuse to go?" she demands, her anger growing.

"Then they are brought back by force," he says through gritted teeth.

"They are raped and beaten," she hisses, "sometimes to death. They are terrorized and humiliated. I have seen it myself. Your people are animals, Jackson, the basest of animals."

"Then come and train them!" he demands, placing his palms on the table forcefully. "Even the basest of animals can be trained! I can only work with what I have. I can only do so much. This is why I need your help."

"I am needed here," she says. Jackson's eyes change, and

he leans back in his chair, exhaling deeply.

"Is it the ship you don't want to leave, or Seth Harris?" he asks. Liz can feel her anger rise, sensing that once again, he is presenting her with an ultimatum.

"Why does it have to be one or the other?" she demands, knowing that he has read the answer in her eyes already.

"Lizzie," he says softly, "don't you know that it's only a matter of time before you have to let him go?"

"I don't," she says. "Perhaps you should clue me in."

"You have no future with him," her brother says gently.

"What do you know of my future?" she demands.

"It's not about your future." His voice remains soft. "It's about his. This doesn't end well for him, Lizzie. I won't pretend not to see what you like about him, but there will be other men."

"What do you mean? What do you intend to do?" Liz's gut is frozen in a ball of ice, although she should not be surprised at anything she's hearing.

"He's the captain of the Green Grow 3," Jackson says. "And he is responsible for taking away the greatest hope our country has for survival. There is no place for him in the New Generation, and clearly Green Grow has abandoned him as well."

"If there is a place for me, there is a place for him." Liz is surprised even as she speaks the words, as if some knowing voice within her is finally telling her that it's only a matter of time before the New Generation dominates everything she knows.

"No," he says firmly, "there is not. There can't be."

"Why?"

"Even if I could spare him, why would I?" he demands, leaning forward again. "He's tried to take everything away from me—you, the Green Grow 3, the loyalty of my people, all of it!" Liz feels her mouth fall open, her anger eradicated as a wave of disbelief crashes over her.

"How has he done that?" she asks.

"I would have the ship by now if he hadn't left orbit," he says, eyes narrow. "I could have taken it quickly and easily, and we would be feeding the surface again."

"You can't blame him for that!" Liz says, incredulous. "If you hadn't tried to overtake the ship, we wouldn't have been flung out into space! If you had contacted us like a civilized human being, instead of overrunning depots and trying to hijack shuttles, we wouldn't have felt the need to leave in the first place! Don't blame Seth for decisions you made."

Jackson's mouth opens, and then closes again. He looks angry but says nothing.

"Did you come here to kill him?" Liz demands, leaning forward.

"He's safe for now," Jackson replies, seeming unabashed. "I'll admit, I wasn't sure when I arrived, but I see now that I need him to get the ship back to Earth."

"And then what?" Liz asks. "You plan to dispose of him, just like you disposed of me when you left all those years ago?"

Jackson leans back in his chair as if she hit him. His eyes go wide, but he says nothing. She glares at him, waiting for an answer.

"I can see that you're angry," he says, "and I'd rather not discuss my leaving with you when you're angry. *When* you decide to come back to Earth—because it's only a matter of time until you see it's what you need to do—let me know. I know you'll need some time to process all this, but when you're ready, I have someone I'd like you to meet. A real man of vision."

Liz is dumbstruck, but only for a moment. "You don't

get to tell me what I need, Jackson. Nor do you get to act like you are the only one capable of shaping the future. You don't have that right, not after leaving me alone for so long. Why didn't you find me? You posted notices recruiting spies on the very same billboards I used to try to find you. You must have seen them, or your men must have seen them. I searched and searched for you. Why didn't you look for me?"

He studies her for a moment, his lips pursing.

"I didn't need to look," he says. "I knew where you were. I knew you were safe and healthy. I did want to contact you, but the time never seemed right. And then I started hearing from Willow and others how much you hated the New Generation, and how you had allied yourself with Seth Harris."

"Seth is only reason I made it aboard the ship!" she cries, oblivious to anyone who might be around them, although everyone within earshot vacated the area when she first raised her voice. "He smuggled me onboard and fabricated records so I could stay. And yet, you find him so vile. What's vile is that you never tried, Jackson. You never tried!"

"I was afraid, Lizzie," he says softly, shoulders slumping in defeat. "I was afraid you'd despise who I became, and now I'm afraid I was right."

"Afraid? Bushwa. I don't believe you're afraid of any-thing." She expects him to reply, but he only laughs. It sounds bittersweet and sad.

"Perhaps not," he says, looking down into his hands, which are once more folded into his lap. "In the end, we re-ally only fear what we have to lose, and I've had very little to lose for a very long time."

Liz is confounded. She wonders if he's trying to manipu-late her, but she doesn't think he is. She gets the sense that he's only being honest, and isn't this what she's wanted—honest vulnerability? Part of her wants to laugh at his sorrow, to find just the right words to hurt him. The rest of her wonders if, despite everything that has transpired, he is worthy of some compassion. She thinks again of the boy who cut his sandwiches in half to share, of the boy filled with conviction that he could make a difference in the world if he only set out to try.

"Fresh hell, Jackson. Why is everything an ultimatum with you? If you force me to choose between you and him, I will choose him."

"There is no choice to be made," he replies impatiently. "Harris made the choice the moment he decided to abscond with the ship." Fresh anger surges over her. Jackson is right about one thing—she cannot bear to see what he's become.

"There is always a choice," she says, leaning over the table as her eyes narrow, "and you need to make it right now. Promise me that you will not orchestrate any attacks against Seth. Promise me now, or I will do everything in my power to see that you don't survive the night!"

There is no trace of fear or surprise in Jackson's eyes as he studies Liz.

"I can see how deeply attached you are to him," he replies. "I accept responsibility for that. I should have come for you sooner—much sooner."

"Promise!" Liz growls, hands clenching into fists. Jackson sighs.

"I already told you I need him to get the ship back to Earth," he says, sounding impatient. "I promise to take no action against him until then. But when the ship returns to orbit, I cannot and will not defer his reckoning any further."

"Fine," Liz says, relaxing her fists. She's surprised to feel relieved. She's surprised to realize that she believes Jackson will keep his word, even though she's only beginning to understand the depth of his hatred for Seth. Clearly, his feelings run too deeply to be changed, too deeply for him to promise anything more than a deferral of his vengeance. But he's giving them time, time to find another way.

Of all the agreements she's reached with her brother over these last two months, this is the one that matters to her the most. This is the agreement that might be the first step toward trust. For the first time, Liz believes that Jackson may truly care for her, that he may be capable of honest compassion. When they were kids, he was a stern teacher. He wanted Liz to be strong. He required her to be strong. But he also loved her deeply, cared for her with flawless devotion. For the first time, she believes it's possible that he might still feel that way, and the idea of it makes her want to cry.

"Did you get enough to eat?" she asks him, meeting his gaze for only an instant. This seems to take him by surprise—his mouth opens, then closes again when he finds nothing to say.

"Yes," he finally says, "thank you."

"You haven't told me how you got that scar," she says, "or your command."

"True," he says, smiling gently, "but it's a sad story, and aren't we both sad enough right now? Perhaps your tales of searching for me are more uplifting?"

"No," she says softly as they rise to go.

They walk in silence back to Jackson's room, where she leaves him at the door. She turns to go, ready to be alone with her thoughts, when she feels his hand brush lightly against hers. She looks back, and they exchange no words. His eyes are blue, like an ocean of sorrow, lapping gently against her shore with seventeen years of apologies.

"Come back to Earth with me, Lizzie," he says softly.

"Together, we can build the future we both seek. Think about it."

Liz squeezes his hand gently, wondering what their mother would think about her children now.

***

"Acceleration to commence in three, two, one ..." The automated voice counts them down. Liz closes her eyes, as she does during each acceleration. She imagines herself wrapped tightly in a heavy blanket, buffered against the inevitable cold of a dark night on Earth's surface as she searches for Jackson. When she imagines it this way, the pressure on her body seems more like a comfort than a burden, and she needs it to seem that way. She nearly freaked out during her first controlled acceleration, having no idea what to expect as it became harder and harder to breathe and nearly impossible to move. Even when the ship slowed, the world was spinning around her, her heart racing as she gulped air and wondered if she'd survive the ordeal.

She replays her conversation with Jackson, hearing him ask her again and again, *Would you consider coming back to Earth with me?* She realizes that she has no desire to return to Earth, to revisit the dusty, ashy, barren land. Earth is a one-act venue, and the only performance is suffering. She doesn't care to witness it, not anymore. Hasn't she seen enough, endured enough?

She believes that Jackson wants her to see Earth from his perspective, that he wants to win her approval, or loyalty, or forgiveness, or whatever else of value he thinks she has to offer. But does she want to see things differently? Is she even willing to try?

She could tell herself to have an open mind, but is it

actually possible? Liz thinks about Gabriella, about the raiding party outside the fence, screeching like demons as they tried to descend on the Fifty-Two. Are those the people she is supposed to teach about harvesting produce? She remembers one of them was missing a tooth. She shot him without hesitation, and of all of her regrets, she hasn't given that particular death a second thought.

Besides, what does Jackson think she has to offer him? What does he actually want her to do? He can't possibly really need her to teach people how to care for plants. *Maybe he just wants me out of the way,* she realizes, wondering what he might have planned for Seth or the rest of the crew if she were to depart the ship. If nothing else, she's proven herself a worthy adversary, a formidable shield.

She rewinds her memories, skimming through the chapters of her life, looking for some valuable skill or knowledge she has to offer, something that doesn't involve fighting. But she can think of nothing she excels at besides surviving. *Surely I can be something more than a weapon.* But isn't that what life has required her to become? Liz didn't choose to be a fighter. She was responding to the world around her.

Yes, I was responding to the world around me. Suddenly, she realizes something she never took the time to consider before. *I'm too busy reacting to make my own choices.* She rewinds the memories of her life again, considering them from this new perspective. Her mother dying, compelling her to go to the depot and never return. Her jobs on the Green Grow 3 and the missions she ran for the council after Seth took command. She was a member of the council, but she made no decisions. *No one told me to look for Jackson,* she reminds herself, but didn't she want to find him in part because he always seemed to know what to do?

I saved the Fifty-Two, she thinks, and her train of

thought pauses. She did save them. No one told her to do it. That was her choice, and her choice alone. And look what happened—fifty-two people are still alive who wouldn't be otherwise. They are healthy and vibrant and full of life. She thinks about the play the children wrote for her, and her heart warms. *You chose to save them. Make more choices like that. Make your own choices.*

Liz realizes once more that she's been focused on the wrong thing. She's been focused on what everyone else is doing, instead of deciding what she wants to do. What does she want to create? How does she want this to end? She doesn't know, but she needs to begin by understanding the truth—all of it.

***

Liz knocks quietly, dreading the conversation she knows she must have.

Ruth answers warily, opening the door to her quarters, and something in her eyes seems to surrender when she sees that it's Liz. Perhaps it's the way Liz is looking at her, or perhaps she simply knew it was inevitable, but Liz gets the sense that Ruth knows exactly why she's here.

"I want to know the truth," she says. "All of it."

Ruth's eyes drop to the ground, and suddenly she looks old—even frail. "Can we talk somewhere else?" she asks. "I'd rather the children not hear."

Liz nods, her words stuck in her throat in a ball of fear and anxiety. They walk in silence to the lift, and when the doors open, Ruth shuffles on ahead of her, apparently resigned to wherever Liz chooses to go. She presses the button for Level 20, and Ruth seems surprised by this.

"It's not easy being a leader," Ruth says as they walk

down the path. "People look to you for answers you don't have, comfort you can't provide. They look to you to make things right, even if the whole world is wrong. There is much you cannot do, not even if you want to."

Liz can't look at Ruth's tan face, varnished with layers of wrinkles. She can't look into her pine-bark eyes with the fuzzy ring of blue around the edges. Liz stops in front of a bench, placed near one of the lilac bushes she knows Ruth loves. She's come to know many things about this woman, but is any of it true? Ruth sits, and Liz perches on the bench next to her. She wants to remain standing, but her legs feel weak and she doesn't know if they will hold her. Not now.

"What do you want to know?" Ruth asks, sounding weary.

"How long have you been working for Jackson?" Liz asks, unable to meet her eyes.

"What I told you before was true," Ruth says. "The New Generation raiding parties started patrolling closer and closer to our cave. I knew it was just a matter of time before they found us. We were scouting new locations, but not fast enough. Jackson showed up alone one morning, appearing in the cave right behind me like an apparition as I was taking the daily inventory of our food."

"What did he offer you?" Liz asks.

"A head start," Ruth replies, and Liz tilts her head in confusion. "I suppose that's not the full truth, though. He gave us a chance to join the New Generation."

"And isn't that what you did?"

"No," Ruth replies, shaking her head. "He gave me the night to talk it over with the group, because it wasn't a deci-sion that I could make for everyone." *We'll go,* Liz remembers Ruth saying at the depot. *All fifty-two of us.* She didn't hesitate to decide then.

"A few people chose to stay," Ruth continues, "but I

knew I couldn't stay. I'd seen too much to believe that we'd have any chance of a life worth living in the New Generation."

"Who stayed?" Liz asks, trying to ignore the ball of emotion growing in her stomach.

"Three women and one man," Ruth answers. "The rest of us took to packing, planning to be out of the cave before Jackson came back the next morning. We set out, going deep into the cave to a back entrance I thought no one knew about. It was dark by the time we emerged, and Jackson was waiting for us. He gave me the memory stick. He agreed to wait until the following day to send his raiding party after us, if I agreed to take the stick to the depot and attempt to get it on board the shuttle he said would arrive."

"He knew I was coming?" Liz asks, feeling numb.

"I don't know how much he knew," Ruth replies, shaking her head, "but he knew a shuttle would land, and when."

"And you believed him?" Liz asks.

Ruth seems to ponder this. "I didn't believe or disbelieve him," she says. "I only knew we needed to leave, that we had to try to find another way, if only for the children."

"What else did he tell you?" Liz asks.

"He said if we got the memory stick on board the ship and delivered it to the person he designated, he would make sure the people who stayed behind remained together."

"Chub?" Liz asks.

Ruth nods. "I was only trying to help my people, Liz. That's what you do when you are responsible for others—you try to take care of them."

"Where did you hide the memory stick?"

"I started off by sewing it into the hem of Zachary's shirt." Ruth's voice is choked. Liz wonders if she's crying but can't bear to look at her. "I thought you might at least take one child. I didn't think you'd save all of us, but when you did, I ripped the drive out of Zachary's shirt and hid it in my sock, in the arch of my foot."

The ball of emotion in Liz's stomach blooms. She remembers the security procedures at the dock when she brought the Fifty-Two back, the bloody strips that might have once been socks when Ruth took off her shoes for inspection. The guard looked at her shoes, but not the soles of her feet. No one wanted to look at them, ravaged and raw.

"Liz, I am to blame for this," Ruth says emphatically. "I, alone, should bear the consequences of what I've done. The others don't deserve to be punished for my choices."

"Why did you keep helping him, though?" Liz asks. "You manufactured parts for his machine. You passed messages and altered security video. Why didn't you come to me? Why didn't you tell me?" *I would have kept you safe,* she thinks, but her lips refuse to articulate such an empty promise.

Liz can feel hot tears running down her face as her fists clench in her lap. A wave of hurt and anger crashes over her, all the emotions she's deferred by refusing to acknowledge Ruth's betrayal. But who is she angry at? Who hurt her? Is it Ruth, or her brother?

Jackson has a way of forcing his choices on others, like when he refused to negotiate with anyone but her, and then again when he showed up in the conference room. *Ruth had no real choice,* she decides, although her heart can't move past the fact that this woman did, in fact, have options. But Jackson already had spies on the ship. Why did he have to use these people? Why is he trying to take away the closest thing to a family Liz has found since their mother died? Why does he think he can do that? And more importantly, why does he want to?

Liz marinates in the pain of betrayal until her body shudders, wondering if this is her punishment for all the careless things she's done in her life.

"I didn't know what would happen," Ruth says quietly, her body folding into itself as she sits with her shoulders hunched and her head bowed. "I didn't know what he would do to the people I left behind on the surface. I didn't know what you would do if I told you. I suppose I hoped each time would be the last time. What he asked for seemed so trivial, at least until I looked at it from a broader perspective. I wanted it all to go away, and I was a coward. I should have kept refusing him."

Liz's eyes narrow. "What do you mean by *kept* refusing him?"

"I didn't do everything he wanted," Ruth says in a quiet, hoarse voice. "He wanted me to kill Captain Harris, and I refused."

Liz's eyes go wide, her wave of emotion overtaken by numbing shock as her mouth falls open.

"I wouldn't have any part of it!" Ruth cries frantically, looking alarmed by the reaction.

Liz wants to rail against the old woman, furiously and savagely, for everything she withheld. She wants to blame her for every advantage Jackson gained because of her duplicity. She wants to scream at her to choose a side. But as she looks into Ruth's eyes, the brown ringed with a soft gray edge of age and weariness, her anger dissolves into sadness. Ruth did the best she knew how to do. Liz thinks about the play, the one the children wrote in her honor, and she is washed in hot tears again.

"Was it all a lie?" she asks the old woman. "All the time we've spent together—at story time and in the garden? Was

I just a means to an end?" Ruth starts to speak, but Liz blurts out, "I would have helped you anyway! You didn't have to pretend to like me! Why did you pretend to care about me?"

Ruth sobs as she roughly wipes her weathered face with her gnarled hands. The old woman's body shudders as she draws in breath to speak.

"I do care about you, Liz," she says. "I love you. We all do. You are the leader I want to follow. You are the person the children want to become. You are the best person I know!"

Liz raises an eyebrow. "Don't try to flatter me. Tell me the truth!"

"That is the truth! You are the only person helped us without exacting a price. That day at the depot, you asked nothing in return for saving us. You just did it, and you keep doing it. You've asked for nothing in exchange for everything you've done for us, not that day or any day since. You are the part of humanity worth saving, Liz. You love without conditions. You give without a price. That's why we are your people, Liz—your Fifty-Two. Any of us would do anything you ask, anything!" Liz doesn't know what to say. *That's not who I am,* she thinks, but it's true that she asked for nothing in return when she helped the Fifty-Two. Which matters more—who she is or what she's done? Thinking of herself in this new way makes Ruth's betrayal hurt more.

"Then do this much for me," Liz says fiercely. "Stop helping Jackson. Stop playing both sides. I want to know if he contacts you again."

Ruth nods, eyes wide and filled with emotion. It looks to Liz like fear, and that sends a stab of hurt through the shards of her heart. She looks away and wipes her face with her sleeve.

"Liz?" Ruth asks tentatively, as if she's the child and Liz the teacher. "What's going to happen to me now? Will Captain Harris make an example of me, like he did those other two people?"

"No," Liz says quickly, not sure how much more pain her heart can hold. "No one will be punished, but you need to stop communicating with Jackson. Tell me if you hear from him again—immediately."

"Of course," Ruth says, her voice shaking, her hands trembling. Liz feels like part of her is dead, the warm, comfortable part that Ruth seemed to nurture in her so easily. She is numb but not callous, and she doesn't want Ruth to be afraid. Hasn't she lived with enough fear? Liz feels broken, but she manages to put an arm gently around the old woman's shoulder. Ruth flinches and then seems to melt, finding Liz's other hand and squeezing it with her own.

"Do you want your people back?" Liz asks, wishing she could make all the pain in their lives disappear as she rises from the bench. Ruth looks up at her in surprise as she makes her way to her feet. "The four people who stayed behind."

Ruth seems bewildered, eyes darting wildly as her mouth opens. "Of course," she says. "If they want to come, that is."

Liz laughs wryly.

"I'm pretty sure they'll want to come," she says, wrapping herself in the familiar desire to protect these people and everything they've come to mean to her. Liz aches with pain, but it doesn't diminish her love for them. *Is this what love is?* she wonders as they walk in silence back to the lift.

CHAPTER 20

NIGHTMARE

***

Seth sits on the cool ground, leaning against the trunk of an apple tree, one arm cradled around Liz. What remains of their lunch sits beside him, the tray resting on the soft green grass that grows between the rows of trees. The orchard is empty, and by Seth's estimate, they should have at least thirty minutes before the crews return for their afternoon shifts.

Seth wants to imprint this moment with Liz on his memory with all his senses—the way she feels and smells, the sight of her shiny blond hair falling in wisps across her face. He loves how she molds herself to his body, the weight of her head resting on his chest. There is much he needs to tell her and much he wants to hear, but for now it's enough to sit here together, to share a moment of peace.

"Jackson asked me to go back to Earth with him," Liz says, breaking the silence as she traces a finger along the silver buttons of his uniform. His breath hitches as his ears register her words, but he doesn't think Liz notices.

"Do you want to go?" he asks, breathing in the smell of her hair.

She doesn't answer him right away. "I'm not sure any-one should go anywhere in that machine of his." Seth considers accepting her response, this non-answer that could buy them more time to avoid the subject. But his leaden heart knows it's better to talk now.

"Do you want to go?" he asks again, twirling a strand of her hair around one index finger.

"It's intriguing," she admits. "It's not a choice I ever imagined needing to make."

"You didn't imagine being in the New Generation high command?" he says playfully, trying to mask the wave of pain stabbing his heart.

She raises her head to look at him, eyes narrowed. "I certainly did not. But maybe if I went, I could make a differ-ence somehow—make things easier for us."

You make all the difference to me, he thinks, remem-bering the skinny girl with freckles he locked eyes with at the depot all those years ago. He saw everything in her eyes, her strength and fire, her innocence and pain—all of her contra-dictions that attracted him like a bee to a flower. He's learned so much from her since then.

"What do you think it would be like back on Earth?" he asks, mostly to fill the empty space. His heart feels heavier with every beat. Will he really have to say goodbye to her, to this woman he's come to need more than the air he breathes? His heart aches as he remembers how he told her he'd protect her, how he swept her up in his arms just a couple of months ago, not far from where they currently sit. He carried her to the lift and then again into his quarters.

Seth remembers caressing her face and her hair, deli-cately at first and then hungrily as he began to undress her, wanting to know every inch of her—every freckle and scar.

She had so many scars. He tried to heal each one with his love, exploring them first with his fingertips and then with his lips, kissing and touching and worshipping everything about Liz that made her unique—everything she was and everything she inspired him to be.

That single spark of passion ignited an eternal blazing love. He wrapped her in his arms, and she enveloped him in return. Seth doesn't think time or circumstance could ever untangle the knot of love, passion, and unity they've woven so intricately. He hopes not, anyway. He doesn't want to ever be untangled from her. And yet, he knows he cannot protect her if she stays with him. He doesn't see a path forward for himself, but at least he can help her onto whatever path she chooses, even if it's without him.

Liz's voice draws him back to the present.

"It won't be like anything, Seth. I'm not going." Her eyes are inquisitive, her beautiful eyes that see him so clearly.

He studies her for a moment, his stomach suddenly getting tight. The only thing worse than losing her would be for her to get hurt because of him. However his story ends, he needs to know that she's still out there, living and breathing and carrying on with her life.

"You shouldn't stay because of me," he says softly, looking away from her. "If you think you can make a difference going with your brother, then that's what I want for you."

Liz sits up, trying to meet his gaze, but he can't bear her to see the pain he feels in his heart. He closes his eyes.

"I don't want to go with my brother," she says. "I can't trust him—none of us can. All those years, he didn't look for me! It would have been easy for him to find me, but he didn't even try. If he wants me to come back with him now, it's for some purpose he isn't telling me. I'm not interested in being his pawn, and I don't want to leave you."

Seth faces the inevitable task of opening his eyes.

"Z," he says, finding it hard to get the words out of his head, "it might be best if you go."

"What do you mean?" she asks.

"I promised to protect you." He wants to say more but loses the rest of the words somewhere in his throat. She hesitates for a moment before asking the questions he knows will come.

"Seth, why do you want me to leave you? Aren't we better together? What are you not telling me?"

He feels the intensity of her gaze, and that only makes it harder to contain his fear and sadness. Seth doesn't want her to see him cry. He doesn't want to think about everything he will lose if she leaves with Jackson. Gathering his breath, he hopes it will give him the strength he needs to tell her everything, and then to bear the consequence of whatever it means.

"I want you to live. I want you to have the best that life can offer you. When I look at all of our future possibilities, it looks like the best and safest place for you is as far away from me as possible. I see a way forward for everyone but me." She looks away, and he cannot tell what she's thinking.

"Jackson isn't undefeatable," she says. "We stopped him from overtaking the ship. We've survived this long, despite him. Look at everything we've accomplished—together. There is a way forward for us. We just don't see it yet."

"It's not just about him." Seth falters again.

"What haven't you told me?" Her voice is urgent, and Seth knows her patience is waning.

"I received communication from the Green Grow executive board."

A moment of silence hangs over them. Seth knows he should say more, but he can't bring himself to do it.

"That's great news," Liz says, eyes searching his with growing confusion. "Isn't it? They can help us. Right? Can't they?"

Seth searches for the right words to explain everything. "They've charged me with mutiny, and theft of the ship. They ordered me to return to orbit immediately for a hearing."

Liz stares at him, dumbfounded. He waits for her to process his words.

"But that's ridiculous," she says cautiously. "Are you sure it's really them? Maybe Jackson sent the message, to confuse us."

"I don't think it's Jackson," Seth says, the words flowing more freely now. "The messages came from Green Grow, and they're broadcasting on a loop."

"Messages?" Liz asks. "You got more than one?"

"Yes, the first one arrived a week ago, right after we started the controlled accelerations. They asked for a status report on the ship's systems and confirmation of our location."

Seth can see the question written on Liz's face— *Why didn't you tell me?* He continues, "I assumed it was one of Jackson's ploys, so I ignored it."

"When did the second one come?" Liz asks.

"The morning Jackson arrived," Seth replies. "That's the one detailing the charges against me. I haven't responded, even though now I get copies of both messages every half hour. Jarrod thinks it would be a mistake to respond, that they could pinpoint our location more easily."

"Jarrod?" Liz asks.

"I didn't tell anyone about the messages at first," he explains. "I wasn't sure they were real, and we already have so many problems to solve. But when Jackson showed up, I figured I needed to know where they came from. I didn't know how to track back the signal, so I asked Jarrod for help."

Liz nods. "What does he think?"

"He thinks they're real," Seth continues. "He tracked the origin of the signal to the Green Grow 2. It appears to be hovering behind the dark side of the moon, which is why we never picked them up on our scanners. Jackson was right—the executive board is hiding."

"But we're so far away," Liz says. "What difference does it make if they know where we are?"

"It may not make any difference, but Jarrod thinks it's risky to respond. He's been digging into our control systems, and he already found a back door that would give them access to our navigation. They have the ability to override the course I set. Apparently, they also created a back door into our life support systems as well. Jarrod thinks the code has been there since Captain MacAbee left for the peace summit, maybe longer."

"Can they control the propulsion drive?" Liz asks, eyes widening.

"I don't think so," he says, "but they could do other things—like disable our air scrubbers or lock down levels. They could jettison the growing levels altogether, and that would be disastrous. We could live for a while in the Survival Saucer, but not more than a few months."

"Why would they do that?" Liz asks. Seth can see the confusion in her eyes, her brow furrowing as her mind churns.

"I don't know, Z. They could be baiting me, waiting for me to reply and defend myself so they can pinpoint our location. Maybe they'd offer me leniency if I return the ship, or they could simply wipe all of us out and reclaim the ship another way."

"I don't understand," Liz says, shaking her head. "Why were they silent all this time? Weren't they worried about the ship?"

"Z, they didn't abandon the ship—just us. They could have taken control of the ship at any time. Maybe Jackson is right about that too. Maybe we were bait, or maybe there's some other reason they didn't intervene. They felt threatened enough to leave Earth's orbit, but they didn't seem to want to go far. They've been hiding behind the moon."

"Maybe they couldn't go any farther," Liz says.

"That's a possibility. Jarrod suspects they were also tapped into our drones and the video monitors, although now we're well out of their range."

"They were watching us?"

"Probably." Seth shrugs. "And if they were, they know we were building the propulsion drive. We took a lot of risks getting the materials and specifications for the drive—maybe they were waiting for us to finish it before they intervened, to see if it worked."

"If they could see all that, they must know Jackson tried to overtake the ship. They would have seen his broadcast. So how do they even know you're still in command?"

"I don't know. Maybe they don't. I have a lot more questions than answers." Seth's brow furrows deep in thought. He feels the frustration rising at his own ineptitude, filling the hollow space in his chest.

"Okay," Liz says, sitting up straight and pulling her knees close to her chest. Her eyes sparkle like water diamonds, intense and alive. Seth wants to remember her eyes like this, forever. "So, what's the immediate threat?" she asks. "We'll deal with that first."

"That would be your brother," Seth says, a corner of his mouth lifting into a smile as she casts him an irritated expression. "As far as the executive board goes, they may pose no threat at all, as long as we don't give away our location. Even if they knew where we are, it's unlikely they could override our systems given the distance."

"Unless they have real-time communication, like Jackson," Liz adds.

"Yes," he agrees, "which is why Jarrod is working to close the back doors. I don't want to make assumptions about their capabilities. But Jarrod is also building new thrusters and managing many of the ship repairs and overseeing the propulsion drive. It all needs to be done, and he says he has to do a lot of it himself."

Liz nods, brow furrowed in thought. Seth considers whether he should continue, wondering if she will think less of him when he tells her his real concern. It's a chance he has to take. "My biggest concern about the executive board involves what happens when we get back to Earth. It's only a matter of time before Jackson overtakes the ship. If we had allies, it might be different. But we can't stand alone against his technology, or his manpower, or frankly, his resolve. I think I can hold on to my command until we get back, but once we're back in orbit, the only option I see is escaping—taking a shuttle to China or India before Jackson makes his move, and negotiating sanctuary."

Seth pauses, studying Liz's face intently, looking for any sign of derision or disgust. She's not one to run from a fight, and he doesn't want her to think him cowardly. But she only looks at him, waiting for him to continue, so he does.

"If what Jackson says is true," he explains, "the executive board is already negotiating with China and India, and the board has more to offer than I do. I might be turned over if I seek sanctuary there, and I'm not sure where else to go. There may be other places, or other possibilities, but I don't see them."

"So, maybe we face the board," she says, her words sharp with ferocity. "You don't have to go alone, Seth. In fact, I won't allow it. You have people who would fight for you, people who have already fought for you, by your side. Maybe it's not an army, but it's something."

"But fight against what?" Seth asks, overwhelmed with hopelessness and panic. "I have no idea who or what I'd be facing if I went back. We know nothing of their alliances or their numbers. We know nothing of whatever weapons or technology they've developed or acquired over the last two years. All I know is what's happened on this ship, and that's not nearly enough!"

"Jackson knows things," Liz says, looking at him with conviction. "Maybe I can use my leverage with him to get information we need." Her passion makes him want to be stronger, to fight harder. But he's not stronger, and he can't fight harder. Liz doesn't change the situation. He pulls her to him again, wanting to hold her so close that they melt into each other.

"We have to be honest with each other, Z," he whispers in her hair, feeling tendrils of hopelessness grasping and tugging threads of his heart, "and with ourselves. You do have leverage with Jackson, and I think you should use it. But we both know I will always be a liability Jackson cannot afford. He won't stop until I'm dead."

Liz's eyes flutter closed for a moment. "Jackson needs you to get the ship back to Earth," she says softly. "No one else can do it, not him and not the executive board. You're not disposable to anyone—not yet. We won't be back to Earth for years, Seth. We have time to figure this out."

"Do we?" Seth asks. "Two days ago, we thought we'd have months or years to figure out how to deal with Jackson, but then he defies everything we know about science to show up and prove us all wrong. This means the possibilities are now endless, Z. Jackson could transport a new captain to the ship, or a whole army for that matter. We can't stop him. Or maybe he's grooming someone already here to take my place. He might be working with Green Grow, for all I know. Too many impossibilities have happened—I can't assume anything I know to be true anymore." *Except you,* he thinks, as the possibility of being without her pierces his heart once more.

Liz seems to consider this, biting her bottom lip the way she always does when she's deep in thought.

"He promised me that you'd be safe until we get back to Earth," Liz whispers fiercely. "We have time to figure this out." She presses herself even closer to him, leaving no space between them for doubt or fear or hopelessness, yet somehow the heaviness remains.

"I said I'd protect you," Seth says, "and the safest place for you right now is as far away from me as possible." He doesn't want to feel sorry for himself, nor does he want to look weak. But he's failing on both accounts. He doesn't want to cry, but he cries anyway. Tears run down his face and into her hair, and she squeezes him tighter and tighter until she finally lets go, freeing her hands to wipe away his tears.

Liz washes his face in soft kisses, whispering again and again that she won't leave him. Seth wishes he could live in this moment forever, this sacred eternal moment where the love they share is enough. But like everything else that matters, it will pass much too soon.

***

Liz lies on Seth's bed, curling herself into him and surrendering to his arms and his heat and the movement of his breath as it deepens. She tries to sleep as well but finds herself unable, her mind still spinning from the events of the day.

She dozes fitfully for a few hours before finally collapsing into a heavy sleep, the kind that always gives her strange dreams. This time, she's back at the depot. She is going toward the fence, to speak to the Fifty-Two. But it isn't Ruth at the fence. It's Seth. All of the faces belong to Seth. The Seth where Ruth should be is older, worn down. The Seth where Zachary should be is just a boy. The Seth where the New Generation should be is so savagely fierce, she hardly recognizes him.

She opens the gate to let them in. Seth after Seth after Seth spills in. She saves him. Then she kills him, as Seth after Seth after Seth barrage her savagely with homemade clubs and knives. Liz knows the folly in it, saving him just to kill him.

Then, from the abyss of her mind, something new overtakes the putrid fog of her dream. It comes as a whisper, a voiceless whisper. It doesn't come from her dream. It comes from somewhere else.

Hello, it says. Liz almost wakes but doesn't. She breathes in deeply, then exhales, trying to expel whatever insanity is taking root in her fractured mind.

Hello, it says again, louder this time. It seems to be coming from the far corner of the room. Liz sits up suddenly, eyes open and reaching for her bedside light, but she isn't in her own quarters. She listens but hears nothing, except Seth's heavy breathing as he lies beside her. The voice is gone, and the room seems different—not just quiet, but empty somehow.

CHAPTER 21

HELLO

***

As Liz sits in the captain's conference room, it's almost as if things are normal again. The council is gathered—the *real* council, without Jackson or Shelby—and they are discussing what they intend to transport to Earth using her brother's machine.

It's early, or whatever version of early exists on the ship, and her head is throbbing. Memories of her dream stain her thoughts, but she tries not to focus on it. They only have fifteen minutes before Jackson and Shelby will join the meeting, and they have reached no meaningful conclusions about the shipment.

"I told you, Harry," Claire says furiously, "my lab is perfectly capable of producing more biofilm. Don't blame me because you can't manage your end of the process."

"Don't insult me," Harry says. "It's not about me managing the process. It's about the volume of algae you're requesting to contribute to this goo. I'm not comfortable harvesting that much that quickly. Frankly, I think you're being dramatic. All I asked is for two additional days."

"We don't know how long Jackson will be able to stay here. We can let the algae recover later. We need to prioritize this food shipment."

"Do you hear yourself? Let the algae recover later? Do you realize that the algae provide the majority of our oxygen and is indispensable in our water purification system? It's not like we can just go down to the neighborhood pond and collect more."

Liz can sense that Seth is about to intervene. She looks toward him and sees him begin to move his hand, to call for order, but it's as if time has slowed. It seems to take him a full minute to blink his eyes, and when he begins to speak, the sound doesn't match the movement of his lips. It's slow and his voice is distorted. Then the world before Liz starts to blur. The edges of Seth's blue eyes get fuzzy, and then she can't make them out at all. The world turns into a fiery blur, and she loses track of his voice altogether. A different sound booms through her head—a single word that echoes in her skull breaking every fragile fiber as it ricochets in her head. *HELLO*, it says. Liz feels something wet escape her lips, and then her world turns to black.

***

A steady beep. The soft hum of equipment around her.

Liz opens her eyes slowly, taking in the dimly lit room filled with medical equipment and three other beds. She has a strange feeling that she's been here before.

"Z?" she hears. *Seth.* She registers his face in the dim light, the pressure of his hand squeezing hers. Then her eyelids become too heavy again and she drifts back off the peaceful abyss from which she arose. She falls and falls, too tired to even be thrilled by it, until she lands somewhere, somewhere sweet and fresh.

She's on the ground, in some kind of tall, sweet grass. She reaches for a word to describe the grass, or perhaps its name, and finds she doesn't know. But she knows she loves it. She lies there, and then, much to her own surprise, she starts to roll.

It's a glorious feeling, engaging all her senses. She can feel the grass on her back, scratching all the spots she can't reach. She can smell the sweetness as her body crushes its blades under her weight. She can see a sky above her, a perfect, blue, sunny, real sky. The day is real, not simulated. And even though she can't see it, she knows the night is real too—a real sky filled with real stars and two very real moons. But that is later. Now it is day, and she knows without being told that she has a mission—a desire.

She must collect more of this sweet grass, the best grass from a special place. She knows she shouldn't linger, and so she rises to start her day, surprised to find that she walks on four feet instead of two. *Who am I?* she wonders, knowing that she has a name—an identity—even if no one has ever told her what it is. *Cyril,* she thinks. *My name in this place is Cyril.* She finds herself torn between knowing more about herself and simply being—soaking up the joy and contentment that seems to flow through her so freely.

Without being told, she knows that she will go to a marsh. That's where the best, strongest grass grows. And so she starts off, padding along and soaking up the little glow of life she feels every time one of her small feet presses against the ground, pushing her farther through time and space, closer to the marsh where she will find the sweet grass she seeks.

Suddenly, she stops. She listens. A humming rises, and a new feeling comes over her—apprehension, or perhaps even fear. She breathes in the air, the ozone-tinged smell of danger filling her lungs. Someone is angry—she knows this, without being told. *Who?* she asks herself. *The Knower,* the answer comes. *The Knower? Yes, the One Who Knows.* A flash of lightning forks out across the cloudless sky above them, and the fear rises to panic.

She—Cyril—is running, as fast as she can on her four short legs. She must get back, back to a place she knows is home, even though she doesn't know where it is. She must get back to the others who are her family. *I have a family,* she realizes, just as the vision slips away and she dissolves back into the abyss of solitude.

Liz feels her awareness rising again, and she opens her eyes. She's in the medical unit, the room still dim, the equipment still humming softly. This is a different hum, an impersonal but comforting hum, not the hum of danger.

"Cyril," she whispers, trying to hold on to the word even as it begins to dissolve in her memory.

"Z?" She feels the pressure of Seth's hand on hers. "Is what real?"

"What?" she asks, her eyes focusing on the blurry mass she can see to her left.

"You asked if it's real," Seth says quietly, coming into focus. "How are you feeling?"

"What happened to me?" Liz asks. "Where did I go?"

"You had a seizure," he says in a quiet, soothing tone. "You're in the medical unit."

"No," Liz says, "I was somewhere else." She tries to keep the memory, to grasp it tightly as it dissolves. "There was grass, and sky, and a noise—some kind of humming."

Seth rises from his seat beside her, cracking open the door to the hallway just enough to wave to Claire. The beam of bright light sears Liz's eyes, so she closes them. She can't remember now where she was before, only that she was happy and that she wants to go back. A wave of despair washes over her, a feeling she's always been able to stave off before. She doesn't see the point in fighting it off now, tears welling in her eyes as the pointlessness of her life and the hopelessness of her future settles on her.

She doesn't care who sees her cry, at least until Jackson enters the room. As usual, he stands tall, as if he has no questions about his own life. She squints her eyes and quickly wipes her face, wrapping her feelings in a blanket of gritty numbness. Seth raises the head of her bed.

Claire and Jackson talk between themselves as if they're the only people in the room.

"Her brain activity is stabilized, although she still has an unusually high level of activity in the parahippocampal gyrus."

"And did the bloodwork come back?" Jackson asks.

"Yes," Claire says. "I see no sign of infection or any other identifiable cause. All we can do at this point is continue to monitor her." Jackson seems to remember that Liz is in the room, right in front of him, and he quickly spans the distance to the side of her bed, taking her free hand in his. He speaks to her as if no one else is there.

"Lizzie, you had a seizure. Have you ever had anything like that happen before?" She can feel Seth's hand tighten on hers, the slightest hint of moisture between their skin. His palm is sweating.

"I already said that she hasn't," Seth says, his voice tinged with anger. "She's been here on this ship for thirteen years, and she's never had any seizures."

Jackson squeezes her other hand. His skin feels cool and dry.

"She can answer the question herself," he says coldly.

"Actually," Claire interjects, "she may not be up for questions right now. How do you feel, Liz?"

"I want to go back," Liz says feebly, allowing both her hands to go limp.

"Go back?" Claire asks, looking puzzled. "Back where?"

"She thought she was somewhere else," Seth said, letting go of her hand and resting his fingers gently on her forearm. "She mentioned grass and the sky, and she asked me if it was real."

"She's hallucinating," Claire says to Jackson, as if Seth isn't worthy of a response. "That's not uncommon, given the severity of her seizure."

"Don't worry, Lizzie," Jackson whispers loudly, leaning in close and squeezing her limp hand. "You're going to be fine. I'm here now."

Is that supposed to make me feel better?

"I'm tired," Liz says, wanting to be alone even though she's unsure if she can sleep.

"I'll stay with you until you fall asleep," Jackson says.

"But what about Shelby?" Liz asks, wanting him to go away.

"Oh, I have no doubt she's under the watchful eye of our security team," Jackson says somewhat sourly.

Liz senses that Seth might be on the verge of speaking. She can feel tension radiating from his body, pulsing through his fingertips still touching her arm. Then she hears a buzzing noise—his tablet. Seth hesitates and then turns, taking his fingers off her arm to check the screen. He sighs angrily before leaning down to caress her forehead with his lips.

"Z," he whispers, tracing his fingers along her arm one last time, "I have to go see Jarrod. You rest as long as you need to. I'll be back as soon as I can."

"Leaving so soon, *Captain?*" Jackson says. Liz doesn't like how he spits out that last word. She remembers clearly now—Jackson wants to kill him. Not yet, but soon enough. Her head starts to throb, and she desperately wants to go back to the nothingness of sleep.

"I'd be happy to stay," Seth says, eyes narrowing in the dim light, "and perhaps you could explain to me why we've been having electrical surges on the ship ever since you arrived."

"I'm not sure what you're referring to," Jackson says, "but if you are incapable of maintaining your ship, perhaps I can explore the problem later, when my sister is better." Liz shifts in her bed, desperate for this conversation to end.

"Seth," Claire says pointedly, "this is upsetting Liz. She needs to rest."

"Yes, *Seth.* Do as your mother says."

Liz feels her heart beat faster, squeezing her eyes shut. She expects to hear Seth's voice next, but no sound comes— only the soft closing of the door as he leaves her room. Then Claire speaks.

"I'll check on you later," she says softly. Liz opens her eyes when she hears the door close again and feels the dimness on her lids. She sees her brother's form next to her bed.

"Do you remember what happened?" he asks her softly. Why can't he be this nice all the time? Why does everything with him have to be so complicated?

"No," she says, wondering if her voice is actually echoing in the dark room or if it's only her imagination. "I remember sitting in the conference room, and then I woke up here."

"You had a seizure," he says softly. "Apparently it started without warning, but thankfully Claire was there when it happened. I apparently wasn't invited to that part of the council meeting, so I didn't know what was happening until you were transported to the medical unit. But I'm here now, and I'll make you better."

Liz starts to cry, turning her head away from Jackson to hide her tears. How can anything be better now?

"Look what I brought," he says softly, producing a leather bag and reaching inside. In the dim light, she can make out a worn book. "It was your favorite." She squints to make out the cover. *The Velveteen Rabbit.*

She turns away again, tears spilling over her cheeks. Memories sweep through her mind—Jackson reading to her by the light of a candle, or sometimes a battery-operated lamp, pointing to a word as she'd sound out the letters. She would squint her eyes in the dim light, just like she's doing now. They were so different then, children with a world of possibility at their feet.

"You rest," he says, brushing a strand of hair off her forehead. "I know this will put you right to sleep. You rarely made it past the fifth page when you were tired."

"Jackson, is something wrong with my brain?" she asks.

"No, I'm sure there's not, but even if there was, we would fix it."

"But what about my parahippo … What about that part?"

"It's just an unusual place to have elevated activity, that's all," he says, caressing her hair gently. "Don't worry about it. You don't need to worry about anything right now."

But don't I? Liz curls up on her side, turning her back to her brother as she pulls her knees toward her chest, pillow under her chin. He begins to read, and she closes her eyes.

At first the words shred her heart, forcing her to admit that things will never be the same as when she was a girl. They can never return to trust without question, faith without doubt. And yet, he's here now, reading to her. Is that worth holding on to? It might be, but then she thinks of Seth. He's the one she will choose, if choosing is required.

Why does it have to be this way? She squeezes her eyes shut tightly, not wanting to think about it. She can't think about it. Neither can she avoid reality forever, but for now— just for today—she will try to forget the inevitability of what is to come. She finds herself comforted by Jackson's voice. He's come so far to see her. He's worked so hard so they can be together. Her eyes start to droop, and she feels her body begin to relax. She thinks she feels herself start to doze, and that's when she hears it.

Hello, the whisper comes. She knows this voice, but how?

Liz remembers now. It was the same voice booming in her head right before everything went black, the same voice she remembers from her dream. It's soft and feminine. Liz reaches back far into her memories, wondering if it's her mother's voice, but she cannot remember.

"Hello," Liz whispers back, too quietly for Jackson to hear over the hum of his own words.

Can you hear me? Liz can discern the words, but barely. She knows the voice is only in her head. She remembers that Claire said she might have delusions. This must be a delusion. And yet, the voice seems so real. Liz finds it appealing to have someone to talk to—someone who isn't her brother or Ruth or the council, someone who has never betrayed her. She doesn't care if the voice is real or not.

"Yes," Liz whispers, "as long as I focus on your voice."

I don't want to damage you again, the whisper replies. *I think I damaged you last time.*

"Yes," Liz whispers, "I think you did, but I'll be okay."

I need your help. Will you help me? Something terrible happened, and I need you to fix it. Liz thinks back to that day on the surface, when she first met Ruth. The woman asked for her help too—*Don't you have room in your heart for one little baby?*

"Who are you?" Liz asks. "What's your name?"

I am who I am. I have no need of any name.

Liz doesn't know how to respond, so she waits. Silence fills her head until she asks, *But what should I call you?*

Silence remains, stretching long enough that Liz begins to wonder if she really heard a voice at all. Perhaps it was a figment of her imagination. All she can hear now is Jackson, still reading in the background. Then, suddenly, the voice is there again.

You may call me Abby, the voice says. *How may I call you?*

"My name is Liz." *Shouldn't you know my name if you're in my head?*

I only know what you are willing to tell me, the reply comes.

"Can I sleep now?" Liz whispers, not ready to process the fact that she's talking to the voice in her head, and it has a name.

I don't know, Abby whispers. *Can you?*

"I think so," Liz replies, her eyes so heavy she cannot open her lids.

Sleep well, Liz. Then, just as suddenly as her head felt full, it feels empty—blissfully empty.

CHAPTER 22

MEANWHILE ON EARTH

***

Slowly and laboriously, Jackson rises from the bed. By his estimation, there are two minutes remaining in the 4G acceleration, but he can't bear the thought of remaining immobile another second. Lizzie is in the medical unit, and he cannot be with her. Neither can he return to Earth with the first shipment, as he'd hoped. The shipment will be ready in two days, but that won't be enough time to treat Lizzie. If he is to stay on the Green Grow 3, as he must until she is well, he has affairs to tend, and he is determined to see to them now.

He glances at Shelby, so deeply asleep that she barely even shifts toward the warm space he leaves. Good—she's comfortable. She's never seen such luxury as they now have in their Level 1 quarters on the Green Grow 3. In truth, Jackson has never known such either. But he knows it would be easy to become accustomed to it.

He reaches deep into the leather satchel he brought with him, containing only the most essential of belongings, and pulls out his tablet, this one newly upgraded to accommodate his current needs. He clicks open the application he needs and waits for Alex to answer his call. He starts to feel the pressure on his body begin to ease, and he ponders for a moment the miracle of relativity—compared to the 4G acceleration, his body feels light at 1.5G.

A face fills the screen.

"Alex," Jackson says, not bothering with a smile or any other such forced body language to make the man feel comfortable. "How goes it?"

Alex wears his typical serious expression, balanced by his innocent blue eyes, and rugged features that have transformed slightly with the gene therapy Jackson continues to administer. He has infused Alex with hybrids of Jackson's own DNA to repair the damage to his body, damage he incurred during the transporter tests. And Jackson hasn't merely repaired him—he has improved him, giving him strength and intelligence, and perhaps even loyalty, that were not his own. He wants Alex to be the best possible mate for Lizzie. He wants them to have strong children, especially since Jackson is beginning to wonder if Shelby is able to have children at all.

"Captain Goeff," he acknowledges with a somber nod. Jackson likes how Alex always uses his formal title, out of respect. "Operations are proceeding per your instructions. The growing teams are introducing the modifications to the hydroponic mixture in the new cave farm, and the first round of data from the gene therapy cancer treatment program should be here in a few days."

Jackson nods. "And the scouts?"

"Well," Alex hesitates, and Jackson is sure he knows what's coming next. "Most of the crews are still out, and the team transporting the bone mender to the Eastern faction is checking in regularly. But Zack Butler's crew returned early, and he's been vocalizing doubts about whether you will really be returning with the food shipments you promised everyone."

Jackson sighs deeply. None of this surprises him. He's only been gone three days, and Zack is already causing problems, trying to turn the crews against Jackson. *Some people are never satisfied,* he thinks, feeling a seed of anger trying to germinate in his belly.

Jackson has done so much for his people over the last two months, since he has been communicating with Lizzie and the Green Grow 3. First, there's the hydroponic farm in the cave the old woman abandoned—well, mostly abandoned. The few people who remained turned out to have very little helpful knowledge, even after Jackson subjected them to enhanced methods to extract information. But everyone can be used for something, even if it isn't what they wanted. The women in particular are young and healthy enough to serve the purpose of bearing children.

The farm itself is promising and has already yielded substantial improvements in the food supply, since Claire helped him enhance the hydroponic solution. He also built his own bone mender, which has been labeled "miraculous" by the numerous people it's helped. Injuries are common in his camp, and broken or fractured bones are a serious problem, especially given the amount of time his people have been malnourished. Cancer is another problem, and he's already healed at least a dozen people using the gene therapy research Claire shared.

In the eyes of many of his followers, he is a god, worshipped with adoring eyes as he promises even more miracles, if they can just stay the course a bit longer. But opinions are fickle. Jackson has seen firsthand how easily people are swayed, how they will follow any dream as long as they don't have to be responsible. He needs to be there with them, to remind them which dream they are following, to remind them that he is their captain.

He remembers President Greene, the founder of the New Generation. *Such a shame,* Jackson thinks, a familiar stab of sadness piercing his heart. Jackson had so admired Greene—he was a dreamer, and Jackson jumped headfirst into the dream. Maybe he was young or naïve. He thought he could change the world at the age of fourteen, and the president assured him he could make a difference.

But change was already on the wind. The dreamer was overthrown, smothered in his sleep before Jackson was powerful enough to do anything about it. A new leader came with a new vision—a vision that changed the New Generation from an organization of principles and ideals to a wolf pack. It's still mostly that way. Status is obtained through cunning and strength, often physical strength. Dominance is established and seniority defended against challengers. Failed challengers, if they survive, skulk back into the ranks, shamed and subjugated, or they take whatever followers they have and split, forming a new pack. That's how the New Generation went from one national organization to four factions—Western, Midwestern, Southern, and Eastern. Indeed, that's how Jackson created the Western faction.

Not even this structure is completely stable or permanent, and the factions could combine or further split as surely as drops of mercury. While Jackson hoped that eventually they would rejoin into one organization—after his position in the organization was secured—he now knows that he will always stand on the precipice of change, with people like Zack Butler eager to push him from behind into an abyss from which he will never rise.

"What's he saying?" Jackson asks, reminding himself that this is Harris's fault. If it weren't for Harris, he would already have a smooth operation—regular food runs from the Green Grow 3, which would still be orbiting Earth and under Jackson's command.

"The usual," Alex says with a wave of his hand. "That you've run your course. That, important as your prior accomplishments are, everyone is still hungry."

Jackson sighs. Alex is right—it's the same argument his prior opponents made. No one discounts what he's done, only whether he's the best leader going forward.

"What else?" Jackson asks.

"He's telling people you've given too much away by sending technology to the east. He claims you've sent them food, and that's why we don't have enough. He also says you're lying about taking possession of the Green Grow 3, and that Lizzy has bewitched you, muddled your thinking."

"He's bold, isn't he?" Jackson mutters in anger. He knew Butler would become a problem, but he didn't expect it to escalate this fast. *He must see the window of opportunity my absence creates,* Jackson thinks, feeling a twinge of admiration for the man's insight. *Formidable.*

Alex continues, "He says we need to join forces with Mackey and migrate south, to force our way across the Mexican border." Mackey. The very sound of his name fills Jackson with disgust, calling forth a vision of President Greene, fighting and struggling under the weight of Mackey's body as he smothered him with a pillow in his own bed. Jackson saw it with his own eyes, hiding in an alcove filled with books. Now Mackey rules the Midwestern faction with a sadistic iron fist. Jackson knows he wouldn't have hesitated to kill Lizzie when she landed the shuttle outside

Minneapolis to retrieve the antimatter, except that she was too smart and fierce to get caught.

"Are people listening?" Jackson asks.

"A few are," Alex replies, "and the rest of the crews will be back in two days, sir. Will you be back in time to head this off?"

"Regrettably, no. I need to stay a few days longer."

"Do you want me to deal with Butler? I could take him out. I don't want him to cause problems with the rest of the crews."

Jackson considers this. There are reasons he hasn't eliminated the man yet. For one thing, he's good at leading the simpler-minded men, although perhaps this is also what makes him such a dangerous adversary. Jackson wants to benefit as much and as long as he can from Butler's strength.

"No," he says. "I still have a use for him."

"Very well, sir, but I'd be happy to deal with him." Alex's face exudes a fierce and innocent loyalty, one that has made Jackson even more fond of the man.

"I know you would, but here's what we need to do. Tomorrow, the first food shipment will arrive. I want you to close off the main cavern, and put the kitchen staff on standby. Shelby and I will return before the crews get back, and when they arrive, we will feast."

"A feast, sir?"

"Yes, I'll send you further instructions shortly."

"Very well, sir. And how is the lady faring on the Green Grow 3?" Alex asks, although Jackson is sure this isn't what he really wants to know.

"You know Shelby," he says with a smile. "She is formidable, no matter what the circumstances may be."

"Yes, sir, I'm glad to hear it. And your sister? How is Lizzie?" Alex's eyes take on a softer quality.

"Frankly, she's why I'm still here," Jackson replies. "I believe the extended time in space has adversely affected her health, so I've stayed to care for her."

"Can you help her?"

The question sounds more like a plea. Jackson may not be able to control what Lizzie thinks and does, but it was quite easy to help Alex fall in love with his sister, even though he's never met her. A few pictures, a few stories, and a promise that if Alex could win her heart, Jackson would approve of their union.

"Yes," he says in a gentle tone, "I believe I've identified the source of her illness, and it's only a matter of time now before she is better."

"Perhaps space does not suit her," Alex says. "Perhaps she should return to Earth and take her place with us here."

"Indeed. We are discussing that very option. But don't get your hopes up. There is still important work to be done here on the Green Grow 3. She may need to stay a bit longer." Jackson won't admit that his sister has refused to come. He won't break Alex's heart by telling him that Lizzie is madly and deeply in love with Seth Harris, misguided as it may be. He won't mention any of that, because nothing is immutable. Jackson is sure that he will make this come together the way he wants, as he has made everything else come together. And in the meantime, he'll send Alex some new pictures of Lizzie, pictures he's taken with the small camera sewn into the lapel of his leather jacket. And he knows Alex will love her all the more, because Lizzie only seems to grow more beautiful every day.

"I'm sure you know what is best," Alex replies. "I'll await further instructions, and sir—I'm here for whatever you need."

"Thank you, Alex. I know." Jackson gives him a reassuring smile before he terminates the call. He glances toward the bed and sees that Shelby is awake, studying him with her exotically dark and beautiful eyes.

"Is all well on the surface?" she asks.

"Zack Butler is making a move," he says, trying to quash the anger he still feels growing in his belly.

"How will you respond?"

"I still have work to do here, my love, but we need to go back to the surface. I know that none of this has been easy, but will you go back with me, just for a short time?"

"Of course," she replies. "How short of a time?"

"Dinner. We'll be back here before anyone knows we're gone." He can see a hint of disappointment on her face. He knows that she's ready to go home. But, just as he knows she will, she agrees anyway.

"How about a bath?" he asks, moving to sit next to her on the bed and kissing her head gently. "I had some lavender and roses delivered, and some milk too. Will you let me run you a bath, my love?"

"I suppose," she says with a sigh.

"I know you're disappointed," he offers in a soothing voice, "but I promise, a bath will lift your spirits."

Her expression changes in an instance as she snarls in return, "We cannot allow ourselves to grow soft, Jackson! We cannot allow the wasteful frivolities of this ship to distract us from our purpose."

"Indeed," Jackson says softly, "but we must also keep our spirits high, and you deserve a special treat."

"Fine. Don't make it too hot."

Shelby follows Jackson into the bathroom, perching on the edge of the tub as Jackson fills it with lukewarm water.

"We should be home by now," she growls. "Not just for dinner, but for good. Lizzie should be with us, and Seth Harris should be dead. Have you forgotten the plan?"

"Of course I haven't forgotten!" Jackson barks. "It's my plan! How could I forget it?"

Shelby steps into the tub, casting him a dispassionate look.

"Why are we still here?" she asks. "And why is Seth Harris still alive?"

"I don't yet have the Walkabout 2 data," Jackson replies, "and I'll deal with Harris when the time is right."

"The time is now!" she insists, sinking into the milky, flower-laden water. "The crews demand his blood."

"And they shall have it, but not yet. I still have need of him."

"And then?"

"And then, I shall dispense with him in the cage."

Shelby closes her eyes, sinking further as her lips curl into a smile.

"I like that," she says. "I like that very much."

"You see, my love? Even the best of plans can benefit from periodic reassessment." Jackson laces his fingers into her hair, tightening his fist as he pulls her close for a kiss. Her eyes fly open as he presses his lips firmly to hers, for only a moment before he releases her. She leans her head back against the tub as he hisses with narrow eyes, "Do not question my resolve again."

CHAPTER 23

BEST FOR EVERYONE

***

OCTOBER 28, 2059—TUESDAY

Seth is determined to complete the business before him, although it doesn't feel like a council meeting without Liz. She's still in the medical unit, groggy and recovering from the seizure she had yesterday at this very table.

If he closes his eyes, he can see her as she was before it happened. Alive and vibrant. Ready to take on the world. She was a wellspring of resilience, infusing Seth with hope that together, they would find a way to survive.

But now she lies in the medical unit, listless and vulnerable, her mind wafting between reality and whatever dreamland she discovered while unconscious yesterday. He feels so very alone.

Scanning the faces around the table, Seth knows that Harry and Jarrod are his allies, while his mother and Jackson are his adversaries. That leaves Mathilda—who seems to reside in whatever version of purgatory Jackson's arrival created in her heart—and Shelby. Seth doesn't pretend to understand her agenda, although he's sure it's probably complicated and does not work in his favor. Without Liz, the balance is tipped against him.

He glances at the sheet of paper in his hand, an inventory of everything he believes they can send to Earth using Jackson's transporter. He is surprised and pleased at how much there is, enough in fact that it has to be divided up into two separate shipments. Surely it will make a difference to someone. He hands copies of the report to Jarrod, who sits on his left.

He's in no mood for bickering or talking past each other. He wants to reach an agreement about the list, get the staging of goods underway, and go back to the medical unit to sit with Liz. That's where he wants to be. Even if she's sleeping, holding her hand is a better use of his time than anything he can accomplish with this group.

"I hope to keep this short today," Seth begins as everyone's eyes settle on the list. Before he can continue, his mother interrupts.

"Seth," she says, "I'd like to update everyone on Liz's condition. We all witnessed her seizure yesterday, and I'm sure the council wants to know how she's doing."

Seth's eyes narrow. Something doesn't seem right about this. But he can't pinpoint what's wrong, so he nods for her to continue.

"She's stable at the moment," Claire continues, addressing the group, "and Jackson and I are working closely together to monitor her condition and identify the root cause of her seizure. We've noticed unusual brain activity, but we're still running tests to determine what it means." She looks at Jackson, giving him an almost imperceptible nod, as if she's cuing him.

"Yes," he agrees, "and although I intended to return to Earth with the first shipment and transport the second shipment remotely, I now see that I need to stay a bit longer, to continue with Lizzie's case. We need to find out what is wrong with her." He quickly glances back to Claire, another cue in what appears to Seth to be a rehearsed presentation. His eyes narrow again, wondering where this is headed.

"We will continue to monitor her and run tests," Claire says, "but our working hypothesis is that the seizure was triggered by our acceleration. Unless we find some other explanation, we feel it will be important for Liz to return with Jackson to Earth. Jackson can oversee her treatment in consultation with me on video chat."

The shock of his mother's words lasts only a moment before rage surges from Seth's stomach to the top of his head. Earth is the last place Liz needs to be right now. It would be dangerous enough if she were perfectly healthy. Seth won't stop her if she wants to go back with Jackson, but she says she doesn't want to go, and in her current condition, she'd be completely helpless—totally at his mercy. Seth would have no way to help her.

Jackson might be her brother, but he's still New Generation. Who's to say he wouldn't hold her hostage? And he'd most certainly do his best to brainwash her. Seth clenches his teeth together to stay the flood of words he wants to unleash on his mother. He cannot bear to look at her right now, so he turns his attention to Jackson.

"Liz informed me yesterday of your discussion about returning to Earth," he says. "She made it clear that she does not wish to go. She wishes to continue her work here, so that's what she will do. I am certain we can provide whatever care she needs."

Seth expects Jackson to get angry, to reply with one of his typical cutting, sarcastic remarks. But he doesn't. Instead, he only nods his head in agreement, appearing thoughtful.

"I agree," Jackson begins. "We should respect her wishes. I spoke with her yesterday about returning to Earth with me, and she declined. While I think it's a shame to waste the potential her presence on Earth offers, I accepted her decision. The offer stands if she changes her mind."

Seth's eyes narrow again. What is he missing? He's ready to declare the matter settled when his mother speaks again.

"But her judgment may have been impaired, even then!" Claire insists. "The seizure was most likely the culmination of damage over time. She's clearly incompetent now, given her hallucinations, and we cannot know at what point her judgment was compromised. She is not capable of knowing what's in her best interest and should not be allowed to make this decision herself."

Seth is stunned. "You have no basis for declaring her incompetent!" he says. "Nor do you have any basis for your diagnosis." He glances between Jackson's placid face and his mother, whose jaw is set like she's ready for a fight. The reality of what's happening hits Seth hard.

Jackson doesn't have to argue about this—my mother will do it for him! She's trying to take Liz away from me. For the first time in his life, his anger transforms into hatred, a malice so intense that it scares him. It blinds him to any altruistic motives she may have. All he can see are the times she dismissed him, treated him like a fool—like a child.

"We must do what is best for her," Claire snaps, "what is best for *everyone*." She never liked Liz. She wanted to blow up her shuttle when she brought back the Fifty-Two, and railed against her at every council meeting when problems arose during her missions.

She's been working against me for a very long time, Seth thinks. *I just haven't seen it for what it is.* And now Claire is trying to force her will on him, to humiliate him and make him look weak in front of Jackson.

Seth's mind spins. Then it settles into a cold, calculating fury. He no longer sees his mother before him. That woman is lost, replaced by an enemy, someone working with Jackson to defeat him. His teeth are clenched, but he relaxes his jaw. His fists are tight balls under the table, but he loosens them, stretching his fingers. He can feel his heart rate slow, his face cool. He turns his attention back to Jackson, dismissing Claire just as she has dismissed him so many times.

"Are the shipments acceptable to you, Jackson?" Seth asks, motioning to the report. "Can your transporter accommodate them the way we propose to package them?"

"Yes," he says smoothly. "This is a good start to improving life on Earth, and my transporter can accommodate the two shipments. I still plan to stay until the second one, though, to assist in Lizzie's care."

"Fine," Seth says, rising from his chair. "Department heads, stage the goods for the first shipment." He turns to go, wanting to be anywhere his mother is not, but she stands and follows him out, nearly running to catch up to him. He nods to the security officers standing outside the conference room, the ones who will escort Jackson and Shelby back to their quarters for the controlled acceleration. Then he heads toward his office. If his mother confronts him, it will be in a place of his choosing.

And so it is.

"Close the door," he barks as she storms in after him. She looks furious, but abides his command.

"You're not seeing the big picture," she says. "Jackson wants Liz on Earth with him. Think of how useful she could be there, not just to him but to you!"

"She doesn't want to go," Seth tells her, through gritted teeth. "I know you've never liked her, but it's not your decision to make."

"Like her?" Claire asks, not hiding the contempt in her voice. "No, I don't like her, but that's not the point. She can help you if she goes back with Jackson, but here, she only clouds your judgment!"

Seth feels his face burn, cheeks flush with anger.

"My judgment is fine, Mom. In fact, I think it's clearer now than it has ever been. If Liz wants to stay, she's staying. I won't allow you to use your position to control me, or to tear us apart."

"Tear you apart?" She looks at him with disgust. "You sound like a child! Grow up, Seth. See the situation for what it is."

"I grew up a long time ago. You chose not to notice. But rest assured, I do see the situation clearly. This conversation is over."

He knows by the look on her face that she's hurt, angry, and frustrated. Maybe she does love him, but it's no excuse for what she's doing. Seth refuses to look at her as she leaves, sitting heavily in his chair to let his anger pass before he returns to Liz's room in the medical unit to spend the few minutes that remain before the morning acceleration.

***

Hello. The voice comes softly again, increasingly familiar but still disconcerting. Liz's body is heavy, nearly unbearable. She recognizes the feeling—they must be accelerating. She remembers now that she's in the medical unit. Her eyes remain closed. She doesn't need them at the moment.

Abby?

Yes, she responds. *Are you restored?*

I don't know, Liz thinks, unsure what restoration would mean in her case. *I am better than I was.*

You're fragile, Abby says, *so easily damaged. Like the creatures here, although you're different in many ways. I thought your vibration was higher than theirs, but now I realize—it's only more complex.*

Creatures? Liz asks, the sound of Abby's voice swirling with ribbons of confusion in her mind.

Yes, the creatures who live here, in this place you sent me.

Who sent you? Where? Liz doesn't know what to make of Abby's words, and a feeling of helplessness threatens to overwhelm her.

Yes, Abby says emphatically. *This place, this time. You sent me here.* The words make no sense to Liz.

What? Where? she asks, feeling helpless to understand. The confusion of it nearly overwhelms her.

You don't know what you've done, Abby says gently. *Now you're getting upset, and it's lowering your vibration. I will explain what happened, and then you will understand. All you need to do right now is listen.*

What have I done? Liz asks.

It wasn't you, specifically. At least, I don't think it was you. But it was one of your kind, someone in your vessel. Someone in your vessel pulled me out of my world, into this world with time and space.

Liz tries to understand what Abby is telling her, but her mind spins in circles. *How is that possible?* she asks.

I don't know. I was with my teacher, preparing for an ascension, and then I felt a strange energy. I tried to perceive the energy, to understand its nature, and I saw a tiny creature, with such a dense little body that it was barely aware of its own consciousness.

A creature, like the ones where you are? Liz struggles to hold on to some detail that makes sense to her. Her consciousness folds in on itself, trying to wrap around some piece of information she can comprehend, making her insides feel like they might implode.

No, Abby replies, *a different creature.*

What creature? I don't understand. Liz starts to panic. Her heart races, and her labored breathing quickens. She wants to move, but she can't.

Calm yourself, Liz. Abby's voice is gentle. *Calm yourself. Raise your vibration, or our connection will fade.*

Would I know this creature? Liz asks, needing to ground herself in some familiar detail, something real.

I—I don't know. Let me see if I can recall it in a way your eyes can perceive. Liz hears a hum in her head, and she isn't sure if it's overwriting Abby's words or merely filling the silence. But a moment later, an image flashes into her mind.

The image is blurred and distorted, as if Liz is seeing it through wavy glass. It looks like a ball of colored light, but then something happens. Liz feels the sensation of zooming into the image, focusing the blurry edges. But in fact, the image is changing right in front of her, into something more discernible. It's like watching a plant grow in fast forward, seeing it turn into something recognizable, but only because it's changing. She can see metal overlayed on flesh, and then she becomes dizzy with vertigo. She wants to close her eyes, but they are already closed. She has no escape from the image

Abby shows her. It fills every space in her mind, crowding out her own thoughts and memories.

Liz feels like one eye is on the verge of popping. She wants to vomit, but she can't. She can't move. She can't breathe. She can't stop looking at the creature in front of her, the sickening swirl of light and form. The image changes again, and she can see four small feet. She can see a round ear, and a tail. The metal parts start to look like electrodes, or some kind of sensors. She can hear Abby's voice echoing somewhere behind the image, telling her to raise her vibration.

What does she mean? Liz wonders, the thought echoing loudly in her mind. The humming sound grows, drowning out the echo. She thinks that Abby is telling her something, but she cannot make out the words. Confused, Liz realizes that the image before her is a mouse, and then the humming is gone, Abby's voice silent. She feels a wet trickle across her lips and down her chin. She wants to wipe it away, but she cannot control her body.

She doesn't feel as heavy now. The acceleration must be over.

Her world fades to nothing as she falls unconscious.

When Liz wakes up, she cannot tell how much time has gone by. Her body hurts, like she lost a fight to a giant. Maybe she did. She starts to cry.

CHAPTER 24

RIGHT AS RAIN

***

Liz knows even before she opens her eyes that Seth is there with her. She can feel his energy, radiating steady and strong but also quiet and sad.

"How long have I been here?" she asks, finding her throat so hoarse that she can barely speak. The light is dim, but she sees Seth's form lean in, her nostrils filled with the scent of his skin after he showers.

"A day," he says softly. "It's Tuesday now, close to lunch." A day seems like a long time. Under different circumstances, Liz would try to rise and reenter life on the ship. But not this time. Her head feels empty, blissfully empty, and all she cares about now is enjoying the relief.

"Can I have water?" she rasps. Seth raises the head of her bed and lifts a cup to her lips.

"How do you feel?" he asks.

"Right as rain," she says, although every fiber of her body protests.

"I doubt that," Seth says tenderly, placing the cup on a nearby table. "My mom and your brother think the accelerations might be causing your seizures."

Liz considers this, then shakes her head. "No, it's not the accelerations. It's her."

"Who?" Seth asks, and Liz briefly wonders if she should tell him about Abby. She knows it will sound crazy. *But I'm not crazy. Abby is real, and she wants us to help her.*

"Someone needs our help, Seth," Liz says, choosing her next words carefully as he waits. "She calls herself Abby. I don't know who or what she is, but she talks to me, in my mind. If she talks too loud, or if I panic, my brain seems to overload. I think that's why I have the seizures."

"Did this voice, who calls herself Abby, ask you for help?" Seth asks.

"Yes, she asked me to help her go home. She said we didn't know what we did. She said so many things, and I can't make sense of most of it. But she's real, Seth—as real as you or me."

"Is she talking to you now?" Seth asks.

"No, she's gone."

"How do you know?"

Liz wonders if Seth believes her, but he only sounds curious.

"My head feels different," she says. "When she talks to me, it feels … full, I guess. I don't know how else to describe it. And there's a humming noise. Sometimes it's loud, nearly unbearable." She pauses, trying to find better words to describe her experience, but she can't. "I think it has to do with Jackson's machine. Abby says that someone on this ship created energy, energy that pulled her somewhere she doesn't belong. She showed me an image. It was a mouse, covered in electrodes."

"A mouse?" Seth sounds surprised.

"I think Jackson sent a mouse through his machine, and somehow Abby was pulled in with it."

"Where is she?" Seth asks. "Is she here on the ship?"

Liz considers this. "No, I don't think so. She says there are fragile creatures where she is, but it sounds like she's somewhere else."

"But then how can she talk to you?"

Liz knows how her story sounds, and that awful feeling of panic starts to overtake her again. "I don't know, Seth!" she cries. "I don't know!"

"It's okay," he says softly, reaching out to brush a strand of hair from her face. "You don't need to have all the answers." They sit in silence, and Liz closes her eyes, wanting to lose herself in the blissful emptiness of her head.

"Am I crazy?" she asks.

"No," he says, and then he chuckles. "Well, maybe, but not because of this." She smiles at him weakly.

"I don't think it's impossible," he continues. "Jackson's wormholes could leave an energy signature, and you didn't hear this voice before he transported himself to the ship, did you?"

Liz shakes her head.

"We still don't know what's causing the electrical surges, either," Seth adds thoughtfully. "Maybe they're connected somehow."

"Maybe," Liz says weakly. "Now that Abby can communicate with me, I think she expects us to help her."

Seth appraises her for what seems like a long time.

"Okay," he says finally. "How do we do that?"

***

Seth watches his mother and Jackson enter Liz's room, Jackson sitting opposite from him and holding Liz's free hand while Claire opts to stand at the foot of the bed. Liz still looks diminished, so small in the bed that Seth never thought of as large. But he thinks the parts of her that matter most—her vibrance and resilience—are still there, only muted by the suffering this voice called Abby seems to cause her body.

When Liz told him about the voice just minutes before, he knew they would eventually have to tell Claire, if for no other reason than the fact that she's overseeing Liz's medical treatment. But he didn't imagine it would happen so fast. He thought that he and Liz would have more time to talk about it, to gather data and see if the voice persisted. But Liz was convinced that Jackson was the only one who could help Abby, and that helping was the only way to make her voice go away.

Admittedly, Seth could have tried harder to persuade Liz to wait, to see if the voice went away on its own. But he didn't want to push her too hard by arguing—and what if Jackson really could help her? In the end, Seth couldn't deny her pleading eyes. She summoned Jackson urgently to her room, and Claire insisted on accompanying him, no doubt to further her agenda of labeling Liz as incompetent.

Seth doesn't doubt that Liz hears a voice, or that this voice calls herself Abby. Liz says it is so, and so it is. But is it real, or is it a delusion? He isn't ready to draw any conclusions yet. The idea of an alien being invading Liz's mind sounds far-fetched. But Jackson's machine alters the very fabric that creates time and space, so isn't anything possible?

Did that monster trap an entity who is now communicating with Liz telepathically? Seth can't rule it out, not after everything he's seen. Besides, Seth knows that he'd rather believe Liz than admit that the accelerations might be causing her seizures. If an entity is, in fact, communicating with her, going back to Earth with Jackson won't help her condition.

"Jackson," Liz begins slowly, "did you transport mice with your machine?" Her eyes are wide, unsure and endearing. Seth can almost see the little girl she used to be, and he wants to sweep that child up into his arms and keep her safe forever.

"Mice?" Jackson looks perplexed. "Lizzie, I thought you wanted to talk about your seizures."

"I do," she says quickly and firmly, "but I need to know. Did you test your machine on mice?" Jackson's eyes dart around the room, bewildered. He looks at Seth, then at Claire, as if he's deciding what to say.

"Did you?" Liz asks again, quietly.

"Yes," he says. "I ran several tests using mice. It's how I developed the biofilm."

"So, you put electrodes or sensors on their bodies as part of the test?"

Jackson nods.

"Where did you transport the mice?" Liz asks. He laughs, a loud nervous sound.

"What does this have to do with your seizures? Why does it matter?"

"It matters because I'm asking you," Liz says angrily, sitting up in bed. *There's my fiery girl,* Seth thinks. "This isn't the time for half-truths or insinuations. Where did you send them?" Seth keeps his expression neutral as Jackson's eyes dart between him and Liz, suspiciously.

"I wanted to confirm the exact coordinates of the turnaround point," he says in a hushed tone, "so I sent them to Omega."

"To Omega?" Liz asks.

"Yes, to the turnaround point. You see, I had some questions about its coordinates, and I felt it was important to…"

"I don't care why you sent them," Liz interrupts, "only where you sent them."

"I sent them to Omega," Jackson confirms.

"How many?" Liz asks. Jackson looks perplexed, opening his mouth as if to speak but then closing it again. *She has a way of making him do that.* Seth notices yet again how differently Jackson interacts with Liz. *Almost human,* he thinks wryly. Jackson waves his hand in a dismissive flourish.

"What does this have to do with your seizures? Tell me, Lizzie, before my patience wears thin."

Seth can see Liz appraising her brother, undoubtedly trying to decide how to phrase what comes next.

"Jackson, I know this may sound strange," she begins, "but I need you to listen to me. During one of your tests, when you transported a mouse to Omega, something happened. A being, who calls herself Abby, was pulled into the wormhole. She saw the mouse, and then she was pulled into time and space. She's telling me we need to fix our mistake. We have to send her home."

Jackson sits frozen, eyes wide and mouth hanging open. Seth can appreciate how he feels, or at least he knows how he felt when Liz told him about Abby. But he doesn't care about that now. He only wants Liz to get better.

"How do you know this?" Claire asks, the sound of her voice triggering Seth's anger. *She doesn't care how Liz knows,* he thinks. *She's just stockpiling evidence that Liz is incompetent.* Does Liz know she's being set up to fail? The nervous expression on her face tells Seth that she might.

"Abby communicates with me telepathically," Liz whispers. "That's what triggers the seizures."

"You're hearing voices?" Claire asks. She sounds concerned, but Seth knows that she's not, not really.

"Lizzie, it's not real!" Jackson cries. "The seizures are making you hallucinate. That's all. There's no voice. Come back to Earth with me so I can help you!"

"Abby is not a hallucination!" Liz insists. Jackson's mouth falls open again, speechless.

"Then let's talk to her," Claire says quickly. "Is she here now?" Anger rises in Seth's throat. How dare anyone mock Liz? But Liz doesn't seem angry.

"No, she's not," she says, "but maybe I can call her. She told me our connection fades when I get upset, that my vibration lowers. But if I raise my vibration …"

"Raise your vibration?" Claire exclaims. "Seth, this is ridiculous. Can't you see? We need to put an end to this and help her."

"You well know that all matter vibrates!" Seth says in return, knowing that's not her point but refusing to affirm the condescension infused in her words. Jackson sits dumbfounded, oblivious to everyone but Liz, lying in front of him.

"Jackson?" Claire asks. Jackson blinks rapidly, jolted from his stupor. Seth doesn't care what the man thinks about her words, but he knows his mother does.

"What does it hurt to let her try?" he asks weakly. Seth is surprised to detect sadness in his voice that seems quite genuine. "Maybe we'll gain some valuable insight." Claire nods stiffly, and they all wait as Liz closes her eyes, breathing deeply and resting her hands in her lap.

"Abby?" she whispers. Seth watches her chest expand and contract, drawing in breath and then letting it go. "Abby?" she whispers again, over and over. Part of Seth hopes the voice comes through. The other part hopes it never speaks to Liz again.

Seth can sense his mother preparing to say something when Liz's hands suddenly fly out, pressing firmly into the bed on either side of her body, as if she's bracing herself.

"She's here!" Liz gasps, her body rocking like a small boat on a vast ocean. Her eyes are clenched shut. "Abby, are you on the ship now? Are you here?" Seth holds his breath as they all wait in silence. "She says no," Liz whispers in a rush of words. "She says it's only her tendrils of awareness, that she has to spin a thread very fine and match my vibration to connect. Tell me again what happened to you, Abby."

Liz's body stills for a moment as she continues, "She says she was with others of her kind, preparing to ascend. She felt a strange energy and perceived the mouse, and then she was alone … in linear time. She says we pulled her into linear time."

Liz's eyes flutter open, and Claire leans in to look at them. "Her pupils are completed dilated!" she exclaims. "We need to get her into the body scanner right now. I'm going to sedate her."

"No!" Liz cries, and Seth leaps to his feet, putting his body between his mother and the woman he loves.

"Seth, she's hallucinating!" his mother screams. "She is psychotic!"

Suddenly, two of the ceiling lights explode, sparks and bits of glass and plastic raining down. Seth throws himself onto the bed to cover Liz, and Jackson shields his head with his arms. Claire shrinks to the ground, taking cover under a rolling table.

"Is she psychokinetic, too?" Seth demands, scared and angry. Only Liz seems unmoved. Her eyes are closed again, her body swaying like a flower in a gentle breeze.

"Jackson," Liz says, her voice cutting through the darkened room, "she knows it was you. The energy that pulled her away from her home is the same energy she detected when you transported yourself here. That's how she found our ship. She wants you to fix your mistake and send her home."

"Fix my mistake?" Jackson shouts, arms still folded over his head. "I didn't do anything wrong!"

"She says you've done everything wrong," Liz squeaks in a high-pitched rush of words. "She says you've taken everything from her. She's angry, Jackson, so very angry …" Seth can feel her body convulse beneath him—another seizure. Around him, sparks begin to fly out of the walls, from every electrical outlet, and the screen starts to melt on the monitor next to the bed. He can smell the burning plastic. Will it explode?

Suddenly, the room quiets. Liz's body still trembles below him, but the only thing he can do is hope that she's in that place she wanted to go, that nice place in her mind with grass and sky.

***

Jackson is surprised when the door to his quarters opens and Claire walks in, a medical kit in hand.

"Claire? What's happened?" He rises from his chair. Then something surprising occurs. She shushes him.

"We need to talk," she says in a low voice, "and the only way I could get in here was to tell the security officers that Shelby needed medical help, that she experienced symptoms from the controlled acceleration this morning."

Jackson can hear the urgency in Claire's voice, and he can see the irritation on Shelby's face. He finds it endearing that she's so easily irritated by any label of weakness, even if it's a ruse.

"Well, love," he says to her gently, "I suppose it would have to be you, because I was seen coming from the medical unit in perfect health just moments ago. I know, it's ridiculous that Claire needs to provide any explanation to visit us." Shelby seems to accept this but says nothing as he turns his attention back to Claire. "Are there new developments?" he asks.

"Liz is fine," she says quickly, and Jackson is dismayed that she would make such a comment. He understands her meaning, but Lizzie is anything but fine. Jackson doesn't yet know how to interpret everything that transpired in her room. He hasn't even had time to remove the bits of glass and plastic from his hair, much less come to a level of understanding.

"You need to take her back to Earth with you," Claire says forcefully.

Jackson feels his own irritation begin to stir—no one tells him what he needs to do. "Do I?" he asks sharply. "She's been clear about her desires."

"She is in no state to make a decision for herself," Claire replies, then pauses before she speaks again.

Yes, Claire, Jackson thinks, *choose your words carefully.*

"I know that Liz is a vibrant young woman," she begins in an even tone, "full of life and conviction. I want her to be healthy, and she may respond better to treatment on Earth, given the enhanced gravity here." She looks at Jackson, brimming with emotion. "But you and I both know that there are other reasons she should go. We cannot build the partnership, or the future, we both desire as long as she and Seth are together. They must be separated."

Jackson's irritation is displaced by intrigue.

"I can envision many benefits to Lizzie returning with me," he says thoughtfully, "but I have no intention of abducting her against her will."

"You won't have to," Claire replies, piquing Jackson's curiosity even more. He briefly wonders if her words are simply bait for a trap he doesn't wish to fall into, so he only looks at her, waiting for her to continue, appraising her silently as she grows flustered, or perhaps nervous.

"The first shipment will be ready for transport tomorrow," she explains hastily. "The second shipment shouldn't take more than a few days to package and stage. No doubt, like the first one, we will transport it before the morning acceleration. This will give me the time I need, when the ship is quiet, to sedate her and transfer her to your capsule."

Jackson's eyebrows rise in surprise. Is he hearing what he thinks he's hearing? Certainly, he likes what Claire is saying. Lizzie would wake up on Earth in his best medical facility, and he could explain what happened in mostly truthful terms. Then, his only problem would be delaying her inevitable demand to be returned to her beloved Seth Harris. But surely, he could create delays in sending her back, even if it means disabling his transporter for a while.

Claire will be the target of her fury, not himself. And once she's on Earth, Alex will help him pivot her views on where she should be and what she should be doing. Perhaps between the two of them, they can persuade her to change her way of thinking—if he can keep her on Earth long enough.

"Why do you want her gone so badly, Claire?" Jackson asks, indulging his curiosity. He's pleased when she appears thoughtful, because he will not abide undue criticism of his sister.

"It's not about her," Claire says quietly. "It's about Seth. He doesn't think clearly around her, and he needs to see his situation for what it is."

"Oh?" Jackson asks, startled. Harris is despicable, but even Jackson can see that he makes his own choices. If anyone's judgment is being influenced by the union, he's certain it's his sister's. "What is it that he needs to see?"

"That you are not his enemy," Claire says urgently. *Aren't I, though?* Jackson suppresses a laugh. "I intend to prove that to both of you before we return to Earth."

"Do you?" he asks, hoping she will tell him more.

"You must know that he was only trying to do the job he was given. He didn't ask to be captain of the ship. The responsibility was thrust upon him—he was practically still a boy. He wants the same thing as you, Jackson—to help the people of Earth and make the world a safe place again."

Jackson briefly wonders how Claire has the intelligence to do such great work while also maintaining such grand delusions about her son, despite all the evidence before her. But he chooses to save his energy for more important questions. Whatever Claire's delusions, they are irrelevant to him. Nonetheless, he feels he owes her some measure of reality, if for no other reason than the contributions she's already made to his agenda.

"Claire," he says, trying to be gentle as he reminds himself that, regardless of how he feels about the brat, Seth Harris is her son. "You must know that when the Green Grow 3 returns to Earth, I cannot promise the safety of its captain, no matter who it is. Not after all the hardship his decisions have caused my people. They are angry and will demand consequences for his choices."

Claire bites her bottom lip fiercely, eyes moist. Jackson is sure she's suppressing a response he doesn't care to hear. She seems to come to some decision as she studies him intently.

"In that case," she says with conviction, "he won't be the captain when we return to Earth."

"Oh?" Jackson asks, surprised once more. "What will he be?" He can see that the question makes Claire angry, but her emotional state has no bearing on the reality before them.

"He is a biochemist by training. He will work with me in my lab, like he was planning to do before Captain MacAbee foolishly left him in charge and then disappeared." *A scientist? The brat is a scientist? Who knew?* Jackson wants to laugh aloud. But that would likely end the conversation, and there are still things he wants to know.

"And what do you think he will do when he realizes Lizzie is gone?" he asks Claire, wondering if she has a brilliant plan to address this colossal problem or whether she really is that ignorant of her own son's nature.

"I'm sure he'll be quite upset," she says thoughtfully, her gaze distant as if she's weighing the consequences of her proposal, "but what can he do? Only you can activate the transporter, and he will feel obligated to continue with his duties to get the ship home. I didn't raise a shirker, you know." Claire smiles weakly, a poor attempt at humor that only makes Jackson further question her knowledge of who she raised.

"Perhaps it could work," he says noncommittally. "Who do you envision the captain to be when the ship returns?"

"That's my problem to solve," Claire says sharply. "Do you want my help transporting Liz or not?"

Jackson is surprised by her pluck, but he doesn't chide her. "The capsule is too small to accommodate a third person," he says, "but if Lizzie happens to be in one of the crates when we return to Earth—safely and securely, mind you, in a crate clearly marked as requiring immediate attention—I'll do what I can to keep her there."

Claire studies him with fiery eyes, perhaps considering whether this is a wise arrangement, or maybe only ticking through the things she'd like to say but won't. He's certain his response is less than she hoped, but it's what he'll give.

"Fine," she hisses, "I'll sedate her and get her into a crate. I'll give her enough to keep her under at least twelve hours after you arrive on Earth, and I'll mark the crate as containing perishable medical supplies." Her eyes are defiant as they meet Jackson's, an invitation to challenge what she says next.

"Let's not forget that this benefits both of us. I expect you will remember this when we get back to Earth."

Jackson smiles in that way that people seem to find warm. "Rest assured," he says, "the people of Earth appreciate everything you have done and everything you will undoubtedly do. You are making an immeasurable difference."

Claire looks at him suspiciously, a mix of emotions written on her face. She nods and turns to go but stops before she reaches the door. "Jackson?" she says, looking tired and vulnerable as she turns back toward him. "Please don't take my son from me. For the sake of everything I've done to help you, for the sake of everything I will do. I will do anything. Please."

Jackson can't help but feel sorry for her. He knows that loss can be very hard, and Claire has been useful. He needs her to remain hopeful, at least for now.

"You are a brilliant woman, Claire," he begins, "and you have time to develop a plan. I intend him no harm as the ship travels back to Earth." She only looks at him before she turns and leaves the room.

As the door begins to close behind her, Jackson sees her exchange words with one of the security officers posted outside. He's certain it's that man, Ellis—the old woman's man.

If Ruth discovers Claire's plan, she will surely interfere. *But she won't find out,* Jackson tells himself. The walls are thick on this level, and too well insulated for eavesdropping. And Jackson clears the room of any listening devices each time he enters it, with his pocket-sized EMP. If anyone finds out about Claire's plan, it will be by her mistake, and Lizzie will have no reason to suspect that he has any responsibility for stripping her away from her beloved Seth Harris.

"Are you reassessing the plan, my love?" Shelby asks, pulling his attention back into the room.

"No," he says, "this changes nothing."

"Good." She smiles. "I can't wait to see the brat in the cage." Jackson smiles back at her, thinking of the large cage in his camp where disputes are resolved—in favor of whoever survives, of course.

"I've come to realize that he is formidable," he says. "It will be a good fight."

"Who will you put in with him?" Shelby asks eagerly, excitement building in her eyes. "Shall we invite the other captains? I'm sure Mackey would relish time in the cage with him. After you, of course—if there's anything left of him when you are done. And I'd like to see my mother. We'll have enough food for everyone, and I know the crews would enjoy the celebration."

"Maybe you should have the first round with him," Jackson says affectionately. "You, too, are formidable—ferocious. I haven't forgotten that."

"Hmm ..." she says, cocking her head. "I hadn't considered it, but I like the idea."

"We have time to hash out the details."

"And Claire?" she asks.

"No." Jackson shakes his head. "She must be spared. She still has much to offer. I'll hide her away in a lab, I suppose." Shelby looks disappointed, but he knows she understands.

"She doesn't know her son at all, does she?" she asks, sounding curious.

"No, love, I don't think she does. But whatever dissension follows from her act can only work in our benefit."

"Indeed." She goes to the bed to stretch herself out, much like a cat. He loves the way she moves. "But how will Lizzie respond?"

"I will need to handle the situation carefully," he says, already working through various possibilities and scenarios in his mind.

"Alex will be pleased," Shelby says, and this makes Jackson smile.

"Yes, he will, but let's not mention anything to him yet. I don't want to get his hopes up. Lizzie is crafty, and we cannot yet know if Claire's plan will work."

"Yes, love," Shelby agrees. "She is much like you— strong and powerful."

Jackson smiles, not because of Shelby's words but because of how she looks at him when she says them, like a wild cat who can't wait to pounce on him. Even here in this place, this place where she can barely tolerate the gravity, she looks at him with desire—voracious desire.

He goes to her, extending his hand to lightly caress her hair.

"It's all coming together, love," he whispers in her ear as he lies next to her on the bed. "It's all coming together."

"And what about Omega?" she asks as he trails his fingers down her neck, dipping his chin to touch her skin with his lips.

"Nothing yet, but I'm sure we'll intercept the feed soon." He moves closer to her body as he wraps his arms around her, loving the feeling that he still has so much to discover about her even though he's had her so many times. It never gets old. He hears her gasp as his lips reach her collarbone, her back arching slightly toward him, inviting him to discover her anew. He's careful not to lean into her too heavily, to place too much weight on her already-taxed body. And then he lets his desire carry him, away from his thoughts, away from the Green Grow 3 and away from all of the steps still remaining in this journey—at least for a little while.

CHAPTER 25

EMPTY SEAT

***

"Why would Jackson transport mice to Omega?" Seth asks, striding into Mathilda's office and closing the door behind him. She looks up, startled, and he can see the fatigue on her face.

"What are you talking about?" she asks, turning away from a keyboard and one of several monitors to face him.

"Mice," he says briskly. "Mice. Jackson told Liz that he sent mice to Omega when he tested his transporter. Why?"

She sighs deeply, leaning back in her well-used office chair. She takes off her glasses and rubs her eyes, motioning to a chair covered in a stack of paper. "You might as well sit down," she says.

Annoyed, Seth roughly moves the papers to the floor, wondering how Mathilda can stand to be in such a cluttered space, much less be productive, as he squeezes himself between two stacks of file boxes to sit.

"When Jackson sent us the Hubble data, the most obvious information was Omega's coordinates," she begins. "We used those to set our course and plan the accelerations. But the data set contains much more information about the planet, information that suggests that Omega may be capable of supporting human life." She pauses, looking at Seth expectantly as if she knows he needs a moment to process the implications of this. He does. His mind is reeling.

"How long have you known about this?" he asks, feeling his confusion morph into anger. She seems surprised at the question.

"Since he sent the data," she says, as if it should be obvious. "The information is right there—I knew in a matter of hours."

"And you didn't think to mention it?" Seth demands.

"Really, Seth?" she retorts. "When should I have mentioned it? When you had me confined like a prisoner? Or perhaps after Jarrod finished pleading with you to shoot me, like you shot Willow and Zag? Besides, you never asked!"

"I didn't realize it was my job to ask." His voice is icy. "I thought it was your job to tell me things I need to know."

"Oh, come on," Mathilda says in disgust. "You didn't wonder about Omega? I mean, why that planet? Why that location? You didn't think Jackson had some reason for sending us to a place light-years away? Maybe if you hadn't been so busy villainizing me, it would have occurred to you."

How could Mathilda withhold this from him? He has no idea how this information would have changed things, but he's certain it would have. *Is she still loyal to Jackson, or is she being petty?* he wonders. He finds both possibilities equally infuriating.

"Perhaps it didn't occur to me because I have no intention of traveling to a planet light-years away. The only reason I've cooperated with Jackson's demands this long is because he seems to be the only person with any constructive ideas about how to get us home! But, as soon as we verify that the new thrusters work and that we can generate fuel, I'm putting a stop to this charade and turning the ship around."

Mathilda's mouth drops open as she looks at him with wide eyes.

"What?" she demands. "You think I've been withholding relevant information, but you don't find it relevant to share this plan of yours with the council?"

"Perhaps I would find it relevant if the council supported me. But if they aren't outright working against me—as you did—they waste everyone's time bickering. Someone has to lead this crew, and it's apparent to me that my best decisions are the ones I make alone." Seth only realizes he's screaming when Mathilda shrinks back, biting her lip as if she's afraid of him.

He inhales deeply, raking his fingers through his hair, his elbows tucked tightly against his ribs to avoid toppling the boxes on either side. Now isn't the time to be angry. Maybe the time has passed, or maybe he can be angry later. But at this moment, Liz is lying in the medical unit, her brain under attack by what Seth now believes is mostly likely a sentient being trying to communicate through her. He needs information, not an argument. He closes his eyes. *I choose to be calm. I choose to be calm.*

"So," he begins in an even tone, "Jackson transported mice to Omega. Why?" He's surprised to see that his change in tone has an immediate effect on Mathilda, who relaxes back into her chair and begins to speculate.

"To see if they'd survive, maybe? To gather data? I'm not sure. I mean, the Hubble data makes it look promising, but that's a far cry from knowing whether humans could live there. What did he tell Liz?"

"He claimed he was trying to confirm Omega's coordinates, but I doubt that's the real reason. The mice were fitted with some kind of sensors, but he didn't say what they were for."

"Probably one of his half-truths," Mathilda mutters, glancing back to her computer monitor for a moment before her eyes drift off. "You know, I don't think he ever actually lied to me. When he showed up here with Shelby, I was sure he'd lied to me. But when I started thinking about it—really thinking about it—I realized that he only let me believe what I wanted. He told me just enough to read into his words whatever I wanted them to mean, and he never actually promised anything. He never even told me he loved me."

"Mathilda," Seth says, feeling exhausted and older than his years, "I wish I could tell you that I'm sorry Jackson deceived you, but what I'm actually sorry about is that you fell for it. He is who he is, but I thought you were smarter than that."

He can see he's hurt her, but she doesn't protest. "Apparently not," she says sourly, "and I don't know why Jackson transported mice to Omega, not precisely. But I may know at least one of the reasons he transported himself here. Would you like to hear it, *Captain?*"

"Yes," Seth replies, ignoring her sarcasm, "I would very much like to hear it."

She draws herself up in her chair and begins to explain. "When Jackson transmitted the Hubble data, I noticed a notes file in one of the data fields. I doubt he meant to attach it, but it would have been easy to overlook given the intricacy of the file structure. The notes related to a deep space probe, called the Walkabout 2. Somehow, Jackson reprogrammed it to head toward Omega. Based on my calculations of its speed, location, and the transmittal speed of the data, I think we may be close enough now to tap into its data feed.

"The probe is streaming information back to Earth, but it takes time to travel through space. Since we're closer to the probe, we could receive the data first, before it gets back to Earth. I think Jackson came, at least in part, because he wants to see the data."

"But why come here?" Seth asks. "His tablets communicate in real time."

"Yes, but the Walkabout 2 doesn't," Mathilda replies, smiling for the first time since Seth arrived. "His tablets require special hardware, an antenna the Walkabout 2 doesn't have. The probe has been flying in space longer than we've been alive, so he can't upgrade its hardware. I doubt he was even able to send its course adjustments in real time, although given what I saw in the notes file, it was already headed in the approximate direction of Omega. Relatively speaking, it would have been a minor correction."

"What would the data tell us?" Seth asks, his mind racing with questions and implications. Does the executive board know about Omega too? *No,* he thinks, *we didn't even know we were going toward Omega until after we left orbit. The executive board doesn't know where we're going.* Or do they? Seth can't be certain, and the weight of this terrifies him.

Mathilda's voice pulls him back to their conversation. "I'm sure it will give us more detailed information about Omega, but we can't know what until we see the data. The Walkabout 2 is closer to Omega than we are, but it's still pretty far away. I'm sure it's outfitted with powerful cameras and an array of sensors—it was built to explore space and send back data. But who knows? It could tell us a lot, or nothing at all."

"Does Jackson know you have this information?" Seth asks, and Mathilda's eyes instantly narrow in anger.

"I don't know what Jackson knows! I don't know why he does what he does, or what he thinks! He doesn't communicate with me anymore, not since he's been talking to you and Liz. And he never was fully honest with me, anyway, although I'm sure you'll interpret that statement of fact as one of self-pity."

Seth studies her for a minute, realizing that she must feel very alone. But that isn't his responsibility.

"Can you intercept the data stream?" he asks, and she waves meekly to one of the computers behind her.

"I've already written a program to scan for the probe's signal. It's been running since Jackson arrived. When we intercept the data stream, I'll know."

"I'm sure you will," Seth says quietly. "And I would like to know, too."

"Sure," she says bitterly, "since you asked. I guess you still need me after all, don't you?"

"Of course I need you," Seth says sharply. "I always needed you! You're the one who broke our trust, not me. You're the one who chose to put the ship and the crew at risk when I needed you the most! And every time you withhold information, like you did about Omega, it's another reminder of why I can't trust you."

"So, you need me but you don't trust me?" she whispers, blinking tears away. "Well, I suppose at least you're honest about that."

Seth doesn't know whether to feel sorry for her or be disgusted. Regardless, he can't concern himself with it now, not after everything he just learned.

"I want to know when you access the data," he says, rising from the cramped chair and leaving her cluttered office to return to his own.

***

"Acceleration to commence in three, two, one ..."

Seth closes his eyes, trying to forget that the place Liz normally occupies on the bridge is empty. She's still in the medical unit, where she will undoubtedly remain for the foreseeable future. He repeats the mantra he knows so well, trying to still the flutter of panic in his chest as the acceleration begins to compress his body. *I choose to be still. I choose to be still.* He feels trapped, like he's suffocating.

An image of Liz flashes into his mind, looking so small and vulnerable in the medical unit bed. His panic grows. *Stop it,* he tells himself, forcing himself to think about anything but her, but she's all he can think about.

He turns his attention to the voice she hears—Abby. As crazy as it seems that Liz's mind is being invaded by a telepathic entity, Seth believes it's true. It explains everything he's been unable to explain—the electrical surges and her seizures—and the timing aligns with Jackson activating his transporter to come to the ship.

If Jackson trapped Abby when he used his machine, he's probably the only one who can send her home. But, so far, he's been too arrogant and, ironically, narrow-minded to believe that Abby is real.

When the lightbulbs exploded and the medical monitor melted, Seth assumed it was evidence enough for anyone to believe Liz's story. But as soon as she was moved to a different room and a maintenance team was deployed to deal with the damage, the discussion between Jackson and Claire picked up right where it had left off—exploring the connection between the 4G acceleration and her brain, and discussing the merits of treatment on Earth.

Their discussion continued until Seth insisted that Ellis escort Jackson back to his quarters. But then, not even fifteen minutes later, Seth got a report that his mother was in Jackson's quarters, supposedly treating Shelby, clearly a ruse. He could have interrupted the secret meeting, forced his mother to leave, but why? Wouldn't that make him just like her? Besides, separating them won't solve the problem at hand.

Seth remembers his mom mentioning Liz's parahippocampal gyrus in the brain scan, and he remembers from articles he read years ago that psychic phenomena were linked to activity in that part of the brain. He doesn't remember if the research was conclusive, and what would it prove anyway? That Liz is psychic? No, that's not the problem he needs to solve. So what is the problem?

Mom doesn't believe that Liz is telling the truth.

He has no way to prove, beyond all doubt, that Abby is real, or that she's communicating with Liz. He can't afford to waste his time or energy convincing people who do not want to be convinced that Liz is telling the truth. Surely there is something he can do to help her, but what? His mind spins, flailing for answers but finding none.

Later, Seth sits on the edge of his bed, looking at its vast emptiness. He can't sleep here tonight, not without Liz. It's not her absence that makes it unbearable—they each have their own quarters and sleep alone as much as they sleep together. It's the knowledge that Liz *can't* be here that makes it unbearable for him to lie down, to rest his head on the pillow that Liz tends to bury her face in after he gets up. He's seen her do it, although she hasn't noticed him watching.

Seth runs his fingers across the pillowcase, where Liz's head should be, and something occurs to him. If Abby was pulled into Jackson's wormhole when he transported a mouse to Omega, does that mean she's on Omega too?

Does it matter if she is? For some reason that he can't articulate, he suspects it does matter—a great deal.

CHAPTER 26

FREE WILL

***

OCTOBER 29, 2059—WEDNESDAY

Ruth takes in the scene around her, unsure how the task at hand can be accomplished before the morning acceleration. Her eyes scan the disarray of crates and people, interspersed with makeshift pens of livestock and heaps of produce, and she wonders if Captain Harris will consider canceling the acceleration. It seems the only sensible option, but what is sensible about any of this? *I'm sure he'll find a way to proceed,* she thinks, admiring his determination while regretting it at the same time.

Ruth has been here for hours, watching Level 37 transform from a silent, barren place to a busy, bustling one, the kind of busy that feels frantic and chaotic. The lights seem too bright, and for the first time since she arrived on the Green Grow 3, she cannot deny that she's on a space ship. The only thing separating her from a freezing, suffocating death is the hull, and it doesn't seem nearly thick enough to protect her. The thought of it makes her shiver.

Until now, it's been easy to forget where she is. The growing levels are lush and Earth-like, and the residential areas feel much like the inside of a dormitory. Sure, there are large, round windows along the corridors, where anyone can look at the stars sprinkled across a backdrop of nothingness. But Ruth never wanted to look, and the windows were easy enough to ignore. To her, they were nothing more than a contrived anomaly, artful adornments meant to break up the empty walls of the corridors. They weren't really a lifesaving barrier, separating her from a deadly void on the other side.

But she cannot ignore what lies before her now. The trees on Level 37 have been cleared—all of them—to make space for Jackson's machine, and for the staging and packaging of everything he will allegedly transport to Earth. She can see the entire level, from hull to hull. She can see the curved walls that enclose them, and the sky-like ceiling that feels artificial without the trees. The large tube in the center of the level, with the passenger lifts and an entrance to a large airlock, is the only familiar point of reference, and even that seems alien now. All that remains of the earthy forest that used to be here is the smell of cut wood and the dirt floor, covered in pine needles and compacted under the traffic of the feet and busily working machines.

The trees were leveled yesterday, the stumps ground to make the surface safe and easy to traverse. Now, the pile of logs, which seemed so large before, continues to shrink as the trees are processed by a lumber mill. The mill hasn't stopped running since it was assembled a few hours ago, chewing through the wood with a violent whine as it reduces what used to be living trees into uniform planks of lumber.

It feels chaotic, but Ruth can see a rhythm and a process in the activity around her. The mill transforms the trees into planks. The planks are then moved to another work station, where they are cut to length and nailed into crates. The crates are delivered to yet another station, set up close to the utility lift on the outer edge of the level, where they are filled with a variety of goods and nailed shut. Then, the packaged goods are moved to the station with the green goo, which Ruth has gathered must be sprayed on each crate to a thickness of two inches. The stuff hardens as it dries, much more quickly than Ruth would've thought, and then the crate is delivered to the platform, where Jackson is directing the loading of the crates onto his machine. He looks like a gleeful child, playing with large, green blocks.

Ruth turns her attention to the station where the crates are filled. The utility lift doors open, and a tractor drives off, pulling a trailer full of produce. Ruth finds it strange, how the utility lift always seemed so much bigger than the passenger lifts in the center of the ship, but now it looks small. A group of people, including some of her own, converge upon the tractor to unload it. Some take down sacks of corn and wheat. Ruth heard that rice will come later, once the land is prepared and planted. Others pass box after box down an assembly line of hands—apples and peaches and cherries, delicate items that have somehow withstood the 4G accelerations. She sees bags of mangoes, papayas, avocado, and pineapples, mixed with small boxes of kiwi and berries. She sees oranges, lemons, bananas, and limes.

Did she even know they grew this many different things? She must have known, although she hasn't worked on all the levels. Some of the fruit is dried, some of it fresh, stacked neatly next to bags of nuts. She sees potatoes and sweet potatoes, onions, cabbage and kale. It's hard to imagine sending this much food back to Earth, although she thinks of the depots and knows that shuttle after shuttle used to come daily to restock the shelves. She sees Dr. Singh checking an open crate full of medical supplies, giving instructions to a man who's stacking bolts of cloth to ensure that he doesn't crush the supplies. She sees reams of paper, and even stacks of lumber that apparently don't need to be sprayed in green goo. It seems strange that they would send lumber, but what isn't strange about any of this?

Captain Harris is standing near Jackson, his eyes scanning the entirety of the operation. He hasn't left Jackson's side, even though Ellis and Will stand watch over him and the woman whose gaze makes Ruth want to shrink. *Where is Liz?* she wonders. Ruth hasn't seen or spoken to her since their conversation three days ago, and she's getting increasingly worried.

In fact, Liz is the reason that Ruth is here, watching everything transpire even though she's been assigned no task in this melee and has no official function to perform. Liz is the reason that Ruth will stay until the shipment is sent. All of the Fifty-Two working here today have been alerted to watch out for a prepackaged crate marked "perishable medical supplies," but Ruth feels the need to be here, anyway, to watch with her own eyes as each crate is packed and loaded. She has to make sure Liz isn't transported back to Earth against her will, even though she's certain that Dr. Harris told Jackson that she would send Liz with the second shipment, not the first.

Ruth hasn't yet figured out how to tell Captain Harris about the conversation the children overheard between the doctor and Jackson yesterday while they listened from the vent shaft. She's still trying to wrap her own mind around what they reported, although she knows they speak the truth. Ruth wants to redeem herself with the captain, but she's not sure that reporting his own mother's betrayal will endear her to him. She has no idea how he'll take the news, and thought it might be better received with more information to report. But so far, Jackson has revealed nothing else useful, and Ruth must tell the captain before the next shipment is scheduled, regardless of how he reacts.

The remaining crates are filled, sealed, sprayed, and stacked quickly, and the noise across the level starts to die down. Even the lumber mill stops screaming, as one final crate is delivered to the platform and stacked on top. Captain Harris refers to a clipboard, nodding thoughtfully before handing it to Jackson. Jackson studies it and then nods once, both men somber. Ruth nearly jumps as a goat bleats from a makeshift pen behind her, breaking the heavy silence.

Captain Harris raises his eyes, addressing the crew, who wait silently for him to speak.

"Good work, everyone." His voice booms across the empty level. "We have thirty minutes to get the livestock loaded. Let's get it done, so you can all get back to your quarters for the morning acceleration."

His voice lacks its usual vigor. It contains no notes of encouragement or hopefulness. It's as dead as the level around them. The crew return to motion, loading the livestock into large crates already waiting near the pens. Everything is going according to plan. Ruth watches the seemingly oblivious animals walk into the crates with little fuss. In a few short minutes, the crates are sealed and sprayed with goo, needing only a few more minutes to harden and dry before they're lifted onto the platform. Ruth wonders if the animals are afraid. If they aren't, they should be.

As the last crates are loaded, emanating muffled cries of pigs and cows, Ruth watches Jackson reach into a leather satchel and produce a laptop. He huddles over the keyboard, furtively scanning his surroundings as if worried about who may be watching. Ruth thinks this is probably the truest expression she's seen on his scarred face. He reaches into an inner jacket pocket and produces a small box, which he carefully opens to remove a small vial that appears to contain liquid metal. He holds the vial in one hand and types on his laptop with the other. A small door opens in the base of the machine, and he inserts the tube before closing it again.

He dramatically scans the crowd, proclaiming loudly, "I shall activate the transporter now! Make sure you are at least ten feet away from the platform." Ruth watches several of the crew members step back, even though the only person within ten feet of the machine is Jackson.

Jackson backs away from the machine and returns his attention to the laptop, typing furiously. Ruth hears a sound—something between a hum and a whoosh. She feels a strange sensation of gravity, pulling her the wrong way but only for a second. She blinks quickly as the crates on the platform appear to evaporate, going wavy and transparent like a mirage on a hot desert horizon, and then they are gone. The process concludes with a brief popping noise, although Ruth isn't sure if the sound is inside or outside her head. The platform is empty, as if nothing was ever there. All that remains is the smell of ozone, so strong that it overpowers every hint of the cut wood that permeated the air before.

She sees Captain Harris exchange a few quiet words with Jackson, his expression unreadable, and then he turns away from the machine to face the crew, huddled together in much the same way Ruth's own people huddled outside the fence at the depot, waiting to be saved. But before the captain can speak, Jackson addresses them first.

"Thanks to each of you for your help in this momentous task!" he says loudly, arms outstretched. "I cannot express how important this is, how appreciated by the people who are barely surviving on Earth. I cannot express how necessary this is, for all of our survival." He takes a breath, as if he plans to continue, but Captain Harris interjects.

"Yes, thank you everyone." His booming voice carries easily across the level. "We are planning a second shipment, which will be ready in a few days. Check with your department heads about assignments, and in the meantime, prepare yourselves for the morning acceleration. Everyone is dismissed."

Ruth watches as Captain Harris guides Jackson and the woman to the passenger lift, followed closely by Ellis and Will. Ruth wonders if it's safe to be this close to Jackson's machine, if they should be anywhere near it when he activates it. She wonders if the livestock will survive the trip, if the food will be safe to eat when it arrives. Of course, she knows it will be eaten anyway, possibly by the very men who chased them down at the depot, those who survived Liz's fury, anyway. So what does she care if it's safe? There was a time in Ruth's life when she would have chastised herself for a judgment like this, for judging the worth of another human as less than her own. But that time is long gone, that gracious part of her smothered by everything she's witnessed since the world fell apart.

She waits a minute longer before stepping onto a crowded lift headed to Level 3, to return to her quarters for yet another miserable ten-minute acceleration. She knows she will spend the time wondering about Liz, and wondering how she will tell Captain Harris that his mother is planning to betray him.

***

Liz, you need to wake up now. Abby's voice penetrates the darkness of Liz's dreamless sleep. She doesn't want to leave the void, the peace of nothingness that makes her forget everything bad, along with everything good, but Abby's voice persists. *Liz, I know you're tired. I know you're damaged. But it's important to wake now. You must wake.*

Liz's eyes flutter open to the familiar dimness of the medical unit.

"Hello there, sleepyhead," Jackson says, smiling at her in a way that makes her want to like him as he leans in to brush a strand of hair off her forehead.

"Jackson," she whispers, "what are you doing here?"

"Waiting for you to wake up of course," he replies, smiling. "Claire wants to scan your brain again, but I told her we should at least wait until you …"

He did it again, Abby whispers, overwriting whatever Jackson is saying.

"What?" Liz whispers. "What did he do?"

He used his machine, she says, *the one that pulled me away from my home. Why did he use it again, before he corrected the mistake he made in bringing me here?*

"What do you mean, Lizzie?" Jackson asks, looking confused.

"Abby," Liz whispers.

"The alien?" Jackson asks. "Is it talking to you again?"

It? Abby snaps, sending a shard of pain through Liz's left eye. *I am no "it." I am divinely created from the great black womb of nothing, and I am no alien!*

"Her name is Abby, Jackson. She says you used your machine again. Is it true?"

"Yes," he says softly, "we sent the first shipment of goods to Earth, a shipment that will feed many people."

"Abby wants to go home. Can you use your machine to send her home?"

"Of course!" Jackson nods. "I only need the coordinates."

"Coordinates?"

"Yes, I need to know the location of her home, so I can connect the proper wormhole."

My home is not defined by coordinates! Abby's voice gets louder with every syllable. Liz's ears ring, and she closes her eyes to fight a wave of nausea.

Raise your vibration. She doesn't know if she's talking to herself or to Abby, but she thinks it again and again. *Raise your vibration.* After a moment, or possibly an eternity, she feels a sense of calm permeate her mind.

I come from beyond linear time and space, Abby says, her voice soft once more. *I have no coordinates.*

"Can't you just send her back to wherever she entered?" Liz asks her brother.

"Lizzie," he responds, laughing, "surely if this alien is advanced enough to communicate telepathically, it's advanced enough to know where it comes from! Coordinates are a simple matter."

Liz gasps at the sudden wave of searing pain in her head. She presses her palm tightly over her left eye to keep it from exploding in its socket.

"Her name is Abby," she snarls at Jackson, "and you're making her angry!" A video monitor on the wall across the room suddenly turns itself on, the screen alternating between a sheet of blue and waves of static. Jackson looks at the monitor briefly before turning his attention back to Liz.

"I only connected two points with a wormhole. If *she* came from somewhere else, if *she* saw the mouse and then came through the wormhole, it's because she chose to do it. I cannot be responsible for her choice."

Liz braces for another wave of pain, but it doesn't come. Instead, Abby seems to consider Jackson's words. *He speaks of free will,* she says. *I will accept this answer for now, while I consider the relevant implications. But I do not concede.*

What does that mean?

But Jackson speaks again. "I will happily send her wherever she wishes to go, but she must provide coordinates."

I must do nothing! Abby's voice booms once more in her mind. *How dare this insufferable creature place such demands upon me? How dare he continue to use his machine so arrogantly when he cannot know the implications of what he is doing? How dare he deny accountability for what he has done?* Liz feels her hands fly to her temples, pressing against her head as if she can somehow contain her mind as it once more explodes into pieces. *I should destroy him,* Abby roars. *I should destroy him like the inconsequential piece of matter he is.*

"If you destroy him, you'll never get home," Liz cries out, her high-pitched voice echoing in her head. "If you destroy him, I will not help you, no matter what you do." She can sense her hands pressing hard against her head, but they do nothing to contain Abby's anger. Then, it's suddenly all gone—Abby's voice, the pain, the room in the medical unit and Jackson's form beside her. She is falling again, back into the void where there is no pain or joy or awareness, back into that place of nothingness where she suffers no more.

CHAPTER 27

THE MASTER RETURNS

***

"I'll go first, my love," Jackson says, flashing Shelby a grin he doesn't have to force. He carefully props the large grate against the wall, tucking his multi-tool back into his leather bag before slinging it over his head and onto his back. Shelby crouches next to him and peers dubiously into the ventilation shaft.

"I know, it's a bit unorthodox," Jackson says, placing one hand gently between her shoulder blades, "but we don't have far to go."

Shelby looks at him, her thoughts a mystery. She moves back from the opening. "Let's just say it's part of the adventure."

"Indeed!" he says, pleased that she's always so willing to support him. "Soon enough you'll be feasting and celebrating like the queen you are. You'll feel light as air, like an angel with wings." He kisses her lips, lingering for a moment to soak up the spark he feels every time he touches her, then he crawls into the ventilation shaft, pausing a few feet in to make sure she's behind him. It's ridiculous, and he's glad that no one apart from him and Shelby ever need know that he had to skulk around the Green Grow 3 like a rat. But he cannot have his business, or his whereabouts, known to Seth Harris. He won't give him a chance to somehow interfere with his plans to come back or otherwise take advantage of his short absence. Besides, he wants Harris to think his affairs on Earth are under control, not on the brink of spinning completely out.

The day's final 4G acceleration is done, and he and Shelby have been shut in for the night. They will be back before anyone knows they're gone, but even still, Jackson is pleased to give Shelby's body a break from the heaviness of the increased gravity on the ship. He knows her circulatory system is struggling. He's noticed fluid pooling around her ankles and in her hands.

He hopes the short break on Earth will be enough to revive her, because he doesn't know how much longer he'll need to stay on the Green Grow 3. He thought they'd be well within range of the Walkabout 2, but he still hasn't picked up the feed. And now there is the issue of Lizzie's seizures, or perhaps—as she claims—the alien. That scenario is almost as confounding as folding the space-time continuum.

He crawls on, trying to be as quiet as possible, amazed at how silent Shelby is behind him. She's so graceful, in every way. He turns a corner and crawls the remaining distance to the vertical maintenance shaft. He climbs down the ladder, squeezing into the horizontal shaft on Level 2 that will lead them to the abandoned quarters where they exit the ventilation system and catch the lift down to collect the biocapsule, still stored in the airlock on level 37.

Jackson is pleased with how well the capsule is holding together. It's only slightly tacky, and he's certain it's safe to transport them back to Earth. He can make a new capsule for their return trip in his lab. Time is short, but he cannot cut corners.

Shelby perches herself on the transporter's platform while Jackson sets up the biocapsule, carefully checking it over one last time to make sure there are no nicks or chips. He offers her his hand as she climbs inside. Then he programs the machine, inserts a small glass tube of rubidium, sets a timer, and quickly climbs into the capsule with Shelby. He has just enough time to seal the hatch with a tube of bioglue before he hears the familiar hum and feels the buzz that he knows will carry him back to his headquarters on Earth.

***

Jackson can hear the cheers even as he pops the seal on the hatch. He knows he needs to exit with flair, stand up straight and proud to greet the people who have chosen to follow him, who have put their fates and lives in his hands. He kicks the hatch open and leaps out, standing up to his tallest height and glad that once more he is the tallest man in the room. He can smell the earth—it smells different than the soil on the Green Grow 3. Now that he's here, he realizes that he's missed it. Or maybe what he's really missed is the devotion of these people who actually want him around.

The cheers and screams erupt as he raises his hands high, bellowing out a greeting to his people. Then he turns back to the capsule, extending his hand. Shelby reaches out to take it, then steps out lightly, smiling with the radiance that only she can exude. The cheers turn into a roar of clapping and yelling. Here in this place, things are as they should be—he is royalty.

"The master of the house returns!" Alex bellows, standing off to the right. "And he brings food!"

Jackson smiles and bows, soaking up all the attention. Nothing can be heard over the roar of the people. In this moment, he is no mere man. He is a god.

He turns his attention to the wall of the cave behind him, striding over to the stack of crates still covered in the bioglue. This is where he transported the goods, to the large cavern in the old woman's cave. Mirrors hang all over the stone walls and ceiling, an interesting albeit low-tech idea to increase the yield of the plants by reflecting light.

He picks up a hatchet and brings it down hard on one of the crates. The biofilm makes a sharp cracking noise as it splits. He hits it one more time and the front of the crate falls open, hitting the ground with a sharp crack. Four goats tumble out, bleating in terror as the crowd screams even louder. He scoops one up in his arms, raising it high, before setting it down on the ground, stroking its back gently before ushering it back toward the others. Shelby kneels down, petting each of them.

"A small tribute from the Green Grow 3!" Jackson cries, raising his hands to quiet the crowd. "As you saw with your own eyes, Shelby and I have just returned. Didn't I tell you it was conquered?"

The crowd screams.

"Did you doubt me?"

Waves of laughter wash over the crowd.

"No! Never!" they scream. He soaks it up for a moment before raising his hands to quiet the people.

"Good," he says, as the room becomes so quiet that he can hear the echo of his own voice. "I'm glad you still believe in me. At least most of you." He pauses, feeling the tension in the room grow as the silence lingers.

"Regrettably, there is someone here who doesn't believe in me, who doesn't believe in *us*," Jackson says, casting a sidelong glance at Zack Butler. The man's ruddy face flushes, betraying his otherwise unflappable expression.

"We are only as strong as our weakest link!" Jackson bellows. A dissonant murmur snakes through the crowd. "It's our strength that has gotten us this far. It's our strength that keeps us alive. Weakness will only get us killed, and I won't do that to you. I won't do it to myself. Not when we are so close!" He turns spreading his arms dramatically, motioning to the crates behind him. "We are so very close!"

He turns to face the crowd again. "You've chosen me to be your leader, and in return, I've made impossible things possible. Food. Medicine. Security. Transportation. Can anyone else here do what I've done?" His voice makes the mirrors vibrate, but no one makes a sound.

"Does anyone here challenge me for leadership?" He turns to face his opponent squarely, looking down on the man who could never be his equal. "Do you challenge me for leadership, Zack Butler?" He waits as the silence stretches on, the intensity of the crowd's gaze burning hotly on his skin. He can feel their energy rising, taking on a life of its own. These people only know one way to solve problems—Lizzie isn't wrong about that.

Butler's gaze falters. He hasn't had enough time to build the support he needs, and there's no way he can compete with the awe-inspiring fact that Jackson transported crate after crate of life-giving sustenance from a spaceship an unfathomable distance away into this very room.

"Why are you looking at me?" Butler demands. Jackson is amused that he intends to bluff his way out of this. He only smiles and turns to face the crowd.

"Why am I looking at him?" Jackson asks.

"Because he's a liar!" a voice cries out from the back of the crowd. "He told me yesterday that you abandoned us, that you weren't coming back!"

"He's lost his faith, and he's trying to take us down with him!!" another voice screams as the crowd begins to press forward.

"He's the weak link!" Others echo the cry.

Jackson can feel his power returning. He is regaining control of his people, and he revels in the satisfaction of everything he's accomplished since he transported himself to the Green Grow 3. Three days ago, these people were slipping away from him, their confidence in his vision waning. But now everything is different. He's delivered the impossible—a whole storehouse of food from the Green Grow 3. No one in the New Generation can doubt now that he's conquered the ship, even if he knows there are still wrinkles to be ironed out. And now he's provided a new outlet for everyone's fear and anger. He's offering them a traitor, a scapegoat.

"We are only as strong as our weakest link!" Jackson cries, quieting the crowd. "If this man is your standard for strength," he says with disgust, motioning to Butler, "then follow him. But I will not have him any longer. I see now that he has become weak with greed and doubt. If you want to follow me, dispense with this weak link, and then we will feast!"

Jackson's ears register the terrified bleating of the goats behind him, and then the roar of the crowd drowns out every other noise. He can feel the heat of their bodies as they rush the traitor. The man is formidable, and it's a shame he chose this path, but not even he can stand against so many pressing and crushing him, wanting to taste his blood and have a hand in his demise. Butler was a good leader, but Jackson knows that his dissent is by far the most valuable service he could possibly provide. Crushing the heretic will bind Jackson's followers together, and further into his service. At least for now.

Jackson turns his back to the fray, to Shelby who holds two small goats, rubbing her nose on their fur. Alex holds the other two, looking attentively at him and unabashed by the mob that is crushing and beating a man to death just a few feet away.

"Shall we open the doors to the feast?" Alex asks, pointing with his chin toward the large solid doors, locked and guarded at the far end of the.

"Give them a few minutes," Jackson says, taking a white goat from Shelby, who seems more interested in one with black and brown spots. "Let's take these goats away from this madness, and then we will open the doors."

Thirty minutes later, Jackson sits at the head table in the dining hall, looking out across the hundreds of faces reveling in joy and hope and loyalty that desperately needed rekindling. He knows that this feast is a temporary patch, like the biofilm that protects him in the wormhole but quickly degrades. But isn't all support temporary? People are foolish, and Jackson has seen firsthand that most of them will embrace any dream. They go whichever way the wind blows, wherever conditions seem most favorable, oblivious to the consequences of the endless cycle of mistakes they make again and again and again.

President Greene's ignorance of human nature got him killed. He naively thought that his pleas for patience could bind together starving people of mediocre intelligence. The president didn't realize that average people don't follow dreams—they follow men. His own followers chose to look the other way when he was murdered, and they blindly embraced the lunacy that followed. Greene's dream was forgotten before his cold body was even placed in the ground.

Jackson refuses to make that mistake. He knows that the loyalty of his army is a beast that requires regular feeding. It's exhausting, but he still needs these people—at least for now. And so, he will keep feeding the beast, literally and figuratively. He has to, because he's closer now than he's ever been to getting what he wants, or at least the first thing he wants—immutable control of the New Generation. He must control the wolf pack so that he can rise above it, and not just his faction but all of them. Then, and only then, he can start a conversation with the Green Grow executive board—if he still deems them worthy of conversation, that is.

It now seems strange to Jackson that he used to think of Green Grow as the gold standard, not just for science but for civilization as well. He used to want so badly to be accepted among their ranks, to work together to expand the boundaries of scientific knowledge. But that was before he discovered Omega. Soon, he'll have a solid foothold on the new planet—assuming its habitable. He will control the exploration of Omega, as well as access to his transporter, and Green Grow will have to prove their value to him if they want to be included. It's only a matter of time.

Jackson looks out across his feasting horde, letting their adoration saturate him like a dried sponge. It fortifies him to return to the Green Grow 3, where his only supporter is Shelby, and even his own sister still seems to detest him. He finishes his meal and exits quietly with Shelby and Alex, letting the festivities continue as he returns to his new lab. It's much nicer than the last one, spacious and airy and full of equipment he didn't previously have. He's looking forward to spending more time here, but for now it's just a stopover—a place to collect more rubidium to fuel his machine. He gathers four more vials, hoping he won't need to use more than three. His supply is getting low.

He looks at the transporter assembled in his lab, thinking about Lizzie's claim that he mistakenly transported an alien to Omega. Part of him still desperately wants to convince her that it's a delusion. Maybe she will finally consent to appropriate medical treatment. But perhaps, farfetched as it seems, the alien is real. How else would Lizzie have known about his mouse trials? How else can he explain what happens when she claims to hear the voice?

But this alien is not behaving like Jackson imagines an advanced life form would behave. If it were real, wouldn't it communicate with him directly? It's his transporter, after all. And why isn't it more curious about humanity? Surely an intelligent entity would realize they have much to learn from each other, but this alien exhibits no curiosity. It only demands to be returned to its home. Does it truly want to return from where, or when, it originated, or does it intend to lay some claim to Omega?

Jackson has no desire to battle an alien for possession of Omega, but returning it to its point of origin could be an equally difficult problem. He has no idea where such an alien might have come from, no clue what coordinates to use for his transporter. The alien needs to tell him where it wants to go. And it—or rather, she—doesn't seem to know.

Jackson knows he needs to handle this carefully, especially after witnessing the alien's ferocious temper. He has no doubt it could destroy the Green Grow 3, and Jackson cannot allow that to happen. But neither can he transport the alien with no coordinates. Unless …

What if he calculates the farthest possible coordinates and sends the alien there? Based on what Lizzie conveyed, the alien didn't detect the transporter's energy signature until he arrived on the Green Grow 3. Earth must be too far away for it to sense, which means the alien's reach is limited.

Jackson knows what he must do. He will transport the alien far away, too far away from both Earth and Omega for the alien to sense. It should be simple enough to find appropriate coordinates, if he uses the star charts stored in his wrist implant.

He refills a tube of bioglue and appraises Alex one final time.

"I hope to be back in a few days," he says, taking in the man's continuously somber face, "but I'll let you know."

"Will there be another shipment?" Alex asks.

"Yes," Jackson replies thoughtfully, "I'll send you details when I have them."

"And the scouts?" Alex asks.

"Send them back out. Send a group with food and supplies to the maternity complex. The other groups can go on patrol—I want to know if any of Mackey's people are encroaching on our area. If Zack Butler was colluding with him, we'll need to keep our guard up. Oh, and also, set up a meeting with the other regional captains. I'll take it from my laptop on the ship, after the day's work is done there."

Alex nods resolutely and pauses, as if he's considering saying something else. Jackson waits. "Thank you for the pictures of Lizzie," the man finally says, and Jackson knows what's on his mind. He wants her to come back—to meet her in person. He wants the chance Jackson has promised him to win her heart. But he will be patient, Jackson knows. Alex takes him at his word.

"You're welcome," he says, deciding to answer his unasked question. "Hopefully you can meet her soon."

He inserts a fuel capsule into his transporter and sets the coordinates and the timer. He helps Shelby into the new capsule, and then steps in himself, feeling fortified as he seals the hatch with bioglue and waits to be transported to the Green

Grow 3. To make sure no one knows they left, he's programmed the machine to transport him back into the airlock on Level 37.

He's not looking forward to the heaviness of his body as the ship hurtles through space. He's not looking forward to crawling through the air vent up from Level 2 back to his assigned quarters on Level 1. But perhaps Shelby is right—he should simply call it adventure and be glad to do it. No one needs to know. And when they get back, he'll run another bath—for both of them this time. He still has milk and flowers to make it special, and he needs to use them before they go bad. Such things are far too extravagant to be done here where clean water is so very precious and milk far too rare to use for anything other than nourishment, but he might as well enjoy the amenities of the Green Grow 3.

He hears the familiar hum and feels the capsule buzz as they span the universe in a way no other human knows how to do. When it subsides, he pops the hatch, his body heavy with the increased gravity on the Green Grow 3, but his mind and heart are light once more.

CHAPTER 28

QUICKLY AND QUIETLY

***

OCTOBER 30, 2059—THURSDAY

Ruth hasn't been this nervous in years. She's known fear and determination. She's known worry and sadness, but this anxiety is different. It's the anxiety of waiting and watching as seconds tick by, knowing that it's almost time to admit to what she's done. She tells herself that she'll speak her piece, and whatever happens will happen. She won't have to be afraid. Will she feel any better? She doesn't know, but she won't have to wonder anymore.

She's certain Captain Harris must already know about her helping Jackson. Liz wouldn't hide the truth from him. They seem too close for that. Besides, Ellis thinks they were already under suspicion. Well, not *they* exactly. *She.* She was under suspicion. Ellis didn't come out and say it, but Liz must know that nothing happens among Ruth's people without her knowledge and approval.

She hopes the captain can at least appreciate her position, but it doesn't matter. She knows what she needs to do, and no matter how it makes her stomach churn, her breath flutter, and her heart pound, she will do it.

She asked Ellis to make introductions with the young man, to set up a time when she could see him. And the captain seemed to be gracious enough about it. He suggested Ellis bring her to his office after the morning acceleration.

She knows Jackson Goeff is there, somewhere on Level 1. It makes her nervous being this close to him, even though she doubts she'll see him. He is confined—contained. Even if he saw her, what would he conclude? She reminds herself that she cannot care any longer about what he thinks. She's chosen her side, and it's not his. Time to accept that he will be her enemy now, that whatever bridge connected them will be burned. Ruth thinks back briefly to the people who remained behind. They made their choice, and they are New Generation now—if they are still alive, that is.

Giving Ellis's hand a final squeeze in the lift, she tries to draw as much strength as she can for what she knows she must do. It steels her, reminding her that she's not a naïve girl anymore. She's an old woman, with years of experience. People are depending on her now. They always depend upon her now.

Ellis motions her toward the door of the captain's office. She knows she must go alone. Ruth is in charge of the Fifty-Two, and the leader in her knows that this is her responsibility. But the more human part can't help but think of that young woman, Willow Brown, as she screamed and covered her face with her hands right before the captain executed her in front of everyone. Ruth won't beg, if she's executed. She won't scream or cry. She will accept her fate with as much grace as she can muster. It's how she wants to be remembered, how she wants her people to see her at the end. Hopefully she'll be brave enough to keep that promise to herself, if the time comes.

Rather, when the time comes.

Captain Harris smiles at her warmly, but it doesn't reassure her. Despite the executions, she thinks he's he a relatively kind man. He's certainly more empathetic than Jackson Goeff. But Ruth doesn't know him well. Who is he beneath the veneer of his easy smile and good looks? She thinks he's a good leader. Fair. But that won't save her. She deserves accountability, and she's certain that with accountability comes her condemnation. It's worrisome, but she's tired of all this—tired of being afraid, tired of wondering and waiting for her reckoning. Let it be now.

"Ruth," he says, extending his hand in an invitation for her to sit. If she were younger, she might decline. But her age and the increased gravity make her grateful for the gesture. She tries to perch lightly on the edge of the seat, instead of falling heavily into the refuge of the cushioned support as she'd like to do.

She closes her eyes and takes a deep breath. Beyond the sound of her breathing, she can hear his voice. He might be asking how he can help her. He might be asking how she is. She can't comprehend the words, nor does she try. She's not here for pleasantries or small talk.

Opening her eyes, Ruth meets his gaze, determined to hide her fear and weakness.

"I suppose Liz has told you what I've done, that I smuggled a memory stick onto this ship that contained the specifications for Jackson's tablets, the ones he used to coordinate his attack. My actions allowed him to hack the broadcast system and attempt to access the propulsion drive." Ruth feels so very expendable. Many of her people can make important contributions to this ship, but she is old and tired. She wonders if her purpose now is simply to atone for her treachery and redeem everyone else.

"I understand the gist of it," he says, his voice even and neutral. His expression offers no clue as to his thoughts, and this frightens her even more. She studies his eyes. She likes the color of them, a deep, muted blue. She's seen so much feeling in them before, but not now. Now she finds them nothing more than an empty canvas—nothing to decipher and nothing to understand.

"I won't offer any excuses for myself, Captain," Ruth says, hearing more emotion in her voice than she wants to express. "I will bear whatever consequence stems from my actions. I alone made decisions on behalf of my people, and I hope you will hold them harmless."

The captain presses his lips together. Is it contemplation or annoyance? Ruth cannot tell. Perhaps she should say more, but she doesn't know what.

"Why did you want to see me, Ruth?" he asks, his tone still even. Guarded, perhaps. She dismisses all of her speculation about how he might perceive her. It's clear that he doesn't intend her to know. She could waste more time trying to gauge where she stands with him, but her message is too important to play those kinds of games.

"I have information about Jackson Goeff," she says. "I've learned things you need to know."

Captain Harris maintains his neutral expression, but Ruth can see that he's leaned forward in his chair—enough to let her know that he's curious.

"How did you obtain this information?" he asks.

Ruth pauses, a stab of guilt piercing her concentration. It hits her in the chest, so badly that part of her wonders if it's a heart attack. She dismisses the thought and presses on.

"We've been surveilling him in his quarters."

Surprise washes over the captain's face. "Oh? Did you bug his room?"

"Not exactly, no. I wouldn't know what to do with that technology even if I had it. We've been doing it the old-fashioned way. We've been listening."

"Do you mean the security details?"

"No, Captain. Ellis has nothing to do with this. We've been listening in the air vents."

Ruth watches the captain's eyebrows lift.

"You've posted spies in the ventilation system?" he asks.

"Yes, Captain. I believe he's dangerous, and I want to do my part to help manage him."

Ruth feels naked under his gaze, humiliated and afraid, but she knows she's earned his scrutiny. She refuses to look away.

"What did you hear?" he asks.

Memories of the children giving her reports flash through her mind. It had to be them. They were the only ones small enough to move quietly and quickly through the shafts, the only ones who could get close enough to hear what he was saying and stay there for any length of time. She tries to dismiss her guilt. Such things are the cost of survival these days, or so it seems.

"We heard something important, but before we get there, you need to know that Jackson and the woman used the ventilation system to leave their quarters last night."

"They snuck out? Did they spot you?"

Ruth finds this question interesting, but doesn't know what to make of it.

"No, Captain. The children can move quickly and quietly in the shafts, so …" Ruth can't finish.

"The children?" Captain Harris asks, another wave of surprise dissolving his composure.

"Yes, Captain. Adults can crawl through the shafts, but it's not feasible for them to stay in there. Nor can they move quickly. I know, Captain, it's unforgivable, but ..." *I've already done unforgivable things.* Her mind finishes the sentence her mouth refuses to complete. "Jackson and the woman exited on Level 2. We followed them to the lift, but I don't know where they went after."

The captain spins his chair and activates a large screen mounted on the wall.

"What time was this?" he asks, typing commands into a keyboard.

"About two hours after the evening acceleration," Ruth replies, turning her eyes to the screen. She sees a security camera feed, trained on lift doors. Soon enough, Jackson and the woman enter the frame. The feed shifts to the inside of the lift. She can see the captain staring intently, and she can tell that he will have crow's feet around his eyes when he gets older. This makes her think of Ellis, and her stomach lurches as she realizes that things may seem to be going well now, but she's still a traitor. The captain's verdict has not yet been rendered.

"Level 37," he says softly, typing vigorously once more. The picture shifts again, and Ruth can see a large, egg-shaped object, the same shade of green as the goo they sprayed on the crates yesterday. She watches Jackson pick it up and carry it, as if he has superhuman strength. Ruth can't help but think of ants and how they can carry objects many times larger than the size of their bodies. She'd like to crush him like an ant, if only she could. The picture shifts again. Ruth recognizes the machine—the platform where she watched the crew stack food and supplies. She watches Jackson help the woman into the capsule and then climb in himself.

Ruth turns her attention to Captain Harris, whose attention seems to still be glued on the screen. He says nothing, but she can see his mouth is a thin line—even thinner than before. His right eye twitches, and he blinks it away. She sits in silence, thinking it best to not interrupt him. On the monitor, the platform appears to be resting in silence too, empty and peaceful, until the capsule appears once more. The hatch cracks open. Jackson and the woman exit, and the captain cuts the feed, turning to face her.

"There's something else," she says quickly. "We overheard him talking with someone about Liz. When he returns to the surface with the second shipment, I'm afraid he means to take her with him, by force if needed."

A storm blows across the young man's face, giving him an intensity that makes her feel nervous again when he fixes his gaze upon her.

"Who did he speak with?"

Ruth cannot bear to see his expression when she tells him. Her eyes close.

"Dr. Harris."

She waits. But she hears nothing—not a word or grunt or even a sigh. When Ruth opens her eyes again, the captain is standing motionless—statuesque—turned away from her with his hands folded behind his back. She waits, her own back beginning to ache from sitting so straight and rigid in the chair, wondering if she should leave. But just as she braces herself to rise, he turns to face her again. His expression is neutral, although she can see the remains of a flush fading in uneven blotches.

"What did she say?"

Ruth's heart pounds.

"S-she said she could sedate Liz, and hide her in a crate marked 'perishable medical supplies.'"

The captain sits again, exhaling deeply and rubbing his eyes as he leans heavily into the cushioned back. Ruth begins to panic, wondering if it was a mistake to tell the captain about his mother's betrayal. Words begin to tumble out of her mouth.

"She must believe Liz will be safe in the crate. I am sure Dr. Harris only means to help you, misguided as it may be." Ruth bites the inside of her cheek hard, knowing she can say nothing else that is useful. It's hard to breathe as the young man looks at her.

"Thank you for telling me this, Ruth." His voice is not unkind, but neither does it seem forgiving. "Liz is free to leave at any time, but I believe she wants to stay here with us. I hope if you hear anything further, you will let me know. Ellis knows how to reach me at all times."

"Of course," she says, pausing for a moment to consider what she plans to say next. She reminds herself that she decided to support him, to help him, and so she continues. "Captain Harris, I intend to continue monitoring Jackson, and I intend to do whatever is necessary to make sure that Liz is not taken against her will. Regardless of what she thinks of me, my people and I will always help her."

"And what does she think of you?" Ruth is surprised by this question, intrigued at the way the man can converse with her without revealing his own thoughts.

"I haven't seen or heard from her in four days," she says carefully. "I assume she's angry, or disappointed." She doesn't want to say any more, to rehash her confession of betrayal. And so she waits, watching the captain's eyes change and wondering what will happen next.

"You could ask her," he finally says, after what feels to Ruth like eternity. "She's in the medical unit, but you could visit her."

The medical unit? Ruth is horrified. How did she not know this, even in the midst of all the chaos of Jackson's arrival?

"Thank you, Captain. I'll go directly there, if I may." She rises.

"Before you go," he says as she starts to turn. She freezes, wondering if her reckoning is at hand. Surely not now, not after he told her about Liz. "I have a question that I hope you'll answer honestly."

Ruth feels her stomach drop, and the strength begins to drain out of her legs. She's determined to remain standing, not to show her fear, but she lightly touches the backrest of the chair to keep herself steady.

"Why did you keep helping him? After you delivered the memory stick to Chub, I mean. And even after you fought next to Liz to keep him from overtaking the ship. Why did you keep helping him?"

His voice is softer than it was before, quieter and infused with curiosity. Ruth looks at his impassive face, certain he must be thinking and feeling something. Whatever it may be is well-guarded. She considers what to say and reminds herself again of her promise to herself to stop doing anything to help Jackson. The captain doesn't seem threatening to her, even though she now understands that he knows everything. She sits back down in the chair and folds her hands in her lap, studying her knobby fingers as she searches for the right words.

"I suppose the most honest answer I can give is that I don't know," she says, losing herself in the wrinkles of her hands. "I've asked myself the same question so many times, and I came up with so many answers. But at the end of it all, I realized that all the reasons I thought of were really just excuses."

"I heard that four of your people remained on the surface," Captain Harris says, his voice still soft and curious.

"Yes, and that was a factor in the beginning. But I'm sure Jackson has done whatever he intends to do to them, and I can't help them any longer. In the end, I believe I helped him because I was weak. Even after Liz brought us back from the depot and after everything you've done for us here, I was afraid Jackson could still hurt us. I suppose I thought that he might be merciful if I helped him, and the things he asked for seemed so inconsequential ..."

She stops because she doesn't want to start with the excuses, and she knows the relative insignificance of each act she was asked to complete is an excuse. She looks at the captain again, but his expression hasn't changed. He has an inquisitive look she might find endearing under other circumstances. It carries her back long ago, back to her days of teaching school. It reminds her of some of her best students, whose desire to learn burned brighter than any of the distractions most children succumbed to.

"You were fawning." It's a low whisper that Ruth isn't sure she was intended to hear.

"Fawning?"

"Yes," he says, clearly addressing her this time. "It's a trauma response—ingratiating yourself with someone who has hurt you."

Ruth isn't sure what to make of this, although it certainly fits her behavior. "Well," she says with resolve, "no more. I cannot help him anymore, no matter what it costs me."

"Why?" he asks, that curiosity still ablaze in his eyes.

"Because it might make the difference between winning and losing," she says, losing her desire to talk about this. Impatience grows in her belly. Whatever he intends to do, she needs him to get on with it.

"What will happen to me, Captain?" she asks in the sternest voice she can muster. "Will I be tried? Executed like those other people?"

He appraises her for a moment, the curiosity in his eyes giving way to the blank and guarded canvas.

"That would be a terrible loss, Ruth. And if I tried and executed everyone who helped Jackson at some point, I doubt I'd have enough people left to operate the ship. It's a sad state of affairs, but it benefits no one for me to delude myself about it. However, I need to know—are you done helping him?"

"Yes, Captain. I am done." She says no more, knowing that nothing can undo her actions, and isn't though how people should be judged? By their actions?

"I hope so," he says, his voice grave. "I have failed this crew in many ways, and the consequences of my failure are mine to bear. But regardless of what I have or haven't done, Jackson is who he is. Whatever dream he's selling isn't one he intends to deliver on."

Ruth only nods as she turns to go. She thinks they understand each other. Her people are safe, at least for the time being. She will think more about this later, but for now she only wants to go to the medical unit, to see what has happened to Liz.

Ellis meets her outside, his eyes asking the question he doesn't articulate with his voice.

"It went fine," she whispers, and he nods in acknowledgement. "But Liz is in the medical unit, and I'd like to go see her. Captain Harris says it's okay." Ellis rides with her on the lift, standing in silence but clasping her fingers in his.

CHAPTER 29

DREAMS AND MEMORIES

****

Liz knows without being told, without even opening her eyes, that she is in that other place—that place that smells and feels more real than anything she's ever considered real before. It's the place where she is herself, but—strangely— she is also Cyril. She knows without opening her eyes that it's still dark—so early that it's still late, even though it's time for Cyril to rise. She can feel the warmth of bodies curled around her—others. The air is saturated with smells: soil, water, the bodies of those curled around her, even the smell of the coming dawn. Liz didn't know until this moment that dawn had a scent, but now she realizes she's known it her whole life, or rather, Cyril's whole life.

She creeps out of the lodging, surprised to see that it's made entirely of dried grass. She breathes in deeply, taking in the still-dark sky and the sweet grass that she still loves now as the first time she smelled it. Looking around, she wonders if she will roll in a clump of the sweet grass, but she remembers that it doesn't grow here. The family built its house away from the grassy plain, which burns sometimes when struck by lightning. The ground here is mossy, cool, shaded by a large rock overhang near a stream that cuts through the base of a hill.

She will roll in the tall grass later today, covering herself in the sweet smell of its broken blades. But that will be later—it's still wet with dew. Rolling in it now would leave her damp and cold, and the grass crushed into mud.

For now, Cyril will work. She loves her job, gathering grass and flowers and fruit from high in the trees—things the family needs. It can be dangerous, but she would not choose any other job. This is who she is, and this is what she loves.

Others begin to emerge from grass houses as Cyril makes her way to the edge of the settlement. They are familiar to Liz, but she cannot remember their names, or what they look like. She acknowledges them, knowing that they sense her presence in the dark.

The sun begins to peek over the hill under which she lives, and Cyril stops for a moment to commune. Her eyes close as the sun climbs, brighter and brighter and warmer on her face. A glow permeates her closed eyelids as the sun warms her furry face. She loves this part of the day, breathing in deeply as she opens her eyes.

Cyril scampers down the far side of the hill, eyes vigilant and legs fast and strong as she tunes herself in to any danger. Liz knows there is a forest to her left, and a marsh straight ahead. But Cyril turns right, toward the rocky cliffs that line the shore of a large and angry sea. That's where the fruit grows—on a thorny vine that communes with a tall, leafy tree. Cyril isn't sure if the fruit is ripe, so she'll check and see. If it is, she'll get her cart—the one she built herself. It's stored nearby—not in the settlement. The elders would find that worrisome, although they tolerate the cart as long as Cyril uses it modestly.

Why are they concerned about the cart? Liz is flooded with knowing. The elders don't like change. The family has ways of doing things—ways that work and, according to the others, do not require improvement.

But aren't things always changing—the land, the water, the trees, the sky? Yes, but Liz realizes it's not the same thing. Those changes have rhythm and flow. They have always been and will always be. It's the unknown changes that are a problem—the sudden idea that a basket could be pulled on special rails much more easily than it could be carried on a back, the realization that it only works if the strap of the basket turns into a harness. It's that kind of unnatural change that concerns the family, making Cyril's curious mind and strange innovations an enigma—tolerated but not embraced.

Liz's focus shifts to the sweet, crisp, clean air. Cyril breathes deeply, filled with joy. It's the joy of a strong body that isn't yet tired. The joy of breathing and running. Being alive.

She arrives at the tree, pausing to study the ropy vines that embrace the trunk. The vines themselves are poisonous, but the fruit they bear is nourishing and delicious. She climbs carefully, with graceful ease and experience, perching on a solid branch close to the fruit. It's not yet ripe. *Perhaps tomorrow,* she thinks, descending with the same ease and grace. There is no rush.

Cyril rests at the base of the tree, listening to the sound of waves crashing against rocks. It's familiar, but fearful. She can smell the sea. Water and salt. Birth and decay. It is volatile and treacherous, communing with no one but its own inhabitants. Cyril will not go to the sea. She will go back to the forest, familiar and welcoming. There will be nuts to gather, a stream where she can have a cool long drink. Liz can almost taste it. So refreshing.

She's thirsty, but it's not urgent. The day is long, and she has plenty of time. Cyril's eyes feel heavy, and she closes them if only to feel the warmth of the sun on them for a moment—another communion. Only a short nap.

For a moment, Liz knows she is safe. Then, darkness envelopes her—pulling her through what feels like a dizzying sea of empty space and time. She doesn't want to leave, but she has a sense that there is something urgent she needs to do, someone waiting for her. She can't remember what or who, but she relents nonetheless. Struggling would be futile. Liz falls and falls until she falls no more.

***

Ruth sits by Liz's bed, studying the young woman's peaceful, sleeping face. It reminds her of her daughter Suzie, sweet and loving. She had an angel's heart—too good for what the world became.

Ruth once had three children. They gave her wonderful memories, memories she forces down, so deep inside her heart that she almost forgets they are there. She can't bear to think of her children—the memories are too sad. But here, sitting in the dim room next to Liz's comatose body, she lets them bubble up.

She remembers Travis and Suzie and Billy playing in the sprinkler, in the green grass Ruth so often took for granted. She wishes now she would have appreciated it more, her quaint cookie-cutter post-World War II suburban home, replete with all the trimmings of a nostalgic middle-class life. Her husband, Bill, maintained their manicured yard, cutting the grass while Ruth tended the flowers in the window boxes, usually brightly colored annuals she planted every spring. She remembers the back yard, mostly consumed by a large cottonwood tree, although one corner got enough sun for a lilac bush to grow and bloom. She remembers sitting in the porch swing Bill built, smelling the lilacs and watching the children play their games.

Three children in five years wasn't easy, but she remembers fondly how much they all loved to play together, how they helped each other climb into the low branches of the tree. Ruth used to admonish them to be careful, although now she regrets it. What would she tell them if she could go back in time? Enjoy every moment. Laugh. Play. Choose the adventure. Climb the tree. Dig the dirt. Chase your dreams. But she can't go back in time, and no regret can change that.

It was hard to watch her children leave the nest, but she bade them each farewell as they made their way into the world and into adulthood, pretending to be happy for them. Did they ever suspect how lonely she was after they left? Did they know how much they had become her identity? All that remained, when they vacated the space of her heart, was the silence of her own company. Life had been so busy raising three children, and then—poof—they were gone. She learned to adapt over time.

Ruth thinks of Suzie again. She had Bill's blue eyes and Ruth's dark hair. She died in the Midwest quake, in Chicago where she'd gone to attend an orthodontia conference and visit her brother, Travis. She and Travis and his new wife were all crushed in his second-floor Chicago condominium when the building collapsed on top of them. Within moments, two of Ruth's children were gone, and all she could do was hope the end was quick and painless.

Her son Billy lived longer. He was somewhere in the Himalayas when the volcano blew over New Mexico. Maybe he tried to come home, but Ruth has no way to know. She couldn't reach him after the eruption, and then her husband Bill died the following year.

The deaths were hard on Ruth. No one wants to outlive their children. But over time, she came to see the mercy they received in dying, the suffering they'd been spared. What would have become of her sweet Suzie in the hell each new day brought after the world of yesterday disintegrated? Would she have been strong enough to survive? Who would she be now? Would she be as strong as the young woman lying before Ruth?

It used to hurt too much to think about her own children, but it doesn't hurt now. They're a dream of a dream, a soft feeling in her weary heart—a place of refuge, perhaps? No, there is no refuge in the memories, only the numb remnants of a loneliness she has no energy to sustain.

For many years, Ruth wished she'd died with them, but even that wish has faded over time. New children filled the space her children left, knitting together the great chasms in her world where her own three used to reside. Children like Zachary and Sophia, Logan, Axle, and baby Luke. Like Ruben and Gabriella and Will and Melissa. Aren't they all her children, no matter their age?

Ruth studies Liz, wondering why she's here and why she's unconscious. No one will tell her anything useful, although no one seems to mind her sitting here by the bedside. She waits and watches as Dr. Harris and the others check on her periodically, making notes as they study the machines that measure her heartbeat, her breathing, and even her brain waves. She doesn't appear to be injured—no bandages or casts, no incisions or staples. She looks timeless in her slumber, like a blond-haired doll with a scattering of faded freckles across her nose.

Eventually, Liz's fingers jerk, and then her eyelids flutter open. Her eyes dart right and left, looking confused and unfocused as they settle on Ruth. A fleeting glimpse of contentment dissolves as soon as the air and light hit Liz's eyes, as if she were coming from a happy place, from somewhere better than here.

"I understand if you want me to leave," Ruth says, "but I need to know how you are." She places a hand on the bed, next to Liz's and is surprised to feel the girl take it in hers.

"I had a seizure," Liz says, and Ruth can feel her own brow furrow.

"Will you be alright?" she asks, her mind racing from epilepsy to brain tumors, wondering again whether Jackson's technology is putting them in danger.

"Yes," Liz says, eyes going soft as if something just occurred to her. "I believe I will, after I …"

"After you what?" Ruth asks, but the end of the sentence never comes.

"How are the children?" Liz asks, her voice filled with urgency as she squeezes Ruth's hand weakly.

"The children?"

"I saw them hiding under the bench," Liz says, softly, as if she can't muster the breath to be heard. "At story time, after Gabriella ran away with Luke."

Does she know that was five days ago? Ruth decides not to press the issue.

"Everyone is fine. There's nothing for you to do now but rest." It's a lie, of course. Sophia and Logan have woken up screaming each night, and Zachary started wetting the bed, which has been especially problematic since he refuses to sleep anywhere but between his parents. Gabriella spends her time locked in her quarters, clutching baby Luke to her chest. It's been a struggle to get her to eat, and Ruth is terrified she might smother the baby in a panic, shushing him when he cries as if their very lives depend upon his silence. Perhaps there was a time when that was true, but now? Have their lives reverted to such a fearful state?

Liz closes her eyes again, sighing out her breath as if it's too hard to hold in.

"I need to keep everyone safe," she says, legs shifting in the bed. Ruth quietly strokes Liz's fingers—they feel so delicate in her own. She tries not to cry and then wonders why she's trying. When did it become so wrong to cry? Why bother fighting when it's this hard to hold back the tears?

Liz's breathing deepens, smooth and regular. Hopefully she's somewhere peaceful. Ruth lays her face on the bed beside Liz's sleeping body and sobs. Who will the children look up to if something happens to this remarkable girl?

Liz is still sleeping when Ruth runs out of tears. She washes her face at a nearby sink and prepares to leave, to face her people and the world around her once again.

***

Liz can sense Abby's presence as she begins to wake once more in the medical unit. Her head feels extraordinarily full, and she can hear the soft humming noise that always accompanies Abby's communications. When she opens her eyes, she's surprised to find no one by her bedside, or in the room at all.

Abby?

I am here, Liz. I didn't want to wake you.

Has something happened?

I want you to know that I regret the damage I've caused you. Abby's voice is soft in Liz's head. *I never intended to create suffering for you, but I know my anger does. I don't intend to get angry, but it can be difficult to control when I lower my vibration.*

What does it mean to lower your vibration? Liz asks.

I suppose it's like devolving. Beings with low vibrations have more primitive concerns and perspectives.

And beings with higher vibrations?

They know the truth of who they really are.

Is my vibration low?

I cannot say, Abby replies. *It's lower than mine, which is why I have to lower my vibration to communicate. But it's higher than the mouse I perceived—much higher.*

Can I raise my vibration? Liz asks.

All beings grow through learning. If you are willing to learn, your vibration will rise as you begin to understand the truth of who you really are.

Is that what you mean when you tell me to raise my vibration, when we are talking?

No, in those moments, I'm asking you to disentangle yourself from forces that pull your vibration down—like fear and anxiety.

And anger?

Yes, although I see now how difficult it can be to disentangle oneself from anger.

It seems hard for you to disentangle yourself from your anger at Jackson, Liz muses, *but he doesn't make it easy.*

I find him insufferable.

Liz smiles. *Sometimes, I do too.*

But you protected him. Why?

He's my brother.

What does that mean?

Liz tries to articulate the connection she feels to Jackson. But how can she explain something that she herself doesn't fully understand? Lost for words, she summons to mind her memories of Jackson when he was a boy—teaching her to read, pushing her in the swing, cutting his sandwiches in half, telling her to be strong.

Oh, I see. Abby sounds startled. *He cared for you when you were vulnerable. That's the part of him you choose to remember. Your memories have so much feeling. I can sense joy and contentment, but also suffering and loss. And there's something else—something that permeates everything you remember. A feeling of … I don't know, but it pushes you forward and holds you back at the same time. It gives you both suffering and wisdom. What is it?*

Sadness, I suppose, Liz replies, and Abby seems to consider this for a long while.

Liz? Abby's voice comes softly. *I don't understand— why won't you help me?*

Aren't I helping you?

No, you are asking Jackson to help me. But you have the ability to help me yourself. I can see it right there, in your coding.

Coding? Liz is confused.

Yes, your coding. Your DNA.

What's in my DNA?

You have the ability to work across many dimensions, Abby explains. *It's there, in your DNA. You don't need a machine to see across time and space, or even beyond it.*

Liz isn't sure what to make of this, but she can sense Abby waiting for a reply.

If I have that ability, I am unaware of it. I wouldn't know where to begin or how to use it—if I have it.

Liz waits for what seems like a long time.

The ability is there, Abby finally says, *but I sense you are telling the truth. You don't know how to access it. Perhaps if your vibration were higher …*

Are there ways other than learning to raise my vibration? Faster ways?

I don't know. Learning is the natural way. Raising your vibration without knowing the truth of who you are might be damaging.

Like your anger?

Perhaps, or perhaps even more damaging. I do not know.

I want to help you, Abby. I'll talk to Jackson again. Surely, he can find a way to help you go home.

Thank you, Abby replies after a long silence. Liz senses there are things Abby isn't telling her, but she doesn't ask. She feels helpless to do anything useful, so what's the point of knowing? She closes her eyes and feels Abby's presence slip away, leaving her head blissfully empty.

***

Even before Liz opens her eyes again, she knows that Seth is sitting beside her. His energy radiates steady and strong, quiet and sad.

"What day is it?" she asks, noticing that her voice is raspy, her throat hoarse.

"It's Thursday," he says, gently stroking her hand. "The evening acceleration is done."

"I'm glad you're here," she says, taking a sip from the cup of water he raises to her lips.

"Oh?" he asks playfully. "Are you ready for me to break you out of this place?" She smiles weakly, relishing the cool, wet water flowing down her parched throat. She knows she should say yes, that the person Seth knows so well would be fighting her way out of bed. But what's the point of fighting now? She's come to appreciate the dim, cool room, the blissful emptiness that fills her head between conversations with Abby.

"I'm glad to be here too," Seth says. "Did Abby contact you again?"

"How did you know?"

"There's a pattern to her contact," he says vaguely. "What did she say?"

"She wants to know why I'm not helping her."

"What does she expect you to do?" Seth sounds surprised.

"I don't know. She says I have the ability to see across many dimensions. She says it's coded in my DNA." Seth doesn't reply, and Liz knows he's considering what she told him by the way his fingers move on her skin. She turns her attention to the sensation, diving into the pleasure of it.

"Even if that's true," he says, "how does it help us?"

"I don't think it does." Liz leans back into the pillows and closes her eyes again. "She says I can't access it." She sounds crazy—even to herself—but she doesn't have the strength to be concerned about it. Her energy is consumed by breathing and existing, and she has the sense that she wants to be asleep. If she can only go back to sleep, she can find that nice place again, the one she knows but doesn't remember.

"I'm worried about you, Z," Seth says, and the urgency in his voice pulls her attention back to his hand holding hers, his energy radiating at her bedside. "I don't know how much more of this your body can take. We need to find a way to get her out of your head."

"She wants to go home," Liz says weakly, "and as far as I know, Jackson is the only one who can help her. I told her I'd talk to him again, but I can't do it with her in my head. He makes her so angry. She called him insufferable."

"I understand the feeling," Seth mutters absently, tracing one of her knuckles with his thumb. "I don't want you to worry about it, Z. I'll talk to him." He caresses her cheek, leaning in to kiss her forehead.

Liz closes her eyes, feeling the warmth of his lips, the energy of his skin connecting with hers. It's like a drop of rain on desert sand, instantly absorbed and gone much too soon as he pulls away to sit by her bedside once more. So she focuses on the sensation of his hand touching hers. She wants to remember how it feels, to hold it apart from all the other moments running together in her mind—sleeping, waking, the blackness that follows the seizures, and the blissful emptiness that fills her head when Abby is away. She's still imprinting the feel of his hand on hers when she falls asleep again.

CHAPTER 30

FREE WILL

***

She Who Needs No Name, known to Liz as Abby, studies the being she's come to blame for her predicament—Jackson. His thoughts are heavily veiled, impenetrable to her. But she can still observe him as he sits in a chair, studying a holographic image projected from one of his hands.

Abby knows that it's a map of the stars. The points of light in the hologram align perfectly with the form Abby knows to surround the ship in every direction. Like many of the other records these beings maintain, the map is rife with information about the stars and planets and comets and gas clouds scattered across the cosmos.

Jackson seems preoccupied as he studies it, using the fingers of his free hand to mindlessly scroll through the map, eyes soft as he takes in the landscape of space farther and farther away from where the tiny vessel currently travels. The look of longing on his face might suggest that he was searching for his home planet, but Abby knows that the expanse of space he studies in his hand is even farther from his home than it is from the vessel.

Abby knows now where Liz and the others like her originated. She tracked the location the last time Jackson used his machine, the one he continues to use with insufferable arrogance and no regard for how it might affect others. She was curious to experience where they were from, having studied thoroughly all of the information the vessel contained about their home planet. But nothing she studied prepared her for what she encountered when she cast out her tendrils of awareness.

Abby expected Liz's planet to be different from her own. She knows that life manifests in a variety of forms, each with a unique level of awareness. But she assumed that, like her own, the planet would be vibrant and alive. She expected abundance, partly because Liz's vessel has such abundance and partly because she knows the universe to be fundamentally abundant. Her assumptions couldn't have been further from the truth.

Liz's home planet isn't dead, but it's sleeping—deeply. It rests in a comatose slumber, oblivious to the needs of its wilting life-forms, and Abby can sense that it will not awaken for a long time. She can sense that portions of the planet are more nurturing than others, places where creatures like Liz are living in relative harmony, at least for now. But the place Jackson went is barren and desolate, filled with privation and suffering instead of life and abundance.

Abby can see that life here is onerous, and it's caused her to reconsider many of her insights and assumptions about Liz and her kind. In this place they call home, it's much harder to survive than it is to perish, so why do they try? Why not succumb to the planet's deep sleep, instead of scarring themselves to the core of their beings with pain and struggle?

After seeing their home planet, Abby thinks she can better understand the reason for their complex vibrations, and she no longer questions how or why they block their gifts and abilities. They are too busy struggling, suffering under the weight of their pain and a sleeping planet. They cannot ascend while they feel so much agony.

Under other circumstances, Abby would revel in such a profound insight. Knowledge is generally a good thing, but this knowledge feels heavy and worrisome, perhaps even sad now that she has some insight into what that means. She understands now why Jackson flails blindly and recklessly, seeking a lifeline to a better existence, but she also realizes that this makes him dangerous. He is unaware of his own power, oblivious to the ramifications of his actions, and too desperate to care. She cannot trust him to help her.

Abby considers everything she's learned since her great aloneness. Her rate of learning has grown exponentially since she started communicating with Liz. It's taught her that she's capable of ascending without direct guidance from a teacher.

She could choose to break her connection to Liz and start her own journey of exploration, seeking out new experiences that would give her knowledge. This knowledge should push her toward ascension, as long as she is careful to remember who she really is and that her intention is to return home. Perhaps with enough experience and learning, she could find her way. It might be possible, although it wouldn't be easy. She would rather return home the same way she came—instantly and completely—but that may not be an option.

Abby thinks about Jackson's assertion that she chose to follow the small creature Liz calls a mouse through his wormhole. If she chose to follow the creature, then she is responsible for her presence in linear time and space. She cannot expect someone else to change the consequence of a decision she made, but did she choose to follow the mouse? She didn't intend to do it, although she cannot rule out the possibility.

Still, it doesn't seem right that she should suffer the consequences of a reality she didn't intend. Nor does it seem right that others should suffer the consequences of her choices, even if they are uninformed or unintended choices. But just as she did not intend to follow the mouse, it seems clear that Jackson did not intend to pull her into linear time and space.

Abby doesn't know what implications these insights have for her current situation. Clearly, she has much to consider as she recalls her tendrils of awareness, pulling her energy into a tight ball as she dims her awareness into the humming churn of her own planet, her vibrant, abundant planet. The only thing she knows for certain is that she needs to go home, and if Jackson doesn't help her, she will kill him.

CHAPTER 31

MIRANDA

***

"Why did you call this meeting?" a low, gravelly voice calls out, speaking much louder than necessary.

"Do we not meet regularly, Mackey?" Jackson asks, keeping an even tone.

"Yes," Mackey replies, "but we're not due to meet for another month. Why did you call us together?"

Before Jackson replies, another box pops up on the screen of his laptop.

"Reverend," Jackson says, suppressing his disgust for both faces he now sees on his screen. He's known these men a long time, and likes them less by the day.

"What's this about, Goeff?" demands the man who calls himself the Reverend T. Jones.

"Let's wait until we're all here," Jackson replies. They don't have to wait long. The final box pops up on his screen, and the final guest appears. Her face is lined with age, her hair mostly silver. But her eyes are still dark and alive, alert and intelligent.

"Jackson," she says, disregarding the other two men, "is all well with my daughter? Why the ad hoc meeting?"

"Yes, Miranda," he says, "Shelby is fine. She's here with me on the Green Grow 3." Jackson can feel the heat of Shelby's body approaching from his left. Her long, dark hair tickles his cheek as she leans down, looking at his monitor to see and be seen in return.

"Mother," she says, "it's good to see your face."

"Are you really on the Green Grow 3?" Miranda asks, as if they are the only two on the line.

"Yes, Mother," she says, smiling. "Jackson transported us here to conduct important business. I've never seen anything like it."

"Well, isn't that sweet?" Mackey's voice is sarcastic, and still gravelly. "Did you call us together so you could gloat, Goeff?" Jackson squeezes Shelby's hand outside the range of the camera, an unspoken promise that she can talk to her mother later.

"I called us together to discuss issues of mutual concern," Jackson says tersely, "and to make sure we all know the state of affairs across our various organizations."

"So, you figured out how to get yourself in outer space?" Jones asks, his beady eyes and nasally voice reminding Jackson once more of a ferret or weasel. His personality could match either creature.

"Indeed. Did I not tell you I would come aboard, and take command of the ship?"

"And have you done that? Have you taken command?"

"Yes," Jackson says without hesitation, "but it serves my purpose to leave the current team in place for the time being."

Jones laughs, and Mackey follows with a hearty chuckle.

"That's rich, Goeff. Do you not know how to run the ship? Is there something Jackson Goeff cannot do?" He knows the reverend is fishing, and trying to aggravate him. It's working, but he won't let it show.

"I cannot divide my attention between this ship and my affairs on Earth," Jackson replies in his coldest voice. He can see the mirth on Mackey's scarred and craggy face, the scorn on Jones's. "I've lost my head scouting captain—Zack Butler." Jackson sees the slightest shift in Mackey's eyes. Yes, he was responsible.

"I'm sure we're all sorry to hear about your loss," Jones says, "but so what? We all lose people."

"Indeed, and some of us may be losing a few more."

"What do you mean?" the reverend asks, eyes shifting like a cornered rat. Mackey's expression freezes.

"I dispatched patrols two days ago," Jackson says, narrowing his eyes and summoning his coldest voice. "If I find the men you sent to help Zack Butler overthrow me, I will skin them alive and send their remains home."

"Don't be dramatic, Goeff!" Jones says, flashing a broad smile filled with rotted teeth. He looks nervous. Jackson is certain now that Mackey wasn't acting alone. It's not surprising. Mackey isn't capable of original thought, only anger that has no direction and no purpose. The reverend is the one who ordered the move against him.

Jones has been lusting after the Green Grow 3 ever since he found out that Jackson was communicating with Lizzie two months ago. And, of course, he's been looking for new territory since Miranda made it clear that he was no longer in charge of the southern region. He's nothing more than a body keeping her chair warm when she's not there, and Jackson is certain this infuriates the man. He wants his own sandbox to play, even if it does implode again and again at the expense of the people foolish enough to follow him.

Foolish, indeed. People like Mackey and Jones don't create anything new. They only take from others—the kind of men that feed Lizzie's hatred toward the New Generation. She's not wrong, but regardless, men like Mackey—and even Jones—can be useful, if they are managed properly.

Miranda, on the other hand, is a whole different matter. Jackson doesn't know whether to respect or fear her. She smoothly and seamlessly took command of the reverend's operation, and she's the only captain besides Jackson with any real vision. But she's hard to read, and Jackson doesn't like that—not at all. She may be as cunning as he is, and he'd be foolish to dismiss the idea that she may actually be more cunning. It's part of why Jackson married her daughter. Fortunately, it was an easy alliance—Shelby is everything he ever wanted in a woman.

"Boys!" Miranda says curtly, as if cued by Jackson's thoughts. "Don't waste my time with your pissing contests. Why are we here?"

"I'll be arranging food shipments soon," Jackson says, "regular shipments from the Green Grow 3. Put together your priority lists, and we can negotiate."

"Negotiate?" Mackey laughs. Jackson ignores him.

"Miranda, did the bone mender arrive?" he asks.

"Yes," she responds. "We've used it several times, all with good results. I've sent the train back full of the steel beams you requested."

"Excellent," he says, just as Mackey jumps in.

"Train? You're sending a train through my region? Don't you think you should tell me when, so I can make sure it passes through safely?"

Jackson cannot suppress a smirk.

"My mistake," Miranda replies, with no remorse. "I'm certain it's cleared your region by now, but I'll try to remember for next time."

Mackey probably regrets allowing the tracks to be repaired, connecting the West and the East, but there's nothing to do about it now. Besides, his region benefits from the corridor as well, without having to expend any effort of his own. *It's probably the only reason his people haven't starved yet,* Jackson thinks, wondering how long he or Miranda will allow Mackey to remain in control. In truth, they probably would have ousted him already, except they don't yet have the right person to replace him. Many of his people have devolved into the very animals Lizzie thinks they all are, and whoever takes the brute's place will have to be vigilant and careful to turn things around.

"How's it going with the Canadians?" Jackson asks.

"We're holding them at bay," Mackey says gruffly. "I could use more food and weapons to sustain my troops."

"Oh?" Jackson asks, feigning surprise. "I heard you abandoned the northern front."

"That's ridiculous! Don't insult me!"

Jackson watches Miranda's eyes narrow.

"Is that why Detroit has gone dark? Mackey, have you lost Detroit?"

"If Detroit has been overrun, it's news to me!" Mackey roars in a voice that would frighten most people. Jackson isn't frightened. He can see right through the man—weak and pathetic. Miranda clearly sees through him as well. Will this be enough to push her over the edge? It might be. A Canadian invasion could break their newly established transportation lines, undo the work they've done.

"Get. It. Back," Miranda hisses in a searing tone that makes them all go quiet. "Cleveland is in my territory, and if I get any reports of Canadian forces, I will have your head."

"Let me see what I can find out," Mackey offers, as if he really doesn't know. "I'll be in touch."

Miranda only glares at him. Jackson terminates the connection, happily handing the tablet to Shelby so she can call her mother privately. Her face radiates eternal and vibrant youth as she describes the room and the food and the fields and orchards. He didn't realize she found so much joy in this experience. It eases his guilt about the suffering she's endured coming here. It frees up space in his mind to think about his own desires and priorities.

He's tired of managing men like Mackey and Jones. He's tired of working so hard to gain so very little ground, trying to turn the tide of progress. To get humanity moving forward again instead of backward. It's too heavy, too burdensome. Surely, he can fulfill some other purpose, can't he?

He sets those thoughts aside for now.

Jackson presses the top of his wrist, activating the microchip with his maps, scrolling and zooming until he finds the star chart he is looking for. He wants to confirm the coordinates one more time, the coordinates he intends to use to dispatch with that pesky alien Lizzie seems to be channeling. He lets his mind spin as he stares absently at the hologram of stars emanating from his palm, waiting for Shelby to finish her conversation with her mother.

He's still sitting in the chair, mind spinning with possibility, when Shelby hands him the tablet, looking blissful—she always does when she talks to her mother. "Here, my love," she says as he takes it, "I know you need this to scan for the Walkabout 2 feed."

"The scan is running," he says, setting it to the side. "Perhaps I will retire and check it in the morning."

"Oh?" she asks. Her voice is sharp. "Are you unwell, my love? You were so intent on seeing the data the moment it arrived."

Jackson sighs as he takes in the concern radiating from her dark eyes. "I'm fine," he says, "and—as usual—you're right." He picks up the tablet as Shelby dims the lights, telling him goodnight as she kisses the top of his head. The scan still hasn't detected the Walkabout 2 feed, but he has plenty to keep him busy while he waits. A man of his intellect need not be idle.

He sees a message from Alex. It's the report he wanted on the possible locations for expanding algae production—he depleted his supply making the biofilm, which is worrisome given his plans for using the transporter. He opens the file and begins to read.

It's not until Shelby is fast asleep and his own eyelids are heavy with fatigue that he sees the pattern. He remembers mild interference in his earlier video call—short flashes of static that he thought were random. But are they recurring? He sits motionless in the chair, eyes glued to the screen. Thirty minutes is a long time to stare at the screen, but he cannot afford to get distracted, or to miss any minor instance of the interference. His other concerns evaporate as he watches the clock, waiting to see if it happens again. Right on time, the flash of static reappears.

Someone is transmitting a signal, he realizes, *and it's on a loop.* His fingers fly into action, opening programs and typing commands, until he finds it. *It's not even encrypted!* he realizes, as he runs a decoding program.

His eyes go wide when the results populate his screen, his mind reeling to assimilate what he sees, and then his heart grows wings. He cannot suppress a giggle, nor does he try, as he cries out, "I knew it! Shelby, my love, you must see what I've found!" He carries the tablet to the bed so that she doesn't have to rise, her eyes heavy with sleep and her face waffling between alarm and anger.

"What is it, Jackson?" she says, squinting as the bright light of the screen hits her face.

"I was right! The Green Grow executive board is hiding on the Green Grow 2. They must be behind the moon. They simply must be. And look—they're demanding that the brat return to orbit for a hearing. They've charged him with mutiny and stealing the Green Grow 3!" He giggles again, wanting to leap for joy, to dance a jig with his heavy feet.

Then his mouth falls agape as he realizes something else—Seth Harris has been receiving these messages for days. No matter how many times he deletes them, more arrive! He loves the way it makes him feel to think about the brat reading these messages, squirming in his captain's chair, knowing he's boxed in by Jackson on one side and the Green Grow Executive Board on the other. No one will give him refuge now. He has nothing to offer and nowhere to go.

"What does this mean for us?" Shelby asks, stifling a yawn.

"I will have to consider it more fully," he says, containing his glee because Shelby looks tired, perhaps even a bit irritated. He strokes her dark hair, wanting nothing more than to lie beside her and hold her close.

"Did you connect to the Walkabout 2?" she asks, and Jackson knows he must return to work.

"Not yet, my love, but you rest now. We can discuss this later."

Shelby goes back to sleep, and Jackson goes back to the chair. He's still marinating in the joy of Harris's misery when his tablet begins to beep. His eyes grow wide as he sees blocks of numbers flowing across his screen. It's here—the Walkabout 2 data! Much to his surprise, his heart falls.

I'm afraid to know, he realizes. If Omega can support human life, new possibilities will open for him. He could choose to leave Earth altogether. Never return. Leave it all behind. It's appealing, but he's sacrificed so much to get here, to earn his place. He's worked so hard to build a life on Earth.

He glances over at Shelby's sleeping form. What would she do if he told her he wanted to leave the New Generation? Then a far more relevant question occurs to Jackson. What would Miranda do? She's the one he worries about, the one who might be cunning enough to find a way to hold him accountable for turning his back on her. He doesn't know how she would do it, but she'd be furious if he broke their partnership. He can't rule out the possibility that she might find a way.

Jackson closes his eyes and leans back deeply into his chair. His mind can accommodate nothing more, and he decides to wait until tomorrow to analyze the data that might change everything about his future.

CHAPTER 32

OWLS AND ELEPHANTS

****

OCTOBER 31, 2059—FRIDAY

"Tell me what you found," Seth says, walking into Mathilda's office barefoot, still wearing his pajamas. It seemed like a poor use of time to get dressed in the middle of the night, given the importance of what this woman may know. Her note was cryptic, only telling him that she'd accessed the data they discussed and that he should come to her office.

Did she know he'd be there moments after she sent it? Did she know he was wide awake in his quarters, sitting on his sofa with his tablet on one side and a printed copy of the packing list for the second shipment to Earth in front of him? Maybe. She doesn't look surprised to see him, although he can see her eyes briefly scanning him, taking in the sight of his pajamas and bare feet. She, on the other hand, looks as she normally does, dressed in the same clothes she wore the day before, hair disheveled and face forlorn.

Her office is as cluttered as Seth remembers it, and he briefly wonders how her piles of paper and stacks of file boxes manage to survive the controlled accelerations intact. *Maybe they don't,* he thinks, wondering if perhaps that's why the loose papers have the shape of a pyramid. Mathilda stands and moves to a conference table, lifting a stack of papers out of a chair much like Seth imagines a mother would lift a baby. She motions for him to sit down as she trades the papers for a stack of printed photos that she places before Seth. Then she sits across from him.

Seth begins to look through the stack, first flipping quickly, then looking at each image in more detail. He doesn't know what to think or what to feel, and so he thinks and feels nothing as he spreads out the images, placing them side by side in the small space Mathilda cleared on the table.

"I thought you'd want to see the images first," Mathilda begins, "although they aren't the only data coming through. Omega is larger than Earth, but not substantially. The gravity appears to be comparable, and best I can tell, the days are approximately twenty-six hours. It is orbited by two moons, although one orbits the planet more closely than the other. The images reveal land and water, as well as polar ice caps." She waits for him to process what he's seeing.

"Two moons," he says absently.

"Yes, my preliminary analysis suggests that when the moons oppose each other, the planet experiences very little tide. But they do periodically align, and the effect of their alignment is likely much more dramatic than the lunar effect we experience on Earth."

Seth studies the photos before him. He sees two land masses and a lot of water. He sees clouds, which appear to be moving across the land. The larger land mass appears to occupy nearly a quarter of the planet's surface. The shape is vaguely familiar to Seth, and he realizes it resembles a picture he saw once of an owl swooping toward the camera—a large, squarish body flanked by sturdy wings with tremendous span.

A smaller land mass sits to the southeast of the owl, across a relatively small channel. Seth smiles, thinking that it resembles another animal photo he saw in a book—a baby elephant. The elephant is facing away from the owl, the curved peninsula of its trunk pointing toward the vast ocean that covers the rest of the planet. Its chunky legs are perfectly defined by water inlets on the south side of the island.

"The smaller land mass is approximately the size of Asia," Mathilda says. "The larger one is approximately four times larger, and it's almost exactly twice as wide as it is tall."

"That's a big owl," Seth whispers as too many thoughts try to occupy his mind at the same time. *Run,* he wills the baby elephant, who cannot see the huge owl swooping in from above.

"An owl?"

"Don't you see it? It looks like a large swooping owl and a baby elephant."

Mathilda looks at the pictures, then shrugs.

"It's green," he says, pointing to the island. "Plant life?"

"Possibly, although we can't be sure without further samples."

"What else could it be?"

"I don't know," she says plainly.

Seth's eyes settle on a photo of the larger land mass—the owl. He can make out a mountain range in the center of the land mass, traveling from north to south like a spine. To the left of the mountains, close to the far shore, he sees something strange. It's a small but perfectly circular anomaly that looks flat and barren, starkly golden against a mottled backdrop of what might be a high desert. He points to it, looking at Mathilda quizzically.

"Yes," she says, "it's strange."

"It looks like a perfect circle."

"It's an unusual shape," she admits. "Possibly the remains of a meteor crater, or maybe a volcano."

"I don't think so," Seth whispers, breathless as he thinks about his conversation with Liz. He wonders how much he should say to Mathilda. He doesn't trust her, but Jackson already knows about Abby, as does his mother. What's the point in keeping the information from Mathilda, or the rest of the council for that matter? Is he waiting for more proof that Liz isn't delusional, and if he is, isn't he holding the proof in his hands? He takes a deep breath, realizing that there's no easy way to convey the situation.

"Liz's seizures aren't caused by the controlled accelerations," he begins. "They are caused by an entity who started communicating with her telepathically after Jackson arrived. The being calls herself Abby. When Jackson ran the tests on his machine, the ones with the mice, somehow Abby got sucked into the wormhole and transported to Omega. She's trapped there, and she wants us to send her home."

Mathilda's eyebrows are frozen in a quizzical expression, but otherwise her face is deadpan.

"An entity?" she asks. "Communicating telepathically with Liz?" Her face remains frozen.

"Yes," Seth affirms. "Her name is Abby, and she is an energy being."

"An energy being?" Mathilda asks, face still frozen.

"I know how it sounds, but these pictures only support Abby's assertion. If she's an energy being, and she's residing on Omega, perhaps she emits radiation that kills surface life. This can't be a natural phenomenon." He motions to the perfect circle that appears devoid of life.

"An energy being?" Mathilda asks again. "Seth, what am I supposed to do with this information?"

"For the moment, nothing." He takes in her bewildered expression. "But when the council meets this morning, I intend to discuss with Jackson how we can send Abby home. Liz can't take many more seizures like the ones she's had."

"Of course she can't," Mathilda mutters.

"What else did you learn from the data?" Seth asks, ignoring her venomous tone.

Mathilda's eyes blink rapidly as she focuses again on the photos.

"It's still streaming," she says. "There's a ton to decode and interpret, and I don't want to speak prematurely. I can't say Omega can support human life, but I haven't seen anything that rules out that possibility either. It's promising, and the data I've seen so far make it seem more promising."

"Mathilda, if Omega can sustain human life ... what are we supposed to do with this information?"

"I don't know," she murmurs. "It's monumental, but for now all we can do is continue to monitor the data. The Walkabout 2 should enter Omega's orbit in fourteen months, at which point it will deploy drones to collect surface samples. I suppose we'll know more then. Are you sure you want to turn around and go home, Seth? I mean, this could change everything."

Seth bites his lip, mind spinning with overwhelming possibilities. Mathilda is right. This could change everything, which could be a good thing. Or, it could be catastrophic. He doesn't know how to even begin to think about this. He can't think about it—not right now.

He rises to go, feeling the cushion of the plush carpet beneath his bare feet. It's the only thing that feels real at the moment.

"Keep this confidential," he says, motioning to the photos. Mathilda's face turns wry, and she lets out a bitter laugh.

"Who would I tell, Seth?" she calls after him. "Who even talks to me anymore?" He closes the door behind him when he leaves, the images of Omega in his mind leaving no room for the woman's self-pity.

***

Seth watches Jackson stroll into the conference room for the council meeting. The man shows no sign of exhaustion, even though he was probably up most of the night poring over the Walkabout 2 data. Once again, he sits in the seat Liz usually occupies, and Shelby settles next to him. Seth takes a deep breath, knowing there is no good way to begin as he scans the faces around the table.

"We need to discuss Liz's condition," he says. "Some of you may be hearing this for the first time, while others of you already know. Liz believes that her seizures are triggered by telepathic communication from an entity, an energy being who calls herself Abby. Abby claims to have been pulled through a wormhole to Omega, by way of Jackson's transporter, and she wants us to send her home. I'm sure it's hard to believe—it was hard for me to believe when Liz first explained it to me. But I believe she is telling the truth, and I want to discuss our options for getting Abby home."

Jackson nods somberly as Seth lets his words settle on the council.

"I, too, have come to accept Lizzie's reports as valid," he says. "The alien has communicated information Lizzie would have no way of knowing, and the communications coincide with the electrical surges that I have now witnessed firsthand." Jarrod's eyes dart between Jackson and Seth, and Harry looks confused.

"An alien?" he asks. "Claire, did you know about this?"

"I've been treating her seizures," Claire replies curtly, "but I have no ability to prove or disprove her claims about alien communication."

"The alien has a name," Mathilda murmurs through gritted teeth.

"You refer to her as an energy being," Jarrod interjects, looking at Seth intently. "What do you mean by that?"

"Her nature is beyond my understanding," he replies quickly, before Jackson can interrupt, "but according to what she tells Liz, she has no physical body. She says that when she communicates with Liz, she does it through tendrils of awareness—threads of consciousness that she seems to be able to extend across the universe."

"So, she's not fully present on the ship when she communicates with Liz?" Jarrod asks, brow furrowed. "If mere threads of herself are responsible for the surges, I'd hate to see what she could do if she showed up in her entirety."

"We have no reason to believe the alien is hostile," Jackson says quickly, raising his hands in a conciliatory gesture, "although it does seem easily frustrated."

Harry speaks again, still looking confused. "What does this being—this *Abby*—have to do with your machine, Jackson?"

"I wasn't sure at first," he begins, "but after scrutinizing my records, I think I see the connection now." Seth leans back in his chair, crossing his arms against his chest. *I can't wait to hear this,* he thinks, setting his mouth in a thin line as Jackson continues.

"The alien claims that when I was testing my machine, it was pulled through the wormhole and into linear time and space, away from wherever—or whenever—it was before. At first, I thought it was impossible for such a thing to happen. The wormholes I create only connect the two points in space that I designate. But in studying my detailed notes, I noticed an anomaly in one of the tests—a variance in the energy readings. To put it in lay terms, the alien didn't enter the wormhole from the beginning or the end, but rather from the side. I didn't notice it before, the variance was so slight, but after further examining the data, I believe I know where the alien originated and how to send it home."

"So, you *did* strand a being on Omega?" Jarrod asks, eying Jackson suspiciously. "How long has she been there?"

"It's hard to know for sure. It claims to have been for a long time, but I don't get the sense it has a good grasp of linear time."

"She!" Mathilda says. "She has a name—Abby."

"Yes, so I hear," Jackson responds, looking annoyed. "Folding the space-time continuum is a delicate, complex matter. I didn't expect to encounter an alien when I tested the transporter, much less accidentally suck it into the wormhole. It seems many things are possible—things I haven't yet considered fully."

"Abby!" Mathilda cries. "Her name is Abby! Stop calling her *it!* How many times have you done this, Jackson? How many other beings have you trapped?"

"Mathilda," he says sternly, "are we here for you to chide me, or are we here to solve the problem of dealing with this alien?"

"She has a name," Mathilda hisses, "and perhaps you should be accountable for your recklessness! You're tinkering with the very fabric of the universe, with no regard for the consequences!"

Funny, that's what Abby says, Seth thinks as he watches the exchange, waiting to see how Jackson will respond.

"People on Earth are starving," he snaps, leaning forward in a threatening manner. "Perhaps you don't understand all that entails, but I know firsthand. I'm willing to take a few risks to solve the problem. No one could have foreseen what happened to this alien, who chose to enter the wormhole. It—*she*—entered of its own accord. I pulled no one nowhere."

"Abby!" Mathilda screams, rising to her feet, fists clenched at her sides. "Her name is Abby! She's not an *it.* She's a *she*—a sentient being!" Seth watches as Shelby leans forward in her chair, perching herself on the edge as if she's ready to spring at Mathilda like a wild cat. Mathilda doesn't seem to notice as her narrowed eyes burn into Jackson's. The man exhales, slumping back into his chair as if he's bored.

"Do you want to hear how I propose we solve the problem, or not?" he asks to no one in particular, waving his hand dismissively.

"I'd like to hear," Claire says, casting an angry glance to Mathilda, who seems to wilt under the gaze and fold back into her chair.

"This alien, *Abby,* seems to have limited understanding of time and space," Jackson begins, "but it seems that *she* can move easily across vast distances. If she comes here, I'll transport her from the platform back to where she belongs."

"You're certain of the coordinates?" Seth asks, finding it unlikely that the solution came so easily when Jackson was adamant before that it was impossible.

"As I said, I know exactly where she needs to go."

"I don't like it," Jarrod says, shaking his head vigorously. "We don't know how Abby coming here might affect the ship. How do we know she won't destroy us?"

Jackson looks perplexed and dismayed, evaluating the other man as if he were slime on his shoe.

"We can't know," Seth says firmly, "which is why we need to be careful. But we have to help her—she's a threat to all of us. What if we do it from the bridge? Will the shields buffer the rest of the ship?"

"Perhaps," Jarrod says thoughtfully, "although the shields were designed to keep energy out, not contain it. There are servers and systems we need to protect, but I may be able to relocate them, to reroute the controls."

"Will we still have full control of the ship?" Seth asks.

"I'll have to make sure we do," Jarrod replies.

"We would also be required to relocate my transporter to the bridge," Jackson says curtly.

"I'm aware," Seth responds, "but I'm sure the bridge can accommodate it."

Jackson opens his mouth to speak again but seems to reconsider. He offers a tight smile instead, responding, "Very well, although we may need to delay the second shipment of food to Earth."

"We may," Seth agrees. "Jarrod, how much time to you need to prepare the bridge?"

"I don't know. We might be ready as early as this evening, but I'll have to confirm that after I review the system specifications in greater detail. Let's talk after the morning acceleration."

"Good," Seth says, thinking back to the perfectly barren circle on Omega. *If that's the effect Abby has on the planet, then what effect will she have on us?* He looks across the faces in the conference room gravely. "Let me be clear," he says sternly, "if anyone has concerns or reservations about what we're doing, I expect you to voice them. I will make myself available if you prefer to speak privately. We need to act quickly, but this is no small undertaking."

"How can we know if we have concerns or reservations?" Claire says brusquely. "We have no idea what or who we are dealing with."

"Liz has been interacting with Abby," Jarrod replies. "How has the experience affected her?"

"You mean besides her grand mal seizures?" Claire snaps.

"She only has seizures when the alien communicates with her telepathically," Jackson says, wagging his finger at Claire. "Other than the electrical surges, which seem to result from the alien directly applying energy to the ship, we've experienced no adverse effects from its presence."

"Abby!" Mathilda cries, rising from her chair and storming out of the conference room. "Her name is Abby!" Seth wonders if Mathilda has completely lost her mind, but haven't they all?

***

"Hey there, sleepyhead," Seth says gently as Liz opens her eyes to greet him. She wasn't actually sleeping when he came into her room, but she's come to appreciate the peace she feels when her eyes are closed. It's another layer of protection between the blissful emptiness of her brain and the too-bright, too-loud world that lies beyond the door to her room.

"Are you hungry?" Seth asks, setting a tray down on a rolling cart next to her bed. "I brought you ravioli from the cafeteria." Liz manages a smile, remembering that it's his favorite dish.

"You eat it," she replies in a hoarse, soft voice.

"I think you need it more than I do," he says, but she only shakes her head.

"I can't bear the thought of food right now."

"When did you last eat?" Seth asks, not unkindly. Liz manages a laugh.

"I don't even know what day it is, much less when I last ate. But I'm really not hungry. You eat it. I know it's your favorite."

He sighs deeply, a tired anguished sound, but he doesn't argue.

"I talked to Jackson and the council about Abby this morning," he says, taking a fork in his hand and moving the ravioli around the plate. "Jackson claims he found the coordinates to send Abby home."

"Really?" Liz asks, interest piqued as she pushes herself up in bed. "But didn't he say it was impossible to know?"

"He did say that," Seth agrees, "but now he says he found the coordinates. He says that she needs to come here, to the ship, and that he can transport her home. We're planning to relocate his transporter to the bridge, to try to shield the rest of the ship from her energy."

"The bridge?" Liz asks.

"I know," Seth says, stabbing a ravioli with the fork and taking a bite, "but the bridge has the best shielding. If it can keep energy out, surely it can keep energy in."

"Isn't that where the servers are for the propulsion drive?"

"Jarrod is relocating them, and he has to reroute other systems as well so we can maintain control of the ship. But I don't know what else to do, Z. We have to do something to help Abby, and we have to try to protect the ship from her energy. You know more about her than anyone—can it work?"

"It might," Liz says, chewing her bottom lip. "As long as she stays calm and keeps her vibration high. She's been all over the ship—in our data files and all our systems, but the only damage she's caused is when she gets angry or overly excited. Even when she's in my head, it isn't unbearable until she gets angry. How can we be sure Jackson found her coordinates, though? If he's not sure, or if he hasn't actually found her home, it might make her angry—angry enough to destroy all of us."

"We can't be sure," Seth says gravely. "None of us are qualified to question Jackson's claim. But what else can we do?"

Liz considers this for a moment, her brow furrowing as she shakes her head. "I don't know, but I don't have a good feeling about this."

"Do you want us to find another way?" Seth searches her eyes, desperate and pleading. "Say the word, and we'll stop."

Liz leans heavily back into the pillows.

"I'm not saying that. I don't know what we should do. I don't know what we can do. I don't have any better ideas." She closes her eyes, trying to calm the anxiety washing over her. "As far as I know, Jackson is the only one who can help her. So, I suppose we have to try. What do you need me to do?"

"At the moment, all you need to do is rest," Seth says. "We're relocating the transporter to the bridge now, and Jarrod will move the servers for the propulsion drive and reroute the other systems after the evening acceleration. We'll do it then."

CHAPTER 33

LIZ'S GIFT

***

Liz has never ridden in a wheelchair before, and she doesn't particularly want to now. But her legs refuse to support her weight, and she knows she cannot walk the distance between the medical unit and the bridge. And so, Claire pushes her, an IV cart rolling along beside her.

Liz has only been in the medical unit for five days, but it feels like she's always been there. She's almost forgotten her previous life on the ship, the people she knew, the things she did. She's almost forgotten about story time and the play the children wrote in her honor. Her life consists of visits from Seth and Jackson, conversations with Abby, and the blissful emptiness in her head that fills the space between. She could have changed out of her medical gown, but why? Liz has a feeling she'd only be wearing it again.

Everything looks different than she remembers it—the empty corridors, the bright lights, the large round windows looking into the abyss of space. *Abby is out there somewhere,* she thinks, unsure if this comforts or scares her. What will happen when Abby comes?

Liz can't rule out the possibility that Jackson is hiding something. He was certain that he couldn't help Abby before, so what changed? But surely, he's telling the truth. Surely, he knows how important this is, and how foolish it would be to lie about the coordinates. Liz wanted to impress this upon him when she spoke to him privately in the medical unit, after Seth left. "Don't try to deceive her, or mislead her in any way. You've seen what happens when you make her angry, and if she's fully present here, it will be worse—much worse. She could destroy us all."

Jackson only assured her that he was aware, and that he knew what he was doing. "I've got to do this, Lizzie," he told her. "It's the only way I can help you. We need to get her out of your head."

And now the time has come. The bridge seems different to Liz, although she tells herself it's because Jackson's transporter takes up the center of the room. The four poles that sit in each corner of the platform rise within inches of the ceiling, and Liz can see that entire workstations have been removed to make way for the machine. Even the large panoramic window looking into the darkness of space before them seems small compared to the machine.

Jackson sits to one side, holding his tablet in one hand and a glass vial of what appears to be liquid metal in the other. Shelby stands behind him, casually taking in everything around her. Seth is in the captain's chair, and the rest of the council are scattered among the remaining seats. Seth flashes Liz a smile that seems meant to reassure her, but it doesn't. She wants to go back to the medical unit, away from the bridge and Jackson's machine, away from the task she knows she must perform—summoning Abby for one last conversation.

"Jarrod, seal the bridge," Seth commands.

"The bridge is sealed, Captain," he replies. "The shields are activated."

"Disengage all systems," Seth says.

"Systems disengaged," he confirms.

"Jackson, are you ready?"

"Indeed." He inserts the glass vial of liquid metal through a small door in the platform. "The coordinates are set, but I will wait to activate the transporter until we know the alien is here."

"Abby," Mathilda mutters. Liz looks at her forlorn and broken face. *She must feel very alone.* The thought makes her sad in a way it didn't before. She glances over at Jarrod, looking nervous and attentive, and then to Harry, whose craggy face always looks so kind. *He's always been there for me.* Liz realizes that he may be the closest thing to a father she's known. *Is that what a father does?* She cannot know. Her own father left so long ago she can't remember what he looked like, much less what he did or how he acted. Liz looks away from Harry, her eyes falling on Shelby. Something about her seems off—wrong in a way Liz can't explain. She doesn't want to think about it now, so she looks quickly away.

Turning her gaze to Seth's face, she takes in his dark, sleek hair, his finely cut features. This is who she wants to see. This is who she wants to remember. He looks back at her, his own gaze full of worry and doubt. She smiles, and a corner of his mouth raises in return. They share a glance until Jackson interrupts.

"Lizzie," he says with an air of authority, "it's up to you now." But Liz knows it's not up to her—not really. It's up to Abby, and to Jackson. All Liz believes for certain is that this will be her last conversation with Abby—Jackson will send her home, or Abby will realize he can't and shred her brain with rage. Either way, the end is near.

Liz closes her eyes and calls her name, *Abby. Abby. Abby.*

I am here, the reply comes, in the soft, feminine voice that now feels familiar, almost comfortable. *What has happened?*

Jackson found the coordinates. He knows how to send you home. He's ready to do it now.

But he said it was impossible.

He did say that, but he studied the data from his tests more closely. He found an anomaly, the place from which you originated.

Interesting, Abby replies, and Liz can detect a hint of suspicion in her tone.

Will you come? Jackson believes you need to come here, to access the wormhole from the platform on his machine.

He has no ability to trap me, Abby replies sternly. *If he intends to lure me into a trap, or deceive me in any way, he will fail.*

Abby, your vibration … Liz feels her left eye begin to pulse painfully. *Raise your vibration. I want to help you get home, but please don't hurt me. I don't want to hurt anymore. Will it hurt if you come?* Liz's head begins to hum, and she braces herself for pain. But it doesn't come.

I intend you no harm, Abby replies, *but I cannot be certain. Are you certain of your brother's intentions, Liz? Are you certain it's wise for me to come?*

I don't know. Liz feels her heart quicken with panic. *I cannot know, but I think this is our best chance to help you.*

I will come, Abby says. Liz waits with her eyes closed, not able to bear inquisitive looks from Seth and Jackson, nor derision from Claire, nor sadness from Mathilda. She cannot bear the thought of the question she knows they will ask—is Abby here?

Liz doesn't know how long she waits, only that she is waiting and then there is a sensation. It's the same sensation she imagines a magnet feeling, as if the very threads of her life are being pulled to the edges of her body. Abby is coming, wrapping more and more tendrils of awareness around Liz's consciousness to home in on her precise location, to pull them together with the full force of her being.

Liz's ears fill with white noise, and her eyes flutter open to a panoramic window full of crackling static. The stars are gone. The void of space is gone. Abby is coming. Liz can see her, a flaming hydra with many arms. They all reach for her, yearning to anchor Abby's arrival.

Abby's tendrils set Liz's mind afire, but they do not burn her skin. They wrap around her, eagerly but gently, in a sacred communion that cocoons her from everything she knows to be real. She can feel Abby moving closer, or is she farther away? Liz feels herself moving faster than she's ever moved before, faster than light or thought or feeling.

Down, down, down she goes, Abby's tendrils braiding around her and washing her in a sea of energy. Together, they fall into places Liz could never imagine, places where contradictions live in harmony, oblivious to any other way of being—she is full yet empty, moving but still, filled with light and dark. She wonders if she can hold on to her mind, to some shred of identity that is hers alone, but she knows it's futile. She knows without being told that if she struggles, she will suffer. *Raise your vibration,* she tells herself, unsure what she's asking herself to do but finding comfort in the words.

"Do you see her?" Liz cries. She isn't sure who she's talking to—maybe Jackson, maybe Seth. Maybe herself. She hears murmurs around her, grasping only pieces of the conversation. A snippet of Jarrod's voice, sounding urgent as he says something about sensor readouts and energy levels. Seth bellows out commands, but she cannot comprehend what he says. Nor does it matter. Abby is coming, with all of her energy, and Liz knows now that nothing can contain her. No shield can deflect her. No mind can accommodate her. Suddenly, she's afraid, not for herself but for Jackson, her brother who angers Abby with such ease. He has no idea who he's dealing with, no idea of her power.

Liz's own train of thought begins to vaporize into specks of sand, time wound backward and then forward, constructing and deconstructing before her. She hears herself screaming, "She's here! She's here!" Then she wails in fear as she feels her now-fragile mind begin to crack like glass that's been heated and then cooled too fast. She doesn't know if the scream reaches her lips, only that she can sense a flurry of activity around her.

Liz hears her brother humming as he begins to bring his own machine to life. He doesn't need to sing the words to the song—she can already hear them in her head, superimposed as time once again blurs and compresses. *Hush-a-bye, don't you cry. Go to sleep my little baby, and when you wake, you shall have, all the pretty little horses.* She can see Jackson as a boy, feel her mother brushing her wet hair into a braid. Liz wants to step into that world, the world where they are still a family, a world where things might turn out differently.

Suddenly, everything around her is displaced by Abby's voice. *I know what he intends,* she brays, her voice fracturing into many voices, some high and some low. Abby's anger is rising, filling Liz's mind and her body with a fire that threatens to consume her. *I warned you. I warned you not to deceive me!*

Liz opens her eyes, frantically searching for her brother, but all she can see is his machine. It glows with color Liz cannot describe, color she doesn't think human eyes can see. *Is this how Abby sees it?* she wonders, overcome by the nausea of standing between two mirrors that reflect eternity. She closes her eyes, flailing to orient herself and failing.

"Jackson, what have you done?" she screams, eyes shut tight. "What have you done?" But Liz already knows. She knows that what lies on the other side of the wormhole is not Abby's home, but a place almost too far away to perceive, a place dark and empty. She knows because Abby knows, and Abby is furious.

Abby, she pleads, *your vibration—raise your vibration.* Liz is vaguely aware of a console exploding next to her, the sensation of heat and sound on her skin. Her eyes register Claire diving to the floor beside her, curling into a ball and covering her head with her hands, as if that will save her. Her ears register more commands, urgency in Seth's voice. The humanity that remains in her sifts through the chaos, searching for the face that matches the voice she loves. Her eyes lock with Seth's for a moment, those blue eyes that she knows so well—sometimes lightning, sometimes steel. She registers a fleeting thought that he is in danger, very serious danger, and then all she can perceive is Abby. Abby's voice displaces everything else in Liz's awareness. *I have no desire to raise my vibration, Liz. I have no desire to try. My only desire is to make him pay for what he has done.*

Abby is on the brink of losing control. Everyone around her is teetering on the edge of annihilation. Liz can sense her brother, clutching Shelby to his chest and cowering in the wake of his deception. He cannot save her now, and even if he could, Liz knows he won't. He's lost in the haze of his own convictions, his own sense of right and wrong that is more important to him than any person could ever be.

Liz loves him anyway, not for what he's done or hasn't done, not for who he is or who he isn't. She loves him because she knows who he can be, if he chooses. She loves him without conditions, requiring nothing in return. She cannot trust him. She doesn't even like him now. She's not sure she ever wants to see him again, but she loves him, nonetheless, and she knows she always will. Despite what he's done, she won't watch him die. In a flash, Liz knows what she must do.

She cries out, holding on to what may be the last shred of independent thought she possesses, *Abby, raise your vibration!* It's not a request or a suggestion. It's a command that echoes through their collective awareness and shutters out everyone and everything around them. *Raise your vibration,* she commands again. *Forget about Jackson. Forget about his machine. It doesn't matter now. We are together, and together, we can find your home. We can activate my gift.*

Liz feels herself floating, disembodied and wrapped in Abby's embrace. She knows that somewhere, a world away, her body is collapsing, falling onto the ground in convulsions. She knows that Seth is rushing toward her, fighting for every step through the chaos of Abby's destruction on the bridge. She knows that she may not survive what is to come, that in fact she probably won't. Liz can accept dying now, but she cannot accept everyone else dying, not if she has the ability to save them.

And now she does.

Why? Abby asks, her voice softer now. *You know what might happen. Does your brother mean that much to you? Do you find him worthy of such a sacrifice?*

I will not judge his worth, Liz replies. *Nor will I watch you destroy everyone I love. You have no right to do so, not if I offer you another way. I've made my choice, to offer you my gift. What choice will you make, Abby? What consequences will you create for yourself?* Liz waits for Abby to choose. A few moments pass—or perhaps it's an eternity—and then Abby replies.

Thank you, she says. *Thank you for reminding me of who I really am, and for offering this gift. I choose to accept it.*

Suddenly, Liz has no ears to hear, no eyes to see. She has no body, no mind—only Abby. She is consumed in light and fire and sensations she cannot categorize into anything familiar. Then she understands—it's a vibration. Abby's vibration, her vibration—they are one now, and they are getting higher.

A new way of being unfolds before her like a fiery rose, beautiful and deadly powerful. They rise higher and higher, and the last part of Liz that remains herself is extinguished, like a flame with no oxygen. She sees what Abby sees—everything. Time and space mean nothing. Matter is nothing, and nothing matters. She is indescribably powerful, and then suddenly, she is overtaken by a wave of exhilaration truer than anything Liz has ever known.

I am free, she thinks, although she has no mind of her own. She is Abby, and Abby is she. She takes in the vastness of space and time, and then she flies higher and higher, through realities she cannot comprehend, realities that are so foreign to her that she knows trying to comprehend them will break her. She doesn't need to comprehend them. She only needs to search, to perceive something familiar. She casts out her awareness in every direction, until she finds it. It echoes with memories that bubble up from the core of her being, memories of home. She is home.

Then, suddenly, Abby lets go. Liz is herself again, and she is falling, falling, falling, into an abyss she has no energy to escape. She registers the sensation of her human body—pain. Lots of pain. She opens her eyes for what she knows might be the last time. Everything she wants to see is right in front of her. Seth's eyes are bright and alive. He tries to pull her close to him, to shield her with his body, but she resists, not wanting to take her gaze off his face. If this is the end, his face is the last thing she wants to see. She tells him she loves him, or perhaps it's only a thought, and then she is falling again, into blackness that promises relief.

***

Liz feels an immaculate peace wash over her. She knows where she is even before she opens her eyes. She can smell the sweet grass, feel the warmth of the rising sun on Cyril's eyes. The taste of dew carries on the morning air. She opens her eyes to commune with the sun, knowing it's a new day. It's a special day, and Cyril has a special job. There is new life in the family—babies. It's time to celebrate.

Are they my babies? Liz wonders, and for some reason this question strikes her as odd. Why is this odd? She finds herself amused by the question. Then she realizes. She cannot have babies in this place because Cyril is male.

Besides, I would have to be chosen, by a female. Liz considers this, feeling a twinge of something like disappointment on the periphery of her bliss. She waits for more knowing to come—Cyril has not been chosen by a female, because he's different than the others. He's curious and inventive, and the rest of the family isn't quite sure whether he should reproduce or not. What if his babies are as different as he is?

Liz can sense that the family's doubt hurts Cyril, but not very much. He is content to enjoy his life, and he can still enjoy the babies. From the moment they arrive, they are full members of the community. Their mothers must nurture them for a period of time, but they are everyone's babies.

Just last night, six were born, and tonight they will celebrate. The family will feast, and dance, and the babies will be anointed. They will feel the joy of communing for the first time, even if they aren't quite old enough to understand what it means.

The elders gave Cyril a special job to prepare for the celebration—gathering flowers for the babies. It's a dangerous task, but Cyril is happy to do it. He's proud to do it, in fact. Not everyone is capable, but he is.

He scampers toward the forest. Liz loves how the air fills his lungs, sweet and nourishing. She can feel the strength of his legs moving underneath him, the dexterity of his body as he runs through the grass toward the trees, filled with joy and determination.

Liz feels a familiar coolness as Cyril enters the forest. The ground is covered with thick layers of what appear to be pine needles, soft and pungently fragrant under his feet. His steps are silent in this cool, immense place, but the forest itself is not silent. There is singing, creatures perched on branches and flying through the air.

Liz recognizes a familiar detour, to collect the cart stored in the large hollow of a special tree. Cyril pulls a patchwork of small branches away from the opening of the hollow and reaches inside, grabbing the strap woven from the sweet-smelling grass to pull the cart out. The polished wooden rails slide effortlessly over the thick cushion of needles on the ground, filling him with pure joy.

Liz feels Cyril slip into the harness, scampering off feeling strong, proud, fierce, and intelligent. He is unique—a gatherer of flowers and the creator of this cart. No one is like him. He has a lot to offer, even if he is strange.

Liz knows that the family recognizes his contributions—appreciates him, even. But they don't want more of him. How can he accept such judgment without malice? But Cyril is unwilling to dwell on the question further. There is much to appreciate about the moment, about what is happening now. The forest floor is soft on his feet. His body is strong, and the harness presses comfortably against his chest. Liz's misgivings don't exist in this moment, because Cyril is happy and free.

He scampers, breathing deeply, until he arrives at the tree where Liz knows without being told that he will find the flowers. He sits to rest at its base, the trunk so massive that it blocks out the rest of the world. Leaning back against the tree, he wiggles and achieves the most delectable scratching sensation. The day is long, and there is plenty of time to do everything that needs doing.

Something flutters by—a creature that reminds Liz of a butterfly. It's beautiful, although she knows that it's best avoided—dangerous. *Only if you anger them,* she remembers as Cyril prepares to climb the tree. It's easy enough, once he extends his claws on all four feet. Liz would have appreciated claws like this back on Earth, but she dismisses the thought as quickly as it comes. She's not on Earth anymore.

I never want to leave, she thinks as Cyril climbs and

climbs, closer and closer to the sky. She's surprised to sense a different voice responding to her.

How can you leave? it asks. *You're not here yet.*

But I am here.

You're not here—not all of you, anyway.

Liz considers this but doesn't want to dwell on it. In this moment, the questions seem inconsequential. It's more important to feel the bark under Cyril's paws, to breathe the cool air and watch the canopy of the tree grow closer and closer. Cyril perches on a branch, which jiggles slightly under his weight. *What kind of tree is this?* Liz is sure it has a name, but it seems unimportant now. Only the flowers are important.

Cyril turns back to the main trunk, which is still so large that it takes up his whole field of vision, and begins to climb again, higher and higher until the ground seems like a dream from long ago. Bunches of needles get thicker, branches closer together. They remind Liz of pine trees, but they aren't. She knows the needles are dangerous—they will inject Cyril with poison if he touches them. Not enough to kill him, but he'd be lethargic and useless for days. She wills him to be careful, but he isn't worried.

Cyril keeps climbing, so close to the top of the tree that Liz can see the sky. It's exhilarating. A puffy white cloud floats above the tree. If Cyril stretches his paw up, standing tall on his strong legs, Liz might be able to touch it. Has she ever touched a cloud? She doesn't know, but it isn't urgent. It's enough to take it in with her eyes.

The top of the tree sways in the breeze, but Cyril is unconcerned. All he needs to do is hold on and move in time with the tree. *Is this communing?* she wonders, but before her mind can reach any conclusion, she catches a glimpse of the velvety white petals of one of the flowers she's come to find.

It's beautiful—delicate and exotic. She can detect its unique aroma, even though the wind is blowing the other way. Cyril crouches down on the swaying branch, taking in the scene. He creeps out slowly, determined to disturb nothing. Liz knows this is important, although she doesn't remember why.

Cyril needs six flowers, one for each baby. He chose the proper tree—there are dozens of flowers, each of them blooming with perfect feeling. He waits and watches, choosing which six to collect. He must be fast. He must be accurate. He must be focused. Liz knows Cyril is all of those things.

Then, the moment is right. Cyril hops out onto the branch. Fast as lightning, he plucks two bunches of three flowers. As soon as he breaks the stalks, he leaps into the air, looking down just in time to see the needles of the tree snap closed just beneath his feet. He clasps the stems of the flowers in one paw and lets himself fall, grabbing onto a lower branch with his free paw. He swings himself up on this branch, the one where the needles have been undisturbed, being careful not to crush the flowers. The bouquet is large, six blooms almost as big as his body.

Cyril scampers down the tree, victorious. He arranges the flowers in the cart, carefully so none are crushed. Then he returns to the tree, placing his front paws on the bark.

Thank you, he whispers, and as if the tree has heard, Liz can sense it swaying in the breeze. She can feel a small pulse, the very essence of its life, through the bark, saying to Cyril, *Next time, my little friend.*

This is where I belong, Liz thinks.

She hears the other voice—the voice that she assumes belongs to the part of Cyril that is not her. It says, *Then come, and commune with us.*

Commune? She wonders, but before she can further consider what this means, she is falling again. Falling forever, into the darkness, sadder than she's ever been at being torn away from this place that she wants to never leave.

***

Showers of sparks rain down on Seth's back as he holds Liz close to his body. He can feel her shaking, waves of tremors. He does not know if Abby is still with them or if she is gone. He wants to hit someone—to hit Jackson. He wants to scream at the man in rage and pummel his face to a pulp. Seth should have known it was a trick, that Jackson lied about finding the coordinates to Abby's home after being so adamant that they were lost to him.

His rage is strong and fierce, but it pales next to his fear. He clutches Liz tightly to him, trying to protect her from the lights that continue to explode and the sparks raining down. The way that she looked at him before she went unconscious, the way she whispered that she loved him, as if speaking the words might be draining the last of her life force—Seth doesn't know if even she can survive this. He doesn't know what happened in her mind or her body as Abby was on the verge of destroying the ship.

He can hear Jarrod's voice, overwrought, urgent words spilling out of his mouth too fast to comprehend. The man's fingers are flying, typing in commands on a console, but Seth doesn't know what he's doing. The bridge is in disarray. It smells like ozone, probably from Jackson's machine. Seth remembers the smell after they transported the food back to Earth, but it wasn't nearly this strong. It's much worse now—suffocating.

He sees Harry next, frantically pulling a fire extinguisher off the wall. The man appears to be saying something, but Seth can't make out the words over the ringing in his ears. Harry aims the fire extinguisher at an empty console, and now Seth can see the flames, hidden behind the desk but starting to peek out around. He wonders if anything remains of the ship below them.

Liz feels light in his arms—too light, like she's barely there. *Hold on,* he wills her.

His mother looks stunned, frozen in a crouch beside Liz's wheelchair. He quickly looks away from her, and his eyes settle on Mathilda.

She stands alone, oblivious to the chaos around her. Arms hanging casually by her side, she stares at the panoramic window ahead of her. Seth can see her mouth hanging open, her heavily rimmed glasses askew on her face. He turns his head to see what she's looking at, and his breath hitches. Is the ozone suffocating him, or is it the sight ahead of him, out the window?

He could see it better if he were standing, but he doesn't want to move Liz, or let her go—not yet. But even from his position, he can see what lies before them. A planet. He can see the blue of the water and a tip of land. He's certain that when he looks, it will remind him of an owl, a huge owl swooping down over an island that looks like a baby elephant. Omega.

"How are we here?" he asks, but he can't hear himself over the ringing in his ears. He stands up, lifting Liz. She's light as a feather in his arms, and he realizes the ship isn't moving—not substantially anyway. "We've stopped," he says to no one in particular, holding Liz in his arms as he stands and appraises the unbelievable sight in front of him. He's never seen a planet like this. Did Earth look this way once? It takes his breath away, or is that the ozone?

"Yes," Jarrod says, eyes wild as Seth looks over, surprised that anyone heard him.

"Let me look," Jackson says, standing and beginning to span the distance between them. Jarrod draws his pistol and points it at the man's heart.

"If you come one step closer to me, I will empty this clip into your chest!" Jarrod's eyes are wild. "You did this. You've done all this! You lied to us about sending Abby home. You put all of us at risk, just as you've been doing all along!"

Jackson raises his hands in a conciliatory gesture, although he doesn't appear afraid.

"I didn't lie," he says. "I was certain those were the proper coordinates. I did my best to send the alien home, and I accept no blame for its fury. It had an exceptionally volatile temperament, and most likely intended to destroy us all long. We're fortunate Lizzie was able to develop a rapport with it. I have no doubt she saved us all." He opens his mouth to speak again, but Seth cuts him off.

"Liz needs medical attention. Jarrod, can you unseal the bridge?"

"Captain, I have no readings from any other part of the ship. I'm not sure it's safe."

Harry, still standing by the door, balls his fist and bangs on it three times, metallic booms that stab Seth's ears. Everyone waits, and then the sound comes—two booms in return.

"It's the security detail outside the bridge. If they're still alive, it must be safe."

Jarrod finds Seth's eyes, his own fearful and questioning. Seth nods, and after a few key strokes, the doors to the bridge begin to hiss and then open. Ellis stands on the other side, his face washed in bewilderment as he tries to take in everything before him.

"Have we stopped, Captain?"

"It seems we've arrived," Seth replies. "Go in and take a look if you'd like." Seth sees his mother to his right, pushing the wheelchair. *Is it over?* he wonders. *Is Abby home? Does any of it matter if Liz is gone, too?*

"Captain!" Seth hears Jarrod's voice behind him. It seems so far away. He turns to face him, Liz still clutched tightly in his arms. "I'm getting the systems back online. We need to run diagnostics."

"Captain." This time it's Ellis, standing behind the wheelchair. "It seems you are needed here. Dr. Harris and I can get Liz to the medical unit. I'll call you the moment we know something."

Seth studies the man, his earnest face, his weathered blue eyes. He looks across the bridge. Jarrod continues to stare at him expectantly, and even Jackson seems curious about what he will do, standing next to the platform, putting his laptop back into his leather satchel. Mathilda continues to stand in front of the panoramic window, oblivious to everything going on around her.

Seth knows what he wants to do, and what he must do instead. He places Liz in the wheelchair, taking a final look at her unconscious face and exchanging nods with Ellis. His mother appears behind him, leaning over Liz to feel for a pulse, to search for signs of life.

"I'm sure she'll be alright," she says, looking up at her son. Seth says nothing. He needs Liz to be alright. If she's not, he will drain the life out of Jackson Goeff for everything he's done and everything he hasn't.

"Charlie is coming, Captain," Ellis says, pulling Seth's attention back to the present moment. "He'll take my position outside the door."

"Thank you," Seth says, feeling disconnected from his body, as if all the life has been drained out of him. He turns and goes back to the bridge, sitting back in the captain's chair to sort through everything that has happened and what needs to be done next.

CHAPTER 34

A MOTHER'S HEART

***

NOVEMBER 2, 2059—SUNDAY

It's late, and the ship is mostly settled for the night. Outside the medical unit, Ruth sits on the floor in an alcove. She's hidden underneath a small counter, which houses a phone and a fire extinguisher. Liz is inside the medical unit. Ruth heard she had another seizure, which is worrying. She's heard other things from Ellis that worry her as well, the way Captain Harris carried her off the bridge unconscious, the way Dr. Harris produced a wheelchair as if she knew Liz wouldn't be walking on her own back to the medical unit. It was the same time they had those strange electrical surges, and the same time they passed through whatever wormhole brought them to this strange place.

Ruth doesn't know what a wormhole is exactly, but she understands the concept—a door between two distant places. She's gathered from the chatter around her that the ship passed through some kind of wormhole, although she's not quite sure how they survived. She knows Jackson's machine creates wormholes, but he insisted everything be coated in that strange green goo—presumably for protection. Was the ship protected?

Ruth dismisses the question. She probably wouldn't understand the answer, anyway. All she needs to know is that they have arrived, and having reached their destination, they have stopped.

Ruth has seen the planet through the large, round window. There's something about it that frightens her terribly, an eeriness at seeing a planet that is blue and green as well as brown, a planet with no lights but two moons, sometimes visible and other times not. Perhaps it's the unknown that frightens her, the uncertainty of what all this means. Apparently, this is where they intended to go—the turnaround point. And it's nice that they don't have to accelerate anymore. In fact, she feels light as air now that gravity is normalized, as if she might float away if she's not careful. But she's noticed that they aren't turning around.

Ruth has heard that Jackson intends to go back to Earth, and all signs point to this being true. The children still hide in the vents and listen, and he's been talking to the woman about it. She thinks they'll go tomorrow, so time is running short for Dr. Harris to secret Liz away, an unwilling stowaway to go back with him. Ruth made sure someone was sitting at Liz's bedside continuously, at least until Dr. Harris imposed visiting hours. She said Liz needed undisturbed rest and careful monitoring to recuperate. Careful monitoring, indeed.

Ruth watches the doors to the medical unit, unable to get in and unwilling to delegate the job to someone else—not tonight. Soon enough, the doors open, and Dr. Harris barely looks both ways before pushing a large laundry cart into the hallway. It seems the doctor is actually going through with the plan. Ruth hoped she'd think better of herself, or perhaps change her mind. She wonders if Captain Harris had hoped the same thing—he never posted guards outside Liz's door, although he must have other ways to monitor her room.

Ruth sits quietly as Dr. Harris wheels the cart down the corridor, toward the lift. As soon as she turns the corner, Ruth pushes herself to her feet, her old body protesting the time spent cramped. She lifts the phone off the receiver and dials the number Captain Harris gave her.

"Yes, Ruth?" he says, answering quickly.

"It's happening." She hears a click and knows he terminated the call. She waits, at least one minute, maybe two, before creeping toward the lift. She takes it down to Level 35, and then works her way down to Level 37 via the stairs. She quietly pushes open the door, realizing quickly that she has no need of stealth. The argument underway is loud enough to drown out any noise she might make.

"You have no right!" Captain Harris's voice booms, making Ruth shrink. But Dr. Harris only raises her own voice to match her son's.

"You don't think clearly around her!" Her voice isn't just loud, it's strident and accusing. "Calm down and let me explain to you why this needs to happen."

"No, this is not happening." Ruth can see Captain Harris pull the cart away from his mother, flinging a sheet off the top and peering inside. She moves closer, hiding in the darkness behind a stack of crates loaded and ready for tomorrow's shipment. The only thing left to load is the livestock—and apparently Liz.

She can see Ellis, Charlie, and Ruben standing to one side. Her eyes meet Ellis's, and he gives her the slightest shake of his head, telling her not to come any closer.

"Seth," the doctor pleads, "this is the only way we can make peace with Jackson!"

"What did you give her?" Captain Harris demands. Ruth cringes at the fury in his voice. Did Dr. Harris imagine he would respond differently? Or did she think she'd be able to blame Jackson and hide her role in Liz's disappearance from him? Does she know the man her son is?

"A sedative," she says, her voice deflating. "She'll be out another eighteen hours—long enough for her wake up comfortably in Jackson's medical facility on Earth."

"Comfortably?" he cries. "Comfortably? Of all the things you could have done! Of all the things … this?"

"We have to do this, Seth. It's the only way. You'll realize this in time, when you can see the situation more clearly."

"No, Mom, I won't. You have crossed a line you cannot uncross. Perhaps you will realize this when you can see the situation more clearly."

"Seth, all I want—"

"I don't care what you want! This isn't your decision to make."

"It's the only way I can save you!" she cries. "She must go back with Jackson, and you must relinquish control of the ship."

"I don't need you to save me. And I'm not going back to Earth."

Dr. Harris laughs—part maniacal and part condescension. "What are you going to do? Stay here?"

"That's exactly what I am going to do."

"Seth, that's ridiculous. We know nothing about this planet, and we need to get the ship back to Earth. We can't stay here."

"*We* aren't staying here. *I* am staying here. You will be returning with the ship."

Ruth can see the very moment Dr. Harris registers what her son is telling her. It's palpable, like a spoonful of dry flour gumming up her mouth. Her face drops.

"Seth, you can't be suggesting …"

"After everything we've been through, Mom, how could you do this to me? Of all the ways you could choose to undermine me, of all the ways you could have hurt me, this is the one you choose?" Ruth hears the captain's voice break.

Dr. Harris looks astounded, speechless with her mouth hanging open.

"Seth," she says, barely more than a whisper, "I'm sorry."

"I doubt that very much," he says, his voice filled with an unforgiving fury. "You will return to your quarters and remain there until further notice. You can either go there now of your own volition, or I can have you dragged there against your will."

He turns away from her, wiping his eyes with his hands.

"Seth," she whispers, moving to reach out to him, but Ellis steps in her way. He shepherds her away from the man who used to be her child, beckoning her toward the lift, urging her to walk on her own two feet back to her quarters.

"Please, Dr. Harris," she hears Ellis whisper. "Please, let's go."

She looks numb, disoriented as if she's just awoken from a bad dream. She takes a step forward, looking back again at her son. He will not face her, keeping his back turned as he leans into the cart toward Liz. His mother takes another step, lurching forward, and Ruth thinks she might cry. Ellis ushers her away, firmly but patiently.

Why did she have to do this? She can almost feel the doctor's heart breaking. Ruth was a mother too, once. She knows that children can break a mother's heart in a way no one else can. But why did she have to do this? Is she really that arrogant? Does she really believe Captain Harris to be that easily manipulated? Dr. Harris has miscalculated her son, and now she must bear the cost of losing him.

Ruth moves farther into the darkness of the crates, watching the broken woman shuffle by. Ellis lightly holds her elbow as if she might topple over, or perhaps crumble to the ground.

She hears the captain behind her. "Charlie, let's get Liz to my quarters."

"Should Dr. Singh meet us there?" Charlie asks.

"Yes, thank you," he says, in a voice that Ruth finds broken.

She can hear the wheels of the cart, the soft fall of footsteps coming toward her. Her thoughts are reeling, her head spinning. She has a decision to make, but isn't it already made?

Ruth steps out from behind the crates. Captain Harris looks surprised. She meets his gaze squarely, knowing this is too important to waver.

"We'll go," she says, "All fifty-two of us."

"Go?"

"To the planet," she replies. "You'll need help. We can help you. Don't do this alone."

His expression seems curious, and she hopes she looks strong standing before him. He considers her for a moment before giving her a nod, replacing his hand on the side of the cart and continuing on toward the lift. He motions for her to walk next to him.

"I haven't talked to Liz about this yet," he says quietly as they all load onto the elevator and he swipes a key card to access Level 1. "I can't be sure she'll want to join me."

Ruth is surprised by this.

"Don't you know that Liz would follow you anywhere?"

"Liz isn't a follower," he says, a hint of a rueful smile in one corner of his mouth.

Ruth considers her response carefully, not wanting to be misunderstood. "She's a strong woman. Strong women won't follow just anyone, but Liz believes in you. She will go where you go."

"I hope so," he mutters. They ride to the top of the ship in silence.

Ruth follows him into his quarters, surprised that he doesn't stop her. It's been a long time since she's been any-where this nice. She takes it in quickly, turning her attention to Liz's unconscious body as the captain lifts her carefully out of the laundry cart. It looks so easy, like she's light as a feather. Ruth can see the care with which he handles her, gently.

"May I sit with her?" she asks quickly, just as she hears a knock on the door.

"Of course," the captain says quickly, turning his atten-tion to the door. Ruth sees a chair in a corner and pulls it toward the bed, settling into it and resting her hand on Liz's smooth skin. It feels too cool, and Ruth covers it with her own hand, pressing her warmth into Liz's skin. She can hear the captain's voice, but she cannot make out his words.

Dr. Singh comes in, nodding to Ruth but saying noth-ing, taking Liz's other hand to check her pulse, using her free hand to raise her eyelids one by one.

"I'd like to start an IV," Dr. Singh says, standing to face the captain.

"Can you revive her?" he asks.

"Maybe," she says noncommittally, "but let's make sure she's stable first."

Ruth sits in silence, willing herself to become invisible so that the captain doesn't remember to send her away. She'll be back among her own people soon enough. For now, she wants nothing more than to sit in the darkness with Liz, to sit with what remains of her memories of her own children and infuse them into this young woman.

"Charlie," the captain says quietly, "post a guard outside my mother's quarters."

"Yes, Captain," Charlie replies. He pauses for a moment. "Captain?"

"Yes, Charlie?"

"I'd like to go, too. I may not be the best security officer, but I bet you'll need a good mechanic down on the surface."

The captain doesn't answer right away. Ruth thinks she can hear him breathing, although perhaps it's her own breathing she hears. Eventually he speaks.

"I'd like that, Charlie."

Ruth hears Charlie's breath hitch.

"Thank you, Captain."

CHAPTER 35

COMMUNION

****

NOVEMBER 10, 2059—MONDAY

Liz knows as soon as she sets her foot on the ground that she's home. Seth stands beside her, but she can't see his face. He insisted they wear full protective gear, even though Mathilda confirmed the atmosphere on Omega was breathable.

"We don't know what kind of life is on the planet," he said, unwilling to budge on the point. "We don't know what kind of pollen, bacteria, or viruses might be in the air. We're not doing it." Liz didn't contest. Mathilda didn't either, although they complied for different reasons. Liz simply didn't want to waste time arguing. She wanted to get on the planet.

Now she's here.

If she squints, she can see his eyes through his visor. They are inquisitive but fearless, vibrant in the sunshine. Does he feel as alive as she does? Does he know he's home too, or would his eyes look the same if they were standing on Earth now? Liz doesn't have to reach far to find the memory of Seth on Earth—she only has one, the day she smuggled him aboard her shuttle so he could explore the depot. She doesn't remember him looking this vibrant then, but he wasn't the same person then, either. She realizes that she can't compare the man beside her to the boy she took to Earth. Besides, why think about the past when they're here now, together with the people who came to set up an outpost on Omega?

Liz can feel the energy pulsing through the ground beneath her. She can feel what remains of Abby, the shadow or imprint of her presence there even though she is gone. But a new energy is here also, something different than she has ever known. She can't wait to get to know it better. Literally, she can't wait.

She registers Seth's voice objecting as she unlatches her helmet and removes her breathing mask. She knows he's worried, but more importantly, she knows she's safe. She just knows. The air is as sweet as she knew it would be. It's the smell of the grass. The sun feels so good on her skin, blissful.

She can hear water lapping somewhere behind her, the grass blowing in front of her. This is the way she wants to go. She steps forward tentatively, soaking in the way the grass rustles under her foot, the way it moves as a breeze blows the sweet smell of flowers into her nostrils. Yes, this is the way to the marsh, and that's where the best grass grows. She knows without being told.

Each step fills her with joy, making her steps lighter even though she's so much fuller. She feels her pace quicken, knowing who she seeks. Her steps become longer, her smile wider as she makes her way through the grass. It comes up to her knees, but she knows it would seem much taller if she walked on four legs.

Liz breaks into a run. Her ears register so many sounds, the least of which is Seth's voice calling behind her. She can hear his whooshing footsteps as he tries to keep up.

She stops for a moment, needing to feel the ground beneath her feet more than she's ever needed it. She wants to soak up everything she can about this land into every pore of her being. Pulling her boots off hastily, then the thin socks she wears beneath, she feels the soft grass under her feet as she takes off in a run.

"Z!" Seth calls from behind her. "Wait! Where are you going?"

Liz spins around for a moment, spreading her arms wide as she laughs.

"There's someone I need to see!" she cries back. "Don't worry! I know where I'm going. And I know my way back too."

She runs across the grass, feeling no fatigue. She can see a forest in the distance, but she doesn't need to go that far. She stops when she sees the rustle ahead of her. She knows that he knows she's here.

"Cyril!" she cries, as a furry body emerges from the sweet blades. His dark eyes look perplexed, and she sees a quiver of fear in the spikes of his fur. "Cyril, I'm here," she says more gently. She sits on the grass and then lies back, stretching her arms and legs wide and looking up at the blue sky that is familiar even though it shouldn't be.

A moment later, she sees the furry face she knows so well but has never seen before. He studies her for a moment, and she allows it to happen, waiting for him to recognize her. She sits up when he disappears from her field of vision to find him sitting as well, up on his haunches, clasping his front paws in front of his body as if he's waiting for her to be ready. She can hear his voice in her head.

"Are you here to commune?" he asks, studying her.

"I'm not sure I know how," she replies, feeling the joy heal every ache she's carried for so long.

"I can show you," he says, looking at her for a moment before he sprawls flat on his back, rolling in the grass in a way that Liz knows is utterly delicious.

"Teach me, Cyril," she says, happy to finally be here. Soon enough, she will go back. She will find her boots and her socks. She will go back to Seth and help set up the outpost they are building. She will do what she needs to get them established here and to learn about the planet. But for the moment, she is content to soak up her first lesson on communing. Just for this moment, it is enough.

CHAPTER 36

JACKSON'S AMBASSADOR

***

NOVEMBER 24, 2059—MONDAY

Seth sits in the captain's chair on the bridge of the Green Grow 3, wondering if it will be the last time he ever wears a captain's uniform. It's rigid and stifling, and he would tell anyone who asked that it was a nuisance. But the uniform also makes him feel proud, accomplished. It makes him stand straighter, speak more clearly. Perhaps he even acts more decisively. *It doesn't make me do anything*, he tells himself, even as he sits up straighter in his chair and squares his shoulders. Will he miss it? He rarely wears it anyway.

Jackson's face fills the screen, thankfully from light-years away. He returned to Earth with the second shipment, just as everyone understood he would, so they are back to video chats every few days. Liz hasn't forgiven her brother for what he tried to do to Abby, but he continues to adamantly deny any intentional deception.

Ultimately, no one else knows what he did or didn't intend, and as much as Jackson deserves to have the life pummeled out of him—for many reasons—Seth needs the man to lead the New Generation. Removing him from power could destabilize things in unimaginable ways. Who knows what monster would rise from the deep to take his place? Jackson is the devil they know, and his relationship with Liz gives them leverage they wouldn't have with anyone else.

Besides, now that Jackson has what he wanted—the Green Grow 3—Seth thinks they might be able to coexist, from opposite corners of the universe. He has to make peace with Jackson—because others will come to Omega. Perhaps the Green Grow executive board. Perhaps someone else. It's only a matter of time, and when it happens, the outpost will need all the allies it can get. Jackson is a powerful enemy— can't he also be a powerful ally? Seth hopes so, desperately, even though he's still furious.

"Lizzie!" His voice booms with excitement, although Seth detects a note of desperation, or sadness perhaps.

"Jackson," Liz replies calmly, standing to Seth's left. She could sit, but she never does anymore. She says it's too confining, and that she doesn't expect the calls to last long, anyway. Seth knows she's eager to get back to the surface, back to the strange furry creatures that she ventures into the tall grass to meet. She says there is more groundwork to be laid before he can meet them—some kind of diplomatic protocol he doesn't understand. He's seen them, watching from a distance as they constructed the outpost. They are peculiar creatures, resembling pictures of wombats Seth saw in an old magazine from Earth.

"Did the shipment arrive intact?" Seth asks. Jackson's transporter is back on Level 37, and production is ramping up.

"It did," Jackson responds. "How is the outpost coming?" Not even he knows precisely how they arrived at Omega, whether Abby's energy altered Jackson's wormhole or whether she pulled them through space some other way. No one knows what happened when Abby was locked away in the recesses of Liz's mind, and if Liz remembers, she doesn't admit it. Regardless of how it happened, the Green Grow 3 was transported to the coordinates Abby knew best— Omega. The ship sustained extensive damage, but fortunately, it can be repaired.

"It's nearly complete," Seth says. "I expect the exploration team can move in on schedule."

Jackson looks slightly annoyed, his mouth pressing into a thin line. "Indeed," he says. "When you said Liz's Fifty-Two would be accompanying you to the outpost, I assumed you meant fifty-two people, in addition to your own small team."

Seth shrugs. "They've expanded. What can I say?"

"To two hundred and twelve people?" Jackson demands.

"Apparently so. We've discussed this, Jackson. It will give you a chance to get your own people aboard the ship, to start integrating with the rest of the crew."

"Never assume, Jackson," Liz says evenly. "Don't you know that's where most of our misunderstanding lies?"

Jackson's mouth opens, then closes again. "That's good advice," he responds, looking away from the camera.

"And what of the four people we discussed?" Liz asks. "When are you transporting them? They're overdue."

"The ones Ruth left behind?" Jackson asks with the slightest hint of scorn. "They will arrive as soon as you finish assembling the transporter on Omega."

"Why the delay?" Liz asks. "The machine isn't necessary for their arrival."

"No," Jackson says, "but I want to see it done. And there will be five people coming. I'm sending a trusted representative of mine, to keep me informed of what's happening at the outpost." Seth can sense Liz shifting her weight, undoubtedly a precursor to an angry remark.

"Whatever," he replies quickly, before Liz can speak. "We'll await their arrival. Are you ready to make the call?"

Jackson looks gleeful, but only for a moment before he nods solemnly. Seth is sure he's gloating, as if he's won a contest, or perhaps a war. But that doesn't bother Seth. Jackson needs to feel victorious, but Seth knows he's lost nothing. Nothing that matters to him, anyway. In fact, he feels victorious in his own right. A peaceful transition means that Jackson has no reason to kill him, and in addition to his life, he has the two things he's wanted most—Liz by his side, and a chance for both of them to be who they really are. Together, they will build a new outpost on a new planet. What an adventure. It doesn't undo the things Jackson did—nothing can. But it gives them something to look forward to.

Seth squares his shoulders and steels his expression as Jackson places a video call to the Green Grow 2. As far as he knows, the executive board has no clue who is calling, but it's he who is surprised to see a familiar face fill the screen. It seems Captain MacAbee is alive and well on the Green Grow 2.

"Seth, my boy, is that you?" the bewildered man asks. Seth does not attempt to respond, knowing that Jackson will only interrupt him.

"Indeed, it is," Jackson says, "and I am Jackson Goeff, Captain of the Western Faction of the New Generation."

"Seth," Captain MacAbee says urgently, "what is going on?"

"We are transitioning power," Seth says. "If there are others on the executive board you wish to involve in this discussion, please gather them now."

"Transitioning power?" Captain MacAbee looks confused. "Where are you? What has happened?"

"I'm sure you are well aware that the New Generation attempted to overtake the Green Grow 3 while we were still in orbit," Seth begins, feeling anger rise in his chest. "I'm sure you are also aware that minutes later, in the throes of the attack, the Green Grow 3 left orbit, very quickly. I'm sure you are aware this was possible because we built a deep space propulsion drive, after you and the rest of the executive board cut off communication and left us floating in orbit to serve as bait while you hid yourselves behind the moon." Captain MacAbee starts to interject, but Seth continues, projecting his voice clearly and loudly.

"There are things you may not know, however," he booms. "You may not know where we are, and Jackson—excuse me, *Captain Goeff*—can fill you in on whatever details he finds relevant. You should also know that we have closed all of your backdoors. Even if you know where the ship is, you can no longer access our drones or video feed, or override the navigation or life support systems. Your days of monitoring the ship covertly are over, as are my days as acting captain. As part of our peace settlement, I am turning over command of the Green Grow 3 to Captain Goeff. I will be leaving the ship, to establish an outpost on a planet he discovered that appears to be capable of supporting human life."

"But you have no authority to negotiate with anyone on behalf of Green Grow!" Captain MacAbee exclaims. "Whatever agreement you have reached is invalid! Where are you? What have you discovered?"

"The Green Grow executive board abdicated any authority over the Green Grow 3 when you abandoned us," Seth barks. "Captain Goeff, I hereby turn over command of the ship to you. Do you have further need of me at the moment?"

"Thank you, Captain Harris," Jackson says, looking like he's ready to burst with satisfaction. "I shall take it from here." The large panoramic screen goes black as Jackson cuts their feed. Seth rises from his chair, taking Liz's hand and smiling at her.

"Did he actually call me Captain Harris?"

Liz shrugs.

"Are you jake?" she asks.

"Right as rain," he says, unbuttoning the top button of his jacket. It wasn't as hard as he thought to turn over command of the ship to Jackson. He expected to feel humiliated and defeated. But he doesn't. Maybe he despises the executive board's duplicity even more than Jackson's. Or maybe he's simply happy he's not dead—just a few weeks ago, that seemed the most likely outcome. Maybe he'll feel differently in the future, after the shock of everything wears off. But for now, Seth thinks he's made the right decision.

He pays a final visit to his old quarters, where he changes out of the uniform he never truly wanted to wear. He briefly wonders what Jackson plans to discuss with the executive board, and why he felt it was necessary to call them in the first place. Ego, perhaps? That must part of it, and Jackson must want from the executive board the same thing he wants from everyone—power, knowledge, and perhaps a formidable adversary.

Feeling much more comfortable, and perhaps even more human, in his loose pants and tunic, he waits in the copilot seat of the shuttle as Liz and Charlie do the final inspection of the cargo—building supplies and electronics for the outpost that is almost complete on Omega. He realizes there is nowhere else he'd rather be, and nothing else he'd rather be doing. He smiles at Liz as she takes the pilot's seat, going through her preflight check one final time. *Does she know how beautiful she is?* he wonders, but he already knows the answer to the question. She doesn't, at least not yet. Perhaps one day she will. He turns his attention forward, taking in the dock, then the miracle of flight as they depart. He looks at the planet before them, speechless at all the possibility the future now offers.

***

Liz can see the first of two moons beginning to rise over Omega as she stands on the surface, where Jackson's transporter now rests complete. The sun set nearly an hour ago on the opposite horizon, but the Fifty-Two pressed on in assembling the machine. They want their people back, the four who remained when they fled the cave, and Jackson refused to send them until the platform was assembled.

Now there are three transporters, each one creating its own universe of terrifying possibilities in Liz's mind, but Jackson insisted it was the only way. He told Liz that he would hardcode coordinates into each machine, so they would only connect to the other transporters. He told her this was safer, more reliable, than entering different coordinates each time, that having the three transporters would allow him to move people and goods between Earth, Omega, and the Green Grow 3 with greater precision and reliability. He promised her this arrangement would prevent another mistake, as happened with Abby.

Liz isn't sure she believes him, although she's certain he believes what he's telling her to be true. *He's only human,* she reminds herself, which is the kindest explanation she can offer for why he cannot see beyond his own arrogance. It's a flaw that endangers all of them, and why she must stay closely involved with what he's doing.

She closes her eyes and thinks about Cyril. With a flash of sensation, she knows he's curled up in his grass house, asleep with his family. He expects her at sunrise for another lesson in communing. She mutes the connection between then—something he explained to her during their first meeting—and turns her attention to the tablet in her hand, the one that still has the icon on the home screen titled "Call Jackson." Moments later, she can see his now-familiar face.

"Lizzie, I can barely see you!" he says.

"It's dark here," she replies. "The sun went down about an hour ago. The transporter is complete."

"You're working in the dark?" He sounds concerned. "You're on an alien planet! You can't know that it's safe."

"It's safe enough," she says, knowing without being told that she is in no danger. She glances at Ruth and Ellis, waiting by the platform holding a lantern.

"We'll return to the shelter as soon our people arrive," she says. Jackson opens his mouth, then closes it again, no doubt confounded by her insistence that he return Ruth's people immediately.

"Very well," he says. "They are entering the capsule now. It will take a minute or two for Alex to seal it from the inside, and then they'll be ready."

"Alex?" Liz asks. "Is he your trusted representative?"

"Indeed—think of him like an ambassador," Jackson says. "I hope you won't be unkind to him, Lizzie. He's only trying to build the necessary alliances between us. We must work together for everyone's benefit."

"I know," she replies softly, wondering whether this man's arrival will be a gift or a burden. She dismisses the thought as she smells the familiar scent of ozone. By the light of Ruth's lamp, and the lamps held by the others surrounding the platform, she can see that a large green capsule has arrived.

"They're here," she tells Jackson before terminating the call. The biofilm makes a cracking noise as it splits, and she sees a hatch open. A man steps out, his expression serious but not unkind as he squints, taking in the platform and the ring of people holding lanterns around it.

One by one, four other people emerge behind him, looking disoriented and afraid, thin and ragged. Arms reach up to the platform, helping them down. They are instantly cocooned in the embrace of their people, wrapped in tears of joy and laughter. Only one man remains on the platform, and Liz waits a moment for the crowd to clear before she goes to greet Jackson's representative. When he jumps off the platform to meet her, she can see that he's tall, almost as tall as Seth.

"You must be Alex," she says, and he nods in return.

"Indeed," he replies, in a way that reminds her of Jackson. She sighs in exasperation, hoping this man won't be too much of a hindrance.

"Let's get you to the shelter." She ushers him toward the bobbing lanterns ahead of them. "You can eat, and then we'll meet with Seth."

"Seth?" he sounds surprised. "Captain Goeff told me that you are the director of surface operations."

"Perhaps," she says, unconcerned with the title, "but Seth and I are a team."

"I see," he says as they begin to walk toward the shelter. "If I didn't say it already, I'm pleased to meet you." Liz only smiles, wondering how long he'll feel that way, but she doesn't dwell on the question. Time will take care of itself, and she has no room for worry or doubt in her heart now, only the joy of where she is and the possibility of everything yet to come.

ACKNOWLEDGMENTS

Is writing a sequel easier or more difficult than writing the first book? To quote a brilliant writing instructor and friend—Max Regan from Hollowdeck Press—the answer to everything is "yes." It's easier, while also being more difficult, and I wouldn't have gotten this far alone.

I'd like to extend special thanks to the friends I met in Presidio for keeping me inspired, the people to whom I dedicated this book. You gave me what I needed most—inspiration, and the empowerment that comes from knowing others believe in me. I could mention several people specifically, but I'll limit myself to these. To Maxine, who confidently infused me with more love in a month than my own mother gave me in a lifetime. To Becky, for our great adventures far, far away from everything. To Greg and Tracy, who raise me on a pedestal I doubt I deserve.

To my Patreon subscribers, thank you for believing in me—I hope you've enjoyed the ride. I also want to thank April Kelsoe, for pulling double duty as my sister and my number one fan. I've tried to do the same for you, although you're the more gifted encourager. And I owe tremendous gratitude to my guardian angels, and all the divine forces who watched over me while I wrote. It was no easy task, as I drove my 1-ton Ram truck pulling a 38-foot fifth wheel over 8,000 miles, exploring the western half of the country alone with my pup,

Crash Tailthumper. Thank you for carrying me when I could not walk, and for watching over me while I camped in often-remote places, writing with a pen in a notebook because I had no electricity to power a computer.

Thank-you to everyone who made the book come together in practical ways. To Jennifer Rees, the story is richer and deeper for your editing and encouragement. To Dylan Garity, thank you for attempting to help me align with the known laws of physics—it's a tall order, and I loved the book more with each round of edits. To Dane Low, thank you for the brilliant cover.

If you've read this far, I'd like to thank you, too. I hope you'll bear with me as I peck away at the third book of the trilogy, and that your life is richer or better for having read this story. Until next time, my friends.

ABOUT THE AUTHOR

C.J. Hall's debut novel, *Evolving Elizah: Initiatum*, was named by BlueInk Review as one of the Best Books of 2020, and it was a finalist for the 2021 Book Blogger's Novel of the Year Award. A multi-genre author, she resides in her home state of Texas, where she writes full time in the company of her dedicated and heroic pup, Crash Tailthumper. To keep up with her books, and her adventures, visit www.CJ-Hall.com